# MAITLAND MAIDENS

## THE COMPLETE SERIES

by Cora Lee

*Hymn to Aphrodite* by Sappho, translated into English by Ambrose Philips as *A Hymn to Venus*.

Editing by Jude Simms.

Cover by Erin Dameron-Hill at EDH Professionals.

ISBN 978-1-944477-33-2

Published in the United States by More Than Words Press

# Table of Contents

# SAVE THE LAST DANCE FOR ME

**A pretend courtship and private dancing lessons allow two old friends to consider their future together. Who will confess their growing love first?**

Mr. Benedict Grey is the only heir to a long-standing title, and he knows his duty: find a suitable girl, get married, secure the succession beyond himself. But if a gentleman could be called a wallflower, Benedict would fit the description perfectly. And for the past six years, he's been out of Society more than he's been in it. How will he find a woman to wed and bed when he can barely converse with the ladies of the ton?

Lady Honoria Maitland has promised her dying father that, before he breathes his last, she would find a husband to take care of her. But she wants a gentleman that loves her, not her dowry or her name. When she reunites with her old friend Benedict, she proposes a plan that will help them both: a faux courtship and betrothal. She can teach him how to woo a woman and simultaneously ease her father's last days. But Honoria's clever plan failed to account for Benedict's heart...or her own. Is she strong enough to bear the loss of her father and her friend?

# Prologue

*November 1812*

*B*enedict Grey sat as close to the fire in his library as he could without singeing the book—*Remarks on the Antiquities of Rome and Its Environs: Being a Classical and Topographical Survey of the Ruins of that Celebrated City*—in his lap. It was good to be in his own home again, to sleep in his own soft bed, to eat his favorite foods. To wash in the morning and know that he would not be covered in dust inside of an hour.

But after spending the larger part of six years in Greece, London was *cold.*

There was a knock at the door and, at Benedict's easy "enter", his butler stepped into the room. "The Marquess of Whitby to see you, sir."

"It's deuced dark in here, Benedict," Whitby proclaimed, brushing past the butler and heading for a big wing chair opposite his host. "Why are all the curtains closed?"

Benedict's reply—and nod to the retreating butler—was matter-of-fact. "To keep the heat in."

Whitby laughed. "Of course! You must be positively freezing. Why on earth did you come back to England in November of all months?"

"I came back with the last load of cargo. It was either sail with it, or wait until the winter storms had passed.

With two wars on, I didn't want to become stranded in a foreign country."

"Wish you'd stayed in Athens, now, don't you?"

Whitby was grinning. Benedict found himself rubbing his arms and grinning back. "Absolutely."

"Have you been to see Elgin yet?"

Benedict sobered somewhat at the mention of his patron. "I have—it was his endeavor after all. His lordship bore the expenses, he has a right to hear the particulars first hand."

"But you didn't call on any of your family?"

Benedict shifted in his chair. "I wanted a few days to recover first."

"And to hide, eh?"

Benedict ignored the jibe. Instead, he rose from his chair and placed a marker in his book, stroking a finger gently over the cover as he set the volume on his desk.

He strode toward the sideboard to pour drinks. "What are you doing in Town? I thought you were rusticating in the country with your flock of daughters."

"It's my 'flock of daughters' that brings me here."

Benedict heard the sudden seriousness in Whitby's voice and turned at once. "Is everything well with the girls?"

"Oh, they're hale and hearty. All aflutter about dresses and bonnets and such, I imagine. They're going to visit my wife's sister for a month, and were twittering about what to pack when I departed."

Benedict turned back to the sideboard, feeling his shoulders relax as he poured a clear liquid into two glasses. "What do you need from me, then?"

"Two things. First, my wife is holding a house party while the girls are away to celebrate Christmas and your safe return."

Benedict returned to his place by the fire, handing a glass to his cousin. "Try this—I brought it back with me. And I'll not think you a coward for sipping it."

Whitby took the glass and sniffed at it. "Smells like the biscuits Cook makes on special occasions."

"*Stin uyeia sou.*" At his cousin's blank look, Benedict translated his words. "To your health."

Whitby sniffed again, then tossed back the entire glass.

And came up coughing.

Benedict was obliged to get up and pound his cousin on the back, receiving a scowl for his trouble.

"What the hell is this?"

"It's called ouzo. The Greeks drink it regularly."

"Well the English do not. You should have warned me of its potency—*actually* warned me, instead of provoking me like that."

Benedict resumed his seat, arching an eyebrow at his cousin. "You let your wife give a house party for me."

"*Let* her? You know better than that."

Benedict allowed a small smile to form on his lips. If any wife had charge of her husband, it was certainly Lady Whitby.

"Well, we're even now. What was the second thing?"

"What?"

"You said there were two things you needed of me. The first was the house party—which I haven't yet agreed to. What is the second thing?"

Whitby sat forward in his chair, leaning his forearms against his thighs. "Take a drink of that ouzo first."

Benedict did as instructed before replying. "Please don't tell me you want me to squire around some silly girl at this house party."

"Worse," Whitby said slowly. "I need you to get married."

Benedict looked at his cousin for a long moment, trying to analyze his expression in the dim light of the fire. Was he joking?

"And produce an heir."

He had to be joking. Not that Benedict didn't have a fondness for women. Perhaps he had a bit less experience with them than other men of eight-and-twenty years, but he'd enjoyed every moment of what he'd had.

Before a man could marry a woman, though, he had to first find one of the right class and breeding, the right family and wealth. Then he had to court her.

"Truly, Benedict. I wouldn't ask if it was not of the utmost importance."

Benedict downed the rest of his ouzo in one swallow. "Why?"

Whitby sat back, hands still resting on his thighs. "To secure the succession."

"Of course."

A great, long sigh whooshed out of the marquess. "You're my heir—and the last Grey male. You had to know this was coming."

"Eventually, yes. But not three days after I returned to London. Bloody hell, Whitby, I've been gone for most of the last six years—you couldn't wait a few more days?"

"I thought you could use as much warning as possible."

Benedict pressed his lips together in a tight line. "Your lady wife is planning more than just a house party."

Whitby nodded, his eyes—the same hazel as Benedict's —flicking toward the fire. "She's...she's been having a bad time of it these last months." He stopped and drew in a deep breath, as if steeling himself for the worst. "She can't have any more children."

"Why not?" His mother would likely have elbowed him in the ribs for such a lack of delicacy, but Benedict ignored the thought.

Whitby's eyes dropped from the fire to the floor. "She's past her childbearing years. She's seen physicians and midwives, consulted apothecaries. They all say the same thing."

"She's not that old, is she?"

"I didn't think so—my mother bore her last child when she was nigh on five-and-forty, and Lady Whitby has more than a few years to go before she reaches that milestone. But our youngest is nearly six now, and there's not been even a hint of another babe since. She won't say it aloud, but I can see it all over her face—she feels old and useless. She gave me seven daughters, but doesn't think that's good enough."

"I'm...sorry." Benedict was sure that was not the correct sentiment to express, but he didn't know what else to say.

"Of course, having you as my heir helps. We both know you'll do the title honor when your turn comes."

Understanding dawned. "And now Lady Whitby can turn her attention to my matrimonial prospects."

Whitby's eyes shifted back to his cousin. "It's cheered her up considerably, planning this house party and dreaming up eligible ladies for you to meet."

Benedict realized he was still holding his empty ouzo glass and set it down on the hearth at his feet. "She feels useful again."

"Exactly so."

A long silence stretched between the two men. Benedict took his turn staring at the fire, but he could feel his cousin's eyes on him. He knew Whitby wanted him to agree to the whole scheme, to attend the house party with pleasure and throw himself into a search for a suitable wife.

Benedict, however, knew what he was like around the Society set—or anyone outside his fellow antiquarians.

He bored them to tears.

Each time he had returned home during the expedition to Greece had been a disaster. Once, his arrival had coincided with the height of the Season, and his mother had dragged him to every entertainment she'd been invited to. He'd been polite, of course, and had tried to make conversation with the countless people she'd introduced him to. But when they had asked him breathless questions about his time in Athens, he had inevitably responded with the condition and significance of items recovered during the previous months. When people had asked his opinion of the war against Napoleon, Benedict's reaction had been to condemn it—if Britain had not embroiled herself in armed conflict, he might be able to travel safely to Italy and work on the excavation of Pompeii.

After that, few people had asked him questions. In fact, few people had spoken to him much at all.

But he couldn't bring himself to damage Lady Whitby's delicate mental state. Given his cousin's news and the way in which he'd deliver it, Benedict suspected that if he rebuffed the marchioness's matchmaking machinations she'd sink into a deep depression. And if he could prevent that, or lessen its severity in any way, he was certainly willing to try.

But surely he needn't submit to *all* her machinations.

"Well, I won't deprive her of her house party, then." Benedict paused, making sure to catch Whitby's gaze and hold it. "And I will allow that, under the circumstances, it's time I started looking for a wife. But how and when I do so will be *my* decision."

"That's fair." Whitby was nodding his head agreeably. "A good start, at least."

"Not a start, cousin. That's my line in the sand. You and I have always been like brothers, despite the difference in our ages, and I love your wife like my own sister. But I'll not be dictated to on the matter of *my* wife and the mother of my children."

"Sure, sure. You'll find the right woman. I have no doubt."

There was a slight slur to Whitby's words, and Benedict looked more closely at his cousin. His cheeks were flushed pink, his mouth pulled into a lazy smile.

Benedict grinned, leaning against the high back of his chair. While he was accustomed to Greece's favorite alcohol, Whitby was clearly not. He wondered briefly if he might extract other promises from the marquess, but discarded the notion. It would be dishonorable to attempt such a thing. And Whitby would never do so himself.

Instead, Benedict simply continued the conversation, albeit in a slightly more relaxed tone. "I'm surprised you didn't suggest one of your daughters for me."

Whitby waved a hand at his cousin. "No, not my girls. They're sweet creatures, but flighty...and no sign that any of 'em will settle down. Besides, the oldest is only seventeen—would you want to be leg-shackled to a flighty girl of seventeen?"

Benedict felt himself wince at the thought. "No, I would not. And I thank you for taking that into consideration."

"But there will be a multitude of other ladies for you to look over. Best decide what kind of girl you *do* want."

"I suppose I must," Benedict answered, slumping down in his chair. "And what kind of girl might want me."

"Oh, that's easy," Whitby grinned. "You're the grandson of a marquess, heir to a venerable old title...and you've got some money in your own right. The matchmaking mamas will be pounding down your door!"

Benedict slouched further in his chair. "Perhaps I'll tell them I expect my wife to accompany me on future digs."

Whitby laughed. "That would put off the title hunters!"

And pretty much every other lady of the *ton*. Which would break Lady Whitby's heart, and put an end to the Grey line.

Blast it.

Well, there was no turning back now. "I've never been to a house party, cousin. Tell me how it's going to go, and what I must do."

# Chapter 1



*B*enedict had literally backed himself into a corner.

He felt the ballroom wall bump solidly against his shoulder and discovered he was more than a little relieved. At least no one could ambush him from behind.

No one was approaching from the front, though, either. Here he was with hundreds of people at the first great entertainment of the Season, and even the chaperones and spinsters wanted little to do with him.

Not that he blamed them. Most of the *ton* had heard the details of Whitby's Christmas house party by now. They'd know how tongue-tied and awkward Benedict had been, even with the maids when he'd had occasion to speak to one. They'd know how his face had gone distinctly red whenever his turn came at charades, and how he'd inadvertently insulted Whitby's neighbor with what turned out to be a very politically charged remark. Everyone who cared to listen to the gossip would know that he'd given up after that, and spent the remainder of the party in the library, hiding away where he could neither inflict nor receive further harm.

Not that his cowardice had put Lady Whitby off. She'd been upset, of course. But here in her own ballroom with the crème of the *beau monde* swirling all around her, Lady Whitby was in her element. In fact, she was more determined than ever to find him a suitable wife, making lists of eligible young widows and new debutantes, practically following him around Town as he attempted to go about his business.

And she'd just spotted him.

He watched with a sort of detached fascination as she homed in on him from across the room like a hound after a stag. Even amid the bustle and noise of the crowd, the music of the orchestra, and the myriad of people stopping to speak with her, she remained focused on Benedict. Perhaps if he stayed completely still—

"Oh!" a female voice cried. A weight came down on his foot as the rustle of fabric swept against his legs. His arms reached out instinctively and caught hold of a soft form in a white gown dotted with silver embroidery.

"Thank you, sir," the voice said, a little breathless as its owner attempted to right herself. One pale hand braced itself against the lapel of his black evening coat while the other found his shoulder. A curl of dark hair brushed against his cheek. "My dance partner seems rather too vigorous this evening."

"Honoria?"

Long-lashed lids lifted to reveal a pair of eyes as dark as her hair, and her mouth curved into a surprised smile. "Benedict! I didn't know you'd be here tonight."

Aware that heads were turning their way, he removed his arms from her waist and clasped her hands in his, extracting them from his body with as much subtlety as he could manage.

"Isn't everybody here?"

Her gloved hands slipped from his and he felt a pang of regret. Once upon a time a reunion between the two of them would have included a warm—and deliberate—embrace. They were in public, though, and whatever their relationship had previously been, he reminded himself that it would hardly be the same after his years spent abroad.

Her gaze dropped to his waistcoat—silver silk with little leaves embroidered on it, made especially for this ball—and she smoothed her hands over her skirt, making the silver threads catch the light from the chandeliers above. "No one would miss the marchioness's Black and White Ball, of course. But you were never one for society affairs." Her eyes shifted back to his. "Is that why you're over here in the corner? Do you think to hide from the revelry rather than participate in it?"

Well, at least her directness hadn't changed. "As it happened, you're lucky I was here in this particular corner. If I had been out among the revelers, you would have fallen."

Honoria glanced around and Benedict followed suit, noting that people had turned back to their previous activities—except for Lady Whitby. She had resumed her course and was headed directly for him.

"Then for once I appreciate your wallflower ways." She grinned up at him. "You have saved me from what surely would have been the *on dit* of the week."

"Judging by what I saw on the terrace earlier, you would not have even been the *on dit* of the evening. But you could repay an act of gallantry with one of your own."

"What would you have me do?"

He took her hand and laid it on his sleeve. "Walk with me and pretend you enjoy my company."

Lady Honoria Maitland strolled through the ballroom beside her old friend, hoping this was the turning point she'd been waiting for all evening. She'd run into one aggravation after another since the moment she arrived. The shawl she'd worn against the chilly spring night had caught on the door latch of the carriage and torn. Her stepmother had introduced her to two gentlemen whose acquaintance she had previously made but desperately wished she hadn't. She'd accepted a third gentleman's request for a dance hoping to escape the first two, and nearly ended up face down on the floor.

But then Benedict Grey had caught her, and the evening began to show some promise. It had been months and months since they'd even seen each other, and so much longer since they'd had a real conversation. Perhaps that could be remedied tonight.

"Of course I will walk with you. Perhaps we can evade my dance partner—I have no desire to return to his ministrations. And I always enjoy your company."

They strolled away from his corner refuge with all the dignity of visiting royalty. Or at least Honoria did—spine straight, shoulders back, chin up. Benedict's eyes darted around the room as if he was plotting his escape.

Perhaps he was.

But his voice was calm when he spoke again. "Where shall we walk?"

"Let's take a turn about the room for a start." She grinned. "Because if the activities you witnessed on the terrace are still in progress, we'll want to avoid going there."

Benedict merely nodded, so she wracked her brain for another option and decided that a little forwardness would not go amiss with this man. At least, it never had before. "Dancing is also a good way to occupy one's time at a ball."

He cringed visibly. "You want to dance?"

"I love to dance, you know that." Her mouth and feet both paused while she looked more closely at her friend. His shoulders were slightly hunched as he halted beside her, and she could just make out a red tint creeping into his cheeks from beneath his snow white cravat. "Or, you used to know that. Have you forgotten all those afternoons we practiced together when we were young?"

"The afternoons I remember well." He took a half step closer to her and bent his head toward hers. "It's the steps I've forgotten."

"Truly?"

Benedict's eyes trailed down toward his shoes. "Yes, well, there isn't much call for a reel or a quadrille in the middle of an ancient ruin, is there?"

"I suppose not. "Honoria's mouth curved into a slow smile as an idea popped into her head. "But if you're in Town to stay, you'll need to re-acquire that skill."

She must have looked more mischievous than she realized because he straightened abruptly. "You sound like Lady Whitby."

"Is she the one you were hiding from?"

"I was *not* hiding."

The couple nearest them turned for a moment, and Honoria offered what she hoped was an apologetic look before tugging Benedict into motion. "Very well, you weren't hiding. But is the lady in question acting...rather too zealously for your taste?"

"That would be the most polite way to describe her efforts, yes." They walked along without speaking for a few paces before Benedict inched closer again. "What do you know about it?"

Honoria patted his sleeve. "I know only what news your mother has passed along to my stepmother, and that mainly consisted of your continued health and bachelorhood."

His gaze snapped to hers as if he'd been startled by her words. When he coughed and forced a smile, she knew she'd caught him out.

"Ah, so that's what Lady Whitby is after. She wants to see you wed."

"'To a woman of good breeding, with a pretty face and a head for details'," he quoted in an unnaturally high voice. He cleared his throat and resumed his own tenor. "The succession must be secured, of course."

Honoria grimaced, her gaze drifting toward the people in front of them. "A familiar tale in my home as well. 'You're eight-and-twenty, Honoria. If you weren't a duke's daughter no gentleman would even give you the time of day'."

"Is eight-and-twenty really so old?"

She glanced up at the rather plaintive note in his voice, recalling too late that he was the same age. "It is for a woman. It's ancient for an unmarried woman."

"Then why haven't you married?"

An impertinent question if there ever was one. And one that she was not prepared to discuss in the middle of a grand ball.

"We were talking about you." She spied a set of open French windows ahead and inclined her head toward them.

"Why don't we go out onto the terrace after all…that is, if there are no longer indecent acts being performed out there. I may have an idea that will help you, and we'll want a little privacy to talk."

He studied her face for a long moment, then nodded once and led her out into the night. The darkness was tempered by torches lit at regular intervals along the balustrade and a gibbous moon rising over the horizon.

Beside her Benedict breathed deeply in, exhaling with a gentle "Ah."

The cool air felt wonderful on Honoria's heated skin. But rather than say so she took the opportunity to tease him a little. "Too much for you in there?"

"I'd forgotten what a ballroom full of people *smelled* like. So many bodies crowded together, and every single one of them wearing some sort of fragrance. It's…oppressive. It pushes down upon one until the body can bear it no more."

They found a stone bench to one side and Honoria sat, arranging her skirts about her. "You miss Greece, don't you?"

He settled down next to her, his posture relaxing. "I do. But I didn't mean to be so vulgar about it. Please accept my apologies."

"There is no need to apologize to me for speaking frankly. You've said worse than that in my hearing, and I'm quite sure I have in yours. Or have you forgotten the time we 'liberated' that bottle of wine when we were fifteen?"

"I remember it well. You drank half of it before I could get through a glassful—"

"I did no such thing!"

"—and the next day you proceeded to describe to me in great detail just how very vile you felt."

He was laughing now, not a polite chuckle but a sound of genuine amusement. Honoria felt herself laughing along with him. "And you did the same. If memory serves, you even told me how many times you cast up your accounts."

His eyes rolled skyward. "Promise me you won't tell Lady Whitby that story. I would never hear the end of her etiquette lessons."

Honoria turned toward him, searching his face in the low light. "Has she been that meddlesome, then?"

Benedict shook his head, meeting her gaze as his mouth drew down into a more sober expression. "No. Well yes, she has, but I am trying not to mind—she simply has a vested interested in my future nuptials and wants to ensure they take place."

"Will you tell me about it?"

Honoria held her breath for a moment and waited. They used to tell each other everything, but when Benedict had put actual distance between them by sailing away to the Continent, an emotional distance had been created as well. It was one thing to share a fond memory, but what of the present?

His brows crowded together, the way they had when he'd thought intensely about something as a younger man. "She is the wife of a peer, and has given him no son to inherit. Nor likely will she."

"And so she's turned to matchmaking for you."

Her voice was soft and, when Benedict didn't respond, she thought perhaps he hadn't heard her. But then he nodded, bowing his head slightly. "She has."

"For her good, if not yours." Honoria grasped the stone bench with both her hands. "Well, I did say that I had an idea for you."

He straightened, his hair catching the torchlight—it had lightened considerably during his years away to a soft sandy brown. "I'm listening."

"You need to find a wife."

"Yes."

"But you can't dance."

His large hands clapped down over his knees. "What does one thing have to do with the other?"

Honoria put on the air of patient authority she used when conversing with her eight-year-old half-brother. "You must dance with a lady in order to court her. How else will you determine if you can even stand her company?"

"Can I not talk to her?"

Honoria shook her head, setting the ringlets on either side of her face to swaying. "Talking is not enough. One only discovers a person's true character when one speaks with that person alone. But when does a gentleman have the opportunity to speak alone with a lady?"

"We're alone now."

She looked for the twitching of his lips or crinkling of his eyes to suggest he was being facetious, but his serious expression remained fixed.

"We are. But how much longer will that last, do you think? How long before my stepmother begins to look for me?" Her fingers clenched the bench seat with more force. "And what would happen to my reputation if we were found together out here?"

"I see your point."

"Dancing accomplishes so much more. There is time for talking, of course, but there is also a chance to flirt, and to touch. One can study a partner's appearance without being rude or vulgar, and discover if said partner is graceful or clumsy or featherbrained or bookish."

Benedict sighed. "It's a necessity, then."

"Yes. And I will teach you."

"You?"

She tilted her head slightly to the side. "Me. Or you'll have to hire a dancing master."

She watched his fingers tense on his knees as he digested that bit of information. But he didn't reply.

A light breeze rustled the flowers in the garden nearby. The torch flames flickered, casting peculiar shadows across the terrace. Then all was still once more—including Benedict. She waited for several more minutes but he remained silent.

"Think it over, why don't you?" Honoria rose from the bench and smoothed the fine cambric of her gown. "Take me driving tomorrow, and we can discuss it further if you like."

Benedict stood and offered her his arm. "I'll call for you at four."

He fell quiet again escorting her back into the house, and she wondered if she'd offended him. No one liked to dwell on his own deficiencies, certainly. But the Benedict she knew six years ago would have teased her in return about a shortcoming of her own.

Clearly, he was no longer the man he'd once been.

"Honoria?"

She blinked herself out of her musings. "Yes?"

"I would marry you, you know."

She froze. "What?"

"If we were caught together. If I compromised you." His eyes met hers in the half-light. "And not just because I'm looking for a wife now. I would have then, too."

He didn't have to explain when *then* was. She knew he was thinking of the day her mother died. He never did tell her how he'd gained entry into the house or how he found her bedchamber without disturbing anyone, but he'd managed to do both late that night. He'd sat with her and held her hand as she had talked of her mother, then cradled her against him when she'd wept. Only when she had calmed did either of them realize the potential for an immense scandal his presence caused. And even then he'd stayed with her until she fell asleep.

Her fingers tightened on his sleeve in response. Perhaps some of the old Benedict still existed after all.

# Chapter 2

Benedict glanced at Honoria out of the corner of his eye. She sat perfectly straight on the seat beside him with the skirt of her green dress arranged neatly about her. Her shoulders were relaxed, her hands were carefully folded around a reticule in her lap, and a small smile formed on her lips whenever she wasn't talking.

How did she do that?

They were driving in Whitby's curricle through Hyde Park—which is to say they were creeping slowly along in a throng of traffic, looking at other people and being looked at themselves. The driving itself was not a problem, nor even the barely discernible progress along Rotten Row. The sun shone down upon them and the air was still, allowing Benedict to preserve a degree of masculinity and forgo wearing his greatcoat to keep warm. The horses, too, were agreeable: well-matched bays with a calm temperament, quite used to the hustle and bustle of the fashionable hour.

But personal scrutiny under any circumstances made him squirm. Here he felt like one of the Egyptian sculptures on display at the British Museum.

"Ah, Lord and Lady Tiverton. Good afternoon." Honoria discreetly tapped his arm three times, using a system they'd worked out beforehand to indicate the social importance of people they met. One tap was lowest among the *ton*; five taps meant prestige nearly on par with the Prince Regent himself.

Benedict gave a respectful nod to the couple in the slowly approaching barouche. "Lord Tiverton, Lady Tiverton."

"Lady Honoria, how does your father?" Lord Tiverton leaned toward the edge of his carriage, and his driver called the horses to a halt. "I have not seen him in Town yet."

Benedict tugged his own horses' reins as Honoria answered. "His Grace elected to remain in the country, my lord."

"Did he? For how long? I was hoping he would come with me to Tattersall's this month—no one knows horseflesh like the Duke of Alston."

Honoria's expression remained serene, but her body shifted slightly on the curricle seat. "I am not certain when he plans to return. But I will convey your wish when I write to him next."

Lord Tiverton frowned. "Perhaps I will write him myself as well."

She shifted again. "I am sure he would be pleased to hear from you."

They said their good-byes and resumed their tortoise-like pace. Honoria continued to acknowledge passersby with courteous nods, but Benedict noted that her smile was no longer the easy affectation it had been.

"Do you really not know when your father is coming to Town?" he asked in a quiet voice, the better to put off potential eavesdroppers. "It has been an age since I saw him last."

And there it was again—that slight movement of Honoria's person on the seat beside him, as if she were trying to ease an uncomfortable position without drawing attention to the action.

"No, I don't. He does not keep me apprised of all his plans."

"But I should think he would tell his only daughter when he would see her again."

"Well, he didn't." Honoria took a breath and let it out slowly. When she spoke again, her voice was bright with just a hint of scolding. "Why didn't you speak to Lord and Lady Tiverton? They don't have a daughter, but Lady Tiverton could certainly introduce to you any number of eligible ladies."

Benedict kept his eyes on the horses. "I didn't get a chance to speak to them. You and Lord Tiverton carried the whole conversation...all two minutes of it."

He felt her tap his arm twice and automatically looked to the curricle drawing near carrying two well dressed ladies. He nodded to the occupants, his mouth curving into what he hoped was a smile and not the grimace it felt like. The ladies acknowledged the greeting with genteel nods in return.

When the ladies had passed, Benedict addressed Honoria in a low tone. "How does your father, anyway? Has he taken one of his turns again? Is that why he's not in London?"

She paled but offered an artificial smile to a gentleman on horseback as he rode by. "Yes."

"Then why not say so to Lord Tiverton? His lordship knows about your father's delicate health—indeed, the whole of the *ton* knows."

Benedict turned to look at Honoria, *really* look at her. Her smile was still pasted on, but one hand clutched her reticule as if she feared someone would rip it from her, and her posture was rigid. Her eyes, too, refused to meet his. "Something has changed since last I was home."

"Not here." Her voice was nearly a whisper. She took another breath and continued with more authority. "There is a path a little way ahead. Turn down there—we'll be away from prying ears, but still properly within sight of the Row."

He returned his attention to the horses and did as instructed, ignoring oncoming conveyances despite Honoria's arm tapping. What use was small talk when a real problem was afoot?

When they were safely out of earshot, Benedict stopped the curricle and turned to Honoria.

"What has happened with your father?"

"What are you doing? We can't just sit here—everyone can see us!"

Benedict felt his brows draw together. "I thought that was the point."

"But we must appear as though everything is exactly as it should be. If we sit here in the middle of the path talking, all of society will know something is wrong."

"If we drive any further along this path, we'll be alone and out of sight. I didn't even bring a tiger on this outing—you'll be compromised."

She shook her head and gestured with one hand. "It loops around behind those trees, but comes out again over there. We can stop at the trees to talk and only be out of sight for a few moments."

That didn't sound exactly proper to Benedict, but what did he know about it? He'd been focused on stone statues for the last six years, not society gossips. He took up the reins and guided the horses to the place Honoria had indicated.

"Here?"

She nodded.

"Good. Will you tell me what's happened now?"

Her lips pressed together in a thin line and her gaze settled on a spot just to the left of his shoulder. But she didn't speak.

He reached for her hand and clasped it in his larger one, a gesture from their past he hoped she would remember. Words had always been easier for both of them to find when they were touching.

A smile flickered on her lips—recognition of their old form of reassurance or amusement because Benedict had forgotten to wear gloves?—before fading away. "Papa is ill again, yes. But it's different this time...worse. He can no longer walk the length of a room without stopping to catch his breath, and he's been coughing terribly. His physician says his heart is not beating normally, either, and that he complains of severe fatigue."

"Yet you came to London without him." It wasn't an accusation, but a statement of fact.

"He sent me away." Honoria's palm pressed against his, and he could feel the cold of her skin permeating her glove. "He is sure this is his end and wants to see me settled before he dies. I have the means to live independently, but Papa believes the world is a dangerous place for a female with no gentleman to protect her."

"And your brother is still a child. His Grace is right to worry." Benedict covered their clasped hands with his free one, trying to infuse some warmth into her chilly fingers.

"You and I were once like family—you must know that I would always come to your aid should you need me."

"Certainly you would, if you were in the country."

He glanced down at their hands balanced on her knee and felt a twinge of regret. "I'm here now."

"But for how long? And what if something were to happen to you? Then I'd be right back where I am now, without even a widow's rights."

"So His Grace sent you here for the Season to find a husband."

He looked up just as her eyes darted to his. "Yes. But Benedict, who would I marry? This is my eleventh Season and I have yet to find a gentleman I could even spend an evening with, let alone a lifetime. Who could I trust enough to place all my worldly goods—and my very person—under his rule?"

"I could help you search." When she arched a dark eyebrow at him he drew back one hand. "I may not be familiar with the niceties of the *beau monde*, but I know a dishonorable man when I meet one."

"I'm sure you do." Her mouth curved into a wry smile, and her voice regained a note of her old self-assurance. "But I have a plan that will work for both of us."

"Of course you do." His mind conjured up images of Honoria's hastily concocted "plans" from their childhood and he felt the tension rising in his shoulders. But he plunged ahead. "Well then, let's hear it."

"I couldn't fall asleep last night, worrying over Papa," she told him, adjusting her hand in his clasp. For a brief moment she considered removing her own gloves and eliminating that barrier between them. But she dismissed the idea just as quickly—it wouldn't be seemly, and they were already pushing the boundaries of polite society by being out of sight. "So I tried distracting myself with your situation."

"A problem that may be solvable."

"Oh, it most certainly is. But you'll need more than just a dancing master, Benedict. There is dress to consider"—she squeezed his bare fingers—"and deportment. There are social customs to observe after you've met a lady who interests you, too. And I suspect you could use some practice in all of it."

His hazel eyes were steady, but his shoulders sagged a trifle. "No doubt I could."

"I could easily teach you. But what reason would we have for being so much together? The *ton* would wonder."

"We are old friends, Honoria. I don't think the *ton* would wonder too much at our association."

"They might wonder why you were spending so much time with me when you're supposed to be trying to find a wife."

His shoulders dropped a fraction more. "That is certainly possible."

"Which is why you shall pretend to court me."

"What?"

She rested her free hand on their clasped ones. "It's ideal, really. If you're courting me, it will be perfectly natural to call upon me at home, to dance with me at balls, to take me driving and on other outings. We can spend quite a lot of time together without meriting more than the usual notice."

"And you can write to His Grace to say you have a serious suitor."

"One who is more steadfast than the band of silly admirers I have now." Honoria patted their clasped hands. "He would be in transports of delight. You meet all of the practical criteria he has set out for me, and he's always liked you."

Benedict frowned, his sandy brows drawing together as he considered the idea. "But how will I look for a wife if I'm supposed to be interested in you?"

"Think of the courtship as a period of study," she said, knowing he would relate to an academic analogy. "I shall be your instructor in the ways of wooing a lady. When you have learned your lessons well, I'll cry off and you will be unattached."

"Cry off?"

"Didn't I mention the betrothal?" She flashed a grin at him, but then sobered. "I do think, for Papa's sake, we should announce a betrothal. A courtship is not binding, but a betrothal nearly is. I believe he will find it binding enough to content him."

Benedict lifted her loose hand from atop their clasped ones, and held both of hers in both of his. "I can see how a betrothal would ease your father's last days, but I cannot lie to him. And you know if he is to believe the engagement is real, I would need to speak with him in person."

"I am of age—I don't need his permission to marry."

"No, but there would be settlements to draw up. And His Grace would most certainly want to take care of the legalities before his time comes."

"Then what will we do?" She could hear the worry in her voice, try though she might to keep it steady. She needed Benedict's help much more than he needed hers, and she suspected he knew it.

He squeezed her hands and released them, turning to take up the reins. "We've been hidden behind these trees for far too long. And I need some time to think this over."

She faced the front of the curricle, smoothing down an invisible wrinkle in her skirt. "Of course. I've asked a lot of you today."

They drove the remainder of the path and rejoined the crowd, resuming their nodding and arm-tapping and mindless small talk. Benedict kept his expression impassive the whole while, and Honoria wished she knew what he was thinking. He was a man of honor and had been a good friend to both her and her father—which is why she had presented what she was beginning to think might be a foolish plan to him in the first place. But she knew that same sense of honor and friendship would resist deceiving her father, and that notion had kept her tossing and turning in the wee hours.

Because if Benedict refused to participate in her sham betrothal, Honoria would find herself shackled to a man who wanted her only for her bloodline or her dowry. For after eleven years on the Marriage Mart, the likelihood of finding love—going to the same entertainments with the same people she'd known all her adult life—was almost nonexistent.

And love was the only thing she wanted.


Honoria's maid brought a folded piece of paper to her as she sat embroidering with her aunt in the drawing room after dinner. She broke the plain seal and found the message within written in a clear, bold hand:

*H,*

*I still have my doubts, but you asked for my help and I will give it. I will call tomorrow to discuss further details.*

*B*

Honoria let out a sigh that was equal parts relief and affection. Her dear friend had come through for her.

Her aunt must have heard only the affection. "We'll have another gentleman caller tomorrow, then? One whom you'll actually welcome?"

Honoria smiled. "Yes. This one I will welcome very much."

# Chapter 3

Honoria stood in the music room at Alston House a week later, taking stock of the items located there in preparation for Benedict's second visit of the afternoon. The days that had passed since his note had developed a kind of pattern: he would call in the afternoon with the gaggle of other gentlemen hopeful of winning Honoria's hand, then he'd return later to take her driving in the park. He didn't seem to enjoy either activity, so she had tried to impress upon him the need to not only express his attentiveness to her, but to make sure the others noticed it as well. Sympathy would run high for a gentleman who had been thrown over by his lady after demonstrating nothing but thoughtfulness and loyalty to her.

But in an entire week, he never managed to stay in her drawing room for more than twenty minutes. It was probably the topics of conversation, she decided. Her other callers spoke of who was wearing what at which soirée the previous night, the highlights of the latest Minerva Press novel, the beauty of the flowers they sent compared to her own—things they thought she would find interesting. But apparently they bored Benedict beyond reason.

He did show some progress during their Hyde Park outings, though. He'd become adept at asking a question about a subject near and dear to his conversational partner's heart, and listening attentively to the reply. For the brief interviews during the fashionable hour, it was a beautiful strategy—especially with Honoria murmuring ideas to him as they drove. With just a few words he appeared courteous and personable. And, if he was truly paying attention to the answers he received, he was learning quite a lot about the people that moved in society.

Today was going to be quite a different challenge, though. Honoria directed two footmen to move aside this piece of furniture or that, to roll up the carpets and carefully place them against a wall. She shuffled through the music she had laid out on the pianoforte, set it down, then picked it all up again, wondering if any of the pieces would do after all.

Today was to be Benedict's first dancing lesson.

"Mr. Grey has arrived—I told Engle to show him here rather than the drawing room."

Honoria turned to see her aunt gliding through the music room door wearing a bright smile and her best yellow day dress.

Honoria returned the smile and smoothed down her own floral print. Against Benedict's objection, Aunt Cecilia had been told about Honoria's plan—or, at least, the part about Benedict needing dancing lessons. She was residing with Honoria for the duration of the Season, so there was no way to have him in the house for any useful length of time without Aunt Cecilia discovering him. Nor would she have reacted well had anyone questioned her at a *ton* event about his comings and goings.

And somebody had to provide the music.

"Good. I was half afraid he would disappear into another excavation."

Aunt Cecilia snorted. "Not if he's anything like his father was at that age. Lord George Grey would take on any challenge—the more difficult it was, the more effort he'd put into it. And for some men, dancing is more than a little difficult."

"Was Lord George a good dancer?"

"I should say so. He cut quite the dashing figure, too—young ladies were setting their caps for him before they even came out."

Honoria raised an eyebrow inquisitively. "Including you, Aunt?"

"Oh yes," Aunt Cecilia answered without hesitation. "Not only was he handsome, but kind too. Your Mr. Grey is bookish like his mother, but he has his father's kindness."

Honoria was drifting toward one of the large windows that faced out onto the square, but paused to glance back at her aunt. "Do you think so?"

Aunt Cecilia nodded, heading toward the pianoforte and making herself comfortable on the bench. "Did you not see him at the Lambert ball last night? Lucy Drake was sitting all alone during the supper dance—she's nearly as old as you, and her only dowry is those awful smallpox scars on her face. Well, your Mr. Grey went over and sat with her through the rest of the set, and was very attentive to her at supper too. They didn't seem to talk much, but I doubt Lucy minded."

Honoria turned her face toward the sun shining into the room and felt herself smiling. "I did not know, but I'm not surprised. He is very kind indeed. But," she continued, turning away from the window, "you must stop call him *my* Mr. Grey. He isn't—"

A masculine voice interrupted Honoria's protest. "He is. For the next hour or so, at any rate."

Benedict stood just inside the door, and Honoria took the opportunity to look him over. He wore a charcoal cutaway coat over a gray-blue waistcoat and buckskin breeches. His shirt and cravat were crisp and white, his tall black Hessians polished to a high shine. Every stitch on him was unadorned, even plain. But the fabrics were fine and the tailoring equally so.

They suited him remarkably well.

"Your valet seems to have taken our conversation to heart."

Benedict gave her a little bow. "I don't know how he put up with me all those years in Greece. But he's like a new man since you've deemed my appearance to be important."

Honoria felt the corners of her mouth curving upward again. "You look a bit changed yourself—you're standing a little taller I think."

"It's probably my coat. The style is a bit tighter now than I remember. It rather forces one to stand straight with shoulders back." He came the rest of the way into the room and greeted Aunt Cecilia, then settled himself on the largest sofa to pull off his boots—with more struggle than he probably would have liked—and exchange them for the dancing pumps he carried. "There now. If I step on your toes, there's a chance I won't smash them completely."

"You used to be a fair dancer," Honoria reminded him, leading him to the space the footmen had cleared.

"I used to be a passable dancer," he corrected as she turned to face him.

"Then we shall begin with something easy. Aunt, the Beethoven minuet please."

"A minuet? Isn't that rather old fashioned?"

"Yes, but the time signature and tempo are right."

"For what?"

She noticed a woodsy, slightly sweet fragrance as he stopped an arm's length from her. It reminded her of the apple orchard at her father's country seat, where she and Benedict used to read when the weather was fine.

"A waltz."

He took a step back and the scent faded. "Honoria, no woman with any sense of propriety dances the waltz. Even I know that."

"Some do, actually. It's becoming more accepted now." She held out a hand to him. "Besides, there's very little memorizing involved in a waltz. It's more about rhythm than specific figures, so I thought it would be a good place to start your re-education."

He didn't respond, and she briefly wondered if he practiced doing so. Not reacting at all often seemed to be his reply these days. Or did he simply think things over more carefully now?

She wiggled the fingers of her outstretched hand. "You never have to dance it in public if it feels too unseemly to you."

That got a smile out of him, and came forward once more to take her hand. "Very well. You are the dancing mistress today."

The applewood fragrance returned and she realized that Benedict was its source. Interesting considering his condemnation of wearing scent at Lady Whitby's Black and White Ball. She took hold of his other hand and felt....*something.* It was the first time he'd touched her since their talk in the park, and both their hands were bare this time. Was that why it felt different? Or was it something else?

"It's a one-two-three, one-two-three rhythm like the minuet—and you just step." She guided him by the hands slowly around the empty space, counting aloud. "That's right, one big step, two little ones. One, two, three. One, two, three..."

"I feel ridiculous."

But he didn't stop, and so she gave him what she hoped was an encouraging smile. "That's because there's no music."

"Maybe there should be."

"All right, then music you shall have. Whenever you're ready, Aunt Cecilia. Slowly, please." Honoria halted and gave his hands a little squeeze. How warm and strong they were. "Just listen for a few measures and get a feel for it. When you're ready, step off and I'll follow you."

He nodded, his brows drawn together. In concentration or uncertainty?

Both, she decided a few moments later. The song was halfway over before Benedict made a move, and Honoria could see him mouthing "one-two-three" as he stepped with her around the center of the room, his gaze cemented to his feet. When the last note died away, his eyes met hers.

"How was that?"

"Not bad for your first try. Let's do it again."

His nod was matter-of-fact, but his lips curved into a smile that said he was clearly pleased. Honoria signaled and Aunt Cecilia played the piece again, just as slowly as before. But Benedict was ready, and he began his steps only a few measures in this time. He held Honoria's hands firmly and his movements were careful. But each time they repeated the song, Honoria saw his shoulders relax a fraction more and his eyes lift a little from the floor.

"I don't know what all the fuss is about," he said as the last note grew fainter. "There's nothing scandalous about this."

"We aren't to the scandalous part yet. Should we do that next?"

Benedict was rather proud of himself—he was taking to dancing with more ease than he ever imagined he would. Not that he was a particularly clumsy man, but neither had he ever been particularly graceful. He could even imagine himself waltzing with a lady in front of an assemblage of aristocrats without fear of disgracing himself.

Then Honoria dashed his imagined scene to tiny pieces.

His eyes widened as she drew him closer and placed his right hand on the small of her back. When she reached her left hand up to his shoulder, his body went rigid—these liberties were permitted at balls and assemblies in front of other people?

"Relax." She said the word softly, almost under her breath.

He wasn't sure if she was speaking to him or herself, but decided that the idea was a good one in either case. He tightened the muscles in his shoulders and held them so for a moment, then let go. Some of the tension remained, but some of it bled away and he felt his shoulders loosen.

She turned his free hand palm-up and placed hers in it. "There are other positions in which to waltz, but this is the one I like best. It feels the most natural."

"It's like an embrace. You've really danced like this with other gentlemen?"

She tilted her head back and laughed a little. "Yes, though not too many times. And—fortunately—never with someone I wasn't fond of. Are you ready?"

He adjusted his hand on her back, fitting it snugly against the curve of her body. "I think so."

"Step off with your right foot, just like before, and use your hands to turn me. Think of this"—she squeezed his left hand—"as the prow of a ship. You lead with that. This"—her other hand slid down his arm —"is like a rudder. A little pressure one way or the other on my back, and I'll know which way to turn."

He nodded. He could do this, if he could just concentrate on the steps rather than the woman so unexpectedly close to him. "Got it."

She replaced her hand on his shoulder. "We're ready, Aunt."

The music began and Benedict stood still for a few moments, trying to get a feeling for the mechanics of the steps in this new position. Honoria's expression and body were relaxed as she waited in the half-circle of his arm, as if she was perfectly comfortable being there.

That contentment flowed from her limbs into his and he stepped off into the dance, pulling Honoria with him...and nearly tumbled the pair of them to the ground.

The music stopped abruptly and Benedict held tight to his partner trying to regain his balance. "That was not the start I had hoped for."

"No, I suppose not. Let's try again." Her mouth was near his ear, and he heard her amusement rather than saw it.

Once they righted themselves, they did try again. And again. Each time they made it a little deeper into the music without mishap, but Benedict still couldn't shake the intimacy of what they were doing. Honoria's hand had slipped from his shoulder to take hold of his upper arm, possibly because he was six or seven inches taller than she was—he was sure that her hand on his shoulder was an uncomfortable reach for prolonged periods. Or perhaps she had a more secure hold on his arm than on his shoulder. However unintentionally, he'd tossed her about the room a good deal today.

But it felt like more than that...or at the very least, like it *could* be more.

That thought unsettled him. He and Honoria had been friends for nearly twenty years, and he'd never thought of her in any other way. But this sudden search for a wife coupled with the close contact of the waltz set his mind working. On the surface, a union between them would be brilliant. They were of similar rank and fortune—or would be when he inherited—and one of the properties entailed to Benedict's future marquessate adjoined one held by Honoria's father. There would also no longer be a reason to lie to His Grace, which would lighten Benedict's heart considerably. Honoria would make a fine marchioness, too, when the time came. That they were at ease in each other's company only sweetened the deal.

Was that enough, though? Others had married for less, certainly. Benedict had been considering such a marriage himself—was still considering it. But how would Honoria feel about such an arrangement?

"Ready?"

Her voice brought him back to the task at hand. "Yes. Perhaps we'll make it through the entire song this time."

The music started and Benedict focused on getting his feet to go where they were supposed to. One-two-three, one-two-three, one-two-three...

"Your dress keeps brushing against my legs." The words were out of his mouth before he'd even finished thinking them, and he felt heat rising in his cheeks. Why did he have to mention that?

Honoria only grinned. "Just be thankful I'm not wearing one of those huge gowns from the previous generation. Some of them were so wide a lady had to turn sideways to fit through the door."

"That could not have been terribly comfortable." One-two-three, one-two-three...so far, no stumbles...

"No. Nor was it terribly flattering. I can't think of a woman alive who could wear one of those monstrosities and look well in it."

One-two-three, one-two-three... "You could."

"Oh, I doubt it." Honoria had never been one to fish for compliments, and the tone of her voice said she wasn't doing so now. The laughter in her dark eyes agreed. "I'd be wider than I am tall!"

He smiled. "And you'd still be pretty. You always have been."

Once again the words were out of his mouth before they'd fully formed in his mind, but he wasn't embarrassed by them this time. A little confused, perhaps, as "pretty" began to take on a new connotation after his unexpected thoughts of marriage with Honoria. But not embarrassed. He'd only spoken the truth, after all.

And had apparently surprised her with it—her brows had risen for a moment before she replied, "You've never told me that before."

He tugged her into a turn to avoid a side table they'd danced too close to. "I should have done. Not that you didn't hear it often enough from others, but you should hear it from those you're closest to once in a while as well. I'll try not to wait twenty years to say it again."

The last note from the pianoforte echoed through the partially cleared room and Benedict released his partner, bowing low before her. She executed a grand curtsy in return, then clapped her hands.

"We did it! Not a single misstep through the whole piece."

She'd said "we" not "you", and for some reason that pleased him enormously. "We did. Perhaps there's hope for me after all."

He declined tea when it was offered and said his farewells, rather anxious now to be home where he could think in peace. Because he had a great deal more to think about now than when he'd risen that morning.

# Chapter 4

"I'm given to understand you've chosen a wife."

"What?"

Whitby entered Benedict's library, as was his custom, close on the heels of the butler. "You've been paying a lot of attention to one lady," he said, striding across the room and dropping into a wing chair opposite his cousin. "That sets tongues a-wagging."

"You mean Honoria? We have been friends for a long time—you know that."

"Friends who suddenly go driving every day, after the gentleman has called at the lady's home."

Benedict glanced at the book in his hands, then hunted around for a place marker. His cousin was sometimes a little too plain-spoken, but he was also clever and often gave good advice—which Benedict could sorely use. He found the marker and placed the book carefully on the table beside him. "Is there gossip?"

"People have noticed."

"Including your lady wife."

Whitby nodded. "She approves, by the way. She says Lady Honoria would be good for you, balance you out a bit."

"Balance me out?"

Whitby leaned back and chuckled. "You know how academic you can be, how quiet. If it were up to you, you'd spend all your time in here. But the lady has you out of the house. And I daresay you've been more social at entertainments since you started courting her—Lady Whitby says you hold actual conversations with people now."

That was the plan, of course, though Whitby didn't know it. Good to hear it was working.

"I still don't enjoy it. Since socializing is a necessity for finding a wife, I've been making the attempt."

Whitby smiled broadly. "It seems to have worked."

Benedict must have scowled, or at least frowned, because his cousin sat up a little straighter in his chair.

"You do have honorable intentions toward the lady, don't you?"

"I'm not exactly a rakehell, now, am I? And I would never do anything to hurt Honoria." Did Benedict sound as defensive to Whitby as he did to himself?

"Something else is troubling you then. What is it?"

Benedict hesitated, his mind groping for the right words. "How did you know Lady Whitby was the right woman for you?"

"Ah." Whitby relaxed back against the soft upholstery of his wing chair. "It's like that, is it?"

"Like what?"

"You want to marry for love."

And Benedict realized he did. Thoughts of his father crept into his mind, giving a young Benedict facetious advice about how to deal with females. *When she sets her mouth in a firm line like that, son, you'd best do whatever she wants,* Lord George Grey would say while grinning at his lady wife. Or, *One thing you learn when you become a husband is to say the words "yes my love" without even hearing the question. Because the answer is always yes.* But for all his teasing, Benedict's father did impart one important lesson to his son: a good husband loves his wife with all his heart. He never said it aloud, but he never had to; though it wasn't fashionable to be too fond of one's spouse, anyone with eyes could see how deeply Lord George had cared for his bride.

Did Benedict love Honoria like that? If he had to think about it, probably not.

But *could* he?

Whitby was nodding. "It's a tradition in our family, you know. Great-grandfather Whitby was supposed to marry a lady his father had chosen, but he fell in love with another and married her instead."

"And he encouraged his children to follow their hearts, too. I remember that story." Benedict felt his brows crowd together. "It turned out well for him. But what if you don't know what your heart wants?"

"Then you'll just have to wait until it tells you."

"That's not very helpful."

Whitby laughed. "A little too poetic for you, is it? How about this, then. Take note of how you feel when you spend time with her. Then note how you feel when you're not with her. If you'd rather be with her more often than not, your heart is starting to speak up."

"And what if I find I do love her, but she doesn't love me?"

"That, my friend, is when the poetry will start to make sense."

Benedict had been drawn to Lord Elgin's venture in Athens not only because it meant cataloging and preserving the remains of an ancient culture, but also because—if one observed carefully—those remains could tell a person an enormous amount about that culture. It was like putting clues together to solve a mystery, divining what a long-dead civilization might have been like.

Now he decided to turn his skill as an anthropologist on his situation with Honoria.

He was escorting her with her aunt to a concert given by the new Philharmonic Society at the Argyll Rooms, and decided this would be the perfect opportunity to begin a full-scale scientific study. He would take Whitby's suggestion and observe how he felt about Honoria throughout the evening. Taking the inquiry a step further, he also resolved to study *her* reactions to *him* during their time together. Perhaps he could learn not only of his own heart's desire, but something of hers as well.

She was presently engaged in conversation with a gentleman who looked too young to have even begun shaving. Tall and slender, he had curly blond hair that rebelled against the pomade with which he'd attempted to slick it back, and a ready smile for Honoria's every comment. She was gazing up at him, eyes a little wide, both hands gripping the fan she carried, as if he was the most fascinating man in London.

"Have you met Lord Thomas?" Honoria's aunt appeared beside Benedict, nodding in the direction of her niece.

"I haven't had the pleasure."

"Neither have I, but I knew his mother. Shall we go and speak to them? Honoria can introduce us."

Benedict thought he heard a note of mischief in her voice to go with the grin she'd flashed him. Her face, however, held nothing but polite inquiry only a moment later.

He offered her his arm and tried to approach the pair with the eyes of a scientist. Honoria's posture was straight as an arrow, her head tilted back to look this Lord Thomas in the eyes. As Benedict came closer, though, he could see her gaze drop to her companion's shoulder before returning to his face. Her thumb, too, absently strummed a rib of her fan.

"Honoria, dear, who is this handsome gentleman that has so captured your attention this evening?"

Honoria turned toward her aunt's voice and smiled—the same smile she used during her drives with Benedict. "This is Lord Thomas Morgan, son of the Duke of Whittington. Lord Thomas, my aunt Lady Cecilia Maitland, and Mr. Benedict Grey."

Lord Thomas reached for Lady Cecilia's hand, bowing so low over it he nearly brushed his lips across her knuckles. "I see now from which side of the family Lady Honoria's beauty originates."

Lady Cecilia smiled indulgently. "I was not aware you possessed such a silver tongue, Lord Thomas...nor such a keen eye with it."

Benedict fought to keep his eyes from rolling. The ladies and Lord Thomas, however, laughed politely at the little joke.

"Lord Thomas was just telling me about his reading preferences," Honoria said, changing the subject with a glance in Benedict's direction. "Shakespeare, was it not?"

Lord Thomas released Lady Cecilia's hand and flicked his gaze toward Benedict, too, before returning his attention to Honoria. "Yes, my lady. Only this afternoon I was reading *Romeo and Juliet* and thought of you:

But, soft! what light through yonder window
breaks?
It is the east, and Juliet is the sun.
Arise, fair sun, and kill the envious moon,
Who is already sick and pale with grief,
That thou her maid art far more fair than she."

Benedict bit down on the inside of his cheek, just hard enough to keep himself from making a comment, but Honoria seemed pleased. Or was that another version of her society smile?

"Well done, my lord. I would hear more, but I believe it's time we took our seats."

"Allow me to escort you."

Lord Thomas offered his arm to Honoria and strode off with her, which left Benedict trailing behind with Honoria's aunt.

"I wouldn't worry, Mr. Grey." Lady Cecilia laid her hand on Benedict's offered arm as they walked. "The boy has no serious interest in my niece."

"How do you know that?"

"Did you see the way he looked at you before quoting Shakespeare? Lord Thomas is barely two-and-twenty, and a third son with no income other than the allowance he receives from his father. He knows he can't compete with you—probably why he chose such an overused passage. Nor did it seem as if Honoria wanted him to try."

"I thought she looked a trifle bored."

"I suspect she was," Lady Cecilia agreed. "Perhaps she was wondering if *someone* was planning a visit to her father."

Already? "It has only been two weeks, my lady."

"Two weeks in which you've been to the house nearly every day, Mr. Grey. And it's not as though the pair of you were strangers before now."

"No," Benedict replied slowly. He doubted Honoria would have asked him for a pretend courtship if they had been newly acquainted. "But we have been apart for some time."

"That is true. Perhaps, if you aren't otherwise engaged after the concert, you'd be agreeable to a little refreshment at Alston House?" Lady Cecilia winked at him. "It will easier to become reacquainted without a crowd of gentlemen vying for her attention, will it not?"

Benedict allowed himself a smile. Honoria's aunt had been away for much of the time he'd spent with her family when he was growing up, so he hadn't known her all that well. But she'd always been slightly scandalous, and he was grateful for it now. Inviting a single gentleman to your home at night wasn't exactly the done thing, even if Benedict would never be alone with either lady. But he could definitely make use of some real conversational time with Honoria.

"It is certainly easier to speak with a lady when one is not trying desperately not to step on her toes."

Lady Cecilia chuckled. "I daresay you're right about that."

Between listening to the music and socializing at the interval meaningful dialogue during the concert turned out to be nonexistent. So Benedict was doubly grateful when he was seated beside Honoria on a cornflower blue sofa in the drawing room at Alston House later that evening. Lady Cecilia situated herself with a glass of brandy and her sewing basket near enough to the couple to talk to them without shouting, but far enough away that they could speak to each other with a degree of privacy.

Benedict mentally applauded her cleverness.

"Did you enjoy the concert this evening?"

"I did," Honoria answered, her voice full of enthusiasm and pitched just right for her aunt to hear. "The full power of the orchestra when they played the symphony just before the interval...it just isn't something you get from a pianoforte in your home, is it?" When he smiled briefly but gave no verbal response, she discreetly touched the back of his hand. "Did you enjoy the concert?"

Her skin was warm upon his. "I don't know much about music, but I do like to listen to it. And the Society was especially good. The Greek and Roman references were a nice touch, too."

"'Numa Pompilius' and 'Anacreon'? I thought you might find that aspect appealing."

"What about the Renaissance reference? Lord Thomas and his Shakespeare—did you find that appealing?" He said it with a teasing tone, and she laughed.

"Why Mr. Grey, are you jealous?"

"Should I be?" He turned his hand over beneath hers and lowered his voice. "We are supposed to be courting, after all."

She slid slightly closer to him. "He's harmless...merely practicing on me what he hopes will win another. Like you are."

"You must be an exceptional teacher to have two pupils engaging your services."

"Ah, but I was merely a brief test for Lord Thomas, not his teacher." She curled her fingers around his. "You are my only pupil."

He bent his head toward hers and caught the hint of a scent that was both familiar and unknown at the same time. It reminded him of spring and sunshine and books, but he couldn't quite identify it.

"Lucky for me." He closed his hand around hers—it felt good to hold. "And lucky for you. I need as much help as you can give me, I'm afraid."

Her eyes dropped to the cushion where their clasped hands lay. "I didn't think you knew the word 'afraid'."

He gave a short laugh. "Me? Truly?"

"How many times did you board a ship and travel round a continent? How long did you spend in a country where the weather and food and language are so different?"

"You think I wasn't afraid?" he asked softly, giving her hand a gentle squeeze. "I was terrified every moment of every sea voyage. The entire time I was in Athens I lived in fear that something ancient and priceless that I was supposed to protect would be smashed to bits, or that the constant armed conflict in Serbia was going to spill over into Greece."

"But you went anyway. Even after you'd come home to England the first time, you went back."

"The reward was well worth the risk."

Her dark eyes—the same color as the chocolate he'd discovered she liked to drink every morning—lifted to meet his. "You are a brave man, Benedict Grey. Your future wife will either be immensely proud of you, or extremely frightened for your safety."

"Which would you be?"

Her brows lifted in surprise for a moment, before dropping down as she considered her answer. "Both, I expect. Especially when you were off somewhere excavating some other historical site."

"You wouldn't come with me?"

She tilted her head slightly to the side. "I might. It would calm my mind to see you with my own eyes each day. But I would miss the Season tremendously. I like to dance, to gossip, to flirt—"

"I noticed."

Her smile returned and she swatted his arm with her free hand. "What would you know of flirting? I have yet to see you do it once."

"I may not know how to do it, but I certainly recognize it when I see it. Besides, it's you I'm supposed to be smitten with." He caught Honoria's hand as it retreated and kissed it quickly.

Lady Cecilia's gaze flickered up from her sewing, but she said nothing. It was enough, though, to remind Benedict that there was another person in the room.

"Perhaps it's time I take my leave." He planted a swift kiss on Honoria's other hand and released them both. "Aren't we working on country dances tomorrow?"

"We are," she confirmed, her smile growing.

"Then I'll need to rest well tonight." Benedict rose from the sofa and bowed to Lady Cecilia, who acknowledged him with a nod.

Honoria stood with him and lit a candle from the brace burning nearby. "I'll see you out."

She slipped her arm through his as they maneuvered through the house down to the ground level. A sleepy footman came forward with Benedict's hat and gloves as they reached the front door, then melted away into the dark.

Honoria set the candle on a table near the front door and turned to face Benedict. "I can't remember when I've had a more delightful evening."

"I'm not sure that I can, either."

The light from the candle was just bright enough to illuminate her face and he found himself overwhelmed by the desire to touch her one more time. He brushed his fingers over the soft skin of her cheek, then bent forward to allow his lips to follow. When he attempted to draw back, he felt her arms slide around his shoulders and hold him in place. She raised herself up on her toes and pressed her lips against his.

If there was any rational thought left in his brain, it exited right then.

His arms came around her, pulling her snugly against his body as his mouth opened over hers. He was gratified when she followed suit and kissed him back, a bit clumsily but oh so sweetly—once, twice more before lowering herself down.

"Good night, Benedict," she said. Her voice sounded as dazed as he felt.

"Good night," he managed in return.

How he got through the door and down the steps, he didn't know, but he found himself on the pavement, hat and gloves in hand, wondering what to do. Lady Cecilia had insisted they use the Alston carriage for the concert, so the ladies had come to his house in St. James Square before proceeding to the Argyll Rooms. He could probably find a hackney somewhere nearby, but decided walking at least part of the way would do him some good. As usual, he needed to think. Had he the answer to the question of his feelings for Honoria, or hers for him? Or was it simply a physical attraction that had sprung up between the two of them?

Either way, perhaps he should consider more seriously that visit to the duke.

# Chapter 5

Honoria fairly bounced out of bed the next morning, despite the long hours she'd lain awake during the night.

She'd kissed Benedict!

She still wasn't clear on what had possessed her to do such a thing, nor was she terribly sure what his response would be in the cold light of day. But at the moment she didn't care. He had held her as if nothing was more dear to him in the world, and she'd felt so safe in his arms.

She hadn't realized how much she'd needed that safety, that strength, until last night.

"There's a note here from Mr. Grey," her maid said, bustling into the room with a tray. "I thought you might want to read it while you had your chocolate this morning."

"Oh yes, thank you." Honoria poured herself a cup and broke the seal on the letter—he'd used his own this time rather than leaving it plain. She scanned the page quickly trying to get an overall sense of what he'd written, then went back and read again at a pace more conducive to comprehension.

"He's asked me to visit Whitby House with him this afternoon, to take tea with his mother and the marchioness."

"That's exciting," the maid replied with a bright smile.

"Or completely terrifying. I've met them both before, of course, but not..."

The maid nodded. Not as a prospective member of the family. For that is how they would see her, as Benedict's potential bride. Was that how he saw her now, too? Did he feel obligated to marry her after their kiss last night, even though no one knew about it but the two of them?

Or was this just the next logical step in their ruse? It certainly made sense—if Benedict had truly been courting her, an invitation from the female members of his family would be expected. But it was not something Honoria had prepared herself for. She would have to go into their home and essentially lie to them about her future with their cousin and son.

Exactly as Benedict would do with her father.

Well, there was nothing for it—just because she had been blind to its coming didn't mean she could avoid this complication. Especially not when her partner in this business was prepared to do much the same for her. She called for a pen and some paper and dashed off a reply to Benedict informing him that she would be ready at the appointed time.

But what to wear? She and her maid combed through the gowns in her dressing room, considering this one or that one, rejecting others out of hand. Together they pulled out several gowns for Honoria to try, and spread them out across her bed. Each time her maid got her laced in to one, Honoria would stand in front of the cheval glass turning slowly left and right before shaking her head.

She finally settled on a blush-colored muslin sprigged with tiny roses. Ordered last month, she had yet to wear it anywhere so it could serve as a topic of conversation if need be. The color was beautifully feminine and Honoria knew she looked well in it, which gave her confidence a much-needed lift.

She was ready by the time he arrived and elected not to make him wait, though her aunt suggested that spending a few minutes alone in the drawing room wouldn't go amiss with a gentleman. Honoria simply smiled and hurried down the main staircase.

His greeting to her was very correct, his face expressionless, as though he didn't remember that only twelve hours earlier they had been in each other's arms on this very spot. Nor did he reveal any emotion as he helped her into a carriage with the Whitby crest emblazoned on it.

When he settled himself on the seat across from her and not next to her, she decided she'd had enough. She stood carefully, one hand on the ceiling of the carriage for balance, and turned herself onto the plush velvet beside Benedict.

"Honoria, what are you doing?"

"You were pressed against me from shoulders to knees last night, but you can't sit beside me?

He blushed—a full, flaming blush, his cheeks and ears flooded with red. "I can't seem to think when you're close to me."

"That's what every lady wants to hear, that she turns gentlemen to blathering idiots," she replied, crossing her arms.

Benedict leaned forward, resting his forearms on his thighs. "That's not what I meant. I just—the nearer you are to me, the more I think about that embrace. And I need all my wits about me for this visit. We both do."

That he couldn't stop thinking about the two of them together wasn't necessarily a good thing. Was he obsessing about a lack of good judgment? Was he regretting a moment of weakness?

Was he, perhaps, a little bit in love with her?

She relaxed her arms and let her hands fall loosely into her lap. "We need to talk about last night."

He acknowledged her statement with a slow nod. "We do. But that is not a conversation to be rushed—we'll need more time than this drive will give us. Am I still invited for dancing lessons later?"

"Yes, of course. Though I'm not sure what we'll work on. The cotillion is for four couples, which we don't have, and I don't think you're quite ready for a Scotch reel yet."

That drew a small smile from him, though only his mouth was involved in the action. "You're probably right about that. Do you think your aunt would object if we walked in the garden instead? We could talk then."

"Short of leaving us alone in a room with the door closed, Aunt Cecilia is rather amenable to whatever we'd like. I think she'll not object to a walk in the garden."

"Good." He reached for one of her hands and gave it the briefest of squeezes.

Then he moved himself to the seat across from her and rode the rest of the way in silence.

Upon arriving at Whitby House in Park Lane they were whisked directly upstairs to the drawing room. Benedict resumed his powers of speech long enough to introduce Honoria to his mother, Lady George Grey, and his cousin's wife.

"Yes dear, we know Lady Honoria," his mother laughed as she resumed her seat. "There's no need to be quite so formal."

Thank goodness for that. This visit was going to be awkward enough without throwing in uncomfortable formalities.

"Come sit here," Lady George said, indicating a settee near her own chair, "and we'll have a nice, comfortable coze."

Honoria did as she was bid, both relieved and uneasy when Benedict made to sit beside her.

"Oh no, Benedict," Lady Whitby interrupted when he was midway between standing and sitting, "Whitby asked that I send you to him in his study. Something about carriages or curricles or something."

"Oh, yes." He straightened quickly, his ears turning faintly red.

"Are you ordering a new carriage at last?" Lady George asked, clasping her hands together in her lap.

Benedict cleared his throat. "A phaeton, perhaps. A town carriage at a later date." His eyes roamed down to Honoria. "I can't continually borrow conveyances from Whitby whenever we wish to go somewhere."

He was either masterfully selling their imminent faux betrothal, or he was nervous and looking to her to steady himself. Oddly, she was pleased with either motive.

When Benedict had shut the door behind him, Lady Whitby poured tea and began her genteel interrogation.

"Does he often follow you around like that?"

Honoria found she was a little insulted by the question on Benedict's behalf—it made him sound like a lost little puppy. The man had some difficulties in ballrooms and drawing rooms to be sure, but he'd taken over the running of an operation that brought several shiploads of invaluable historic cargo to England. How many others could say that?

"He's a bit protective, I think," she replied, lifting her teacup to her mouth for a sip. Not a lie—he'd always been protective of Honoria—though she'd been doing her share of protecting, too, these past weeks, if in a more subtle fashion.

"That's Benedict," Lady George added with a warm smile. "Do you remember him after his father died? Though he was but a boy, he escorted me everywhere I went—even if it was only from one side of the house to another."

The memory came back to Honoria in images. She and Benedict had been, what? Ten? Eleven? She remembered digging in the gardens not far from one of the old marquess's country houses, looking for medieval battlefields and ancient settlements. And lounging on the terrace when the weather was hot, conjugating Latin verbs together. All this time she thought Lady George had asked Benedict to stay close, when in reality he'd been keeping watch over his mother.

"He's always been mindful of those he cares for," Lady Whitby said, her eyes flickering toward Honoria. "What's your opinion of this phaeton he's purchasing?"

"I was not aware until today that he was considering it." Honoria resisted the urge to shrug. "Benedict is entitled to purchase whatever he likes."

"I heard he was also thinking of refurbishing his house in St. James Square," the marchioness continued with well-practiced casualness. "Or perhaps even beginning a search for a larger home."

"Now that's just gossip," Lady George cautioned.

"But it would be noteworthy if it were true."

Both women were looking at Honoria now, Lady Whitby with stark interest and Lady George with what appeared to be hope.

Drat them.

And drat Honoria's thoughtless plan.

She sipped her tea again. "How nice for him."

Lady George blinked, seeming to realize that she'd been staring. "Honoria, might I ask you some questions of a more...personal nature?"

Oh dear. "You may."

"Do you care for my son?"

"Yes, of course," Honoria responded without hesitation. That she could answer truthfully lessened some of the weight on her conscience.

"And do you want to see him happy?"

"I always have." Another truth, another measure of weight lifted.

Lady George paused, fiddling with her teacup before asking the next question. "Do you think you can make him happy?"

Honoria carefully set her own teacup in its saucer. She knew what she was supposed to say, that she would do everything in her power to keep Benedict happy for as long as they were wed. And if they had actually planned to marry, she likely would have said such a thing. But they never had such plans, and Honoria found she could not lie to his mother after all.

"I-I don't know. I can only hope the decisions we make are the right ones...for both of us." Honoria realized her answer didn't quite match the question, but knew it was the best she could do.

Lady George smiled once more, a little wistfully. "It was brave of you to answer so honestly. But then, you've always been a brave girl. Especially these last few years, else you would not have waited all this time for Benedict to return home."

Double drat—she thought Honoria had remained unmarried in hopes that Benedict would propose, as if they had fallen in love early on and were parted by circumstance.

That was one myth she could not perpetuate. "You make is sound as if we came to some sort of arrangement before he went to Athens. But Lady George, we never did—it wasn't like that between us."

"Perhaps not," the lady said, undaunted. "But I've seen the way he looks at you, and the way you look at him. Your minds may not have settled anything between you, but your hearts have done so some time ago."

Honoria shook her head gently. Her heart had nothing to do with this, even if her body had begun to put forth its own ideas. "I don't think so."

But Lady George would not be dissuaded—another thing Honoria would have to discuss with Benedict when he came to Alston House.

If she ever made it there herself. This visit was beginning to feel as though it would never end.

"Thank heavens you're here, Mr. Grey," Lady Cecilia said as she rushed down the main staircase.

Benedict's head snapped up, the gloves he'd been removing forgotten in an instant at the worry that laced her voice. "What's wrong?"

"Honoria took a letter up to her bedchamber to read when she returned home from her visit to Whitby House, but now she refuses to come out! I can think of only one thing that would have upset her so..."

Lady Cecilia let the word trail away, but Benedict knew what she was thinking.

Honoria must have had news of her father.

He quickly peeled off his gloves and handed them with his hat to a waiting footman. "Perhaps she will speak to me."

Lady Cecilia waited for the footman to make his exit before stepping closer to Benedict and lowering her voice. "I'm more concerned about her well-being than I am about propriety, Mr. Grey. If she will admit you, don't hesitate to enter."

Benedict nodded sharply and headed up the stairs, knocking softly when he reached the closed door of Honoria's bedchamber. When the first knock brought no response, he tried again, with a little more force.

"Honoria, it's Benedict."

He heard a slight rustling before the door was whipped open. "I thought you'd never come."

There were no tear stains on her face, no puffy eyes, no signs at all that she'd been crying. She was a strong woman, but her father's death would certainly have brought intense emotion. What was going on?

She reached for his hand and pulled him into the room, shutting the door hastily behind her and marching over to her bed. "I've had a letter from my father."

He followed her part of the way. "Your aunt suspected as much. How bad is it?"

"Oh, Benedict, that's just it—it isn't bad at all." She took up the folded paper that was lying haphazardly on a brilliant blue counterpane. "The letter is in his own hand, a *steady* hand."

Benedict's brows rose as he strode the rest of the way across the room. "What does it say?"

Her dark eyes lifted to his. "He is recovering."

# Chapter 6

"That's wonderful!" Benedict wrapped his arms around her and lifted her off the ground. The scent of her perfume clung to her skin and he finally placed the fragrance—apple blossoms, like those in the orchard they used to frequent before he went away.

Her hands came down on his shoulders, accompanied by a joyful laugh. "It is! It's beyond wonderful!"

Honoria's momentum carried her back to the ground, but Benedict kept her clasped against him. "There's something else, too, isn't there?

She nodded, the motion setting her curls brushing against the lapel of his coat. "He says that he's recovered enough to come to Town. He cannot participate in the activities of the Season, of course, and he'll have to make the trip in easy stages. But he is coming here."

"It will be good to see His Grace again."

"It will. Oh it will! I thought never to see him again when I left him last." Her smile faded as her hands slid down his chest, pushing herself gently away. "But our plan..."

"Oh. Yes. We are in a bit of a situation now, aren't we?" He helped her up onto the bed and settled himself beside her, mentally sorting through their circumstances. "Well, I believe we have a few options."

"We do?"

He nodded, taking her hand in his. "We could continue on with our plan as you originally conceived it, though perhaps we no longer need the betrothal. We'll maintain our sham courtship and keep working on my dancing and deportment. If your father won't be going out, he won't be privy to gossip. Nor will he know how much time we spend together outside this house unless you or I or your aunt tells him."

"I'd have to have a conversation with Aunt Cecilia." She shifted her hand, nestling her palm snugly against his. "But Papa will be suspicious of your daily visits even if he knows nothing of our time together elsewhere. We were much together before you went to Greece, but that was several years ago. And I'm supposed to have been husband hunting these past weeks."

"You think he'll come to the conclusion all on his own that I'm courting you."

"I do." Her grip on his hand became tighter. "And he'll be so far beyond disappointment when we aren't actually wed that I think it might break his heart."

Which would be bad enough by itself. What if such distress had ill effects on His Grace's already uncertain health as well?

"We could end the ruse now. It's earlier than we had planned but you were always going to throw me over anyway."

She tucked a curl behind one ear. "Do you think you're polished enough to go the rest of the Season alone?"

"It would undoubtedly be easier with your help," he said, running his thumb across the back of her hand. "But I could manage. I suspect there are some ladies out there who like a little shyness in a gentleman."

Honoria grinned. "Oh, there definitely are such ladies. It's endearing when a gentleman summons up all his courage just for you, even when it's only to ask for a dance."

"If I could find but one that suited me, I'll have attained my goal. And my dancing has improved—I can waltz as well as anyone."

"You can." Her gaze drifted away from his, a little unfocused. "And your country dance figures are passable."

"The rest of the dances I can just sit out. Or take a turn about the room with a lady."

Her fingers loosened around his hand. "As long as you don't take her out onto the terrace alone."

"I would never do so—unless it was the lady's idea." He winked, but she wasn't looking. What was buzzing around in that head of hers? "There's another option to consider. We could truly become betrothed."

Her eyes flew back to his and her mouth formed a little O—he'd startled her with those words. Well, blast it, he'd startled himself, too. Certainly he'd been thinking about it, but he hadn't intended to address the subject like this.

"It would solve all of our problems," he explained, wondering if he was trying to convince her or himself. "I would have a wife perfectly suited to become the next Marchioness of Whitby, and you would have a husband to take care of you." She opened her mouth to speak, but Benedict held up his free hand to stop her. "I know that His Grace is on the mend, but I also know that he'll still be adamant you find a husband. He survived this last bout of illness, but he may not survive the next."

"You're probably right about that," she conceded. "I can hear him now, cajoling me to 'see reason' as he always puts it."

"His reasoning isn't wrong, you know."

She ran her free hand down the material of her skirt. "Perhaps someday a world will exist where a female does not need the protection of a husband—or anybody else—if she doesn't want it. And I know that our world isn't so, but..."

Her hand reached her knee and she lifted it to repeat the motion, but Benedict caught it in his. "But what?"

She sighed and let her eyes drop to his shoulder. "But I wanted to marry for love. This is my eleventh Season, Benedict, and I've only encountered gentlemen who were chiefly interested in my dowry or my bloodline. How are two people supposed to build a life together when one is no better than a prized mare?"

"Do you think that's how I see you? As a means to money or a link to the Maitland family tree?"

She shook her head, but still didn't meet his gaze. "To you I am Honoria: friend, dancing master, partner in verb conjugation—"

"—kisser of gentlemen in darkened front halls."

She blushed then, and Benedict watched with fascination as the color blossomed in her cheeks. When was the last time he'd seen her blush?

"I-I didn't think—"

"You always were somewhat impulsive. It got you into trouble sometimes when we were children, but I have always admired that about you."

"You have?"

He released one of her hands to grasp her chin, carefully turning her head so he could see her into eyes again. "I over-think things much of the time, and therefore am often slow to act. Your spontaneity helps me get out of my own head and experience things instead of just contemplating them."

"So you're glad I kissed you?"

He could see the beginnings of a smile tugging at the corners of her mouth and allowed his own smile to grow. "I am. If you hadn't, I'd quite possibly still be deciding if it was a good idea to try." He released her chin and inched closer to her on the bed. "Did you like kissing me?"

Her blush deepened, but she answered in a steady voice. "Yes. I don't think I did it very well, but it was pleasurable."

"If we were wed, I could teach you how it's done...and more." He was grinning fully now—he'd always enjoyed teasing her. "I do owe you for the dancing lessons."

He stood abruptly, clasping both her hands and drawing her to her feet. When he dropped to one knee, her eyes went wide. "Benedict, are you really asking me to marry you?"

"I am. We are good together, you and I, and good *for* each other. There is no other woman I'd rather have by my side. Honoria Maitland, will you do me the great honor of becoming my wife?"

She stood looking down on him, her face a mask of surprise. Benedict had surprised himself once again—he certainly hadn't planned on proposing marriage to anyone today—but this time it was a good surprise. Holding Honoria's hands in his, imagining her presiding over his home and his children, felt so very right. She'd been his best friend since they were eight years old, and he wanted to be with her always.

But she hesitated.

"Honoria?"

"Yes?"

Benedict's brows drew together. "Was that a yes, you'll marry me? Or yes, Honoria is your name."

"The second one."

Her voice was quiet, giving no indication of her feelings, and he began to feel ridiculous down on the floor at her feet. He stood with as much dignity as he could muster and rubbed his thumbs over both her hands.

"Honoria, what is it? If I've horribly mangled this proposal, I'm very, *very* sorry. I've never asked a woman for her hand before..."

Her lips twitched in a brief, sympathetic smile. "No, it isn't that. Your speech was actually quite nice."

"Then what? Whatever it is you can tell me."

She squeezed his hands and looked him straight in the eyes. "Do you love me, Benedict?"

"What?"

"I told you I wanted to marry for love, so I'm asking if you love me."

A question he'd been asking himself and for which he still had no definitive answer. "If you want to marry for love, I should be asking if *you* love *me*."

And that was apparently not the answer she was looking for. She pulled her hands from his and moved a few steps from him, taking the apple blossom scent with her. "Don't do that—don't deflect, or get pedantic. Just answer the question."

"I care about you more than anyone else." That was true, had always been true. "And there is clearly a physical attraction between us." Also true, so much that it took every ounce of self-control he possessed not to go to her, take her in his arms, and teach her more about kissing.

Her back was to him and he couldn't see her face, but her voice was flat. "But you don't love me."

"I don't know what that kind of love is, Honoria—I've never been in love before. I could love you like no other person in the world ever could and not be sure of it. Isn't my respect and affection enough?"

She was still for several agonizing moments, and Benedict finally understood her annoyances with his own long silences. How maddening it was to wait for someone to answer a simple question!

But this question was far beyond simple.

"No." Her voice was so soft he wasn't sure she'd even spoken aloud until she repeated the word. "No. It's not enough." She turned to face him but didn't approach, wrapping her arms around herself as if she were cold. "I want love, Benedict. Real, strong, can't-mistake-it-for-anything-else love. I want to be the center of my husband's world, and for him to be the center of mine."

He ventured a step toward her. "I would make you the center of my world—you practically are already."

"Because you need me right now. You need me with you to navigate the ocean of Polite Society, to teach you to dance, to help you say the right things to the right people. Once you're wed, I doubt you'll go out much and you won't need me anymore."

He took another step. "I will always need you."

She stepped backward. "You managed for six years in Athens without me."

What could he say to that? He *had* managed without her those years, quite well in fact. He'd run Lord Elgin's entire operation without the slightest bit of help from Honoria. And it was entirely possible that he'd be off on another project in the not too distant future. Would he need her then?

His lack of answer must have ended the discussion for her, because she unwrapped one arm from her torso and pointed toward her bedchamber door. "You should go."

What? She was throwing him out? "Honoria—"

Her voice was as flat as her expression, but she was firm. "No, Benedict. I will not marry you. Our business is concluded, and you should go now."

There was certainly no use in trying to argue with the lady when he had no argument she would accept, so he bowed low and left her, not even stopping to collect his hat and gloves on the way out of the house.

Honoria remained standing, statute-like, staring at the empty doorway of her bedchamber. When Benedict asked her to marry him, she had for a moment envisioned herself as mistress of his modest house and mother of his children. She'd remembered the tender way he'd kissed her after the Philharmonic Society concert, and how wonderful it felt when he touched her. But when he couldn't tell her he loved her, she knew she couldn't go through with it.

Her father would chide her, perhaps even scold her. He would say that Benedict was her perfect match in every way, and she was daft to refuse him. But she didn't regret her decision—she wanted a man who loved her and would not settle for less.

Yet tears began welling in her eyes and she wrapped her arms tighter around herself. Would their friendship survive this day? Most certainly the answer was no. Even short formal encounters at *ton* events would be awkward now; there was no way they'd ever be comfortable enough with each other to sit together and share confidences. Nor likely would they drive or walk or dance together again, and Honoria felt a physical pain in her chest at the realization. Benedict said he'd admired her spontaneity, but this time it cost her dearly.

# Chapter 7

He missed her.

> O Venus, beauty of the skies,
> To whom a thousand temples rise,
> Gaily false in gentle smiles,
> Full of love-perplexing wiles;
> O goddess, from my heart remove
> The wasting cares and pains of love.

It had been three days since Benedict's proposal—three days that he'd spent in his library, trying to find solace in books. It was a technique that had worked countless times before, quelling homesickness when he went off to Eton and later to Cambridge, helping him escape from and work through the grief at his father's death, calming his fears each time he boarded a ship and sailed away from safe, stable land.

But his books brought him no comfort this time.

It didn't help that, in an effort to drown his misery in all things ancient, he'd stumbled across a slim volume of Greek poetry. Unable to concentrate sufficiently on the foreign words, he'd distracted himself by hunting for an English translation.

Then he sat down to read it.

*If ever thou hast kindly heard*
*A song in soft distress preferred,*
*Propitious to my tuneful vow,*
*O gentle goddess, hear me now.*

Who knew a person could hurt another person so badly with one single word? Had Honoria said "yes", he would be making preparations to marry the one person in the world who had always understood him. But she'd said "no", and his whole world had fallen apart—just when he was beginning to settle into it.

*Celestial visitant, once more*
*Thy needful presence I implore.*
*In pity come, and ease my grief,*
*Bring my distempered soul relief*

Grief was—surprisingly—the very word to describe his emotional state. He *was* grieving, not for the loss of a comfortable marriage but for the loss of his closest friend, only weeks after they'd found each other again. How would he manage without her?

Honoria had insisted that he got by in Athens without a whit of support from her, but he realized that she was wrong. She might not have been with him, but she had frequently been in his thoughts. Most of the letters he'd received from his mother had included scraps of news pertaining to Honoria. Often they were frivolous things, like the color of her new dress or the way she'd styled her hair. Sometimes there were more serious anecdotes: how she'd sat with her father when he was ill or how capably she handled the household. Whatever the tidings, they always brought a sense of warmth and affection and home.

*Favour thy suppliant's hidden fires,*
*And give me all my heart desires.*

He buried his face in the pages of the book. "I am an idiot."

"We're all a little slow sometimes, cousin."

Benedict straightened to find Whitby standing alone at the door of the library. "How the devil did you get in here?"

Whitby strode to one of the windows and threw back the closed curtains, ignoring the question. "Lady Whitby and I were worried when you failed to turn up for Eleanor's come-out last night."

"What? Oh, right—your eldest's ball. That was last night?"

Whitby went to the other window and dragged open those curtains as well, allowing harsh sunlight to flood the room. "It was. And you disappointed her severely." He turned to face his cousin. "When I arrived here to see what had happened to you, your valet and butler said you were in a sorry state—holed up here with your books, not speaking to anyone, having to be coaxed to bed at night, not eating or sleeping much. You look like hell, too. Have you been drinking?"

Benedict ran a hand over the beard sprouting on his face. How long had it been since he'd shaved? "No."

Whitby dropped into his favorite chair. "Maybe you should. What happened?"

"I asked Honoria to marry me."

Whitby rose and went to the sideboard, pouring out two measures of ouzo from the decanter. He didn't say anything until he'd brought one glass to Benedict and returned to his chair. "That explains your new title—are you Baron Idiot, Viscount Idiot, or something a bit higher up?"

"I believe you may have to start calling me Your Grace." Benedict looked at the glass, then set it on the small table beside him.

Whitby winced. "Ouch. Do you want to talk about it? Or do you want to sit here and brood some more? I'm game for either, but I'm not leaving you alone like this."

"Ironically, this is something I would have talked to Honoria about—especially before I went to Athens. Even when I was at university we remained close."

"But now?"

"But now I suspect she never wants to see me again."

"What did you do?"

Benedict hung his head. "She asked me if I loved her...and I hedged."

"That doesn't sound so bad."

"But it was." Benedict planted his elbows on his knees and dropped his head into his hands. "She told me she wanted to marry for love, Whitby. Then she asked me if I loved her, and I didn't say yes."

Whitby sat back in his chair and whistled. "You *are* an idiot, then. Anyone who's been within a mile of you two knows you're in love with her."

Benedict's hands scrubbed through his tangled hair. "Well, I didn't figure that out until today."

"And if you explain that to her now, it will look like you're telling her what she wants to hear to get her to the altar."

"Precisely."

Whitby grinned. "Did I ever tell you how many times I proposed before Lady Whitby accepted? It was four. Four times I asked her for her hand, and four times she turned me down. I don't even remember the reasons she gave—you'll have to ask her, she tells the story better than I do—but she damn near broke my heart each time. I almost didn't try again, but I'd discovered that life was invariably sweeter when I was with her. And there's that stubborn streak that runs in the family, too—I had to try one more time."

"I'm not asking for Honoria's hand five times, cousin."

Whitby's grin turned into a laugh. "You will if she keeps turning you down."

Benedict groaned. "How did you even find the courage to talk to her again? Or to go out in public when the whole of the *ton* knew what happened?"

Whitby's expression faded into something more serious. "I knew she was worth it. I didn't care what I had to go through, I just needed her with me."

Benedict blew out a heavy sigh. "I do love her, but I don't know if I can handle another rejection."

"You've not recovered yet from this one," Whitby said, rising from his chair and ambling the few steps to his cousin. He clapped a hand on Benedict's shoulder and gave it a squeeze. "Take some more time with Homer, or whatever you're reading. Drink some ouzo, or whisky, or lemonade if it makes you feel better. When you're ready, try again."

"It's Sappho. And next time I'll have a solid plan."

"That's the spirit," Whitby smiled, giving his cousin another pat. "A better plan gives you a better chance."

"That explains this disaster, then—I had no plan at all."

Whitby returned to his chair, his eyes and mouth wide with exaggerated horror. "No plan? No wonder she refused you."

"Shut up." Benedict rubbed his hands over his face. "You know I have no improvisational skills. I didn't intend to ask her to be my wife that day, it just sort of happened. And I've never been good with 'just sort of happened'."

"True, but you're more at ease with people you know well. And you know Lady Honoria better than just about anybody. Don't over-think it."

"Good advice," Benedict said, reaching for his abandoned glass of ouzo. "You know me rather well, too."

"He's here."

Honoria walked into the enormous ballroom at Almack's with her Aunt, her eyes instinctively roaming the crowd of people—as they had for the past week—looking for Benedict. He topped most men by two or three inches, making him easy to spot even among a sea of gentlemen wearing similar dark tailcoats. Whether she wanted to seek him out or avoid him, she didn't know. Nor had it mattered—she'd seen not a whisper of him since she refused him and ordered him from her home.

Until now. To her surprise she found him here in the Assembly Rooms, not in the throng of onlookers but in the midst of the dancers. He was partnering a girl—and a girl she was, looking as though she still belonged in the schoolroom—only a few inches shorter than he was in a country dance. Her chestnut hair glinted in the light from the candles in the chandeliers above, her white gown swirling about her as she moved.

"Who is here?" Aunt Cecilia asked, trying to follow her niece's gaze.

"Benedict. And he's *dancing*."

Aunt Cecilia craned her neck, heedless of decorum. "He is—and doing it rather well. You should be proud of your pupil, my dear."

"Who is that he's with? I don't recognize her."

"I don't either. She must be a new debutante." Aunt Cecilia tilted her head slightly. "He seems to be enjoying her company, whoever she is."

Drat the man, he did seem so. His face was animated when he spoke to his partner between figures of the dance, and when he wasn't speaking he was smiling.

He had never looked that merry during his lessons with Honoria.

She shook off the thought, and the feeling of discontent that it brought. What did it matter to her who Benedict danced with? She had no claim on him.

"Well, good for him," she managed. And a part of her *was* truly happy to see him so much at ease in public—it had simply never occurred to her that he could be so with someone else.

Another part of her, though, longed to be the one he smiled at, the one who took his arm as he led her from the dance floor. She wanted his hazel eyes to light up when they saw her, and to be swept up in his arms and kissed witless. She wanted to share confidences and opinions and plans and...

And she had said no when he offered it all to her.

"Aunt Cecilia, might we return home? I'm suddenly not feeling very well."

"Are you certain? We've only just arrived." Her aunt turned toward her and put a hand to Honoria's cheek. "You do look a bit pale. Perhaps some lemonade and a dance would help?"

Honoria shook her head. "If I wasn't feeling ill, that awful lemonade would surely make me so. And I don't feel like dancing."

Aunt Cecilia's eyes widened. "You must feel poorly indeed. I'll call for the carriage."

They waited together near the entrance, Honoria hooking her arm through her aunt's and holding it more tightly than she meant to. By the time the carriage arrived, Aunt Cecilia looked genuinely worried, seating herself beside her niece and wrapping an arm around Honoria's shoulders.

"It's Mr. Grey, isn't it?" she asked softly.

Honoria laid her head on her aunt's shoulder. "I am a fool. A blind fool. It was never supposed to turn out this way."

"Things rarely end up the way we plan them."

"Nearly everything did this time—but that's the problem."

Aunt Cecilia gave Honoria's shoulders a little squeeze. "What happened?"

"You know about the promise I made to Papa when he thought he was dying. Well, I didn't want to marry just anyone. In fact, I didn't want to marry anyone at all unless he loved me."

"Not an easy thing to do."

Honoria shook her head. "Then I ran into Benedict at Lady Whitby's ball." She smiled in the darkness of the carriage, recalling how literal that statement was. "He needed help polishing his society manners, and I offered him a bargain. I'd teach him to dance and make himself agreeable, and he would act as if he were courting me. We were going to announce a betrothal for Papa's sake, then I was going to cry off after..."

Aunt Cecilia nodded against the crown of Honoria's head. "But your father recovered."

"And Benedict asked for my hand—a real offer, not the subterfuge I'd concocted. I-I sent him away."

"That was the day your father's letter arrived. I wondered why Mr. Grey left without so much as a word."

Honoria turned her face toward her aunt's silken sleeve. "I refused him. He couldn't tell me he loved me so I refused him."

"Then you saw him with another lady tonight."

Honoria lifted her head from Aunt Cecilia's shoulder and snorted indelicately. "Lady? She was half my age if she was a day. What can she give him that I cannot?"

"A 'yes'."

Honoria frowned in the dark. "I deserved that."

"It's true." Aunt Cecilia found Honoria's hand and clasped it in hers. "And you have a decision to make. You can make up your mind to let Mr. Grey go on to whatever happiness he might find without you. Or you can float along like a paper boat on the Serpentine and wait to see if he comes back to you."

"But he was never really mine to begin with. It was all for show."

"Was it?"

*Was* it? Had Honoria missed something her aunt had seen? "Or?"

"Or," Aunt Cecilia continued, "you can play an active part in your future."

Honoria gestured with her free hand, even though she knew her aunt couldn't see her do it. "I tried that, and look how it turned out."

"You did try—once. The question is, are you going to try again?"

Honoria had no ready answer, and leaned against Aunt Cecilia for physical support as well as the emotional kind. "What would you do?"

Aunt Cecilia put both her arms around her niece and hugged her. "It doesn't matter what I would do. It only matters what you will do."


Honoria bid her aunt good night and went to her bedchamber as soon as they reached Alston House. What *would* she do? There wasn't a passive bone in her body, she was certain of that. But when she had tried to take her future in hand, she'd made a complete mess of her oldest friendship. And she loved Benedict, despite his own ambiguity. If she went to him and an agreement was struck, could she spend the rest of her life with a man who very possibly didn't love her in return? Was she settling to try to soothe her heart?

If she let him go, she knew there would be more nights like this one. He would eventually find a woman who was satisfied with his affection and respect. Honoria would see them together when they came to Town for the Season—if they came to Town. Perhaps Benedict would find a lady who was content to spend her days in the country, or the museums. Or one who would travel with him to excavation sites all over the world. She'd never see them together in those cases.

She'd never see him at all.

# Chapter 8

Benedict stood in the morning room of his townhouse, staring at a potted sapling sitting in the middle of the breakfast table—a cutting from an apple tree that lived in the orchard he and Honoria used to frequent. He had sent for it the same day he sent the note to Honoria pledging his participation in her pretend courtship, and it had arrived this afternoon. He'd meant it as a gift to her, thinking a reminder of the good times they'd shared would be comforting when her father was so ill.

What was he going to do with it now?

A footman stepped tentatively through the open door. "Lady Honoria Maitland has arrived, sir."

What? She was in his house? "I'll see her here."

The footman bowed himself out and Benedict combed his fingers through his hair. A thousand reasons for Honoria's visit ran through his head as he straightened his cravat and waistcoat. Was it her father? Had some evil befallen him on his journey to Town? Had one of her suitors offered for her? Had her aunt fallen ill? He hadn't put on a tailcoat this morning. Did he have time to do it now?

"Hello, Benedict."

She stood alone in the doorway, clothed in a pinkish dress with little flowers embroidered all over it and looking as beautiful as he'd ever seen her. Her bonnet was still tied securely under her chin, though, and the brim shaded her face enough to keep her expression a mystery.

At least she had called him Benedict, not Mr. Grey. "Hello, Honoria. Your maid can wait in the kitchen if she chooses. I don't have much in the way of staff, but she'll find some company there."

"I didn't bring a maid."

His brows drew together. "You didn't come here alone...did you?"

She nodded, making the silk rose on her bonnet flutter. "I took a hackney so no one would see the Alston crest on the carriage."

"You don't think my neighbors may have seen you at the door?" He reached for her arm and tugged her into the room. "You've all but ruined your reputation."

"I don't care. I needed to talk to you."

She would care if one of the gossip rags got wind of this. "Very well. But take off your hat—I'll not have a conversation with half your face."

He pulled out a chair from the breakfast table and she sat, carefully pulling her bonnet off. When she began to pluck her gloves from her fingers, he seated himself beside her. But she didn't speak. She kept her eyes on her hands as if her gloves were dangerous items that might go off at any moment.

But he could not take the silence. He turned himself sideways in his chair and leaned forward, inelegantly pulling her gloves off and depositing them on the table where she'd placed her bonnet. The faint scent of apple blossoms clung to her skin. "Now, what would you like to talk about?"

Her eyes remained focused on her hands. "I-I don't know. I didn't get that far in my plan."

He couldn't help but smile. "You risked being compromised—rendered unmarriageable and unfit for society—to come here, but you don't know what you wanted to say?"

She raised her eyes to his, one brow arched with a touch of defiance. "I did."

Oh, did he love her! How could he have ever doubted it? "Why don't we talk about this specimen on my table then?"

"All right."

Her uncertainty seemed to bolster his confidence, and he took both her hands in his. "Do you remember the spring you father and stepmother were wed?"

"I do. Papa insisted we have the wedding at Orchard Lake and turned it into a week-long fête."

Honoria wrinkled her nose, and Benedict laughed. "You liked that estate best out of all His Grace's properties. Don't pretend you didn't."

"I didn't like being dragged back into the country in the middle of my second Season." The expression on her face softened. "You came down from Cambridge for the ceremony."

"Mmhmm. I stayed at Whitby's Westbrook next door. Remember?"

She was leaning slightly forward now, a small smile on her lips. "Half the *ton* came, too, so I got to finish my Season after all. Papa hired that orchestra to play in the little folly behind the house, and we danced outdoors until it was too dark to see. Except when we'd sneak off to the orchard and read when the crowd got to be too much for you."

"*I* used to read," he grinned. "You would sit beside me on the blanket and talk about your beaux, your dresses, the dresses other girls had worn, your new stepmother, how happy your father looked, the weather—"

She freed one of her hands to smack his knee. "I didn't talk that much." Her fingers slid back into his grasp. "Did I?"

"Yes, you did. But I didn't mind. I liked being there with you, having you close to me."

"I liked spending that time with you, too. But what does that have to do with this?" She nodded toward the sapling.

Benedict released her hands and rose from his chair, bending across the table to grab hold of the pot and drag it closer. "We always sat near that enormous apple tree—"

"The one that seemed to have more blossoms on it than the others, every single year. It smelled heavenly."

"Is that why you wear apple blossom perfume?" he asked, allowing himself to be diverted for a moment. It was a question he'd been meaning to ask her.

A pink tinge crept into her cheeks. "I only started wearing that a few weeks ago. I-I noticed your applewood scent during one of our dancing lessons..."

A fluttery sensation flooded Benedict's body and he felt giddy. She wore apple blossom perfume because he wore applewood, and had risked her future with the *beau monde* to talk to him alone.

"Do you know why I chose applewood?"

"I figured it had to do with our orchard."

*Our orchard.* How right she was. "That spring in the orchard? I think that's when I fell in love with you." He pushed his chair back with one foot and knelt before her, clasping her hands in his once more. "And I have loved you with all my heart every since. I was just too addle-pated to know it."

Honoria laughed—a bright, bubbly laugh that sounded like a hundred years worth of happiness in one burst. "I'm afraid I was just as slow as you were, my love. But the important thing is that we get it right at some point in time."

"I believe that point is now." He brushed his lips over the backs of her hands. "I will never be comfortable in society, never enjoy it the way you do. But if you will always save me a dance and sit with me in the orchard, I'll find a way to manage. I love you too much to do otherwise. Will you marry me, Honoria?"

She jumped from her chair and pulled him to his feet, throwing her arms around his neck. "Yes!"

His arms slid around her and held her against him as she lifted her face for a kiss.

He didn't disappoint her.

"Oh my goodness, your mother was right..."

Honoria was nestled snugly beside her betrothed on a sofa in his library, his arm wrapped securely around her. They'd migrated there from the morning room wanting to be more comfortable than the breakfast table allowed, knowing all the while that Honoria should return home as soon as possible. But Benedict's fingers slowly stroking her arm turned "as soon as possible" into just "soon". When she dropped a soft kiss on his jaw and laid her head against his shoulder, he declared that an hour together wouldn't do any harm.

"What was my mother right about?"

Her fingers toyed with the buttons of his waistcoat. "When I visited Whitby House, she said she though you and I had fallen in love before you went to Greece. I told her she was mistaken, but she wouldn't be dissuaded."

"She saw it before we did."

"Or it was wishful thinking," she replied. "You had been away at university, and I'd had a few Seasons—we weren't in each other's company as much in those days."

He kissed her hair. "Either way Mother will be happy."

Honoria sat up, bracing a hand against his chest. "What about you? Are you happy? Truly?"

"Yes," he said, brushing a finger against her cheek. "Can you not tell?"

He had a silly smile plastered on his face and she grinned. "To be sure."

"What about you? Are you happy?"

"It just hasn't sunk in yet, I think." She settled back against him, taking one of his hands in hers and drawing his arm around her. "I made the decision to marry for love during my first Season, and that was quite a while ago."

"And I'm enormously glad of it. I could not imagine myself leg-shackled to a girl ten years my junior. Plenty of gentleman do it, but I was looking for a wife I could partner, not one I had to raise."

That triggered a memory from her brief sojourn at the Assembly Rooms. "Then who was that you were dancing with at Almack's last night? She looked rather on the young side."

"Why, Lady Honoria, are you jealous?"

She felt his chuckle vibrate through her. "Yes, you cursed man, I am." There was heat in her voice, but his amusement was fueling her own as well. "Who was she?"

"My cousin, Eleanor."

She sat up again, releasing his hand and turning herself all the way around to look at him. "Your cousin?"

"Whitby's daughter, the oldest. I was supposed to lead her out for the opening set at her debutante ball, but I was so aggrieved by your refusal that I forgot about the whole thing." Benedict reached for her, letting his hand glide over her skin before clasping her fingers in his. "I escorted her to Almack's to make up for it."

"How did you get in?" She frowned for a moment, realizing how discourteous her question sounded, then backtracked. "I mean, the Patronesses only grant vouches to men they are particularly fond of. I wasn't aware you knew any of them that well."

"I don't, but my mother and Lady Whitby had a word with Lady Castlereagh." His mouth pulled into a grin. "They assured her that my dancing would be impeccable."

Honoria gave him a sly smile. "Too bad Almack's doesn't allow the waltz."

"Better that they don't," he replied. "You are the only woman I've ever waltzed with, and I prefer to keep it that way."

He leaned in and kissed her then, one hand resting on her hip while the other threaded through her hair, scattering pins on the sofa cushions. Aunt Cecilia would notice the difference in Honoria's appearance when she returned home, even after everything was set to rights, but Honoria didn't care. Her arms went around Benedict and she held him close, breaking away to press her lips to his cheek, his temple, his jaw.

"I prefer it that way, too," she murmured. "You will be my 'only' for many things—I'm glad I can be yours for at least one."

"Oh, more than one," he corrected, planting a final kiss on the tip of her nose. "You're also the only woman I ever got drunk with, or learned dead languages with. And the only woman I think of when I smell apple blossoms.

She set her forearms on his shoulders and pushed back to look into his eyes. "Is that what the tree is for in your morning room?"

"It is now." His arms slipped around her waist and held her firmly. "It was originally going to be a gift for you—a cutting from our favorite tree at Orchard Lake."

"Perhaps we can plant it in the garden."

"Here? I thought you'd prefer a larger home."

She let her fingers wander lightly through his hair. "I will prefer any home you happen to be in."

His eyes closed for a moment as his entire face relaxed. "I'll show you the rest before I take you back to your aunt. You can tell me then if you think the nursery is large enough."

She brushed her lips across his cheek. "Are we going to have so many children, then?"

He opened his eyes and she could see flecks of gold and green in his irises. "We must at least try. I am the last Grey male. And there's another 'only': you'll be the only Mrs. Benedict Grey."

"Unless I am Lady Honoria Grey," she reminded him with a smirk. "I can do that, you know."

He slid a hand slowly up her back. "I do know. And I don't care which title you use—as long as it's my name you have and my life you share."

She smiled and drew him closer for another kiss. "Every blessed minute of it."

# Epilogue

*August 1815*

The house was quiet when Honoria entered, in direct opposition to the chaos that had reigned when she left. It was dark, too, except for the candle carried by the butler in the entry.

"Good evening, madam."

"Good evening. Is my husband still up?"

"He retired to the master bedchamber some hours ago, madam. Whether he is still awake or not, I cannot say."

She smiled. "Hopefully he didn't fall asleep reading again, with the candles still burning. And Emily?"

"Sleeping peacefully in the nursery."

He offered to light her way upstairs but she declined, sending him off to bed and climbing the stairs in the darkness. In the two years she'd been mistress of this house she'd come to know all its secrets, and could find her way around blindfolded.

After a stop in the nursery to check on her sleeping child, she reached the chamber she shared with Benedict and gently pushed the door open, peeping through the widening space to see if he slept as soundly as his daughter did.

"Ah, the prodigal wife returns."

He was reclining on the big bed clad only in breeches and shirt, with a book in his lap, as Honoria had predicted, but far from sleeping. He slid off the counterpane and met her halfway across the room, wrapping his arms around her despite the summer heat.

"Welcome home." He bent down and kissed her softly, then kissed her again with more eagerness, as if she had been gone days rather than hours. "I missed you."

"I missed you, too," she replied, rising up on her toes to drape her own arms around his neck.

"How was the ball?"

"Lady Lambert outdid herself this year—every inch of the house was decorated in roses, and she had seven kinds of cake."

He laughed. "Seven? Perhaps I should have gone after all."

"You would have been bored," she told him, massaging his nape. "I nearly was myself some of the time."

"What about your aunt?"

Honoria grinned. "My aunt is so besotted with her new husband she scarcely noticed anything else."

"Hmm, sounds like someone else I know." He planted a big, smacking kiss on her cheek.

She pushed him playfully away. "We are not newly wed anymore."

"But you are still besotted with me."

She liked how he stated rather than asked it. "Yes, I am."

"As I am with you." He brushed his lips against her forehead.

She savored his embrace, but all too quickly the high temperature intruded. "Will you help me out of this gown? If I wear it any longer I fear I'll melt into a puddle at your feet."

He arched a suggestive eyebrow at her, but turned her by the shoulders and went methodically to work on her laces.

"How is the packing coming?" she asked over her shoulder.

She felt the tugging stop for a moment.

"I don't remember having this much to do before I left for Greece."

"You didn't have a wife and daughter to cart with you then." The tugging resumed and moments later Honoria's bodice fell from her shoulders. She stepped carefully out of the gown, laying it over a chair to deal with later.

He pressed a kiss to the back of her neck and began unlacing her stays. "That must be it."

"You're sure you want to take us all the way to Italy?" She'd probably asked him the same question a dozen times in the last month as their departure date drew nearer. "You'd be able to inspect the work done at the Forum much more easily without us."

Her stays peeled off her body and slid to her feet, and he kissed her shoulder. "You know I would expire of wanting the both of you before I ever even crossed the Channel."

She kicked away the corset and plopped down in a chair to remove her shoes and stockings. "Then I fear your baggage train will be disproportionately large."

"I don't care if we have to commission a special ship to carry it all," he smiled. "But it won't be that bad. I had a letter from Mother today—she's arrived safely in Rome and has found us a house. By the time we get there, it will be furnished and staffed. The largest of our trunks are going tomorrow, so they should be there before us, too."

"Good."

He took both her hands and pulled her to her feet. "Dance with me. We'll imagine we're in Lady Lambert's lavish ballroom, with the orchestra playing whatever we want them to play, and forget about trying to move our household across an entire continent."

Dressed now only in her shift, she grasped his upper arm with her left hand, laying her right hand on his offered palm as his free arm came around her. "We cannot dance this close together in public, my love. It's unseemly."

He grinned and drew her even more snugly against him, waltzing her slowly around the room. "Then forget the ballroom. It's just the two of us, here in our bedchamber."

She closed her eyes and nestled her head against his chest. "That is exactly what I want."

His lips pressed against her hair once, twice, before he spoke again. "Then it's exactly what you shall always have."

# BACK IN MY ARMS AGAIN

**Two former lovers unexpectedly cross paths once again under troublesome circumstances. How will they overcome their turbulent past together to protect their future?**

Lady Cecilia Maitland has everything an unmarried woman could want: money of her own, high social status, and the ability to live life on her own terms. What she doesn't have is the only man she ever loved. She turned down James's proposal all those years ago and didn't see him again...until he turned up at a house party in search of a patron. Cecilia knows she can provide him the monetary and social support he needs if they marry, but will he accept such an offer from the woman who broke his heart? And what will it cost her if he does?

Mr. James Fitzsimmons is the son of a well-to-do farmer, solidly among the ranks of the gentry but not privileged enough to move in the same circles as a duke's daughter. Meeting Lady Cecilia seventeen years ago was pure luck, but falling in love with her was pure torment. When she refused his offer of marriage he vowed to put her out of his mind—and his heart. But when James discovers a powerful lord is threatening to take the farm and ruin the Fitzsimmons name, he knows he needs an influential ally. Can James agree to Cecilia's terms and risk his heart once more to save his family?

# Chapter 1

*February 1815*

James Fitzsimmons sat before the fireplace in his best friend's drawing room, staring at the letters in his lap. There were three, each promising ruination and even imprisonment to the recipient should certain conditions not be met by Lady Day—the twenty-fifth of March— namely that a loan totaling the princely sum of three thousand pounds be paid in full.

The sender was the powerful Earl of Grimsby. The recipient was James's father.

"How am I going to come up with three thousand pounds in six weeks?"

Stephen Eddington settled himself on a sofa set at a right angle to James's chair, placing his elbows on his knees and resting his chin in his hands. "Well, you can't borrow against the farm."

James's father had done precisely that, igniting the fire that James was now trying to put out. "I can't ask our neighbors for help. They are comfortable, but not so wealthy they could spare this kind of money even if everyone we know contributed."

"And your father would be none too happy if they found out why he needed the money so quickly."

Because the elder Fitzsimmons had shown exceedingly poor judgment in this financial matter. Grimsby's reputation marked the earl out as deceitful and avaricious in his financial dealings, and less than gentlemanly even with the men of his own class.

James scrubbed a hand through his hair and over his face. "This would be a good time for a long-lost wealthy relative to appear and offer to make this all go away."

Eddington straightened. "That's a good idea. Not a relative, but perhaps you can find a patron who will lend you the money. I'll put up my own property as collateral if it will help."

"You're a good friend, Eddy, but I can't ask you to do that."

"You didn't ask—I volunteered," Eddington returned with a quick grin. "That, together with the ledgers from the farm for the past several years, should be enough to convince a wealthy merchant or aristocrat to lend you the three thousand pounds. Your family keeps the farm and uses some of the income from it to pay back your benefactor. No one loses their home or livelihood."

James turned the scenario over in his mind. The Fitzsimmons Farm had a long history of solid production and the documentation to prove it, so that would be an incentive to a would-be lender. It was probably the inducement his father had used to obtain the three thousand from Grimsby in the first place, though it wasn't worth that much outright. Neither was Eddington's little estate. But if they found a sympathetic ear...

"What is it?" Eddington asked, jarring James from his thoughts.

"What's what?"

"You're wrinkling your nose as if you've encountered some noxious smell. What are you thinking about that's so distasteful?"

James suppressed a sigh. "You know I don't like dealing with the aristocracy. But it appears that my family's very existence now depends on one of them."

"I did say a wealthy merchant would do as well."

"Do you know any merchants who might be willing to help?"

Eddington shook his head. "No. But I do know some aristocrats who might take pity on you."

James felt his nose wrinkle again and his mouth pull into a frown. "I don't want their pity."

"Just their money."

Ouch. But Eddy was right, and James didn't have time to be choosy. If pity was part of the bargain then he'd have to learn to live with it.

"Fine. Where do we find these soft-hearted people with large bank accounts?"

"Phillip Maitland and his wife are having a house party in a few days. They won't have the sum required, but they are well connected—Mr. Maitland is cousin to the Duke of Alston and spent some time in the Commons as an MP."

James felt his body tense at the mention of the Maitland name and the duke's title. He'd known the duke's own sister in his youth—intimately. But it had been nearly two decades since he'd last seen her, and he highly doubted she would welcome him now.

He pushed the thought aside and tried to focus on his family's current predicament. "Can we wangle a dinner invitation one evening, do you think?"

Eddington smiled brightly. "Better. I've been invited to the house party, and Mrs. Maitland just sent a note asking if I knew another gentleman that might be available. It seems she had a last-minute cancellation and needs to even out the numbers."

James hesitated. A Maitland house party? Would Cecilia be there? "Are you sure I'll be welcome? Dinner is one thing, but an entire house party is a bit more presumptuous."

"It's only a couple of weeks. And there's bound to be someone there who can help you. Mrs. Maitland will be so glad to have an equal number of ladies and gentlemen she may even let you court her daughter."

"Two birds, one stone—how efficient. My mother would be pleased," James replied in a flat voice. She'd taken to reminding him that, while James's sister's son could inherit the farm, the boy didn't carry the Fitzsimmons name, and impressing upon James how wonderful it would be to have a grandchild that did. But Cecilia Maitland had hurt James badly the one and only time he'd proposed marriage, and at seven-and-thirty he was no longer interested in the almost political maneuverings some people undertook to make the "right" match.

"There's been no indication that Lady Cecilia will be there—she's only a distant cousin to Mr. Maitland."

James eyed his friend doubtfully. "You can't be sure of that."

Eddy shook his head. "No, I can't. But I can be sure that your farm will be in Grimsby's hands if you don't go."

"You have a point there."

"You'll go, then?"

James nodded, resigned. He could brazen out a Maitland house party in order to save the farm. And perhaps Eddy was right about Cecilia's presence there. "I'll go, and thank you for any information you can provide about the other guests."

Eddington sank back against the sofa cushions. "You're welcome to everything I know about them. Mr. and Mrs. Maitland are excellent hosts, too—you might even enjoy yourself."

James wasn't sure he'd enjoy anything until the farm was safe, but he nodded again to appease Eddington. "I might."

"You'll certainly feel better after some preparation. Come, let's adjourn to my study and we'll see what we can glean from Mrs. Maitland's invitation."

Lady Cecilia Maitland knocked on the door of her cousin's bedchamber, hoping the hour wasn't too late. Cecilia and Margaret had both been asked to arrive for the house party early to help with the preparations, and Cecilia found herself in need of counsel.

The door opened to reveal a fully-clothed Margaret Maitland, who smiled brightly when her eyes met Cecilia's. "I didn't expect to see you this late. I thought surely you'd be abed and sleeping soundly after traveling all day."

"I would be, but sleep has been rather elusive these past few nights."

Margaret took a step back and opened the door wider. "Would you like to come in for a bit? Maybe a nice chat will settle you."

"I was hoping you'd say that." Cecilia entered the room, closing her eyes momentarily to savor the heat radiating from the fireplace. There were two comfortable-looking chairs placed near the hearth, and Cecilia seated herself in the one closest to the window while Margaret took the other.

"So what has been keeping you up these past nights?"

Cecilia suppressed a smile. How very like a Maitland to get right to the point. "I've found myself in some trouble, and I'm hoping you can help me discover a way to get out of it."

Margaret's brows rose. "What kind of trouble now?"

This time Cecilia allowed the smile to form on her lips. She was the unconventional member of the Maitland family, the forty-year-old woman who set up her own household and invested her money rather than marry and depend on a husband. Being the daughter and sister of a duke meant most of the *ton* brushed off what they called her eccentricities, but Cecilia's society life had not been without incident.

But her smile faded as she spoke. "I have a blackmailer."

"What?"

"The Earl of Grimsby has an old letter of mine in his possession. One written to a lover many years ago that would disgrace me and the whole family if it became public. Or so he says."

Margaret sat back in her chair. "You doubt the existence of this letter?"

"I don't, actually. I vividly remember writing a number of letters to a certain gentleman when I was younger, so it's possible that Grimsby does possess one of them. Though I'll never know how he got his hands on it."

"You're worried about the effect on your reputation, then?"

Cecilia shook her head, her blonde nighttime plait sliding a little against her back. "I have position and wealth enough to withstand whatever backlash might occur, and I'm not exactly hunting for a husband. No, my concern is that my brother will find out."

His Grace the Duke of Alston was older than Cecilia by twelve years and had been in delicate health most of his adult life. Over the past few years "delicate" had been supplanted by "dreadful" more often than not, and the family knew it was only a matter of time before he went to his reward.

"You think the shock will be too much for him."

Margaret's voice was solemn and Cecilia gave a little nod, listening to the fire crackle cheerily along as if everything were fine.

"And you came to me because I'm no stranger to scandal."

Cecilia opened her mouth to protest, but saw that her cousin was smiling. Margaret had borne a child out of wedlock when she was nineteen and had withdrawn from Society as a result. Cecilia knew it had crushed Margaret to live as an exile in the country, particularly when she'd been so young and full of adventure. She didn't often refer to her status, but it was good to see her speaking so easily of it now.

"Because you're my favorite cousin," Cecilia returned.

Margaret chuckled. "Don't let Phillip hear you say that."

Cecilia wanted to grin and reply with some witty comment, but instead she pressed her lips together for a moment. "You can't tell anyone about this, including Phillip—the more people that know, the greater the chance someone will tell Alston."

Margaret reached across the space between their chairs and clasped Cecilia's hands in hers. "Of course I won't. Your secret is safe with me." She squeezed her cousin's hands then released them and sat back. "Now what can we do about Grimsby? What is it that he wants from you?"

"Five thousand pounds. For that I get the actual letter in addition to his silence."

Margaret's hazel eyes went round. "Five thousand?" Then she smiled. "If your investments are doing as well as they appear to be, that isn't an insurmountable sum for you. Is it?"

"No, it isn't. But that's not the point."

"You're angry that he's trying to manipulate you."

Margaret's tone was so matter-of-fact Cecilia grinned. "I'd forgotten just how well you know me. Yes, I'm angry that he thinks he can so easily move me. But I can't tell the magistrate what's happened for fear of word getting out, and Grimsby well knows it—is counting on it."

"Are you still in contact with the letter's original recipient? Perhaps you could write to him and let him know what is happening. He may even have an idea or two about how to stop it."

Cecilia pictured James as he'd been when she'd known him, tall and slim yet strong enough to lift her off the ground with little effort. He'd had a dimple in his left cheek —just a fraction of an inch from the corner of his mouth— that she'd been particularly fond of kissing. But it had been nearly twenty years since she'd seen him last, and the encounter had not ended happily.

"We lost touch," she told her cousin, which was a version of the truth. His actual words had been something more akin to *I never want to see you again.* "I suppose I could set my solicitor to searching for him, but he doesn't go about in Society."

"Then he may not care about the letter surfacing, which is just as well. I think the only thing he could really do to help is marry you. That would render the letter moot."

Cecilia nodded slowly, as if it was a simple thing Margaret suggested. Marriage to her former lover would negate the scandal the letter would otherwise cause for all but the highest sticklers, and those were people who didn't approve of her anyway. What she didn't tell Margaret was that James had been more than just a lover. He'd been a close friend, an ally, and her would-be fiancé. If Cecilia had accepted James's proposal of marriage all those years ago, she wouldn't be having this problem now.

Would she have been happier as his wife?

But what was done, was done. For all she knew, he was wed to some other woman and had a full complement of children helping him run the farm.

"Marriage to anyone would probably negate enough of the scandal that little would reach Alston, particularly if he were confined to his home or bed. I am loath to give up my independence, though, Margaret. I've been my own keeper for nigh on sixteen years now, and to sign everything over to a man feels like a defeat."

"You could retain some of your independence with the right settlements...and the right gentleman," Margaret replied with a sly smile. "And marriage would undoubtedly be more pleasurable than giving in to Grimsby."

"His lordship certainly wouldn't see it coming."

"And in a few days you'll have a house party full of gentlemen to consider."

"Half of whom I'm related to," Cecilia quipped. "But at least it's a viable action, if I want to take it. I would just have to find a willing co-conspirator."

# Chapter 2

"You're thinking so hard I can see smoke coming out of your ears."

"If my brain catches fire, at least we'll be warmer." James glanced over at Eddington, who was drawing his big bay gelding alongside James's dappled gray, ignoring the cloud his breath formed every time he spoke. "I'm just worried."

"Worrying isn't going to do you any good now."

Now that James had left the farm in the care of his aging parents and a brand new steward to beg the protection of some bored lord? Probably not. He just couldn't help but be anxious—there were so many things that could go wrong.

"You're sure there will be aristocrats at this house party?"

Eddington nodded, pulling the collar of his greatcoat tighter about his neck against the sleet falling like spoonfuls of freezing porridge all around them. "Phillip Maitland might not be rich and titled, but he has family and friends who are. And the Maitlands are a loyal bunch. The purpose of this house party is to give Phillip's daughter some polish before she makes her come-out this Season, so at least one of the other Maitlands will be there in a show of family support for her. And if there isn't someone at the house party that can help you directly, there will be someone who can introduce you to the right person."

James briefly wondered if the duke himself would attend. How much did His Grace know about his sister's prior relationship with a mere farmer?

"If I have to go somewhere else to beg for help *after* the house party it may be too late, especially if the weather turns ugly. Grimsby's deadline is fast approaching."

Eddy motioned toward a small stately home coming into view among the rolling Cotswold hills. "Well, let's hope there's a duke or marquess here that firmly believes in *noblesse oblige.*"

An hour later James was warming himself before the fire in what was to be his chamber for the next two weeks, trying to decide the most tactful way to ask a complete stranger for a loan. A knock on the door interrupted his musings, and Eddington poked his head in.

"I have good news and bad news."

"Give me the good news first," James said, flopping down into a chair near the hearth.

Eddington took the chair opposite his friend with considerably more grace. "The Marquess of Hadleigh is here."

"And what do we know about him?"

"He's young, wealthy, and eager to prove himself a great lord."

James sat up a little straighter. "Do you think he'd be amenable to aiding an overwhelmed farmer?"

"Possibly."

"Then what's the bad news?"

The corners of Eddington's mouth turned down. "He is the only aristocratic guest. The others are well enough off, but not wealthy enough to produce three thousand pounds...except for Lady Cecilia. But she won't be useful."

James felt like he'd been punched in the chest. She was here! "Lady Cecilia?"

"Yes," Eddington answered slowly, his eyes darting around the room. "I'm sorry. I did tell you at least one member of the family would attend. Unfortunately, it turned out to be a female member with no husband to petition, and one you have a past with."

James sat in silence for a long minute, concentrating on breathing normally. He foolishly hadn't prepared himself for her actual presence, and now he had to contend with a jumble of emotions right here in front of Eddington.

"I can't borrow money from a woman," he managed at last. "And certainly not from Cecilia."

Eddington shook his head. "Of course you can't. Nor could she deal effectively with Grimsby if a problem arose."

James scrubbed a hand through his hair, trying to clear his mind by sheer force of will. "That leaves me with Hadleigh. He will undoubtedly find me vulgar if I lay out my case plainly before him and ask for his protection at dinner. You'll have to help me devise a way to sound like a gentleman when I speak to him."

They spent the next thirty minutes putting together some topics James could use when conversing with the marquess. And both James and Eddington took great pains with their appearances as they made ready for the social hour before dinner, James even allowing Eddington's valet to brush his clothing and tie his cravat.

But when they entered the drawing room at the appointed time, they found they could not locate the Marquess of Hadleigh.

"Good evening, Mr. Eddington, Mr. Fitzsimmons." Margaret Maitland greeted them each with a nod as she circulated among the guests. "I trust you are feeling well-rested this evening."

Eddington took her offered hand and bowed over it. "Indeed we are, Miss Maitland. It seems not everyone is as fortunate as we are, though. We were hoping to speak with Lord Hadleigh for a moment before dinner, but he does not appear to have come down from his chamber yet."

She took her hand back and shook her head. "Nor will he, the physician said. Not for several weeks."

"Physician?" Eddington asked.

"Weeks?" James put in, only half registering the note of anxiety in his voice.

"Did you not hear?" Miss Maitland took half a step closer. "He was conversing with my brother this afternoon," she answered in a quiet voice, "and was paying more attention to his words than to where he was going."

James winced inwardly, knowing that whatever came next was bound to be painful for both himself and the marquess.

"Lord Hadleigh fell down the staircase and broke his leg. He's confined to bed until further notice."

For the second time that day, James felt as though he'd been punched. Not only would a broken leg prevent Hadleigh from participating in house party events for the entire duration, but he would probably be dosed with laudanum to combat the pain.

He would be asleep or insensible.

And James's hopes for Hadleigh's patronage disappeared.

It was as if her conversation with Margaret had conjured him directly into her cousin's drawing room.

Cecilia spotted James from across the room. Even though it had been seventeen years since she'd set eyes on him, she recognized him easily. His hair was shorter now, but still the same golden brown it had been when she'd last run her fingers through it. His skin was not as tanned as she remembered, but his face and hands were still several shades darker than those of the other guests. His clothes were some years out of fashion, but were as neat and well-tailored as they had been during that long ago visit to London.

What was he doing here? She didn't remember his name being on the guest list Phillip's wife had shown her. Nor could she fathom how a farmer from Kent would have an acquaintance with her idle cousins in Gloucestershire.

But then again, no one would have ever guessed that the same farmer had once been very, very close to a duke's daughter.

She circulated about the room, mingling with her cousin's guests and making small talk about the usual nonsense, pretending her heart wasn't beating as though she'd danced a dozen reels. Her eyes took on a life of their own and kept darting toward James, watching as he performed the same rituals. Was he as nervous as she was? Had he even noticed she was there?

And then he was walking toward her.

Dear God in heaven, what did one say to the only man one had ever loved seventeen years after breaking his heart?

"Cousin, are you acquainted with Mr. Eddington and Mr. Fitzsimmons?"

Cecilia focused on Margaret, who was positioned between the two gentlemen as they approached, and forced herself to breathe normally. "I don't believe so. Perhaps you'll do the honors?"

Apparently, one pretended not to know the broken-hearted party at all.

Cecilia offered her hand to Mr. Eddington as Margaret made the introduction, and attempted what she hoped was a genteel smile. "It's a pleasure to have a face to put with the name—my cousins tell me you've been spending a fair amount of time here since you settled in at Westwood."

"I wouldn't say that I've settled in just yet," Mr. Eddington replied politely. "But it has been very pleasant to have neighbors as welcoming as the Maitlands."

"And Mr. Fitzsimmons," Cecilia said, turning to face James and offering her hand. He took it carefully, his brown eyes intent on her blue ones despite his relaxed expression. "I understand you have been visiting Mr. Eddington these past few days. Are you enjoying your stay in the Cotswolds?"

"I'm afraid I haven't experienced much of the region yet." He touched only her fingertips, but stroked his thumb across them before letting go. "My stay has been all business up until today."

"And what kind of business are you in?" Cecilia asked, as if she hadn't heard all the stories about his childhood on the farm.

"I am here to rescue someone," he told her. The corners of his mouth curved upward in what she recognized as his I'm-being-modest smile. "A relation got himself mixed up in a distasteful business matter, and I am attempting to keep him out of debtors' prison."

There was a Banbury tale if she'd ever heard one—who would admit that a family member was in financial trouble? But he hadn't called attention to her lie so she decided to play along with his, raising her brows and forming her mouth into a little O. "How awful," she breathed. "I do hope you are successful."

"So does his relation," Mr. Eddington replied in a rather serious tone.

Margaret's lips quirked and pressed together, as if she was trying to fight a smile. "I'm sure he does. You will let us know how it turns out, Mr. Fitzsimmons?"

"I will."

Cecilia remarked on the weather, hoping—for once—to steer the conversation into more conventional waters. Or at least to a topic she didn't have to think much about. Her mind was busy sorting out a quandary she hadn't seriously considered, despite her conversation with Margaret. Should she tell James about the blackmail? It was one thing to keep the incident to herself when his whereabouts were unknown to her, but here he was in her cousin's home, an arm's length away.

Was he still unattached? If so, would he marry her to save her brother?

Did she want him to?

James and Mr. Eddington took their leave, drifting toward a knot of gentlemen that were talking near the window. Cecilia counted slowly to five, then drew her cousin to a quieter corner of the room.

"That was him."

"Who was whom?" Margaret asked, her brows raised.

"Mr. Fitzsimmons is the man I wrote the scandalous letter to."

"The letter that Grimsby is using to extort money from you?"

Cecilia nodded, her eyes seeking out James before refocusing on Margaret. "Yes."

"He's the lover from long ago?"

"He is."

Margaret frowned. "Wait, didn't I just introduce him to you?"

Cecilia felt herself cringe. "You did. I apparently decided that it would be easier to pretend I didn't know him, or that I'd forgotten him."

"But you haven't."

Forget James? No. Even before Grimsby had dredged up old memories with her letter, James had been in her thoughts more than one would think possible after so long an absence. "Even if I had, Grimsby's little enterprise would have brought him to the forefront again. But things did not end well between us, and I was unsure of Mr. Fitzsimmons's reaction to me."

"He seemed perfectly civil," Margaret replied. "Assuming he remains so, you now have your chance to tell him about the letter and Grimsby's use of it."

"Do you think I should?"

"The way I see it, you have three options. You can quietly pay his lordship the money he demands and get your letter back. You can come up with a plan that results in Grimsby's downfall without harming your brother. Or you can ask Mr. Fitzsimmons his opinion of the matter since, strictly speaking, he is already involved."

Cecilia smiled and touched her cousin's arm. "This is why I came to you in the first place—you can always boil a situation down to its essence. Now all I have to do is come up with a way to put Grimsby in his place."

"You won't tell Mr. Fitzsimmons about the letter, then?"

"I don't believe I will. The only reason he's involved is because his name is on the letter. If I can resolve the situation, he need never know it was an issue at all."

Margaret opened her mouth as if to reply, but was interrupted when Phillip appeared at her side holding out a piece of paper to Cecilia.

"This came in the post this morning addressed to me, but it's for us both."

"Why are you bringing correspondence to the drawing room twenty minutes before dinner?" Margaret asked, her voice a mixture of irritation and concern.

"I only just found it a few minutes ago, when I was looking for the book I wanted to lend to Mr. Hobbes. It's from Orchard Lake."

Orchard Lake was the Duke of Alston's favorite residence. Cecilia accepted the paper from her cousin and scanned it quickly. It wasn't a summons to her brother's death bed, but it wasn't a glowing report either.

"It seems His Grace has taken to his bed again," she said aloud for Margaret's benefit. "The duchess writes that while he is too weak to walk unassisted and his breathing grows ragged, he is still in good spirits with a healthy appetite. She does not want us to abandon the house party, but wishes us to be apprised of his condition in case..."

Margaret nodded. "We are apprised, then. And Her Grace will certainly inform us of any changes."

Cecilia handed the paper back to Phillip. "Thank you. You'll find me again if more news arrives?"

"Of course."

Phillip tucked the paper into the pocket of his cutaway coat, patted Cecilia's shoulder, then threaded his way across the room, presumably in pursuit of Mr. Hobbes. Cecilia's eyes met Margaret's and she suspected they were both thinking the same thing: whatever Cecilia was going to do about the Earl of Grimsby, she had better do it before he decided to make public the contents of her letter.

# Chapter 3

$\mathcal{C}$ecilia made it through dinner, and tea with the ladies afterward, by sheer force of will and good manners. She even managed to participate in the game of Charades someone suggested when the gentlemen joined the ladies in the drawing room. But all the while her mind was spinning, grasping at any possibility that might keep the Earl of Grimsby's mouth shut.

As soon as was polite, she said goodnight and excused herself to her bedchamber where she could move around freely while she tried to think.

"Very well then, Cecilia," she said aloud, "what can you do to keep Grimsby from telling Alston about that letter?"

The obvious answer was to pay the five thousand pounds he required and hope that he kept his promise to return the letter to her. It was the quickest, easiest way to put the whole matter to rest. But it was also predicated on a blackmailer keeping his promise.

She began walking around the room, skirting the edge of her bed and heading for the washstand before turning back toward the fireplace. "I don't like that at all. What's to stop Grimsby from refusing to turn over the letter, or demanding more money?"

She could always even the score later. Grimsby had a wife and daughter who enjoyed the entertainments of the Season, and Grimsby himself had been known to escort them about Town. With Cecilia's social position it would be easy keep Lady Grimsby's name off the guest lists for balls and soirees. A word in the ear of one of the Patronesses and vouchers for Almack's would be withheld. It would be a miserable year for a husband-hunting girl and the mother watching her flounder.

Yet it wasn't the Grimsby women that Cecilia wanted to punish, it was the earl himself.

"He might be indirectly affected, but it wouldn't be enough. And Lady Grimsby has never been anything but kind to me." Running a hand over the footboard as she passed the bed again, she shook her head and discarded the idea.

What else?

"I suppose I could arrange to have him injured."

Cecilia halted abruptly as soon as the words were out of her mouth. No, that was clearly unacceptable. She might feel justified in imagining scenarios where his lordship got what he deserved, but to actually cause physical damage would be unconscionable.

Sighing, she resumed her circuit about the chamber at a more somber pace. "I'm just going to have to pay him. My brother's peace—his very life—is certainly worth five thousand pounds. If I insist on a simultaneous exchange, the chances of getting my letter back are much greater."

Perhaps her cousin's cook would have some pastries hidden away in the kitchen that would make Cecilia's pride easier to swallow. She strode to the door and opened it, pausing in the hallway to get her bearings. As she located the main staircase, she noticed candlelight spilling out from a partially open door further down. A male voice joined the light.

"And there's no one else in a position to help, is there?"

It was James. Cecilia crept closer, gathering the material of her skirts in one hand to quiet the rustle. What was this about?

"No. I'm sorry, Fitz. I thought for sure you'd find your patron here." That was Mr. Eddington, sounding truly sorrowful. Why did James need a patron so badly?

"There has got to be a way to save the farm and keep my father out of debtors' prison. I will not give over my family's livelihood to that man, earl or not."

Keep his father out of prison? Was Mr. Fitzsimmons the relative James had cheekily discussed before dinner? And who was the earl threatening him?

Cecilia's hand went to her mouth to stifle her gasp, but it couldn't stifle her words.

"It's true, then."

James turned and found Cecilia standing just outside the partially open door, her eyes widened with surprise. He gestured her inside and closed the door tightly behind her as she entered, mentally kicking himself for not having done so in the first place.

"Yes, it's true." There was no point in denying anything now. Cecilia was an intelligent woman and he was a terrible liar—she'd see through any story he tried to concoct.

"Who is it?" Her lips pressed into a firm line and her eyes narrowed. "Wait, it's Grimsby, isn't it? He's at it again."

James turned sharply. "Why would you think that?"

"How many other blackmailing earls do you know?" she shot back.

"Blackmailing?"

Cecilia nodded. "That is what he's doing to you, isn't it?"

"Did you say 'again'?" Eddington cut in. "He's done this before?"

"He's doing it currently. To me."

The room went quiet and James tried to understand what he'd just heard. Cecilia was being blackmailed by the Earl of Grimsby?

"He has a financial hold over my father," James explained to her, glancing back at Eddington, then refocusing on Cecilia, "It isn't blackmail, but a loan was made and now he wants full payment or we lose the farm. No one else can know. Promise me you won't breathe a word to anyone."

She nodded slowly and didn't speak for a moment. The Cecilia he'd known all those years ago would have taken a secret to her grave for him. But would she now?

Then the corners of her eyes crinkled as her mouth formed a cheerful smile. "Oh, I can do better than that—I can help you stop him."

"What? You're a woman—what can you do to an earl, a peer of the realm?"

"First of all, I have money to hire solicitors and barristers and private investigators...whatever and whoever is necessary to combat his lordship legally, if such a thing is possible. At the very least, I can pay back your loan."

"That would be helpful," Eddington said transferring his gaze from Cecilia to James. "Neither you nor I have the funds to do that."

"I also have connections to powerful lords, not the least of which is my brother."

"There's your patron." Eddington directed his words to James with a slight nod and raised brows.

"That's assuming I agree to this...this partnership. Eddington is correct in his assessment of our financial situation, but borrowing money from a female is unseemly. And what makes you think that your connections would bother with a lowly farmer you once knew? They certainly aren't going to stick their necks out because you ask nicely."

Cecilia laughed a little. "No, they probably wouldn't. But they would do anything to see justice done for a member of the family."

"Which I am not."

"You would be if we married."

Eddington made an inarticulate noise in his throat and tried to cover it with a cough. "Did you just ask Fitz for his hand?"

Cecilia kept her eyes on James. "You wouldn't be borrowing money from me, then, either—my fortune and all my investments are yours as soon as the vows are solemnized."

Eddington coughed again and James glared at him, prompting the man to excuse himself and hurry out of the room with a mumbled, "I'll just give you two some privacy."

"Marriage?" James asked, dropping into a wing chair near the fire. "We haven't been in contact with each other for seventeen years—after you declined my offer of wedded bliss, might I add. You didn't even acknowledge that you knew me before dinner today. And now you want to become my wife?"

She followed him to the fire and seated herself in the chair opposite him. "It doesn't have to be a real marriage. We would not have to live as husband and wife."

But they would still *be* husband and wife. The dream of his twenty-year-old self come true...too late. "Would your relations help me if I were just a husband of convenience?"

"Probably not," she said, clasping her hands together on her knee. "The money and my status would be yours, though, along with whatever I can do personally." She paused a moment and took a breath as if she were collecting herself. "If we told everyone it was a love match, my family would be more than happy to protect you."

James felt himself shaking his head in frustration. "Why would you even suggest such a thing? You can't love me after all these years—you don't know me anymore, nor do I know you. You can't be out to spite your relations by marrying so far beneath you, since you offered them up as allies. I'd find it very difficult to believe that you long to give up your ways as a grand lady and settle down on my farm. So what is it?"

"I treated you badly, James. I know it was a long time ago, but it still weighs on my conscience. I led you to believe we could have a life together, then cast you aside when you tried to make that a reality."

"Did it hurt you to refuse me?" he asked quietly. The pain in her voice was oddly touching, even after all the time that had passed.

Her eyes darted to his. "Of course it did. I was wounded deeply when I sent you away. That it was a self-inflicted wound made it even worse."

"Then why did you?" The words came out with more bitterness than he'd intended. "Why did you refuse me after encouraging me for months? Why did you let me think you loved me when you didn't?"

"I did love you." The words were soft, almost lost in the popping of the fire. She glanced down at her lap before meeting his gaze once again. "My niece was thirteen and not so far from thoughts of marriage herself. Marrying you, with your social rank so far below mine, would have harmed Honoria's prospects of a good match."

He let out a humorless laugh at that. "You think marrying a farmer would have rendered a duke's daughter unmarriageable?"

"Not unmarriageable, no. But I wanted her to have every opportunity to find a good husband. The scandal we would have created would have touched my whole family."

There was the real reason she'd refused him. "And they wouldn't have approved, would they?"

"No."

"Then why would they now?"

"Because I'm an old spinster," she answered flatly. "And Honoria has been safely married for over a year now. If my brother and my cousins believe marrying you makes me happy, they won't care who you are."

James stood and walked around to the back of his chair, leaning against it. "So this is your chance to atone, to make yourself feel better all these years later."

"That's part of it."

"What's the other part?"

"Grimsby also has a hold over me. He has one of the letters I wrote to you when we were together, and has threatened to make it public."

James felt his face flush with heat. Those letters had been for his eyes only, not for a snake like Grimsby and certainly not for the Society gossips.

"James?"

"I was just thinking about the things you wrote in those letters."

Pink crept into her cheeks, slowly at first then in a rush of color. "Oh."

Oh indeed. She'd poured both her heart and her physical desires into those letters.

She pressed her hands to her cheeks for a moment and cleared her throat. "I, erm, suppose I could weather the scandal well enough on my own. But I'm terribly afraid it would put too much strain on Alston's health."

"He is unwell again?"

She nodded. "I fear the stress of such humiliation would kill him. And I will not let Grimsby tear my family apart."

James leaned more heavily against the back of his chair. "I can't fault you for that. One has to protect one's family whenever possible."

"Then you agree to my plan?"

"I don't know, Cecilia." He ran a hand over the back of his neck. He didn't even know how he felt about seeing her again. How was he supposed to handle her offer to wed him?

"We can do it quickly—a marriage by special license can be arranged while we're here at the house party. Once our vows are solemnized, my letter becomes moot and you have money to save the farm. We both win, and Grimsby doesn't get to revel in our disgrace."

"We will be shackled to each other—and our past—for the rest of our lives."

"We will," she said slowly. "Though when everything has been settled, we could go our separate ways."

"How very aristocratic," he returned dryly. That was the second time she'd mentioned separate lives. Perhaps she was just as reluctant to wed him as he was her.

She sat up straighter. "You'd rather go on living together? Pretending that we can be happy together for the next thirty or forty years?" He watched her press her lips together and take another deep breath. "Let's prioritize. We can marry, safeguarding my brother, and send Grimsby a bank draft, safeguarding your farm. Then once we have that in hand and know your family to be safe, we can re-evaluate our own situation. Does that sound reasonable to you?"

James nodded, hesitant to agree but seeing no other way out of the mess his father had created. "It does."

"We'll have to make my family believe we're in love to secure their protection for you. And it will negate the need to tell them about the blackmail. Will you agree to that?"

He sighed. There really was no other way to save the farm if Grimsby went back on his word. Nor would his father appreciate James telling strangers about his financial situation. "Yes, I will agree to it."

"Then congratulations, Mr. Fitzsimmons, you and I are betrothed."

What had she done?

Cecilia lay sprawled on her bed staring up at the ceiling, wondering how she'd managed to affiance herself to a man who wanted little to do with her.

"It's for the good of us both," she told the pillow beside her. "And for our families."

The pillow was unmoved by her declaration, so she tried again. "Yes, the provision about pretending ours is a love match is necessary. News of my wedding a farmer to give him money would be at least as shocking to my brother as the letter in Grimsby's possession."

Still the pillow sat in silent judgment.

"I wasn't lying when I said our parting weighed on my conscience—I gave James every indication that I would welcome his proposal, then I refused him when the time came." She rolled onto her side and poked her index finger into the center of the pillow. "The worst part of it was that I wanted to accept him. I loved him and wanted nothing more in the world than to be his wife. But I was scared..."

"Scared of what?"

Cecilia planted her face into the pillow as Margaret closed the chamber door behind her, then flipped onto her back. "Have you forgotten how to knock?"

"I'm sorry. I heard your voice but no one else's and wanted to be sure you were well. From what I heard, that may not be the case."

Cecilia sat up and patted the bed beside her, hugging her cousin when Margaret came to sit down. "I am well enough in body, and I may have routed Grimsby. But I fear my heart is in for a turbulent month."

"What happened?"

"I am going to marry Mr. Fitzsimmons."

Margaret's lips parted as if she wanted to speak. When no words came, Cecilia filled her in on the details of the agreement she'd made with James. By the time she was done, Margaret found her voice.

"I thought you weren't going to even tell him about the letter. Why did you offer to marry him?"

"I did it on impulse. He was there before me, and in such difficulty. But he refused the help I could easily give, and I just blurted it out."

"He didn't agree with you so you proposed marriage?"

Cecilia heard the amusement in her cousin's voice and felt a smile tug at the corners of her mouth. "It sounds silly when you say it like that."

"What would you say to Honoria if she did such a thing?"

"Honoria's much more in control of herself than I am," Cecilia replied, picturing her niece at the last party they'd attended together. "She gets carried away with things from time to time, but I'm the impetuous one in the family."

"Is that what you're afraid of?" Margaret asked, taking her cousin's hand. "That you're too rash to be a wife?"

"The consequences of my actions would fall upon my husband and his family, too, not just on me. But that wasn't it." Cecilia felt her whole body tense, but forced herself to say the words. "I sent James away the first time because I was afraid of the consequences Honoria would face, but I was also afraid to live as a farmer's wife. What if I couldn't adjust to his lack of fortune? What if I couldn't do the things I was expected to do?"

"What if you couldn't be the woman he needed?"

Cecilia leaned her head against Margaret's shoulder. "Yes."

"And now you have a safe way to find out—if it doesn't work, you go back to being Lady Cecilia without any consequences."

"And I feel like a coward all over again because of that."

Margaret put her arms around Cecilia. "Then don't think of the escape clause. Put your heart and soul into your marriage as if you were planning to live with him forever. If you're a total failure, you'll know you did the right thing all those years ago. If you're a brilliant success, then you'll vanquish your fears. Either way, you've spared your brother a blow to his fragile health and saved the Fitzsimmonses from ruin."

"Those are terms I think I can live with."

"But if you fall in love with him again..."

Cecilia shook her head against Margaret's shoulder. "It won't matter if I do. He hasn't forgiven me for the way I treated him when we were young, nor is he inclined to try."

"Then that's his loss."

"I only hope it isn't mine, too."

# Chapter 4

"Here comes your bride." Eddington flashed a grin at James over his plate of eggs and kippers.

James pushed his food around his own plate, glancing up at Cecilia as she entered the dining room before his eyes darted to the other guests enjoying their breakfast. "Yes, there she is."

She smiled at him, her eyes lingering on his face just a little bit longer than was strictly necessary. James managed a smile in return, but if it looked as sincere as it felt then he wasn't fooling anyone.

"You should be over the moon," Eddington continued. "You came here to find a solution to your problem and you did. Your father's name will remain unblemished and the farm will remain in Fitzsimmons hands."

"I am very relieved about that. More so than even you might realize."

"So why don't you look it?" Eddington leaned over his plate and lowered his voice. "Is it because help came from a woman? Or because help came from *that* woman?"

James put his fork down and picked up a piece of toast, contemplating the golden brown triangle. "I wasn't expecting to confront a seventeen-year-old heartbreak during my stay...or ever, really. And everything has happened so fast I've barely had time to comprehend it all."

He'd reanalyzed his past with Cecilia the previous night in the privacy of Eddy's bedchamber—how they'd courted for nearly six months, how deeply in love James had fallen, how he thought that Cecilia had felt the same way about him but walked away from the relationship when he asked for her hand. Eddington had been there for it all, his bachelor apartments just a floor above James's when they were both in Town, but saying it aloud had felt necessary.

It all seemed so long ago, but was suddenly very relevant once more.

Cecilia appeared at the table with her plate and took the empty chair beside James. "Good morning, gentlemen."

Her voice was cheerful and her blue eyes sparkled in the morning sun shining through the window. James wondered if she really was that merry or if she was just a fine actress.

Eddington responded first. "Good morning, my lady. Did you sleep well?"

"I did, actually. It took me a little while to settle down for the night, but once I did I slept like a top. How was your night, Mr. Fitzsimmons?"

"Eventful."

"Hmm, is that good or bad?"

He put the toast back on his plate, maintaining eye contact with it rather than her. "More good than bad." Finally, he raised his eyes from his plate—after all, if she was going to be his wife, he ought to be able to look her in the eye. "And there's still a lot to be done."

"Yes, there is. Can you meet me this afternoon? We can settle a number of things today."

"That will remove some of the weight from my mind."

"Good."

She reached over to touch the back of his hand but he reflexively pulled away. "Where and when shall I meet you?"

A hurt expression flickered over her face, but vanished quickly. Was she over the disappointment so swiftly or was she merely hiding it? James suddenly wished he knew.

"I'll be in Phillip's study all afternoon." Her lips curved into a smile and she leaned a little closer. "The ladies are embroidering this afternoon, so I plan to make myself scarce."

"Don't you like embroidery?" Eddington asked.

"I do, but not when there are other things that require my attention." She reached for James again, this time touching his sleeve instead of his skin. "Besides, the ladies here will spend the day talking about the upcoming Season while their fingers stitch, and gossip about who is looking for a spouse. I have no need of that kind of conversation."

She rose from the table, her plate of food still untouched, and nodded to them both before disappearing through the door.

Eddington fixed a sharp eye on James. "What was that all about?"

"I'm meeting Lady Cecilia this afternoon. Weren't you paying attention?"

"I was. Were you?"

"What do you mean?"

Eddington glanced around the room, which was empty now of all but a footman. "Aren't the people here supposed to think that you and Lady Cecilia are falling in love?"

"Yes."

"Then either your idea of love is skewed or you're a dreadful actor."

James considered that for a moment. "I know what love is. Or I did, once. I suppose I need to figure out how to show it when I don't feel it."

"Or learn to feel it."

"What?"

Eddington smiled. "Would it be so terrible to be in love with your wife?"

"In general, no. But when my wife previously decided she couldn't be married to me because I wasn't aristocratic enough, it's a bit harder to fall in love with her again."

"Maybe you don't have to."

James arched an eyebrow.

"Maybe you can summon some of what you felt for Lady Cecilia when you were younger. You don't actually have to love her, just remember how you felt when you did."

"Before or after she left me?"

Eddington sighed. "Before, of course. I remember what you were like when she refused you—possibly better than you do, given how muddled your head was then. But if you focus on the good times you two had together, you might be able to bring some of that joy into your actions now."

James thought about that for a few moments. "It makes sense...if I can ignore the way we parted."

"Can you do that?"

"I can certainly try. And I don't have any better ideas."

James went back to his breakfast with a little more enthusiasm. If he could simply remember how it felt to be in love with Cecilia—truly in love with her—this outlandish plan might actually work.

Cecilia sat at Phillip's large desk in the room he used as both his study and library, writing yet another letter in anticipation of her marriage. She'd already completed letters to her solicitor, her niece's husband, her housekeeper in London, and the Earl of Grimsby.

This letter she'd left for last, hoping inspiration would strike and writing it would be easy. It was for her brother and his duchess explaining why, after years of happy spinsterhood, she was rushing to marry a farmer. She didn't need Alston's permission, but she knew it would hurt him to learn of his only sister's marriage over tea with the neighbors.

"I'd be there to tell you in person if there was time," she said aloud.

"Perhaps we can visit when the dust has settled, so to speak."

Cecilia's eyes snapped to the doorway where James was standing, looking very confident and handsome in sharp contrast to his bearing at the breakfast table. "Would you like that?" she asked.

He entered the room and approached the desk but did not sit. "Probably as much as you would enjoy visiting my family."

"Actually, I think I should like to meet them and see the farm." She wondered briefly if that was true or if she was merely being contrary. "I certainly heard enough about both when we were courting."

His lips curved into a smile sincere enough to produce the infamous dimple. "I did go on about home a bit too much back then, didn't I? But I would be delighted to show it to you, and to visit His Grace when the time comes."

"I will add it to my list of correspondence."

James finally seated himself in one of the upholstered armchairs Phillip kept in front of the desk for visitors. "Is the list long?"

"Longer than I'd at first expected. It turns out there's more to arranging a wedding than finding a vicar and speaking vows."

"Can I help?"

Cecilia allowed herself a smile at that. The tone of his voice was one part polite helpfulness and one part hurt male pride. Now that he was resigned to their impending marriage, she suspected he wanted to take the lead.

"Yes, actually. You can start working on the terms of our settlement. I'm asking my solicitor to draw up an agreement that will include three thousand pounds for the farm loan and a clause specifying that the bulk of my estate will remain in my name, under my administration. I've also made provisions for any children we may have—"

He drew in a quick breath and tried to cover it with a cough. "Is that...a possibility?"

"It's a fairly standard clause in a marriage settlement."

"But how likely is it that we would have children?"

"If you're asking if I'm too old to bear children, the answer is no, not yet. If you want to know if I'll be sharing your bed..." She felt warmth unaccountably rise in her cheeks. Since when did talk of a little physicality embarrass her? It wasn't as though they hadn't been intimate before. "I haven't discounted the possibility. We will be married, after all."

James was silent for a long moment before speaking quietly. "Would you like to have children?"

She didn't answer right away, rising and walking around the desk as she considered. *Did* she want children?

"I don't know, to be honest. I've been a single woman so long I haven't thought about becoming a mother in years." Coming to a stop in front of James, she leaned against the desk and reached for his hand, hoping for a better reaction than the one she got that morning. "What about you?"

He flinched when she touched him, but recovered quickly this time and clasped her hand in his. "I do. Though I wouldn't be devastated if it never happened. I have a nephew to dote on, and he'll inherit the farm one day. There will be other nieces and nephews that come along, too, I'm sure."

Before Cecilia realized what she was doing, she pulled James to his feet. "We agreed to tell my family we married for love, didn't we?"

She reached out and took his other hand, lacing their fingers together. "Then you need to appear as if you enjoy touching me."

His eyes widened slightly. "Do I not?"

"You didn't at breakfast."

"I used to."

She took a step closer, breathing in the scent of his shaving soap and skin. No cologne for James Fitzsimmons—that hadn't changed over the years. "Then let's see if we can bring some of that pleasure back. Or at least help us become at ease with each other again."

She released both his hands and he gave her a quizzical look in return. "What now?"

"Just touch me."

He remained still for several seconds, his eyes trained on hers. Then he slid his arms around her and drew her gently against him, his chest rising and falling more rapidly as his breathing quickened. "It's like the first swim of the summer, when the water's still chilly. If you jump in all at once, it's uncomfortable for a minute but you get used to it pretty quickly."

"That's one way to do it," she smiled, sliding her hands up his arms and resting them on his shoulders. Her heart was pounding and she was sure he could feel it, but she carried on as though she held her former lover every day. "Will you tell me about your nephew?"

"He's my sister's son, ten years old come April. Very intelligent—he's already reading up on the latest farming techniques to help increase our crop production."

She felt James's arms relaxing, his hand splayed across her back. "Do you think he'd like to go away to school? Or to university when he's older? We could set aside some money for his education."

"You don't have to do that. He may very well want to receive a formal education, but his father might not like you paying for it, particularly under the circumstances."

"Maybe we can make it a gift, then, if his parents approve." Cecilia felt his breaths begin to lengthen and slow, though his heart was pounding as hard as hers.

He bowed his head and murmured in her ear, "A gift from his Aunt Cecilia? That might be better received."

A little sigh escaped her as she tightened her arms around him, combing her fingers through his hair. When he spoke to her like that it was almost as if they'd never parted. "Then that's how we'll do it. Is there anything you want in the marriage settlement?"

"The only thing I want right now is to kiss you."

Wait, where did that come from? Had Mr. Eddington said something to James after she'd left the table at breakfast? Or was James daring her to take their pretense further? Either way, it felt good to be in his arms again even if it was a little different this time.

And she dearly wanted to kiss him. "Then do it."

His hand released her back to stroke her cheek as his lips found hers. It was a soft kiss at first and tentative, while they each relearned the contours of the other. Then the familiarity flooded back and Cecilia opened her mouth over his, deepening the kiss the way she knew he liked. He reciprocated, wrapping his arm about her once more and squeezing her bottom.

She broke away laughing. "Well, I supposed we're used to each other again."

He leaned in and captured her lips once more. "I'd forgotten how well we did that."

"You'd forgotten?"

He rested his forehead against hers. "Made myself forget. There was no use dwelling on something I could no longer have."

"Except now you can have it." She pulled him down to her and gave him one more languid kiss.

This time he broke away with a smile. "Then we might not have to make a decision about having children—it might be made for us."

"We'll see," was all she said, but her mind was whirling. She'd offered him the chance to live separate lives after their troubles were settled, but conceiving a child would change all of that.

Or would it?

"Do you think your family will believe we're marrying for love?" he asked in a low voice.

"Think of these kisses every time you look at me, every time you touch me, and no one will ever believe otherwise."

He dropped a kiss on the tip of her nose. "Then that's one thing we no longer have to worry about. Shall we get your letters finished up?"

He released her and dropped back into his chair. The distance between them felt strange after being pressed against each other, but she rounded the desk and took up her pen as she resumed her seat.

"*Is* there anything you want in the marriage settlement, James?"

His body sagged, as if the air had been let out of him. "No. Have your solicitor draw up whatever document you think is best, and I'll sign it. I only want to keep my farm and my family safe."

# Chapter 5

Two weeks later, James once again sat with Cecilia discussing their impending wedding. This time, though, they were seated side by side on the sofa in the drawing room of her Hanover Square home in London.

"Is everything at Mivart's to your satisfaction?"

She'd made arrangements for him to stay at Mivart's Hotel, just a few minutes' walk down Brook Street, until the ceremony. "Very much so. And Eddington asked me to pass along his gratitude—it was very generous of you to secure a room for him as well."

"I thought it would be easier for you if you had a friend here."

James found himself biting back a grin. "My brother-in-law said the same thing to my sister when they were wed. She traveled to his parish church for the ceremony, with my parents and I to follow a few days later. She was so nervous, her betrothed suggested she bring a cousin or close friend to keep her company."

"You were never the skittish type, though."

"I'm not now, either." And that was the truth. James might have misgivings about what he and Cecilia were about to do, but the settlements had been signed and the special license issued. His family's livelihood would be safe in a matter of days, and he wasn't about to jeopardize that.

She smiled and turned toward him, resting her elbow on the back of the sofa. "I expected nothing less."

He reflexively reached for the hand that rested in her lap and gave it a squeeze. Two weeks of pretending intimacy—or as near to intimacy as two people can get with a group of guests at a house party—had made the gesture almost automatic. "I do have a whole new appreciation for would-be brides, though, particularly the younger ones. Everything is arranged for them, and not just the ceremony. Their whole future is settled by their fathers and husbands-to-be."

"Women often give up a lot for marriage, but they often receive a lot in return."

"You said 'they.' You don't count yourself one of them?"

Cecilia shook her head, the blonde curls at her temples swaying gently with the motion. "I'm in a very different position than most women. I'm giving up only my name and a little money for our marriage."

"You are giving up your name, aren't you? For some reason it hadn't occurred to me before now. Cecilia Fitzsimmons does have a nice ring to it."

She gave a rather unladylike snort. "You said you sympathize with brides now, perhaps you should change your name. James Maitland sounds lovely."

He must have given her an odd look, for she adjusted her grip on his hand and explained further. "Sometimes when a man marries an heiress or a lady with a title of her own, one of the conditions in the settlement is that he take her name, or that they hyphenate both their names. It's meant to keep her family name from becoming subsumed by his, when it was her money or title in the first place. It doesn't happen often, but it does happen."

"Is that something you'd want? I don't have a lot to give in this marriage, but I can give you your name."

She didn't reply right away, casting her eyes downward for a moment before returning her gaze to his. "Thank you for that. I don't need to keep my name, but I very much appreciate you considering it. Most men would laugh at the very idea."

He leaned slightly forward. "I'm not most men."

"That's one of the reasons I'm marrying you."

"Is it?" He felt his eyes widen in surprise. "You never mentioned it before."

"You think I'd offer up my family and fortune to just anyone?"

She shook her head again, and James was taken by the sudden urge to wrap one of her curls around his finger. But that act hadn't been part of their repertoire at the house party. Nor was there anyone in the house to impress with their faux devotion to each other.

Yet here they sat, holding hands and sharing confidences.

He gave in and let himself tug a lock of her hair gently through the fingers of his free hand. "You don't have a past relationship with just anyone, either. Do you?"

The distance between them doubled without warning. "James Fitzsimmons, what kind of woman do you think I am?"

"That's just it, I don't really know." He slid closer and clasped her hand again, wanting even that little bit of skin to skin contact with her. "I didn't mean to imply that you were anything but a proper lady. But you were so warm and open with me, I thought perhaps you'd found someone else to share that with."

"Only you. You had a way of making me feel important, James, and not because of who my relations are. And you made me feel comfortable enough to let my guard down. Few people have been able to do that."

"So I'm definitely not most men," he smiled, taking her other hand in his. "You are certainly not most women. You made it easy to forget that our stations were so much different, to just enjoy my time with you and be myself."

She smiled softly. "That bodes well for our marriage, then. I know things between us will never be what they were, but perhaps we can at least be friends again."

Friends who also wanted to bed each other. Cecilia had told him to keep in mind the kisses they'd shared in Phillip Maitland's study to help sell their new relationship, but James had had trouble *not* thinking about them. With her lips on his skin now he abruptly understood how blood could run hot, and his mind filled with images of the two of them tangled in crisp linen sheets. Tomorrow was going to be their wedding night. And they had discussed having children...

But no. A physical relationship with Cecilia was not a complication he needed. Better to remember his family, waiting for news back in Kent, and focus on taking care of them.

"I think I would like us to be friends again." To his surprise, he meant it. He still hadn't forgiven her for casting him aside so easily before, but her efforts toward securing his family and the farm had begun to melt his resolve. And things would certainly be easier between them if they could forge a friendship.

The carriage clock on the mantle chimed the hour and Cecilia released his hands. "You should probably go. The neighbors, no doubt, took careful note of your arrival and will be watching with great anticipation for your departure. You wouldn't want to ruin my reputation, would you?"

The question was asked with a wink and James grinned. She used to say much the same thing to him when they were younger, meeting in secret. "No, my lady, I certainly wouldn't."

He bowed over her offered hand, wondering if the kiss he placed on her fingertips heated her blood as much as her kiss had heated his. If she felt anything she gave no outward sign, but James headed back to his hotel with more vigor in his step than he'd had in some time.

Cecilia's wedding day was cold but sunny. The vicar arrived fifteen minutes early, but fortunately so did her niece Honoria, husband in tow, and the four of them settled in the drawing room with tea and coffee to await the bridegroom.

"Congratulations, Aunt," Honoria said, wrapping her arms around Cecilia. "I'm so happy for you."

"Happiness abounds for the Maitland women this winter," Cecilia replied, hugging her niece tightly, then hugging Benedict, too. "How is my little great-niece?"

Benedict's smile reached almost literally from ear to ear. "As lively as her mother."

Honoria laughed. "She mostly sleeps and sucks on her fingers."

"That's mainly what you've been doing since she was born," he replied. "Minus the finger-sucking, of course."

"If you'd been through what I went through to bring that child into this world, you'd need a lot of rest, too," Honoria said, swatting his shoulder.

He caught her hand and kissed it quickly before releasing it. "It wasn't a criticism, my love. Merely an observation."

Cecilia couldn't help but smile at the two of them. She'd wondered for a long time if Honoria might follow in her own spinster footsteps, but the girl had simply been waiting for the right gentleman to come into her life. Or back into her life, in this case. Honoria and Benedict had known each other as children and only later discovered romantic feelings for one another.

Cecilia briefly considered a possible parallel between her own situation and her niece's, then dismissed it. Benedict and Honoria had parted amicably when Benedict sailed away to Greece to assist Lord Elgin in his preservation of the statuary there, but Cecilia's parting from James hadn't exactly been on good terms. They did rub along fairly well together at the house party, though. And those kisses in Phillip's study...

The butler announced James's arrival and Cecilia smiled as he entered the room. He was dressed in cream breaches and a green tailcoat that matched the leaves of the flowers embroidered on his cream waistcoat. She held out her hands to him, glad she had chosen an evening dress of rose silk rather than the plainer day dress she'd originally thought to wear.

"Mr. Fitzsimmons."

He took her hands in his and kissed them both, his lips soft against her skin. "Lady Cecilia."

Mr. Eddington entered behind his friend and Cecilia introduced them to the assemblage before gathering everyone in front of the fireplace for the ceremony. The vicar took his place before the couple and began the ceremony. Words were spoken and promises made, then James slid a polished gold band onto Cecilia's finger.

"I pronounce that they be man and wife together, In the Name of the Father, and of the Son, and of the Holy Ghost. Amen."

And just like that, she and James were joined together for the rest of their lives.

Honoria was the first to embrace her, whispering more good wishes into her aunt's ear. But when she released Cecilia, Honoria reached for James.

"Welcome to the family, Mr. Fitzsimmons," she told him cheerily as she hugged him. "Or might I call you Uncle now?"

The color rose in James's face, tinting his skin a pink that was only a shade or two lighter than Cecilia's gown. "You may call me Uncle if you wish," he murmured, slipping his arms around Honoria for a moment.

"Honoria, would you show the gentlemen into the dining room? The staff have prepared a scrumptious wedding breakfast—"

"—and the happy couple would like a moment alone," Honoria finished with a wink. She accepted the arm Mr. Eddington offered her and led Benedict and the vicar from the room.

Cecilia turned to James and took his hand. "Thank you for allowing my niece some latitude. I am her father's only sibling and her mother was an only child, so she had no uncles until today."

To her relief, James flashed a smile. "Well, I had no nieces until today. It may take some getting used to, but I suspect I will enjoy the addition to my family."

Cecilia stepped closer and lowered her voice. "Speaking of family, I instructed one of the footmen to carry a message to my man of business as soon as the ceremony had concluded. Payment is being delivered to Grimsby this afternoon, with instructions to have my letter returned to this address. By the time we retire for the evening, everyone will be safe from Grimsby's schemes."

James took her in his arms and held her tightly against him. "Thank you," he whispered, kissing her hair.

She let herself lean against him, breathing in the woodsy scent of cedar he wore. Interesting that he'd chosen to wear cologne this day, particularly one that brought their former favorite trysting place so easily to mind. "It's my pleasure, Husband."

He kissed her hair once more, then she felt his warm lips on her temple, her earlobe. "May I show you my gratitude, Wife?"

She raised her face to his. "And be the first to kiss the bride? Yes, you may."

His mouth found hers with a passion they hadn't shared in nearly twenty years, his hands slowly traveling down her back to cup her bottom. She draped her arms around his neck held him as tightly as he held her, wishing there weren't so many layers of clothing between them.

Wishing there weren't people waiting for them in the dining room.

She broke away reluctantly, keeping her eyes closed as she tried to steady her breathing. "You must be *very* grateful indeed."

His lips brushed her cheek, the corner of her mouth. "Apparently I am."

Cecilia blinked open her eyes and studied his face. "You sound surprised."

"Not surprised to be grateful," he replied softly. "A little surprised by the zeal with which I expressed myself."

"We always had zeal, didn't we? I could send our regrets to our guests and we could find out how much more zeal we can awaken."

He kissed her again, more gently this time, as if they were already ensconced in their bedchamber and had all the time in the world. "No, we should celebrate with them and eat that wonderful meal your staff prepared."

She nodded. He was right, of course. Spending time being affectionate newlyweds in front of guests would help cement the idea of a love match in Honoria's mind, and that would be critical in convincing her father. And becoming physically intimate when they were unsure of each other emotionally was a disaster waiting to happen.

"We'll need our strength if we become as ardent as we used to." He dropped one last kiss on her lips and squeezed her bottom before releasing her.

Cecilia allowed her husband to escort her from the room, her head as fuzzy as her skin was hot. Was James teasing her? Had he purposefully aroused her only to leave her wanting?

Or did he mean to give her the wedding night she'd dreamed of all those years ago?

# Chapter 6

It was another week before James resided in the same chamber as his wife—a week in which he was by turns pleased and frustrated that he kept his body from dictating his actions. As much as he wanted to bed Cecilia, he knew that engaging in marital relations would complicate their already knotty relationship—especially if they conceived a child together.

And the last thing he needed was another complication before meeting the Duke of Alston.

James stood in front of the pier glass in the chamber the newlyweds had been given at Orchard Lake, looking for imperfections in his clothing and person. He could hear Cecilia murmuring to her lady's maid in the adjoining dressing room and wondered if she had the same jittery feeling that was growing in his limbs.

The image of the lady's maid appeared in the glass, and James turned just in time to see her disappear through the chamber door. Cecilia appeared a moment later clad in a pale blue gown that fairly floated around her.

She approached him and brushed imaginary dust from his shoulders. "Nervous?"

"Is it so obvious?"

"No, that's why I asked," she replied, turning him around to face the glass once again. "You look calm and confident."

Her blue eyes peeked over his shoulder and he met her reflected gaze. "Good. Those are qualities I want your brother to associate with me. I've never met a duke before, and I am now related to this duke because of some less than savory circumstances. The blackmail, I mean," he added quickly.

"Blackmail certainly qualifies as less than savory." He could see the corner of her eyes crinkle in what must have been a smile. "Though Alston doesn't know about that part."

"That should help."

She tugged gently at the hem of his coat and smoothed out the tail. "Do you remember when we first met and you found out I was *Lady* Cecilia?"

"I immediately wondered what I'd got myself into."

"You could have turned tail and run, but you didn't."

"I was already besotted with you," he replied slowly. "I didn't want to run."

She stepped beside him and threaded her arm through his. "Do you want to run now?"

"No." He was pleasantly surprised to hear strength in his voice.

"Good. Alston likes to be shown the deference he is due as a duke, but hates being treated like an invalid—even when he is one. It's a fine line to tread, but you managed it with me."

Cecilia had made it clear all those years ago that she expected a certain level of conduct from him, but she'd also maintained that her relations' interests weren't necessarily her own. James had responded by acknowledging her social station to be above his while ignoring the implications of her surname.

Perhaps a similar approach would work with His Grace as well.

"Let's go and find out."

They entered the drawing room arm-in-arm and approached Alston, who was ensconced in a rather throne-like chair upholstered in cream with gilt carvings forming the supports and legs. He was dressed in expensively tailored clothing and looked ready for action, but James could hear His Grace's labored breathing over the rustle of Cecilia's gown.

Alston remained seated and held his arms out to his sister. "Dearest Cecilia, how glad I am that you've come."

"How wonderful it is to be here," she returned, bending to embrace him and kiss his cheek. "It feels like ages since we were last together."

"It was so long ago you were a different person."

Cecilia straightened, but didn't stiffen as James thought she might. "My name may have changed, brother dear, but I am still very much myself."

Alston's lips curled into a smile. "Of course you are. And this must be your new husband."

James executed a bow slightly deeper than was necessary in the drawing room of a close relation. "Your Grace, it's a pleasure to finally meet you."

"And you." Alston gave a shallow bow from his chair and gestured to the lady seated on the sofa nearest to him. "My wife, the Duchess of Alston."

James took his new sister-in-law's offered hand and kissed the air just above it. "Your Grace."

She inclined her head even less than Alston had, but she was smiling. "It's so wonderful to meet the gentleman who finally enticed our Cecilia into wedded bliss."

Is that what his wife had told her family? Well, James wouldn't contradict her—not after she'd fulfilled her side of their bargain with such speed. "It took seventeen years, but now we have the rest of our lives together."

The duchess sniffled and blinked as if she were holding back tears, yet she was smiling brightly. "I'm so glad for the both of you."

Cecilia was invited to sit beside her sister-in-law, while His Grace beckoned James to pull a chair up beside the ducal "throne." He did so, bracing for the grilling he expected to receive.

Alston leaned over the arm of his chair and lowered his voice. "Did you marry my sister for her money, Mr. Fitzsimmons?"

How was James to answer that truthfully without betraying Cecilia? "Her solicitor drew up a marriage settlement that kept her money under her own control, and my farm is very profitable. If my wife ever invests money in the farm—or anything else—it will be her own decision."

Alston sat back with a satisfied smile. "I assumed she would make such an arrangement, but as her older brother it is still my duty to protect her whenever possible. Since that business is settled, we may now speak of much more agreeable matters. Are you interested in music at all?"

Dinner that evening was a quiet family affair, held in the morning room rather than the formal dining room. Alston had required help to rise from his chair in the drawing room, and was slowly escorted by his wife and a burly footman to his place at the table. Cecilia and James had trailed behind, seating themselves across from her brother and sister-in-law in a cozy little square.

But midway through the first course His Grace began coughing, and by the time the second course was being served his labored breathing had escalated into persistent wheezing.

"Darling," the duchess said sweetly, laying a hand on her husband's shoulder. "Perhaps you'd better retire for the evening."

Alston glared at his plate and forced a slow breath in through his nose. But his expression softened when he looked at Her Grace and coughed in lieu of an exhalation. "Perhaps you are right, my dear. Would you..."

James sat in awkward helplessness as two footmen came to assist Alston from his chair and out of the room, wheezing and coughing all the way, while the duchess conferred with a maid.

"Should we do something?" he asked Cecilia in a half-whisper.

She shook her head. "Not yet. The footmen will take Alston to his bedchamber, and Her Grace will get him settled."

His wife not his valet? Interesting.

"My husband will want me to apologize on his behalf," the duchess said, turning to James and Cecilia. "He had so hoped to make it all the way through dinner with the two of you."

"He cannot control his illness," Cecilia replied with a wave of her hand. "If he could, he would have forced its submission to him long ago."

"That's true enough," the Duchess of Alston smiled. "Please enjoy the rest of the meal. When Alston is recovered enough for company, he will no doubt send for you."

She disappeared through the same door her husband had been carried through, and James looked at his wife. "So we're just supposed to sit here and eat as if nothing happened?"

"Eat, yes. Pretend as if nothing happened, no. Of course you can't go on as if you didn't just see your new brother-in-law fighting for every breath he took."

And if it was difficult for James, how hard must it be for Alston's own sister? He reached over and clasped Cecilia's hand, running his thumb over the back. "Nor can you."

"I will manage."

"But you don't have to manage alone. Not anymore."

She didn't respond with words, but her fingers curled around his hand and gripped it tightly. They sat in silence for several long moments that should have been awkward—but oddly weren't—as her throat worked and her eyelids blinked.

Then she cleared her throat and kissed his hand. "Thank you," she said softly. "I don't believe I'm hungry after all. Would you mind terribly if we retired to our chamber?"

She'd said *we* not *I*, and for the first time since leaving his farm, James felt useful again. Needed. "Of course. Perhaps a little reading by the fire will settle us both."

An hour later, they were fetched by a footman to the ducal bedchamber with little fanfare and no context. Were they to say their last goodbyes to His Grace? Cecilia seemed heartened by the summons, though, and when they entered the large room James understood why.

Alston was sitting up in bed, propped up by a mountain of pillows and still laboring for breath, but with a little more ease than at dinner. He was clad only in his shirt and trousers, his discarded clothing being scooped up by a man who was probably the duke's valet. Her Grace sat beside him on the counterpane, leaning against an identical set of pillows as she read aloud from a book that sounded like a farming treatise.

"Ah, there you are," the duchess smiled as Cecilia led James deeper into the room.

Cecilia smiled at her sister-in-law, but directed her question to her brother. "How are you feeling, Alston?"

"Ready for another cup of coffee," came the reply. His voice was weak and wheezy, but steady, and he held out his arms for the embrace Cecilia offered.

Her Grace started to slide off the big bed, but Cecilia stopped her. "I'll get it. This is the tray over here?"

To James's surprise, his wife crossed to the silver tray and poured out two cups of coffee, adding cream and sugar to one before serving the duke and duchess with her own hands. "James, would you like a cup? It's strong, because that seems to help calm Alston's breathing. But I can ring for tea if you'd rather have that."

"Coffee will be fine, thank you," he murmured.

Alston gestured to a chair next to his side of the bed. "Come and sit here, Fitzsimmons. I've a thing or two I'd like your opinion on. My home farm has been struggling to produce these past few years, and Cecilia says you're an expert on such matters."

Her Grace shot a warning look at Alston. "You know talking only exacerbates your condition."

"Then I shall do most of the talking," James supplied with a smile, taking the indicated seat. "Cecilia tells me I can discuss farming until long after everyone has stopped paying attention."

Cecilia appeared beside James, handing him a cup with her brows raised slightly. Was she remembering the last time she'd poked fun at his agricultural ramblings? It had been just days before he'd asked for her hand.

"It's true," she replied, running a hand over James's back after he'd taken his cup from her. "I have never met a man so passionate about any one thing."

James forced himself not to react. That had been the other half of their private joke—that Cecilia was the only thing he was more passionate about than his livelihood. Her hand came to rest on his shoulder and he dared a quick look up at her. A small smile played on her pink lips and her blue eyes crinkled slightly at the edges.

Was she remembering the demonstration of James's passion that had followed?

"Cecilia, my dear, perhaps you could convince my lady wife to take some air," Alston said, shattering the moment. "It isn't good for her to always be cooped up here with me."

Cecilia gave her husband's shoulder a squeeze, trailing her fingers down his arm as she moved toward the duchess. "Of course. How does a walk in the garden sound?"

Her Grace took a long look at the duke, pressing her lips together before answering. "A short one will do us both some good, I imagine," she agreed, pushing herself off the bed. "The cold air will clear our heads."

The ladies departed, and Alston met James's gaze. "My duchess works too hard tending me, but she won't leave me to the care of our servants." His words were slow and somewhat hoarse, as if he'd been shouting all evening. "I'm glad you and Cecilia are here now, though I'd have preferred to be in better health for our first meeting."

James stared, taken aback by the pronouncement. He'd have thought an aristocratic family like the Alstons wouldn't have dirtied their hands in a sickroom. But here was the duchess herself having to be persuaded to leave.

"Perhaps Cecilia will remind Her Grace to look to herself a bit more."

Alston nodded. "It's easier for her to leave me in the company of family, too. Even new family."

"But I'm a stranger yet." James hoped his eyes hadn't widened as much as he feared they had.

"Yes and no," the duke replied. "It's true Her Grace and I don't know you well, but we know Cecilia and we trust her judgment. And if Cecilia thinks you worthy of her hand, we are content to believe so as well."

He shifted on the bed as if he hadn't just turned James's world on its side, trying to adjust one of the pillows at his back. "Now, would you please tell me what can be done to improve my home farm?"

# Chapter 7

"What did the two of you end up discussing?" Cecilia asked, draping herself across the big bed in their bedchamber. She was still fully clothed, but her spirits were low and her body drained. The soft feather mattress would go a long way toward alleviating at least one of those problems, and she hoped a light conversation with her husband would take care of the other.

James moved quietly about the room, shucking his tailcoat and unwinding the cravat from his neck. "Irrigation. From what your brother described, his crops are either drenched or parched—he can't seem to regulate the amount of water they receive. We talked about some different things that could be done to fix that."

She'd been focused on the elaborate plaster ceiling above her, but lolled her head to one side and smirked at James. "Sounds exciting."

"It was, actually," he grinned back. "Solving a problem always gets my heart pumping."

Could that have been why he was so amorous after their wedding? A serious problem had been solved that day for both of them.

She brushed the thought aside. "Then it did you both some good. Alston was considerably more cheerful when Her Grace and I returned."

He hadn't sounded any better with all that wheezing punctuating his every breath, but he'd been smiling when the ladies reentered his chamber. And Cecilia couldn't remember the last time she'd seen her brother smile during one of his attacks.

"What about you?" James draped his cravat over a chair with his coat and hoisted himself onto the bed beside her. "Did your walk cheer you?"

"A little." She'd felt more relief than anything at the chance to escape the sickroom and the helplessness that dwelled there.

Not that she'd admit that to anyone.

James turned onto his side and met her gaze, brushing a blonde curl from her face. "How long has your brother been ill?"

They'd discussed Alston's health at length once upon a time, but perhaps James had forgotten. "He first began to notice symptoms not long after he left university, and slowly declined from there."

"You were still just a girl, then."

Cecilia had been ten years old the first time her brother had his first attack, and younger still when he'd complained of those first symptoms. "I was. Alston has been unwell for most of my life."

The statement hit her like a cricket bat. How had she never realized that before?

Her surprise must have shown on her face because James reached over and clasped her hand, giving it a gentle squeeze. "Did that, perhaps, influence you as you grew older?"

What was he driving at? "Quite possibly. There were many times we had plans to travel here or there, or to participate in some event or other, and had to make last-minute changes because of Alston's health." She drew here eyebrows down as she thought back to her childhood. "It was never something we talked much about as a family. We just did it."

"You and your parents protected him."

She nodded. "I suppose we did."

"And that's why, when I asked for your hand all those years ago, you declined. Because protecting your family is quite literally second nature to you."

Cecilia studied his face, his skin darker against the cream-colored coverlet, his mouth curving upward very slightly. "Perhaps it is."

He drew her hand to his lips and pressed a kiss to her palm. "I didn't see it before. I'm sorry, Cecilia."

"You can't mean to tell me that you'd have taken my refusal with a smile had you known me better."

He dropped their clasped hands onto the bed between them and pressed his lips together for a long moment before speaking. "Not with a smile, no. But I may have spent less energy being angry with you afterwards."

"How angry were you?" The words slipped out in a near whisper. She hadn't meant to ask the question aloud, but she was burning to know his answer. How much had he hated her?

"Too angry," was all he responded, his voice not much louder than hers, "for much too long. But I'm not any longer. I would do anything to protect my parents, my sister and her family, no matter how painful. That's what you did for Alston, for Honoria… I understand that now."

Tension she'd carried in her heart for seventeen years finally eased, and Cecilia felt her body relax into the feather mattress. She sat up, releasing his hand and stroking his cheek as she looked down into his bright eyes. "I'm so glad, James. Truly."

There was another pause in the conversation while their gazes met and held. This was the same James she'd fallen in love with as a young woman, and she had no words to describe how good it felt to have him back.

"Now," he said, clearing his throat and breaking the moment. "When was the last time someone did something for you?"

She chuckled. "You've seen my home. Do you not remember the servants there? Or here, for that matter?"

"That's not what I mean." He snaked an arm around her body and drew her down to him, smiling up at her when she halted herself with a hand to his chest. "When was the last time someone close to you offered you comfort? Alston has his duchess and his children, and Her Grace has you. But you've had a rather fretful day yourself."

"And you're offering to comfort me?" The tip of one finger had landed just inside the open neck of his shirt, and she drew a small circle on his exposed skin. His chest rose beneath her hand as he inhaled sharply.

"If you wish it."

A part of her wanted to peel the remaining clothes from his body and spend the rest of the evening reacquainting herself with its contours. But worrying over Alston and trying to keep up a brave front for her sister-in-law had been exhausting, and her brother was still in danger. Instead, she slid her arm around him and nestled herself against his chest, tucking her head beneath his chin.

"Would you hold me for a while? We can talk or not as you please, but I would very much like your arms around me."

James obliged, planting a kiss on her hair as they sought a mutually comfortable arrangement of their bodies. "My arms are at your disposal. And not just tonight. No matter what happens between us, if you should ever need me—for anything at all—you need only ask."

She turned her head slightly and pressed her lips to his skin, to the same place her fingertip had been. "Thank you, James. That means a great deal to me."

They fell silent once more and Cecilia closed her eyes, allowing the slow rise and fall of his chest to lull her into a dreamless sleep.

When she blinked open her eyes, the bedchamber was dark and James had disappeared. Cecilia rubbed her eyes and sat up, noting that the room wasn't completely dark—there was a fire burning in the fire place. As her vision adjusted to the gloom, the outline of a man came into focus. He was sitting in a chair practically on the hearth, trying to catch the firelight on a piece of paper.

Stretching as she slid off the bed, she crossed the room to join her husband. He looked up at her approach and offered a smile.

"I thought you might sleep all night in your gown and shoes."

His body was turned toward the fire and Cecilia positioned herself behind him, resting her hands on his shoulders. "Is it very late?"

"Nearly midnight."

"You could have woken me."

James shook his head, laying a hand over one of hers. "Extra sleep never hurt anyone. And I suspect you needed it."

"I did," she replied, realizing the truth of her words as she spoke them. Between her brother's health and Grimsby's blackmail, the past few weeks had been more distressing than she'd realized. "What about you? Did you sleep?

"No. I couldn't stop thinking about these." He held up the letter he'd been reading and its companion, folded but with a broken seal.

"From the farm?"

He nodded, glancing down at the paper in his hand.

She slid her arms down his chest and lightly embraced him. "All is well, I hope."

James rested his cheek against hers, and she felt him smile for the briefest of moments. "It seems to be. My father has confirmed everything the steward has reported..."

His voice trailed off, and Cecilia kissed his cheek. "But you wish you were there to see it with your own eyes."

He inhaled deeply and let the breath out on a sigh. "Yes, I do."

"We can—"

"No need," he interrupted. "At least, not yet. Your brother needs you more than my farm needs me right now."

Cecilia tightened her arms around him, dropping another kiss on his cheek. "Thank you. I want to meet your parents, your sister and her family, but I'm reluctant to leave here."

He unwrapped her arms from his shoulders and led her around the chair, snaking an arm around her waist and drawing her onto his lap. "They will be pleased to meet you, and not just because you saved the farm. I think they'll like you."

She dropped her head to his shoulder and smiled, hoping the low light of the room masked the anxiety that suddenly welled up inside her. "I hope so."

"I can't, however make any promises on behalf of our animals," he laughed. "We have one old cow who has appointed herself guardian of the others…"

She felt her body tense and James's voice trailed off. He ran one of his large hands up and down her arm in a gesture that she thought was meant to be reassuring. "But I don't want you to feel like you have to work when you're on the farm. You won't have to deal with the livestock—"

"James." She lifted her head from his shoulder and met his gaze. "Might I confess something to you?"

"Of course."

His eyes were wide in the firelight, his brows raised in silent question. Would he be angry? Would he judge her to be just another spoiled aristocrat?

There was only one way to find out.

"I am terrified of visiting the farm."

His brows rose even higher, but his hand began rubbing her arm again. "What? Why?"

Cecilia wanted to bury her face in his shirt so she didn't have to look at him, but she forced herself to maintain eye contact. "I have only the most rudimentary knowledge of farms in general, and only old stories of your farm in particular. I am afraid that, not only would I be completely useless, but that I would actually hinder operations."

He smoothed her cheek with roughened fingertips, grinning. "Cecilia Fitzsimmons, a hindrance? Never."

"I'm serious, James. I was trained to dance at balls and converse with strangers. I know nothing about cows or crops."

His hand dropped from her face and his smile faded. "I'm sorry. I didn't mean to poke fun at you. But you are the least useless woman I have ever known, and I was trying to picture you bumbling about the stables and fields. The vision was so incongruous with your actual capabilities, I couldn't help but smile."

"What capabilities?" she asked pointedly. "I have no skills that would be useful on a farm."

"You are an excellent manager of people," James replied, the corners of his mouth turning up once more in a smaller smile. "That is enormously useful on a farm such as mine that is worked by a small army. There are always more tasks to be done than can be completed in a day, and someone needs to keep track of which tasks are completed by which people and how well it is done. I saw you do the very same thing at your home in Town."

"Of course I did—that's called managing a home. But your farm doesn't have a butler or housekeeper."

"No, but it does have a steward."

He had a point there. The role of property steward was not unlike that of a housekeeper, and Cecilia had dealt with housekeepers for years. "Are you going to keep him on after you return?"

It was only after she'd asked the question that she realized how full of meaning it was. James wouldn't need to retain the steward if he planned to remain in residence once he returned to the farm. And if James wasn't leaving, that meant Cecilia would be traveling about the country alone, separate from her husband.

Separated from her husband?

"I don't know." James sighed again. "I've spent my whole life on that farm, *given* my whole life to that farm. I love it as much—" He stopped abruptly and dropped his gaze to her lips. Then he cleared his throat and raised his eyes to hers "—as much as I love my family. And it hurts to leave it in the care of another. But I have also enjoyed my time away, being something of an idle gentleman for a few weeks while I spend time with you."

He liked spending time with her, away from his work. Her younger self would have swooned to hear such words from her dedicated farmer. Her current self couldn't help but smile broadly. "Speaking of idle time together, may I ask you one favor before we descend upon your family?"

"Ask away."

"Would you come with me to London when we leave here? From there we can go directly to the farm and stay as long as you wish. But I'd like very much for you to escort me to a ball when the Season opens."

His entire face seemed to frown. "A ball?"

"Just one, given by Benedict's cousins every year. Grimsby will undoubtedly be there—everyone is—and I'd like to have a word with him. In public."

She winked with her last statement and James laughed. "I see. Well, I can't fault you for that."

"You might even take pleasure in it." She leaned in close, her mouth just a fraction of an inch from his ear. "As much pleasure, perhaps, as I will seeing you in your evening clothes."

"When you put it that way..." His warm lips brushed her neck, her jaw. "Maybe we could stay in Town for a bit. A few days alone together might do us some good."

She kissed his temple, but forced herself to draw back. Her body very much wanted to take the next logical step with her lawfully wedded husband, but their future together was still so uncertain.

Perhaps in London they could settle things between them.

"Yes," she agreed with a soft smile, "they might."

# Chapter 8

James and Cecilia stayed two more weeks with the Alstons, until His Grace could almost take a normal breath again. He was still weak and tired easily when they departed, but the rest of his symptoms seemed to have subsided. So, too, had Cecilia's apprehension—or, at least, that's the way it appeared to James.

They'd decided to share the large bed in their chamber and keep nighttime activities confined to sleeping only. Both of them had kept their promises faithfully, but James had been a little overwhelmed by the intimacy of lying in bed beside his wife. It wasn't just that they wore thin nightclothes and fewer layers than during the day, though that was part of it. For James, though, the simple act of being unconscious and the vulnerability that came with that was new. Who else could he be so completely unguarded with?

Who else could she trust with the same feeling?

Despite their firmness about falling asleep on opposite sides of the bed with plenty of empty space between them, James would often awaken with the sun to find Cecilia's back pressed against his. She never put her arms around him as she slept, but if he rolled over and cradled her in his, she would relax into his chest with a little sigh. He'd never felt such contentment wash through him as he had on those mornings.

And he couldn't wait to tell her she snored.

But he kept that bit of information to himself, trying valiantly to rein in his own apprehension. He hadn't been to a society event in seventeen years, and that had been a public assembly with other invitees from the untitled gentry like himself. The event they would be attending, Cecilia explained on the way to London, was the Marchioness of Whitby's Black and White Ball, the first major event of the Season each year. The ballroom would be decorated in black, white, and silver, as would the guests if they adhered to Lady Whitby's rule. And everyone important in society or government would be there, wondering who this upstart was and why he was bothering Lady Cecilia.

As luck would have it, though, Cecilia's niece and nephew-by-marriage were among the first people they found upon entering the Whitbys' ballroom on the appointed evening.

Honoria smiled when James bowed over her hand. "Uncle, how wonderful to see you here."

"We have one more item of business to attend to before I sweep your aunt away for an extended stay on the farm," he smiled back, slightly disappointed that there would be no hug from his new niece due to this public setting.

"How exciting!"

Cecilia laughed beside him, threading her arm through his. "Everything is an adventure to you, isn't it?"

Benedict took his wife's hand and grinned first at her, then at her aunt. "It is when you have the right company."

James glanced at his own wife and smiled. He'd originally planned to take her to the Fitzsimmons Farm after their betrothal when they were young, but that never happened. The circumstances were different now, but he discovered he was still looking forward to showing her his property, his livelihood.

And he very much wanted her to meet his family.

The couples parted after requesting dances from each of the ladies, and James escorted Cecilia around the perimeter of the ballroom.

"Lady Whitby outdid herself this year," Cecilia said, her eyes roaming around the room.

"Has she? I hadn't noticed." His voice was low and he waited until she met his gaze, then pointedly looked her up and down. She'd explained the details of her silver gown when they'd dressed earlier that evening, right down to the material making up what she'd called an overdress. But he saw none of it, only his lovely bride.

She swatted his arm, the tiniest hit of pink coloring her cheeks. "Am I so distracting?" she asked with half a laugh.

"You're beautiful," he answered without hesitation. She'd always been pretty, but tonight her eyes sparkled more brightly than ever despite her visible efforts to hold back a grin.

She leaned her head against his shoulder for an all-too-brief moment before murmuring, "Thank you." When she straightened again, she looked rather serious. "Will you kiss me for luck?"

"Here?" He'd kiss her anywhere she liked, but it was highly unfashionable to show affection to one's spouse in public. Kissing in the middle of a ballroom was unheard of.

"I don't want to lose my nerve."

Ah, she was worried about Grimsby. Cecilia had told James a bit of what she had planned for the blackmailing earl, and that she'd purposely left some of the encounter to chance. That, she'd confessed, made her slightly anxious.

"You'll be just fine," James said with a smile, laying his hand over hers as it rested on his arm. "No one wrongs Cecilia Maitland Fitzsimmons and escapes unscathed."

Her chin lifted and her grin returned. "You're absolutely right." Then she leaned in and brushed her soft lips across his cheek. "But a little luck never hurts."

She released his arm headed into the crowd—it was also highly unfashionable to be always together with one's spouse at a *ton* entertainment—leaving James on his own. He felt a wave of heat flood his body and suddenly didn't know what to do with his hands now that he had no wife to hold. But he took a deep breath and let it out slowly, nodding briefly at an older couple as they strolled past. If Cecilia could take on her blackmailer, James could get along in public without her for a while.

Cecilia couldn't remember the last time she was so tense at a ball—she was normally rather comfortable, even in the crush that was the Whitbys' Black and White Ball each year.

But she hadn't had a blackmailer to call out before.

Not that she was going to challenge him to a duel, of course. But she did plan to challenge his morality and honor before the entire assemblage. If she failed, if Grimsby was too clever to take the bait, then she could be the one humiliated.

And her husband and brother along with her.

But, oh, if she succeeded...

She smoothed her gloved hands down her cloth-of-silver skirt and set her shoulders, moving slowly but purposefully through the ballroom looking for Grimsby.

She paused in her pursuit on occasion to talk to and be sociable with the other guests, trying to maintain a demeanor of gaiety as she would at any other entertainment. She circled the dancers and chaperones and gossiping dowagers, moved past the table laden with punch and lemonade, but the earl was nowhere to be found.

She tried the card room next, hiding a grin behind her fan when she spied James seated at a table with Lord Whitby. Her grin faded in the next instant, however. The Earl of Grimsby was slouching in a chair at the next table, his cards clutched in one hand against his black tailcoat.

"Ah, Grimsby!" Cecilia called, snapping her fan shut and waving it in his direction. "I've found you at last."

He started, straightening in his chair as his eyes widened for the briefest of moments. "Lady Cecilia, how nice to see you this evening. How might I be of service?"

She flitted across the room and halted at Grimsby's side, clasping her fan in both hands. "You've already done so much, finding that letter for me."

His brows rose a mere fraction of an inch. "Letter?"

"The letter I'd written to my dear husband so many years ago." She emphasized *husband* just a little, in case Grimsby hadn't heard about her recent marriage. Cecilia's man of business had forwarded a bank draft to the earl for the discharge of the loan against the Fitzsimmons Farm. But she'd stood on principal and chosen not to give in to the blackmail and pay for the return of her letter.

Grimsby's brows rose to a loftier height, and Cecilia guessed that he hadn't known of her marriage to James. What fun that she be the one to inform him his scheme had no power over her any longer!

"Your husband?" Grimsby shook his head, then stood and gestured to the chair he had just vacated. "Why don't you sit, and we can discuss this matter without disturbing the other card players."

Cecilia ignored his suggestion and made sure her voice carried across the room. "I don't know how it could have gone missing—Mr. Fitzsimmons and I keep our private letters to each other in locked caskets—but I was enormously glad to receive your note detailing your possession of it."

Heads were turning throughout the card room, no doubt in response to her raised voice. But mouths opened and eyebrows were raised at her last statement. She could practically hear the other guests wondering how and why Grimsby had obtained a personal letter belonging to a lady not his wife.

Grimsby shifted in his chair and started to speak but Cecilia cut him off, channeling her growing glee into her ruse. "I would also like to offer you a reward for your discretion, my lord. There are too many people in this world that would have used that letter to try to embarrass me or my family by threatening to make it public, but your only concern was making sure it was returned safely to me."

His expression froze in stony silence, and Cecilia couldn't tell if he was angry, or mortified, or some combination of emotions he'd rather not name. Whatever his feelings, she was absolutely delighted. She'd both exposed and negated his nefarious intentions without accusing him of anything at all.

"O-of course I cannot accept a reward," he managed, clenching his teeth with an audible *click*. "I am honor bound as a gentleman to return your property to you, and that I shall do."

Cecilia suppressed—with much difficulty—the urge to laugh. There went any money he'd hoped to extort from her, too. He could certainly try another private threat, but it would be a threat with no teeth. By appearing at the ball together, the whole of Polite Society now knew that Cecilia and James had wed, so there would be little if any scandal from a love letter between them. And by Grimsby's own admission to the entire card room, he had Cecilia's letter in his possession. If he refused to return it, she could simply ask him for it the next time she saw him...preferably in public.

"You are an honorable man, indeed, and I am grateful to you for keeping my letter safe."

His body seemed to deflate as he bowed to her. "I shall see to it first thing tomorrow."

She acknowledged his bow with a nod and turned, nodding to Lord Whitby and James. She'd intended to simply leave the room then, but James jumped to his feet and was at her side in three strides.

"We're both most appreciative, Lord Grimsby," James said with such sincerity Cecilia almost believed him.

Grimsby flashed a half-hearted smile, and when he declined to comment further, James offered Cecilia his arm. "Shall we, my dear? I believe the next dance belongs to me."

She slid her arm through his, drawing herself much closer to his side than was proper. "Yes, of course. My heart is so much lighter now with this business finally resolved."

She smiled broadly at her husband and allowed him to escort her out of the card room. When they'd cleared the door, James tugged her down the hall and into an open but empty room.

"Nicely played," he grinned, sliding his arms around her in a celebratory embrace.

She reciprocated, throwing her arms around his neck and pressing her cheek against his. "I wasn't sure it would work, but it did."

"You could talk anyone into anything, wife of mine," he murmured in her ear.

Cecilia closed her eyes, tightening her hold on him. "Flatterer," she whispered back with a smile. She held on for a moment longer, then loosened her grip on his shoulders. "Did you truly want to dance with me, or was that just an excuse to get away from Grimsby?"

"What I'd really like to do is return home and sit before a warm fire with you for a little while," he said, with a small smile. "We'll have to be up early tomorrow if we're going to make a good start toward the farm. I know you don't sleep well in a moving carriage."

"That sounds wonderful," she admitted. With her confrontation of her blackmailer concluded, she couldn't think of a reason to stay. "Though we can't leave until my letter arrives—Grimsby promised to send it first thing."

"Certainly not. We've gone to all this trouble to thwart the man, we may as well stay in Town long enough to see this matter concluded."

"My thoughts exactly."

He brushed his fingertips across her cheek and once again offered his arm. "To home, then, where we shall count down the minutes until your letter arrives."

# Chapter 9

To Cecilia's surprise, her letter actually did arrive mid-morning the day after the ball, delivered by a footman in Grimsby livery. She unfolded the paper carefully and scanned the words to be sure it was *her* letter, then re-folded it and found it a place in her reticule where she could guard it closely.

By the time they reached the Fitzsimmons Farm, though, she'd forgotten all about her letter. There was so much to take in: the main house that was larger than her cousin Philip's home in the Cotswolds, the multitude of outbuildings, the adorable little lambs and foals, the friendliness of James's parents.

The biggest surprise, though, was a house tucked back in a corner of the property. Two stories high and built in red brick, it drew a grin from James that was so big Cecilia thought his face might split in two.

"This one is mine," he told her, throwing his arms wide. "The main house is where my parents lived when Father inherited this place, and where my sister and I spent our childhood. But when I came of age, I wanted something for my own."

"It's like a dower house," Cecilia replied with a wink, taking his offered hand as they circled the structure. "Except that the son of the family lives here rather than the dowager."

"Exactly. The property still officially belongs to my father, and this was a way for me to have some privacy and autonomy until the day comes when I inherit."

He escorted her through the interior, pointing out structural features he'd requested and the decorating he'd done himself, all with that wide grin.

"It's very cozy, James. And I don't mean that as a euphemism for 'small' either—this house looks to be the same size as my home in Hanover Square. And every room feels like a place I'd enjoy spending time." She squeezed his hand gently. "You clearly do."

"I do," he echoed. "My parents keep talking about moving out of the main house and giving it over to me, but I keep telling them not to. I'm more than happy here."

They stopped before the entrance to an empty room on the ground floor, and Cecilia peered inside. "Why haven't you furnished this room?"

"I was saving it as a sitting room for my eventual wife."

His words were even in tone and volume, but his eyes locked onto hers as he spoke. All she could manage in response was, "Oh." She released his hand and clasped hers together. "We probably ought to—"

"James? Are you in here?" a female voice called from the front door.

"Mother?"

Cecilia followed her husband back through the house toward the door and discovered Mrs. Fitzsimmons standing in the entry.

"There you are," she smiled at her son. "Your steward is looking for you, and I was hoping to show Lady Cecilia some of the duties belonging to the lady of the manor."

Cecilia shared a look with James and gave him a small nod. Finding out how the farm worked was one of the reasons she'd wanted to make this trip. "That would be lovely, Mrs. Fitzsimmons. And you must call me Cecilia. I am family now, no matter how that came to be."

She felt warm pressure on her hand and James flashed her a smile. "I'll leave you two, then."

Cecilia spent the rest of the afternoon shadowing her mother-in-law as she went about her daily routine. As James had told her at Orchard Lake, there was little difference between running a large farm and a small estate. The Fitzsimmons Farm employed fewer servants inside the house than Alston did at any one of his country estates, but they're number included the usual housekeeper and butler, along with a variety of maids and a few footmen. The kitchen garden was larger than Cecilia's in Town and Mrs. Fitzsimmons was more involved with the care of hers than Cecilia, but that, too, was familiar.

"All these years I thought being a farmer's wife would be completely foreign to me," Cecilia smiled after they'd gone over the dinner menu with the cook. "Yet, the things you've shown me here today are the things I do in my own home."

"It was different for James's great-grandparents," Mrs. Fitzsimmons responded. "The farm was smaller then, and so was the income it produced. They employed one maid-of-all-work and a few field hands, but that was all. When I married Mr. Fitzsimmons, I thought that's what I was walking into, myself."

"Were you terrified?"

Mrs. Fitzsimmons giggled. "I was. My mother-in-law had gone on to her reward before I came here, and Mr.

Fitzsimmons's grandmother was in ill health, so I had no one to show me what to do."

"I would have been overwhelmed," Cecilia said softly.

"Oh no," Mrs. Fitzsimmons replied quickly. "I am a gentleman's daughter and managed without too much trouble. You, having been raised in grander circumstances than I, would have made this house your own in short order."

"I suppose I would have." She glanced around Mrs. Fitzsimmons's sitting room with its oak escritoire and chairs upholstered in powder blue, thinking of that empty room in James's house. Would she choose different fabric for her chairs? A different wood for her writing desk? Would James sit with her in the evenings and discuss the day's business while she embroidered?

"Thank you for taking me under your wing," Cecilia smiled. "If there is nothing else for today, I believe I'll lie down for a while before dinner. For all the traveling I do, I still haven't managed to learn how to sleep well in the carriage."

"Of course. Do you remember the way?"

"I can just follow the path, can't I?"

Mrs. Fitzsimmons's eyes widened. "Yes, if you were going to James's house. Your chamber is upstairs. We assumed that since yours was a marriage of convenience..."

"I see. Well, then, upstairs I shall go."

There was an unexpected twist. After spending weeks upon weeks with James—including a few coaching inns with only one room available—she was to finally have her privacy back.

But did she want it?

James lay in bed that night and tried to sleep, but his eyes remained open and his mind alert. He thought that, between the fitful sleep he managed traveling from London and tramping all around the farm this afternoon, he'd be falling asleep in his supper. But here he was in his own bed at last, with the familiar sounds of his home around him, and he remained wide awake.

"Well, if I'm not going to sleep, then I should do something useful," he said aloud, swinging his legs over the side of the bed. He found a pair of trousers to put on and grabbed a clean shirt from his clothespress, pulling it on as he moved through the moonlit house. A pair of thick stockings his mother had knitted for him completed his ensemble and warmed his icy feet.

He decided to tackle the stack of correspondence that had piled up in his absence, taking out a fresh sheet of paper as he opened the topmost letter. Before he could read a word, he was startled by a noise at the front of the house.

Was someone knocking?

When he opened the door, he was greeted by the sight of his wife bundled in what his mother liked to call a wrapper, her bright hair hanging in a thick braid over her shoulder.

"Cecilia? What are you doing here at this time of night?"

"Perhaps we could discuss it inside? Spring may have come to England, but you'd never know it this night."

He shook himself and held the door wider for her. "Of course. I'm afraid the only fire laid is in my bedchamber, though. Do you mind talking there?"

She smirked at him as she entered the house, twining her arm around his. "How scandalous, Mr. Fitzsimmons! Whatever will the neighbors think if they find out?"

"Let us hope we never have to find out," he replied with mock seriousness. "This way, my lady."

When she was seated before the fire and suitably comfortable, James tried again. "To what do I owe this pleasure, Wife?"

"Is it a pleasure, Husband?" she asked softly.

How was he supposed to answer that? "I have only spent two days with you that were not somehow pleasurable: the day you refused my proposal, and the day you proposed to me."

"Do you mean that?"

The firelight was flickering over her face, illuminating it one moment and plunging it into shadow the next, making it difficult to read her expression. There was no other chair in the room for him to sit in, so he knelt before her and took her hands in his.

"Yes."

She let out a breath as if she'd been holding it, awaiting his answer. "Do you think... Do you think we might have more pleasurable days together?"

His mouth pulled into a wide grin. "I certainly hope so." Her answering grin made his heart flutter in his chest.

"Good. Because I believe we've been given a second chance, my love, and I am loath to squander it. Lying in bed tonight, it was all I could think about. Now that you're back in your own home and the farm is safe, you don't need me any longer. My letter is returned and my brother spared the stress of a scandal, so I don't need you any longer, either."

James felt his face fall. Could she see his disappointment in the dark room? "I suppose not," he replied, keeping his voice as neutral as he was able.

She squeezed his hands and drew them into her lap. "But just because we are no longer dependent upon each other doesn't mean this is the end of our relationship."

"Do you want this to be the end?" He couldn't keep the emotion out of his voice now. Not when his future was being decided, when her chilly hands were warming his very heart.

"No," she said resolutely, releasing his hands and fished around in the pocket of her wrapper. When her hand emerged, it was holding a folded letter with her own faded handwriting. "But I don't think we can have this again, either."

He took the letter when she offered it, sitting back on his heels as his eyes roaming over the old paper. It was a letter she'd written to him during their courtship, not long before he'd asked for her hand, filled with florid descriptions of her love and longing for him. He remembered penning similar letters to her, and how he ached for her when they were apart for more than a few moments.

"I believe you're right about this," he said, gesturing with the letter. "This is not who we are anymore."

"Precisely. But my dearest James, we've already begun forging a new path—together—and I want very much to continue along it with you. Will you stay with me, and remain my husband?"

"On one condition."

He heard her suck in a breath. "What?"

"That you move into this house with me for the remainder of our stay here. We may no longer be young, but I still miss you when we're apart."

She slid from her seat and caught him in a warm embrace. "I believe I can meet that condition."

She kissed him then, with such enthusiasm that the pair of them toppled over. James couldn't stop the laughter, but wrapped his arms around his wife sprawled atop him and managed a few more kisses.

"I love you, Cecilia Fitzsimmons. I have since the day I first laid eyes on you, and I always will."

She rubbed her nose against his, then claimed his lips once more. "And I love you, James Fitzsimmons. I have made some mistakes along the way, and we have had more than our share of heartbreak because of it. But I promise to keep loving you as best I can for as long as I live."

She bent to kiss him again and he rolled them over, propping himself up on one elbow as he looked down into her eyes. "I will hold you to that promise, wife of mine."

Cecilia's answering smile shone almost brighter than the fire. She ran her fingers through his hair and massaged his neck. "You'd better."


Later, when they were cuddled up together in James's bed, Cecilia planted a kiss on his shoulder. "How are we going to manage this?"

"I thought we managed rather well," he grinned back.

To his delight, she laughed. "Yes, I think we did. But that's not what I meant. We have two different lives; yours is here, while mine is mostly in London. I'm happy to spend time here, of course, but you've been so anxious leaving the farm in someone else's hands."

He took a deep breath, studying his wife as she braced her arms on his chest and pushed herself up. She'd spent her share of time in the country, and he had no doubt she'd be happy here. But she'd been so at home in London, and he knew how much she enjoyed the whirl of the social season.

"The steward acquitted himself decently," James allowed, brushing her long hair behind her shoulder. "With Father here to keep an eye on him, I could steel my nerves enough to leave the farm."

"Truly?"

The hope in her eyes helped him warm to the idea. "Certainly. We can make our home here most of the year and spend the summer in Town for the Season. It's a bit far from your brother, but not prohibitively so."

What he didn't say was that, if Cecilia were summoned to Alston's death bed, she might not make it in time from the Fitzsimmons Farm. But he suspected she already realized that. And she might be too far away no matter where—or with whom—she was.

"Sounds like you've put some thought into this plan of yours." She caressed his cheek with her fingertips. "Thank you for that."

"What will it be, then, my lady? Can you see your way to a rural life?"

He held his breath, not even caring how obvious it was with her lying on his chest.

"How could I not?" she said, smiling softly in the firelight. I've waited all these years for a second chance with you, my love. I'm not about to let you go now."

James wrapped Cecilia in his arms and kissed her hair. "That, my dear, is music to my ears."

# KISSING BY THE
# MISTLETOE

**She wants to marry. He wants to marry *her*. Will a faux courtship bring them together or break their hearts?**

Maddie Hayward has been actively looking for a husband for nearly three years, but no gentleman will spare her more than a smile. Everyone thinks she's destined to wed Kit Mathison...except neither of them is interested in a romance with the other. When Kit and his family come to visit the Haywards for Christmas, the whole village expects a proposal—but Maddie has other plans. Can she convince everyone that her friendship with Kit will never be a courtship? Or will she have to choose between her closest friend and the chance at family of her own?

Thomas Mathison has loved Maddie since the day they were first introduced, but can't ask for her hand until he can afford to support a family. When she suggests a sham courtship between them he agrees, despite his misgivings. Being seen with someone other than Kit would shatter the illusion of an arrangement between them and give Maddie a chance at a happy life. But while she would be feigning affection, Thomas would not. Can he conceal his true feelings from her while executing her plan? Will he have the strength to let her go when he returns home?

# Chapter 1

Kent, England
December 1813

Maddie Hayward perched on the edge of her chair in Mrs. Spencer's drawing room, back straight, dark hair neatly pinned up, politely smiling as she sipped from a tea cup painted with delicate pink and yellow flowers.

"I understand the Mathisons will be visiting your family for a few weeks," Mrs. Spencer announced.

The other ladies in the room tittered and Maddie fought to keep her smile from slipping. "That's right."

"Mrs. Mathison and...both her sons?" someone else asked, not quite able to sound nonchalant.

Maddie suppressed the urge to roll her eyes. Kit Mathison, the oldest son, had been Maddie's best friend for years—since before his father died and his mother had taken her children to Edinburgh, where her brother lived. Because Kit was handsome, unattached, and possessed a comfortable income, Maddie was supposed to be in love with him.

She did love him, but as the brother she never had, not as a potential husband. Yet whenever she corrected people's assumptions, her words were dismissed. Apparently no one could conceive of a gentleman and a lady maintaining a close friendship without designs on each other.

"Yes," Maddie responded, hoping no one else heard the slight edge in her voice. "Kit and Thomas will both be accompanying their mother."

"You're so lucky," a younger woman sighed. "How wonderful would it be to dance with Kit Mathison?"

Maddie smiled at that with genuine goodwill. Dancing with the local women was something Kit had mentioned in his last letter. It was one of the things he was most looking forward to. "Perhaps you'll have the chance at the assembly this week. I know for a fact that he's eager to see everyone."

Mrs. Spencer waved her hand reprovingly, but let out a little chuckle. "Miss Hayward, you shouldn't tease. We are all aware to whom Mr. Mathison will be directing his attention."

And there was the other side of the coin—Kit was also reputed to be in love with Maddie.

For his part, Kit was highly amused by the whole situation. The consequences were less severe for him, though. Ladies still swooned over him, and not one would decline his addresses. Maddie, being female, was at a disadvantage: she was supposed to try to attract a gentleman and wait for him to initiate a courtship. But no true gentleman would encroach on what he saw as another man's dominion.

Which left Maddie in a precarious position. She had few practical skills, no wealthy family, and little money of her own. If she failed to marry, her only option was to remain in her parents' home and find some way to contribute to the household, lest she become a burden to them.

She smiled as best she could at Mrs. Spencer, feeling her resistance fade away. There wasn't any use in arguing when no one listened to the argument. "But he can't be by my side all the time."

With Maddie's seeming acceptance of the situation, the ladies of the drawing room beamed at her. Then they changed the subject, and no one spoke to Maddie directly for the rest of the visit.

"How does Mrs. Spencer?" Maddie's mother asked when she returned home. "Did she carry on about her new teacups the way I thought she would?"

"She looked well," Maddie answered, removing her bonnet and smoothing down her hair. "She was very keen on the new teacups, yes, but they weren't the focus of our conversation."

Her mother grinned. "I'm sure I know what was, though. How many ladies asked after Kit?"

This time Maddie let her eyes roll. Not that she didn't expect it from her mother, but she'd been hoping they might get through one day without an allusion to her supposed relationship with Kit.

Apparently it wasn't this day. "They all did, at one point or another."

"You are a lucky girl," her mother said, echoing the sentiments of the drawing room ladies. "To think, in just a few weeks' time you could be Mrs. Christopher Mathison."

"What?"

"Surly he'll make you a pretty proposal at Christmas, with both families here to celebrate."

Maddie's mother was practically glowing at the thought of her daughter marrying the head of the Mathison family. Misplaced though it was, Maddie didn't have the heart to shatter the illusion. Everyone would settle down again when Christmas came and went with no proposal of marriage from Kit. And if she truly was lucky, he would find the right woman and marry her. Quickly.

She kissed her mother's cheek and headed to her bedchamber, putting her bonnet in its usual place in her battered wardrobe. What if Kit didn't marry quickly? How long could she linger with the wallflowers and chaperones at every event, unseen by gentlemen who might otherwise have taken an interest in her?

What if he didn't marry at all?

The thought nearly knocked the breath out of her. All Maddie had ever wanted was to have a home and children of her own, to share her life with a man she adored. If Kit remained unattached, would everyone continue to think of her as his? Would she slip into spinsterhood while the eligible bachelors of Kent looked elsewhere?

Maddie dropped onto her bed, bracing her hands against the pomegranate red counterpane her grandmother had brought with her from Spain when she'd married Maddie's grandfather. What would she have done in this situation?

Maddie laid back and grinned. Gran would have flouted convention and begun asking gentlemen to dance and drive and walk out with her. Maddie wasn't quite so bold, but perhaps there was something she could do to take control of her life—this aspect of it, at least. Perhaps Kit would have some ideas, or maybe his brother, Thomas, could help.

She pictured Thomas as she'd last seen him, tall and lanky, his reddish hair curling every which way when he didn't try to tame it with pomade. That had been the last time he'd visited the Haywards, right before he went off to university three years ago. He'd always been kind to her, quick to offer a helping hand when she'd needed one.

Of course, she'd only ever needed his assistance exiting a carriage or his company walking into the village. But Thomas was clever. If he and Kit and Maddie put their heads together, she was certain they'd come up with some way to uncouple her from Kit's non-existent romantic attachment.

Thomas Mathison sat on the rear-facing seat in his brother's traveling coach, his eyes drifting out the window to watch the scenery roll past as he wiped his palms on his trousers. He'd been looking forward to this visit since Mrs. Hayward proposed the idea two months ago, but the closer they drew to the Haywards' home, the more frenzied the butterflies in his stomach became. He had corresponded some with Maddie in the years since they'd last seen each other, so it wasn't as if they'd be strangers after so much time apart. But what if things had changed for her that she hadn't mentioned in her letters? Was she still interested in gardening? Still fleet of foot when skating on the little pond near the village?

An image of ice skating with Maddie formed in his mind, as clear as if it had happened only moments ago: Maddie skating backward, bundled up against the cold, holding Thomas's hands as he drew her closer with promises to keep her warm. She wrapped her arms around his neck and lifted her face for his kiss, and he obliged with a grin.

One of the carriage wheels rolled over a rock and Thomas's head bumped against the window, dissolving the image. Maddie undoubtedly thought of him as Kit's little brother and nothing else. Perhaps she was even skating with—and being warmed by—someone else, even as the geographical gap between them was closing. The thought pierced his heart and he had to stifle a grunt of pain.

Not that he had any claim on her. He had thought it prudent to wait until he'd found work and saved up enough money to support a wife before he spoke to Maddie of love and marriage. He smoothed his hands over his thighs, attempting to wipe away the sweat that was forming again on his palms. Maybe it would be better if Maddie found someone else, someone who wouldn't have to worry about whether or not he could afford a home and clothing and food for more than just himself. She deserved to be with a man who could take care of her, who could give her not only the things she needed but everything she wanted.

"Thomas, dear, are you all right?"

He turned to his mother, sitting opposite him, and blinked. "Yes, I'm quite well."

"Are you certain? It sounded as though you'd hit your head rather hard."

He heard a quiet chuckle from Kit's side of the carriage. "Don't worry mother. Thomas's head is hard enough to withstand a little bump."

Thomas smirked at his brother. "Not as hard as yours, of course. Didn't you once get hit by a mallet and keep right on walking?" Thomas knew very well about the mallet—he'd been holding it when it had bashed Kit in the temple. Accidentally, of course.

Kit grinned and rapped his knuckles against his skull. "Sturdy as a block of marble."

"I do hope the two of you won't be acting like adolescents in the presence of the Haywards," their mother sighed. "Maddie Hayward will not look fondly on a man who cannot put his boyhood behind him."

Kit laughed. "Maddie is the one who gave Thomas the mallet, mother."

Their mother pressed her lips together for a moment before saying, "Yes, but that was years ago. I'm sure she's become a well-behaved young lady now, and if you want to pay your addresses to her, you ought to consider your own behavior."

It was a common refrain among the Mathisons, that Kit and Maddie would settle down together someday. No one but Kit knew of the hope Thomas harbored regarding Maddie, and that was the way he preferred it. But it still stung to have that hope so easily dashed by his own mother.

"I will promise to behave myself," Kit said, patting his mother's hand as it lay on the seat between them. "But I will not promise to court Maddie, no matter how many times you imply that I want to."

"There's no harm in wanting to spend time with her again before you ask for her hand," their mother smiled. "But you can't have been so close to her all these years without meaning to marry her."

"I can, Mother. And I have."

"What about me?" Thomas blurted out. "I've been close to her, too. Might it be possible that I want to marry her?"

He could feel his cheeks warming, and hoped he wasn't actually blushing. His mother was studying his face as if he might be, but then she shook her head.

"Your relationship with her isn't like Kit's. I know that you're fond of her, but she has always spent more time with your brother. She confides in him."

Thomas knew that was true, but felt himself frowning nonetheless. "You don't think Maddie could ever be interested in me?"

His mother reached across the carriage and took his hand for a moment. "I know that there are several ladies in Edinburgh who have already set their caps for you, my sweet boy—your uncle has told me as much. You've been the toast of his social circle since you arrived, he said, and you'll have scores of women to choose from when you're ready to take a wife."

Thomas could see the pride in her eyes, in the set of her mouth, and it warmed him.

"But," she went on, "Maddie was meant for Kit."

Kit crossed his arms over his chest with a frown, but didn't protest. Thomas wasn't surprised—the family joke about hard-headedness didn't just apply to the two brothers. Their mother could be absolutely single-minded when it came to certain subjects, and arguing with her was often a fruitless occupation.

He went back to his window, noting the addition of a few darker clouds among the puffy white ones. He came back to the idea that it might be better if Maddie did have a beau. That would leave Kit free of their mother's expectations and allow Thomas to put aside a dream that would likely never come true. He'd only have to deal with the pain of seeing her with someone else for a few weeks, then he could get on with the business of living without her. One day, he might even find contentment with one of the ladies his mother had mentioned.

Yes, that would be the easiest way out of this dilemma. He would simply ignore the possibility of impending heartbreak.

# Chapter 2

$\mathcal{M}$addie had tried to stay awake long enough to greet the Mathisons when they arrived, but she'd fallen asleep before their carriage had pulled into the drive. Breakfast the following morning was her first chance to see her old friends and she fairly bounced down the stairs.

A wide variety of foods had been laid out on the sideboard and Thomas was the only person seated at the table, reading her father's weeks-old newspaper, when Maddie entered the dining room.

"Good morning."

He glanced up from the newspaper and clambered to his feet when recognition dawned. "Miss Hayward."

She shut the door behind her and crossed the room, holding her hands out to him. "So formal," she replied with mock solemnity. "You'd never know we once fished barefoot together in the brook."

His large hands were cold when he clasped hers, but he grinned. "It was more than once, if I recall correctly. And Kit was put out the last time because you caught the biggest fish."

Maddie laughed at the memory. "Yes he was. He didn't speak to me for two whole days after that. Fortunately, you were nice enough to keep me company until he came to terms with my fishing abilities."

"It was a lovely, *quiet* two days," Thomas quipped, dropping a kiss on each of her hands before releasing them to pull out a chair for her.

"Is that what you're hoping for during this visit?" she asked, settling onto the hard wooden chair. "Peace and quiet?"

He seated himself and propped his elbow on the table, resting his chin on his palm. "Some." His blue eyes shifted to the cream and pale blue wallpaper behind her. "Edinburgh is lovely, and my uncle has made me feel very welcome. But I miss the serenity of the country."

"Does that mean you won't be attending the assembly in the village this evening?" Disappointment filtered through her at the thought.

His gaze moved back to her, but she couldn't read his expression. Was that a half smile on his lips or a grimace? "Yes, I'll be attending. It's been a while since I've danced, but I am looking forward to doing so."

"I'm sure the local ladies are looking forward to partnering you, too." She winked, slouching back against her chair for a moment as an idea formed in her mind. "Would you, perhaps, want to dance with me tonight? Just once," she added hastily, straightening again and regretting her sudden burst of daring. She'd put Thomas in the awkward position of having to dance with her or risk hurting her feelings, and she knew he'd choose her comfort over his own if pressed. "I wouldn't want to keep you from your adoring public."

His brows rose for a blink-and-you'd-miss-it moment, then his lids dropped and his mouth curved into a smile. "I think the adoring public will be more interested in Kit than me. But I would be honored to dance with you, Maddie. As often as you like."

His eyes met hers as he spoke the last phrase, and she felt...*something.* She broke contact before she could inspect the feeling too closely, and pushed back her chair.

Thomas was on his feet in one graceful movement before she could fully get to hers. "May I fix you a plate?"

Maddie rose and pushed in her chair, touching her fingertips to his shoulders—broader and more muscled than she remembered—as she passed him on the way to the sideboard. "Thank you, but I can manage on my own. Can I fix you a plate while I'm up? Or are you content with tea this morning?"

"You can fix me a plate," a voice boomed as the door swung open.

"Kit!" Maddie changed course and headed for the door, arriving there just in time to be engulfed in Kit's brawny arms. "I thought you'd be sleeping late this morning."

"Not me," he laughed, releasing her. "I prefer to keep country hours, just as Thomas prefers to keep clerk's hours, even when he is not on duty."

Kit winked at his brother, following Maddie to the sideboard and filling a plate for himself.

"Good morning to you, too, brother," Thomas responded mildly.

Kit grinned and carried his and Maddie's plates to the table when they'd made their selections, settling in beside her. "I'm going over to the old house this afternoon if the snow holds off. Would the two of you care to accompany me?"

Maddie returned his grin. At five-and-twenty, Kit was finally old enough to take possession of his inheritance, according to the terms of his father's will. He'd spoken of little else in his last few letters, anxious to re-open the house in which he and Thomas had spent their boyhood. "How exciting! I would love nothing more than to go with you, but I'm afraid my mother won't allow it. I'm to rest today, so I won't look tired at the assembly tonight."

"You'll look lovely whether you 'rest' today or not," Kit scoffed. "Won't she, brother?"

Was it her imagination, or were Thomas's cheeks turning the faintest shade of pink? "Of course," he answered, his voice slightly gruff.

Maddie felt her own cheeks warm unexpectedly. Kit had complimented her more times than she could remember, and certainly with more enthusiasm—why did this bland remark from Thomas provoke such a reaction?

"Thank you both." She picked up her fork and focused on her breakfast, brushing away the thought. "But as long as I reside with my parents, I must comply with their wishes. I expect you boys will have a grand time reliving your past, though. And making plans for the future."

With any luck, Kit's plans would involve finding a wife and Maddie would be free to find her own happiness. What would Thomas do? He had begun working for his uncle, who was a barrister in Edinburgh, after finishing university —did he plan to do so always? Did he hope to strike out on his own some day? Did he, too, plan to marry?

Maddie was surprised to discover she didn't know. She was even more surprised to discover that she wanted to know, though that revelation shouldn't have been so shocking. Thomas was her best friend's brother, and her friend in his own right. It made perfect sense that she'd be curious about his wishes and goals.

"As long as we return in time to go to the assembly," Thomas said, smiling gently at Maddie. "I have a promise to keep."

***

"Come, brother, we must be getting back."

Thomas acknowledged Kit's words with an absent nod. He was staring into the frozen brook that cut across the property—the same brook Maddie had pulled her ire-inducing fish from—purposefully delaying their return. He was nervous about dancing with her, even though he'd never been so before. What if he tripped over his own feet? What if he stepped on hers and crushed her toes? What if she had only asked him for a dance to be polite?

"Yes, of course," he replied, tearing his gaze from the ice and heading toward the stable with Kit.

They readied their horses in relative silence, but once they were both in the saddle and on their way back to the Haywards' home, Kit got chatty.

"You've promised Maddie a dance this evening, have you?"

"I have," Thomas said as matter-of-factly as he was able.

"She told me after you'd gone in search of your boots."

Of course she had. She told Kit everything. "Did she also mention that she asked me for the dance?"

Kit nodded, pulling his beaver hat down lower over his ears. "Yes. She's afraid only we will pay her any attention and she'll be stuck sitting with the matrons and wallflowers all evening." He paused, throwing Thomas a pointed look. "This could be your chance."

"Chance for what?" Thomas hoped his brother would change the subject if he played dumb. It wasn't that he didn't want to talk about Maddie, but the more they discussed her, the more he let himself imagine a future with her.

"Your chance with Maddie, you dolt," Kit chuckled. "She's asked me to stay away for most of the evening in the hopes other men would speak with her."

"Am I 'other men'?"

"You certainly could be. And you've already secured a dance with her."

Thomas licked his dry lips. "It's just a dance, Kit."

"And that is how many happy courtships have begun."

The wind picked up, blowing frigid air down from the north and requiring them both to pull their scarves up over their faces, which halted any further conversation. Thomas was grateful for it, and for his brother's silence on the subject of Maddie once they'd returned to the Hayward house with just enough time to ready themselves for the evening.

The families took two separate carriages to the Flying Horse Inn, the tallest building in the village and the only place with a room large enough for a gathering of so many people. Once they were all together in the dooryard, Mr. Hayward offered his arm to his wife.

"Shall we?"

She smiled and laid her hand on the sleeve of his coat. "By all means."

Thomas turned to his mother, about to make her the same offer, when Kit swooped in and beat him to it.

"This way, Mother," he said, glancing at Thomas for the briefest of moments.

That left Maddie standing alone.

"May I escort you in?" Thomas asked, hoping his voice didn't sound as hesitant to her as it did to him.

It was dark, but her brown eyes were sparkling in the light of the carriage lanterns. "You may."

He'd expected her to formally place her hand on his sleeve, as was the custom. But instead she threaded her arm through his and rested her hand on his biceps. It was likely for show, but it was an intimate gesture all the same and Thomas had to remind himself that tonight was a favor for Maddie, not a prelude to something more.

He had to remind himself again once they were inside to counter his brother's words ringing in his ears. Thomas helped her remove her winter cloak, revealing a wine-colored gown with tiny ruffles along the sleeves and neckline. The rest of the gown was unadorned—some might even call it plain—but she needed nothing else to take his breath.

She glanced at him over her shoulder, then turned her body to face him. "What?"

His eyes widened. Had he gasped aloud? "You, erm, you look beautiful. That color suits you."

"Thank you." She poked a finger into his chest as he shed his greatcoat. "It looks well on you, too."

Thomas's eyes followed her finger and he grinned. Under his chocolate brown cutaway coat, he'd worn a cream waistcoat embroidered in claret red roses. "We're a match."

The words were barely out of his mouth before he realized the double meaning and clamped his mouth shut. Fortunately, Maddie didn't seem to notice and Thomas allowed a small sigh to escape his lips, of both relief and frustration. Was this how he was going to spend the entire evening? Tripping all over himself around Maddie, then chastising himself for it?

No, he wasn't. He was going to enjoy himself and relish a dance with the woman he loved. Tomorrow morning their relationship would return to its previous state, and in a few weeks' time he would be on his way back to Scotland.

"Are you well, Thomas?"

Maddie's words snapped him out of his woolgathering and he nodded. "I was wondering if it might be best to have our dance first or if we should wait a little."

"First," she said resolutely. "The sooner I'm seen with someone other than Kit, the better. And," her pink lips pulled into a smile, "I have been told the first dance is to be a minuet."

"You like minuets?" They were old fashioned and falling out of favor with the younger generation. Thomas couldn't remember the last time he'd danced one.

Her lashes swept down as her gaze dropped for a moment. "They make me feel rather stately and elegant," she confessed in a low voice, leaning close enough for Thomas to notice she'd chosen a different scent for the evening—roses. "Something I tend not to be otherwise."

He bent his head to speak softly in her ear as he offered her his hand. "Then let's go and be elegant."

She took his hand and allowed him to lead her onto the dance floor, a slow smile spreading across her face that sent his heart off at a gallop. The small orchestra began to play and Thomas moved through the steps of the dance with Maddie, to-ing and fro-ing, parting and coming together again. They both wore gloves with their evening wear, of course, but he cataloged every handclasp, every brush of shoulders, every accidental touch so that he might recall them all when he'd returned to his life in Edinburgh. If he could never afford to ask Maddie for her hand in marriage, he would at least remember this dance with her.

The song came to an end and another gentleman approached to ask Maddie for a dance. Thomas bowed and slid away into the crowd, trying with little success to keep from turning and watching her. She moved through the dance with a lightness not so much of body—she managed the steps as one who had practiced them often but not necessarily with any great love for the action—but with a lightness of spirit. His own heart lifted and found himself smiling. He made for the refreshment table, hoping to find himself a cup of good, strong punch to further the warm feeling that had begun to grow in his chest. The music changed once again and Thomas turned back one last time, catching a glimpse of Maddie laughing with delight as she hopped her way through a Scotch reel. Good. Her plan had worked, then, and he'd have memories of her to cherish always.

*Chapter 3*

The Haywards and Mathisons gathered in the Hayward parlor the next afternoon, whiling away the gray day in relative quiet and comfort. Mr. Hayward was sprawled in a chair reading the newspaper, Kit was writing letters at the small desk in the corner, and Mrs. Mathison and Mrs. Hayward were working out of their sewing baskets by the fire with Maddie, whose eyes kept drifting toward the window opposite her.

Thomas tried to focus on the book he was holding, but *The Philosophy of Nature, or, the Influence of Scenery on the Mind and Heart* just wasn't capturing his attention.

"Maddie, would you like to take a walk with me?" he asked across the small room. "I know it's cold outside..."

"Yes," she answered quickly. "I believe I could use some fresh air."

There were the usual appeals from the parents to dress warmly, which they both heeded, wearing heavy boots, thick stockings, and extra layers beneath their long coats when they met at the door. They left the house and walked along in silence for a dozen yards, not touching but not actively avoiding one another either.

"I'm so glad you asked me to walk with you," Maddie finally said, her breath puffing out before her in a small cloud. "I wanted to thank you for last night. For the first time in over a year I danced with two other gentlemen, and had an entire conversation where Kit wasn't even mentioned. All thanks to you."

He'd tried to ignore her dancing partners last night—both well-dressed gentlemen with tolerable manners—but had been unable to ignore the luminous smile she'd worn all evening. He'd have run into a burning building to see that smile, but it hadn't been for him. "I'm glad you enjoyed yourself," he said softly, sincerely. "And that I could be of service."

They walked along for a few more minutes without speaking before he felt her mittened hand on his arm. "I— I don't want to impose, but might I ask another favor of you?"

"Of course," he answered without hesitation. If there was any earthly thing he could do to make her happy, he would certainly do it.

"Would you, perhaps... We're all going to the Duke of Alston's Midwinter Fête a few days hence, and I thought you might..."

Ah. No dancing during this outing, but he could see where she was going. "Might like to escort you? While Kit keeps out of the way, of course."

He said the last with a bit of cheek and she laughed nervously, clasping her hands together at her waist. "I know it's a lot to ask..."

Thomas stopped and reached for her hands, bringing her to a gentle halt before him. "You know Kit would do anything to secure your happiness." He squeezed her hands, wishing for a moment that they were indoors again with no need of mittens. "As would I."

"Truly?"

"Always."

She took a small step closer to him, dropping her gaze to the snow beneath their feet for a moment. "Then might I impose upon you for the length of your stay here?"

He pressed his lips together and raised his brows, trying to discern her meaning. "You want me to escort you instead of Kit...until I depart?"

"More than that," she said, tipping her head back to meet his gaze. "I would like you to pretend to court me until you depart so people will know I'm not betrothed to Kit."

She was trembling now, and Thomas tried to resist the urge to pull her against him. "You're freezing," he said instead. "We should go back inside and warm you up."

Maddie shook her head. "I'm not cold. But I might be slightly terrified."

"Of me?"

"Of what you must think of me for being so forward," she said, releasing his hands and wrapping her arms around herself. "And of what your answer will be."

He glanced around and, noting a copse of pines a few feet away, drew her among them, out of the wind and away from any prying eyes that might be about. "Might *I* be forward for a moment? You look as though you need to be held, and I would like to oblige you."

She went into his arms without another word, pressing her cheek against his coat and holding on to him like a drowning woman to a raft. Her trembling ceased a few moments later, and Thomas felt his own muscles relax as he rested his chin on the top of her head. It was a relief and a boon to be able to offer her comfort, and the embrace gave him time to contemplate her request.

"Better?"

He felt her chest expand against him as she breathed deeply in, then contract again when she exhaled slowly. "Yes. Thank you. I don't know what came over me..."

"You're stuck in an undesirable situation, and need help getting out of it," he said, palming her cheek for the briefest of touches. "I might react the same way in your place."

"I doubt it." She pulled back and offered him a slight smile. "But thank you for saying so. I just— I am also more than slightly terrified that I'll never find a husband. Which I'm sure sounds silly to you."

"Not at all," he said. And it didn't. He knew what society thought of women who eschewed matrimony, regardless of the reason. He also knew how much more independence she'd have as a married woman with the right husband. She'd have a home and possibly children of her own, but she'd also have the freedom to go about in public without anyone else's permission—independence she would never be allowed as a spinster daughter still living with her parents. "I didn't realize Kit's presence loomed so large."

She blew out a breath and took another half step backward, still within the circle of his arms but apart from him at the same time. "It does, even more so now that he's come to claim his inheritance. Eligible men won't even look at me. All they see is Kit's intended."

"But if someone else is courting you, the illusion of your impending marriage to Kit is shattered."

"Exactly." She slid her hands down his arms, clasping his fingers in hers. "There is no one else I can ask to do this, Thomas. But I don't want you to feel pressured into agreeing. If you are uncomfortable with this idea, you may tell me so and there will be no hard feelings."

She might not want him to feel pressured, yet he did all the same. The pressure wasn't coming from Maddie, though—it came from himself. Certainly he wanted to do everything in his power to make her happy. Did that include inducing his own insanity? For him there would be no pretending. Anytime he touched her, looked at her, caught the scent of gardenias she often wore, he would look for all the world like a man in love because he would be one. Then he'd have to forget anything had ever happened and hie himself back to Edinburgh, while she made a life with another man.

Could he do it?

He looked down into her dark eyes and saw hope mingling with fear. If he said no, she'd remain in social limbo as Kit's future wife without actually being Kit's future wife.

But if he said yes he would be giving her a measure of control back. And she would be his, even if only for a few weeks.

"Have you spoken to Kit about this plan?"

"No. This is your decision alone. I came to you first."

So there truly was no outside pressure. No one would ever know if he refused her.

But he would know. "I said that I would do anything to secure your happiness. If a beau for Christmas is what you need, than that is what I shall be."

"You're going to do what?"

Maddie stood with Thomas in the bedchamber he shared with his brother. Thomas wasn't touching her, but his presence beside her was enough to bolster her courage.

"Thomas and I are going to have a faux courtship," she repeated, meeting Kit's gaze with determination. "And we need you to play along."

"You're to play this game until Thomas returns to Scotland after the New Year?"

"Yes."

Kit's brow wrinkled. "Won't people just go back to assuming you and I are betrothed?"

That was a legitimate concern, particularly with Kit remaining at his childhood home not two miles away.

"Not if someone takes an interest in her before my departure," Thomas said.

Kit raised a blond eyebrow at that, but it quickly returned to its usual place. "So I am to stay away from you in public, and I can't spend any time with you alone during our visit."

"I know it isn't ideal," Maddie told him. "I've missed you, and we haven't really spent much time together since your arrival. But if we maintain a public distance, even around our parents, then I may finally have a suitor—a chance at a life of my own."

Kit's eyes flicked from Maddie to Thomas, then back again. "And you've agreed to this, brother?"

"I have."

Maddie smiled at his declaration. She had no idea how she'd ever repay Thomas for his cooperation in this scheme, but she would spend the rest of her days finding a way.

"All right, then. I'll play my part as well." Kit rose from the bed where he'd been sitting and grinned. "I suppose that means we won't be playing skittles together this year, then."

Maddie laughed. They had a rivalry in that sport that stretched back to their first Midwinter Fête as children, and this year was a tie-breaking year. "I'm afraid not."

"Perhaps Thomas will take up the Mathison mantle on my behalf, then." Kit winked at his brother. "Keep the tradition going."

"I'll do my best," Thomas grinned.

The three of them played their assigned parts over the next few days: Kit remaining friendly but never alone with Maddie, Thomas becoming more attentive to her, taking her aside from time to time for a private conversation when their parents were about, and Maddie herself pretending she didn't miss the closeness she had with Kit even as she enjoyed spending more time with Thomas.

By the time the two families arrived at the Duke of Alston's estate for the Midwinter Fête, it was becoming second nature for Maddie to take Thomas's arm and walk with him as if they'd been courting for months.

"Where would you like to go first?" he asked, as their various family members scattered in different directions.

Maddie looked around at the booths and tents that stretched off into the distance. "That way." She pointed to her left, where a booth sat with cakes decorating every horizontal surface. "I can smell the warm cinnamon from here. Perhaps they have Chelsea buns."

"Excellent idea."

They had only made it halfway to their destination, though, when they came upon a crying child. Dressed all in gray wool, he looked to be a boy of perhaps five years old with tears pouring down his cheeks.

Maddie knelt down in the snow, heedless of the cold that immediately began to soak into her own clothing. "Whatever is the matter?" she asked softly.

"I can't find my brother," the child wailed, rubbing his eyes.

Maddie tried to smile reassuringly, thumbing tears off his cheeks. "Maybe we can help you find him."

She turned and shot a questioning look up at Thomas, who dropped to one knee beside her. "I'm certain we can. If I put you up on my shoulders, you'll be taller than everyone here. I'd wager you'd be able to see your brother then."

The boy turned wide eyes on Thomas. "Taller than everyone?"

Thomas nodded solemnly and Maddie felt her heart swell. Many men were awkward with children, but Thomas's manner with the little boy was as easy as if they'd always been friends.

"Yes," Thomas said. "Would you like to try?"

The boy sniffled, but nodded.

"Here, I'll lift you up," Maddie offered, reaching for the child as Thomas sank down onto his haunches. She scooped the boy up and hefted him onto Thomas's shoulders, bracing him until Thomas had a firm hold on him.

Thomas rose to his feet slowly and turned to her. "Where should we start, do you think?"

She choked back a laugh. The boy had his little arms wrapped around the crown of Thomas's head, and Thomas carried on as if the situation was perfectly normal. "Where was the last place you saw your brother?" she called up to the boy.

"By the toys," he answered, knocking Thomas's hat off and leaning down into his curly hair.

"By the toys," Thomas echoed resolutely, smiling at Maddie when she scooped up his hat and handed it back to him. "Let's try there first." He held his hat in one hand and reached out the other to Maddie, which she took with a grin she couldn't smother.

Her grin did fade a bit after nearly thirty minutes of searching. But the child finally spotted his missing brother near the bonfire burning at the edge of the festivities. The brother, they discovered, had gone to procure food for the both of them, confident that his youngest sibling was following along behind...until he'd turned to find the boy wasn't behind him at all.

Thomas hoisted the child up and over his head, setting him down on the ground. "You stick close to your brother for the rest of the night, now," he said, his tone serious but amiable.

"Yes sir."

"But if you do lose him again, we'll help you find him."

The boy smiled brightly. "Thank you!"

He scurried off with his older brother, and Maddie clasped Thomas's hand in both of hers. "That is possibly the sweetest thing I have ever seen."

"The boy? He was rather cute, wasn't he?"

She laughed, leaning in to rest her head against his shoulder. She shouldn't have with all the people swirling around them, but it was less scandalous than throwing her arms around him the way she wanted to.

"The pair of you," she clarified. "You're a natural with children."

He smiled down at her for a long moment. "I do hope to have some of my own one day."

An image popped into her head of Thomas leading a cluster of redheaded children to a brook for a day of fishing, of a tender Thomas bending to instruct the little ones how to hold a rod, smiling over their heads at their unseen mother.

"You'll make a marvelous father when the time comes," she said, pushing the thought from her mind.

"I hope so." He was quiet for a spell, adjusting his grip on her hands but never releasing them. Then, "Do you want children, Maddie?"

Children with curly auburn hair and blue eyes like their father? She gave herself a mental shake. "Erm, yes, I do. Someday."

But, she reminded herself, not with Thomas. He had a life to return to that didn't include her, and she had a future husband out there somewhere waiting to be found.

"Well, we still have some of the evening left to ourselves." She forced her mouth into a smile to cover the abrupt change in subject. "What should we do next?"

# Chapter 4

*M*addie spent the next two days trapped with too many people inside a house that felt too small. For the first time in her life she ached for some time alone but absolutely none was forthcoming. Is this what it would be like as she grew older yet remained at home? Her parents' presence becoming more and more confining? Her total dependence upon them flung in her face at every turn?

A break finally arrived when her parents and Mrs. Mathison took themselves off to bed early one night after dinner, leaving her alone with Kit and Thomas in the parlor.

"You know they're all hoping I'll go to bed, too," Thomas said, glancing from Kit to Maddie.

"Then they will be sorely disappointed," she returned with more hope in her voice than she'd intended to show. "Won't they?"

Kit rose and stretched. "Do you think they'll be disappointed if *I* go to bed? I spent the day climbing around on a roof attempting a repair, and all I want to do is sleep."

"Go to bed," Maddie said, shooing him out the door. "I want to hear all about the work you've been doing on the house, but it will keep until tomorrow."

"You two can discuss the next stage of your plan without my interfering," he grinned. "Good night."

When he'd gone and shut the door behind him, Thomas stood and stretched as well.

"Are you going to leave me, too?" Maddie was unsure how she felt about the idea. She'd finally be alone if Thomas retired for the evening, but the idea no longer held the same appeal.

"Never." He seated himself on the floor before the fire with a small smile. "That is, unless you want me to."

She returned his smile from her place on the sofa, set at a right angle to the fireplace. "I can't imagine ever wanting that."

Maddie could have sworn the expression on his face wavered into something darker, but it disappeared before she could properly identify the emotion behind it.

"Once upon a time, you would have done anything to get rid of me," he chuckled. "The irritating little brother trailing along behind you and Kit."

"You weren't irritating. A little annoying on occasion," she teased, leaning over the arm of the sofa, "especially with that old green cape you used to wear everywhere...even in the summertime. Where on earth did you find that thing, anyway?"

He laughed, kicking his long legs out before him. "It was in some discarded trunk in the attic, I think. I never found out who it had belonged to, but wearing it made me feel older—old enough to tag along after my big brother, anyway."

"You're not tagging along after him anymore, though," she said softly. "You've forged your own path in life while Kit goes on with his."

"I've started on my path," he amended. "I still have some way to go before I'll feel secure on it."

"Do you think you'll ever feel secure? Truly secure?" What would it be like to have control over her own future the way a man did?

"I hope so." He turned to look at her fully, raising one knee and resting an arm on it. "What about you?"

She planted an elbow on the sofa's arm and dropped her chin into her hand. "I don't know," Her words were slow even as her mind whirled. The dimly lit room and his confession about the cape made her want to tell some of her own secrets, but the idea was both frightening and mortifying at once. Thomas would never laugh at her...would he?

He reached out a hand to her, interrupting her thoughts. "You look cold, Maddie. Will you come sit by the fire with me?"

She rose from the sofa without hesitation, clasping his hand in hers as she seated herself on the floor beside him. The flames were still crackling merrily in the fireplace, throwing off heat that warmed her face and began to melt her fears.

"I am afraid that my path will never be secure unless I wed Kit," she said hesitantly, keeping Thomas's hand in hers and drawing strength from his touch. "I– I don't want to, and he doesn't want to be shackled to me. But there are times when I am sure that no one else will have me, that men use Kit as an excuse to ignore me."

She couldn't look up. If she saw derision in his eyes, or pity, or anything but complete acceptance she'd flee to her bedchamber and never come out.

His gentle voice broke through her dread. "No sane man would be looking for a reason to avoid you, Maddie. That I can swear to you."

"Do you think so?" She managed to lift her head and meet his gaze, but only just. She'd never been so candid with anyone except Kit, and the fear of rejection hung heavily around her heart.

"I know so," he said with conviction. "You're beautiful, you're intelligent, you're the kindest person I know..." He brushed the fingers of his free hand across her cheek. "Any man would be lucky to call you his wife."

Maddie's heart fluttered and she leaned into his touch, closing her eyes for a moment to fully take in the sensation. "You are very good at this comforting business," she replied with a little laugh.

"Is it working?"

"Maybe you should hold me again...just to make sure."

It was the boldest thing she'd ever said to a gentleman, but at that moment she didn't care. The only thing she wanted in the world was to be in Thomas's arms.

He obliged, wrapping his arms around her and tugging her closer. It wasn't enough, though. The way they were sitting made the embrace awkward and rather unsatisfying.

"This isn't working..." she muttered.

"I have a better idea." He stood and drew her to her feet, pulling her against his body and walking them toward the sofa. Before she could ask what he was doing, he dropped down onto the cushions and carried her down with him.

She let out a little yelp, then realized she'd settled in his lap. "Yes, this will do," she sighed, her arms encircling his broad shoulders as his came around her body.

He rested his cheek against hers, murmuring, "Good." Then his warm lips were at her ear. "Maddie, may I kiss you?"

Her heart was pounding and her skin radiated heat that had nothing to do with the fireplace. She'd never been kissed before, but she nodded her head faintly, gathering her courage. "I wish you would."

He brushed some loose hair from her face as she closed her eyes again, delighting in the tickling softness of his touch, the scent of leather-bound books that clung to his fingers. She sighed again and his mouth came down over hers, capturing her bottom lip in a caress unlike any she'd felt before.

All too soon he released her, but when he drew back she went forward. "Thomas," she breathed. "May I kiss you?"

"You may kiss me all night if you want to," he replied in a husky voice.

Feelings of triumph, of need, and of emotions she couldn't readily identify rushed through her. Whatever was happening, she wanted more.

Maddie leaned in. "An excellent idea."

Thomas was fairly floating when he rode out to the old house with Kit the next day. He hadn't spent the *whole* night kissing Maddie—they had somehow managed to part before midnight—but he'd finally had her alone, in his arms.

And she'd kissed him back. Thoroughly.

"I take it your evening went well," Kit grinned once they were a safe distance away from their hosts.

"Is it so obvious?"

Kit laughed. "Your feet have barely touched the floor since you woke this morning."

"Do you think mother noticed? Or Maddie's parents?" Thomas asked. They were supposed to think he was courting Maddie, of course, but he wasn't ready to declare his feelings to anyone else just yet. He'd only communicated them to Maddie herself in kisses instead of concrete promises, and barely a handful of hours earlier.

"Mother likely did, but she may not attribute your cheerfulness to Maddie specifically. Mrs. Hayward was too busy asking me if I would leave a room in the house untouched for my wife to decorate as she pleased."

Thomas couldn't help but roll his eyes, until they were stopped midway by a frightening thought. "You don't think they're fortune hunting, do you?" Kit's inheritance wasn't large, particularly when compared to more aristocratic estates, but it would provide him and his future family a comfortable existence. And that was more than Thomas could say about himself.

"If they were, they'd have tried to convince Maddie to throw me over and set her cap for Sir Anthony at the assembly." Kit paused, glancing over at Thomas. "She doesn't need permission to marry, brother. If someone were to ask for her hand, the decision would be hers alone."

"But would she go against her parents' wishes?"

"Have you asked her?"

Thomas hadn't asked Maddie anything last night other than, "Do you like that?" The subject of a possible future together simply hadn't come up. "No."

"Does she know how you feel about her?" Kit prompted.

She had to know he no longer considered her only a friend, but Thomas also hadn't mentioned the word *love* last night, nor any of its kin. "I don't know how to tell her."

That was partially true. Finding the right words to declare a love he'd felt for so long would be no easy task. But what if she was still intent on finding a suitor who wasn't a Mathison? What if she loved him in return, but was swept off her feet by another man while Thomas saved up his money?

"What if you just said, 'I care for you'?"

They turned in to the drive at the old house and trotted the horses to the newly repaired stable. Could it be that simple?

"What if she doesn't return my feelings?"

Kit jumped down from his horse. "What if she does?"

*What if she does?*

The thought rolled around in Thomas's head all morning as his hands performed whatever job Kit set them to. By the time they set out for the Hayward house that evening, Thomas had come up with a plan. Rather than walking through the front door and proclaiming his love for Maddie upon his return, he decided on a smaller first step. He would find a few moments alone with her and ask if she would be willing to make their courtship real, perhaps on a trial basis, for the remainder of his stay in Kent. If she said no, he would put the pieces of his heart back together and play her beau for a few more weeks, then retreat to Scotland and nurse his pain alone.

But if she said yes...

"You're smiling again, brother."

If she said yes, there would be more walks in the snow and kisses in the firelight. If she said yes, they would make new memories together.

"Don't forget we promised to pick up the post," Thomas called as Kit's horse danced away from his on the frozen road. Perhaps he could find a small gift for Maddie while they were in the village, as well. Some ribbon for her hair? The book of poetry she'd mentioned at the fête?

He shopped while Kit went to the post office, settling on a bottle of scent, smaller than he'd have liked it to be but from the heart all the same. He'd chosen one distilled from roses, and also had happily handed over the last of his coin for what had to be the only rose in bloom in England this time of year. The proprietor of the shop had a tiny hothouse in which she grew the flowers used to make the scent she sold, and she'd had a single blossom left. It was pink, not the red of her dress and his waistcoat, but Thomas didn't quibble over that small detail. When they came back in season—and he'd saved a bit of money again—he would buy her claret-colored roses every day if she wanted them.

Thomas and Kit returned to the Haywards' home, flushed with cold and in Thomas's case, anticipation.

"Ah, there you are," Mr. Hayward greeted them when they came through the front door. "We'd begun to wonder if you'd been waylaid at the old house."

Thomas felt Kit's elbow poke his ribs before he saw it, and forced a smile. No need to tip his hand before he spoke to Maddie herself. "We stayed in the village a bit longer than we'd planned, sir."

"But we did remember to pick up your post," Kit chimed in, ignoring the glare Thomas shot his way.

Kit handed over the bundle of letters and began divesting himself of his outerwear, handing his greatcoat over to the maid-of-all-work to be dried before a fire. Thomas, conscious of the bottle and blossom tucked inside his pocket, elected to keep his coat, and carefully slung it over one arm as he made for the staircase and his bedchamber.

"Thomas, wait a moment," Mr. Hayward called after him. "There's a letter here for you."

Thomas retrieved it and brought it upstairs with him, tossing it onto his bed as he looked for a place to store his gifts. Perhaps their parents would attempt to leave Maddie alone with Kit again tonight, and he could give her the scent and rose then.

"Who's your letter from?" Kit asked, strolling into the room with a stack of his own letters.

"Oh, erm, I don't know." Thomas laid his coat onto the bed and took up the letter, breaking the seal with curiosity. "It's from our uncle." Unfolding the single page, he scanned the heavily slanted handwriting to see if it was something important.

"Thomas? What is it?" Kit asked a moment later. "You look as though the world is ending."

"I think mine is," he replied in a flat voice, unable to tear his eyes away from the horrible words. "Our uncle has closed his office and sailed for America."

"What?"

Thomas crumpled the letter and flung it against the nearest wall. "I no longer have employment."

# Chapter 5

"Thomas, would you mind terribly walking with me into the village?"

"Hmm?" He'd been sitting at the desk in his bedchamber, staring at his uncle's letter and hadn't heard Maddie enter the room.

"I know you just came from there," she continued, leaning against the open door, "but Cook needs some things for Christmas dinner and I wanted to do a little shopping anyway."

"Can't she get them herself?" he asked absently. Maddie's brows rose and her eyes widened in response. Thomas shook his head and he stood, closing the distance between them. "My apologies. Of course I'll accompany you if you'd like me to."

She searched his face for a moment before speaking again. "Is all well with you?"

Her voice was hesitant and he instinctively reached out to comfort her, sliding an arm around her waist and drawing her further into the room. "It is now," he smiled.

Maddie's arms came around his neck and she returned his smile, though not fully. "You could tell me if something were wrong."

If it was anything else, he might have told her then. It wasn't as though she was a stranger whose trust he was unsure of. But they'd only just begun this new version of their relationship—if that's even what it was—and he didn't want to burden her with his news until he'd had a chance to come to terms with it himself.

He opened his mouth to speak, then shut it again. What if sharing the burden made it easier to bear?

"You're absolutely right." It did—*might*—concern her, after all. If he couldn't make a living, he'd never be able to ask for her hand. "I received a letter from my uncle today."

"The one who employs you?"

He nodded, glad she was in his arms. He was the one being comforted now, but this was a tradition he was happy to continue.

If she didn't throw him over.

Thomas pushed the thought away. "Yes, the one who employs me. Or did. He's run off with an actress and closed his office."

She sucked in a quick breath. "And you have no employment now."

"No, I don't."

"Oh, Thomas..." She went up on her toes and tightened her hold on him. "I'm so sorry."

Her hair held the faint scent of gardenias and her body was warm against his. He closed his eyes and nuzzled her neck. *This.* This is the reaction he'd been hoping for. They had a long way to go if they were going to make a life together. Hell, he didn't even know if she thought of him as a genuine suitor. Was he still just Kit's little brother who she happened to like kissing?

"Maddie, this may not be the right time, but I need to know..." He loosened his hold on her and set her a little away from him. "Do you think you could ever care for me?"

"I have always cared for you," she smiled, palming his cheek.

He covered her hand with his own. "I don't mean as a friend, or as Kit's brother."

"You mean as a beau. A– a lover."

He nodded, kissing her palm and clasping her hand to his chest. "As a prospective husband."

She didn't respond, and the pounding of his heart filled the silence until he thought the wretched organ might explode. Was there so much to consider?

"You have always been my friend," she said at last. "But when you kissed me...nay, when I asked you for a faux courtship and you agreed without asking anything in return, I let myself consider the possibility."

"And what was the verdict?"

Pink crept up her neck and into her cheeks. "That if you wanted to change the plan, to make it a true courtship..." She paused, flattening her hand against his chest, where she could no doubt feel his poor heart beating to the rhythm of his anticipation. "I would be amenable to that."

His breathing hitched, then he sighed heavily in relief. It wasn't a declaration of love, but nearly so. And it had only been a few days since their night by the fire.

"Even though I have lost my employment? I have no money, Maddie, no home to offer you."

"Then don't offer yet," she said simply.

A surprised laugh burst from him. "Such an easy solution! Your parents won't mind?"

"My parents will mind terribly," she replied all too matter-of-factly, patting his chest. "Not because of who you are, but because of your situation. We don't have to tell them, though. Not until we're ready to."

His relief mingled with a pinch of shame. When he was employed, Maddie was happy to have the world think he was courting her. But this temporary setback—and he sorely hoped it was only temporary—had her wanting to hide their relationship from her parents.

Her thumb traced the lapel of his cutaway coat. "What about your mother?"

He didn't relish the idea of explaining the situation when his mother still seemed to have her heart set on a match between Maddie and Kit, particularly when Kit had his inheritance and Thomas now had only the clothes on his back. "If we're not telling your parents, it's only fair not to tell my mother."

"Should we keep it from Kit?"

He couldn't quite read her expression or body language. Was she uneasy about keeping so large a secret from her closest friend, or relishing the idea? "If I wasn't his brother, would you tell him about us?"

"I might," she answered, her brow furrowed in thought. "I likely would, actually. We tell each other nearly everything. If I wasn't his best friend, would *you* tell him about us?"

"Probably," Thomas admitted. "Kit and I have our shared confidences, too. But you *are* his best friend, and I am his brother. That might complicate matters."

Even as he spoke the words, Thomas didn't quite believe them. Kit had known for at least a year about Thomas's feelings for Maddie, and he'd never been anything but supportive.

"Let's not tell anyone at all," she suggested with a smile, tightening her arms around him and combing her fingers through his hair.

She wanted a clandestine courtship? It was almost too romantic a notion for his heart to bear, overwhelming the twinge of shame. "A secret for just the two of us."

"Does that mean I'll have to steal kisses from you on the way into the village?" She gave him what was probably supposed to be a sly look, but ended up giggling.

"You can't steal what's freely given." He released the hand he still held against his chest and wrapping her in his arms.

Leaning down to brush his lips over hers, he thrilled to his very fingertips when she responded in kind. He didn't know how, but by God he would find a way to make money again if it killed him. He would make himself worthy of her.

With thick mittens keeping Maddie's fingers warm, holding Thomas's hand on the way to the village was no easy task. Instead, she looped her arm through his, her body warming when he smiled down at her and dropped a kiss on the top of her bonnet.

The warmth lasted all the way to the first shop they visited, despite the snow that had begun to fall. They purchased the items Cook needed first, then continued on to the milliner's where Maddie spent a few minutes looking at ribbons in various colors. She wanted to spruce up her bonnet in time for church the next morning, but couldn't decide which color would be best.

"Green or blue?" she asked Thomas, removing her mittens and holding up each ribbon for his opinion.

He thought—or at least gave the appearance of thinking—about it for a moment, then pointed. "The blue one. It matches my eyes."

She couldn't keep the grin from her face, knowing full well that the other patrons of the shop would instantly peg her as a woman in love. But she didn't care what they thought, or who knew how she felt about Thomas.

*Was* it love? Maddie wasn't sure, but she suspected it was. And while Thomas had made no declarations, he had been the one to propose a real courtship between them. Did that mean he cared for her, too, or that he thought he was rescuing her from a life of lonely spinsterhood?

He brushed his hand across her back. "Anything else you need here?"

She turned a little and tilted her face up to meet his gaze, pleased to find a version of her own foolish grin smiling down at her. "No, just this."

She purchased her blue ribbon and they walked across the street to the tiny bookshop where she hoped to find a new novel to add to her collection.

"Mama is not so keen on my reading habits," Maddie remarked, running a finger across the spines of *The Vindictive Spirit, A Novel In Four Volumes*.

"Your mother doesn't like you to read?" Thomas's brows drew down in confusion.

Maddie shook her head. "It's not reading itself she objects to, it's my taste in reading material." She tapped the cover of volume four. "For example, if I brought this home she'd lecture me about the impropriety of reading such things and force me to return it."

"What are you allowed to read?"

"Mostly improving tracts for girls and women," Maddie replied with a frown. "They aren't very entertaining."

He chuckled. "I wouldn't think so. What is it you're after today?"

Maddie tapped the novel's cover again and took a step closer to him. "I already have volumes one and two, and I've been aching to know what happens next."

"Maddie Hayward, rebellious daughter," he quipped quietly. "Your secret is safe with me."

"That makes two, then," she said, sending him a furtive little smile. What other secrets would they share before New Year's Day?

She scooped up volume three of *The Vindictive Spirit* and made her way to the counter, surreptitiously scanning the other shelves for something Thomas might like. She was already halfway done with the scarf she was knitting him for Christmas, but she might be able to save enough of her pin money to purchase a book for his birthday in two months' time.

They made one more stop at the tea shop for the special biscuits Cook wanted to serve after Christmas dinner, then headed back. When they came within sight of the Haywards' house, Thomas stopped her with a hand on her arm.

"Where is your novel?"

Her eyes widened. In the blissful haze that had developed during their walk home, she'd forgotten all about the forbidden book. "It's here," she said, pulling it from the bag Thomas carried containing their items.

He unbuttoned his greatcoat and slipped the book inside. "If anyone asks, I'll tell them it's mine."

"You know what our parents will think of you if you tell them you've been reading a Minerva Press novel."

They'd think something was wrong with his mind, but Thomas only shrugged. "They may think what they like."

Maddie shot a quick glance at the house—still too far away for anyone to recognize them—and drew him down to her for a kiss. "Thomas Mathison, you are the noblest of gentlemen."

"Anything for you," he said softly.

For the rest of the afternoon and into the evening there was always someone with Maddie, making it impossible for her to retrieve her book from Thomas. But when Thomas excused himself from the evening entertainment to go write letters, their predictable parents once again made an effort to retire before Kit did, leaving Maddie alone with him in the parlor not too long after dinner.

"A last attempt to wring a Christmas proposal of marriage from you, no doubt," Maddie teased him, noting that their machinations no longer bothered her the way they had.

"Not from me, at least," Kit returned with a wink, prying himself from his chair. "Thomas asked me to pass along a message to you—he asks that you stay here and wait for him, and that he'll return your book tonight."

"Excellent."

Kit's eyes lingered on her for a long moment, but he didn't ask the questions that were probably running through his mind. Instead he simply smiled and took himself off to bed.

Only a few minutes later, Thomas appeared in the doorway carrying his greatcoat over one arm with the other hidden behind his back. "Would you like some company?"

"Yes," she said, meeting him halfway across the room for an embrace. "Oh! You're cold!"

He draped the coat over a chair and dropped a kiss on her hair, laying one freezing hand across the bare skin of her neck. "Ah, but you're so warm."

She gave a little shriek and pulled away laughing. "I didn't realize writing letters required you to go outside."

"I saw something on our way home from the village this afternoon that I wanted to go back for." He pulled his other hand out from behind his back. "Perhaps you'll help me thaw out by the fire?"

Maddie poked at the mass of leaves and stems Thomas was holding. "What is it?"

"Mistletoe," he said with a small smile. "I didn't have time to make it into a proper kissing bough, but I think this will do."

"Yes," she breathed, wrapping her arms around him. "I believe it will."

His lips were warm and soft when they met hers, and she couldn't help but sigh. "This—you—are more than I ever hoped for, Thomas."

He kissed her once more, slowly, skillfully, until her toes began to curl in her shoes. "I have one more thing for you, darling," he said murmured she'd opened her eyes again.

He left her for a moment and fished around inside his coat, coming up with the novel she'd purchased that afternoon. "I thought perhaps we could read it together. You'll have to tell me what happened in the first two volumes, of course."

"What a wonderful idea."

They settled together on the floor before the fire, Thomas leaning back against the sofa and wrapping an arm around Maddie as she curled up beside him, resting her head on his chest. She dutifully recounted the events of the novel up through the end of volume two, then relaxed against his body when he began to read aloud.

His voice washed over her in warm waves and she let her eyes close. She hadn't realized it until very recently, but if she'd been told she could have anything her heart desired for Christmas, this was what she would have chosen.

The clock struck midnight as he came to the end of a chapter and Maddie savored the contentment washing over her.

"Merry Christmas, my love," she murmured.

She felt his breath catch, his heart pounding in his chest before he answered.

"Merry Christmas, sweetheart."

# Chapter 6

Thomas slept little after seeing Maddie to her bedchamber just before one o'clock in the morning. He'd lain in bed staring up at the ceiling, listening to Kit's breathing fill the silence as he relived every moment of the evening with Maddie. She'd been warm and soft in his arms, calling him "my love" and looking at him like he was the only man in the world for her. Thomas tried to remember the last time he'd been this euphoric, but nothing he'd previously experienced even came close.

By the time the sun began to peek over the horizon, Thomas had decided to ask for Maddie's hand in marriage. Not right away, no matter how badly he wanted to. With a decision this important, it was prudent to wait and make sure what he thought he wanted was truly what he wanted. And Maddie deserved that same opportunity. He had no schedule to keep, but perhaps he could find some time alone with her on Twelfth Night. They could take a walk together back to that copse of trees where he first held her, and he could ask her there.

He finally drifted off to sleep with a smile on his face and the scent of her perfume still clinging to his shirt.

The next thing he knew, Kit was shaking him awake with instructions to wash and dress for church.

"Already?" he croaked.

"Late night?" Kit grinned.

Thomas pulled himself to a sitting position and rubbed his eyes. "Yes."

"Was it worth it?"

Thomas felt his mouth pull into what was probably a foolish smile and nodded. "Yes."

"Good," Kit replied. "I'll remind you of that when you begin nodding off at dinner."

Thomas managed to stay awake during the service despite the vicar's determination to put everyone to sleep. He also made it through the afternoon meal, trading sly glances with his beloved across the table. But once the meal was finished, he retired to his bedchamber hoping to snatch a couple of hours' sleep before the evening's celebrations began.

Once again, Thomas had a difficult time falling asleep. But this time it wasn't euphoria that kept him awake—it was fear.

What happened if Maddie said yes to his proposal? After the excitement died down and they began making arrangements for the wedding, for their life together...what then? The reason he had no schedule to keep was because he no longer had a way to make a living. He had a little money put by, certainly, but not enough to support two people. Maddie would have a dowry, too, but he doubted it was a large one. Would it be enough for them to live on?

Probably not.

He rose from the bed and stumbled over to the little writing desk in the corner of the room. He couldn't ask Maddie to marry him until he could support her, and he couldn't support her until he found work again. The only logical thing to do, then, was to begin writing letters.

Someone he knew, or who had known his uncle, might be in need of a clerk and the only way to find out was to ask.

He was still hunched over the desk when Kit came to fetch him for dinner some hours later.

"I thought you wanted to sleep," his brother said, swinging the chamber door open wide.

"I did," Thomas replied, not looking up from his work, "but I couldn't."

"Well, everyone is gathering in the parlor. You still have a few minutes to dress for dinner, but I'd hurry if I were you." Kit gave him a playful slap on the back. "If I can distract mother long enough, you'll be able to sit beside Maddie tonight."

Thomas lifted his head, meeting his brother's eyes but not really seeing them. "Yes, that sounds good."

He returned to the letter he was composing, determined to finish it before he did anything else. He could walk into the village first thing tomorrow to post it and the others he'd completed.

"I'll see you downstairs, then, I suppose," Kit muttered, shrugging his shoulders as he exited the room.

"I'll be down shortly," Thomas called belatedly after his brother.

He managed to find a clean shirt and his best tailcoat, washing hurriedly in the basin before changing his clothing and dashing down the staircase. The assemblage was just about to go in to dinner when he arrived in the parlor, and Kit had their mother on his arm.

"Excellent," Thomas said under his breath, approaching Maddie. "May I?" he asked her, offering his arm.

Her grin was as large and foolish as his had been the night before. "Yes," she said softly, twining her arm with his.

She was wearing a green gown tonight, but he could smell delicate roses about her instead of her usual perfume, reminding him of the little bottle and accompanying flower he'd hidden away in his bedchamber. If they could find some time alone together tonight, he could give them to her. Even better if he could locate that bit of mistletoe he'd scavenged the day before.

But first, he had more letters to write. He already had letters for his uncle's friends in Edinburgh, but there were other people who might be able to help. Thomas's father had lived in London for some years before marrying—perhaps his mother would remember something of her late husband's friends and business associates.

"Did you hear me?"

"Hmm?"

He glanced in the direction the voice had come from and found Maddie staring at him, her brows lifted in inquiry. "Oh, my apologies. I missed the last thing you said."

"I think you missed everything I said," she replied, placing a slice of roast goose on her plate. "Where is your head today, Thomas?"

"Stuck on practical matters, I'm afraid," he said, poking a bit of carrot with his fork.

"Anything I should know about?"

He shook his head, not wanting to have this particular conversation surrounded by their families. "Not at the moment."

Her eyes flicked back to his and held his gaze, then returned to her food. "Later, then."

He speared the carrot and popped it into his mouth. "Perhaps."

What had happened to her affectionate, attentive Thomas? When Kit said his brother hadn't slept well the night before, Maddie brushed off Thomas's aloofness as fatigue. But dinner progressed and the families moved into the parlor for whatever evening entertainment her mother had cooked up, and Thomas still seemed far away.

Well, there was no rule that said he had to hang on her every word, was there? Neither would she want him to. But such an abrupt change from his demeanor the previous evening made Maddie wonder if something bigger was afoot.

She waited for a break in the revels—singing carols and sharing stories of Christmases past—to try to draw him away from the group for a quick word.

"Thomas, could you help me with something?" she asked, tapping a finger on his shoulder to gain his attention.

"Perhaps Kit should help you," her mother responded from her place on the sofa.

"No, Mama, I need Thomas for this."

His eyes swung to hers and he flashed her a smile—a genuine, warm smile of the kind she'd come to expect from him. "I am at your service."

"Thank you," she said, returning the smile. "It's this way."

Maddie gestured toward the door and Thomas followed her into the hallway, giving her an odd look when she continued on toward the dining room.

"What exactly do you need my help with?" he asked, trailing behind her.

"Nothing," she replied sheepishly, pushing open the dining room door and tugging him inside. "I merely wanted a moment alone with you."

She reached for his hand and he allowed her to take it, but his posture was rigid, the expression on his face somewhere between discomfort and fear.

"Thomas, what's wrong?"

He shook his head. "Nothing you need concern yourself about."

Maddie held his hand in both of hers, taking a step closer to him as she studied his features. "If something has upset you, then it concerns me. I'd like to help if I can."

"Nothing has upset me," he snapped back.

She flinched, releasing his hand. "Yes, I can see that."

"I'm sorry, darling," he said softly, reaching for her hand and clasping it once more. "I'm just having a difficult time dealing with my sudden lack of employment."

Well that certainly made sense. What would she do if someone sent her a letter saying she no longer had access to a home or the basic necessities of life? She certainly wouldn't be cheerful about it.

"I have some news that may help," she said, a hopeful note in her voice. "There was a letter from my grandmother in the post you brought home. Her current companion is to be married, and she wants me to come live with her in the companion's place."

"How is that helpful?" Thomas seemed genuinely curious, though there was a hard edge to the question.

Maddie took a breath and held it for an extra fraction of a second. "In addition to the pin money I have from Papa, I'd have a small wage from Gran, too. She only lives a few miles away, so if you stayed with Kit you could..." She let her voice trail off and tried to scrutinize his expression again. "Are you listening to me, Thomas?"

"Yes," he replied with a weary air. "You're saying that because I can't provide for you, you're going to work for a living yourself."

"What?" For the second time, Maddie broke physical contact with him. "No—this is as much for Gran as it is for anything else. She needs someone to look after her, and she doesn't want to leave the house my grandfather built for her." She squinted slightly, confused by his lack of empathy. "I thought you'd understand that. The money is just an added benefit."

"What am I to do in the meantime?" he asked, pulling out a chair from the dining table and dropping onto it. "Am I to wait until you've saved enough money? Then you'll propose marriage to me?"

She took a step back, her voice quiet when she answered. "You could live with Kit, and give lessons in Latin and Greek until you find something more to your liking."

His only response was to sigh and look past her, and Maddie could feel her hands clenching into fists. "What difference does it make where the money comes from, Thomas? The sooner we save enough, the sooner we can be together."

"Will you still want to be with me when I'm a bitter man who can't provide for his own wife? Because that is likely what I'll become without a real place in the world."

She took another breath, a deep one this time, and let it out slowly. "If I'm earning money, you'll have time to find yourself a new situation. Can't you see that? Then you'll be able to find employment that fulfills you, my Gran will be cared for, and we won't have to wait so long to be wed. That is, if you actually want to marry me."

"Perhaps you'd be better off with another man," he replied in a voice devoid of emotion. "Wasn't that your plan all along?"

Maddie felt as if she'd been struck. She instinctively covered her heart with her hand as if to protect a wound there. "My plan was to find someone who wasn't Kit; someone who would love me and who I could love in return, who would be my partner in life," she choked out. "I thought I had succeeded."

"You have succeeded in finding a man with no livelihood, Maddie," he returned quietly. "I saw you in the village, flitting from shop to shop. You were enjoying yourself immensely. How much will you enjoy wearing the same two dresses all the time because we can't afford new clothing? Or having no books to read because we've sold them all to pay for food?"

"Thomas—"

"I don't think you've thought this through," he continued, rising from the chair. "It doesn't matter how much we might love each other if we don't have enough money to live on. And I don't need to be reminded of how little I have to offer you every day of our lives. Perhaps you should marry my brother after all—he, at least, would be able to take proper care of you."

He strode from the room, shutting the door carefully behind him, leaving Maddie alone with the furniture.

"I think that was the end of our courtship," she told the table, running a finger over its smooth, cold surface. "Thomas, like all the others, thinks I belong with Kit."

# Chapter 7

Instead of returning to the parlor and rejoining the two families, Thomas continued on to the staircase and made for the bedchamber he shared with his brother. He wasn't sure what he was going to do there, only that the very last thing he wanted was to sing songs and celebrate.

He entered the room and sat down on his bed, bracing his hands against the mattress. What had just happened? What had he done?

He'd put his own feelings aside for Maddie's future happiness—that's what he had done. The Haywards weren't wealthy, but the status Maddie would sink to as Thomas's wife was more than he could bear. She deserved better than he could give her. She deserved better than *him*.

A knock sounded on the door a split second before the door swung open. "Are you well, brother?"

"Go away, Kit."

"I'll take that as a no." Kit entered the room and closed the door behind him. "What happened? I found Maddie crying in the dining room."

Thomas tried to ignore the stabbing pain in his chest and concentrate on getting Kit out of there. He knew that if he didn't give his brother at least some information, Kit would remain in the room until he wrung out every detail. "I set Maddie free."

"You what?"

"I told her she was better off with a man who had more money than I do."

Kit stood in the center of the room, staring at Thomas. "Why would you do such a foolish thing? I thought you loved her."

"I did it *because* I love her," Thomas replied, unwilling to lift his gaze from the carpet. "Perhaps I'll find employment again and save enough money to support a wife, but she shouldn't have to sit by and wait to see if that happens."

"Did you ask her what *she* wanted?"

Thomas's gaze dropped lower, to a stocking peeking out from underneath his bed. "She wants to become a paid companion for her grandmother, to make money when I can't."

Kit grunted at that. "And that hurt your pride."

His tone was gentler, more understanding, and Thomas ventured a glance at his brother. "Quite possibly. But that's not what this is about."

"No. It's about your insecurities, isn't it?" Kit crossed his arms over his chest and frowned down at Thomas. "Things were actually going well with Maddie. I may have been keeping my distance, but I saw the two of you together enough to know your feelings for her were growing...and mutual. Then you stumble over one stupid rock in your path and you quit the race altogether."

Thomas took a deep breath and let it out slowly as he stood, starting a list in his mind of the things he would need to take with him. If he couldn't get rid of Kit, then he would remove himself from the house. "There was no race, Kit."

"I know that—it's a metaphor. A poor one, perhaps, but never mind. The point is that at the first sign of trouble, you gave up."

Thomas found his hat and winter gloves, tossing them on the bed, and attempted to don his greatcoat. The deuced thing was acting as if it had a mind of its own. "I didn't *want* to let her go, Kit."

"I believe you." Kit stepped aside as Thomas flung his arm out in an effort to tame his coat. "But it was easier to do that than to face your problems, wasn't it? How afraid are you to allow someone to depend on you?"

Thomas looked at his brother, then yanked on the lapels of the greatcoat. "I can't have Maddie without money."

"You can't have Maddie if you're unwilling to work through your troubles, either."

Thomas rolled his eyes, but didn't respond. The famous Mathison stubborn streak was rising up again—likely in both of them—and he was not in the mood to waste his time.

Kit went on with his lecture as if Thomas was a dolt completely incapable of intelligent thought. "She presented you with a perfectly good way for the two of you to be together, and you pretended as though it was beneath you. Do you know how much that hurt her?"

Thomas felt the pain in his chest again—the last thing he'd ever want to do was hurt Maddie. He shoved the thought away, though, and continued dressing to go outdoors. What he needed right now was to get away from here, away from the judgment of his brother and the wreck of his dreams. If Maddie truly wanted him, she wouldn't have been so quick to throw his inadequacies in his face.

Perhaps she didn't want him that badly after all.

He picked up his heavy winter gloves from the bed and pulled them on. "Does she know how much she's hurt me?"

Thomas snatched up his hat from his bed and marched out the door. He heaved a sigh of relief when he made it to the front door of the house without seeing anyone else about—the only thing he wanted right then was to be alone.

He walked the two miles to his childhood home at full speed, hoping to burn off some of the anger and pain that boiled inside him. But they only seemed to build. Perhaps he should have expected Maddie to act the way she did—he was, after all, a second son with nothing but his mother's love, and one couldn't pay the rent with that.

But Thomas had expected his brother to take his side, and Kit had sided with her. That hurt more than Thomas was willing to admit.

"I really shouldn't be surprised, though," he said to the front door of the old house as he put the key in the lock and turned it. "If he hadn't been so partial to her, none of this would have happened in the first place."

Thomas burst into the house and shut the door firmly behind him, blocking out that thought as well. He was in an untenable situation. He wished he'd never kissed Maddie, never caressed her, never opened his heart to her. He couldn't quite bring himself to wish he'd never met her, but how much less painful would the loss of his employment—and his ability to make his own way in life—be if he'd never come to Kent this Christmas?

Would his uncle's departure have hurt if Thomas had stayed in Edinburgh? Absolutely.

"But I didn't stay," he said through gritted teeth. "I came here and found love. This was my chance to have everything I wanted, and it's gone."

He stomped around the house collecting firewood, kindling, and a tinderbox, shucking his outer garments as he went, the vigorous movement warming him even in the chilly house. Once he got the fire going, Thomas found himself unable to sit still. Well, Kit had showed him how to make some of the small repairs—perhaps that would be a good way to spend the rest of the evening.

Then at least something good would come of the day.

Maddie ran into her chamber and threw herself down on her bed, frustration boiling over into anger. Why wouldn't Thomas just listen to her? Maybe working as her grandmother's companion wasn't going to bring in a lot of money, but it would certainly help. And he'd dismissed the idea as if she'd insulted him by even suggesting it. Was this just a one-time occurrence? Or was this how he would always treat her when there was a problem?

If this was how he dealt with setbacks, then perhaps it was better that they parted.

A knock sounded on her door, and she slid off the bed to answer it. When she saw her best friend waiting with open arms, her throat became tight again.

"I know I'm supposed to keep my distance," he said, his voice low and serious, "but I thought you might need a friendly ear and a good hug tonight."

"I heard footsteps and the front door, and assumed that was Thomas leaving. You didn't go with him?"

Kit dropped his empty arms and shook his head. "He's my brother and I love him, but in this case he's being an ass. I don't know what got into him."

Maddie opened the door wider and gestured Kit inside. "He's more interested in money than he is in me."

"I doubt that very much," Kit replied, closing the door behind him. "I probably shouldn't be telling his secrets, but in this case I think it's justified. He's loved you for some time now, and he was over the moon when you two decided to pursue a romantic relationship."

Her heart did a little flip—Thomas loved her!—until she recalled the way he'd reacted to Gran's offer. "He's not acting like it."

"I know." Kit held out his arms again. "And I'm sorry for it."

Maddie finally allowed herself to embrace her friend, letting the comfort and relief of his arms push the turmoil from her mind. "You aren't the one who should be sorry, Kit, but I appreciate the thought."

He gave her a squeeze and pulled back a little to look her in the eyes. "Is there anything I can do?"

"You're doing it," she said, giving him a weak smile.

"All right, then." He pulled her close again and rested his cheek against her temple. "I'll just stay right here until you tell me to go."

"Good." And it was good. She'd missed Kit so much these past weeks, but she missed Thomas now, too. If he hadn't been such an ass, as Kit had called him, he would be the one holding her tonight. "Do you think he'll come around, Kit?"

"I certainly hope so. No one could love you mo—"

She drew back and tried to read the expression on his face, but he wasn't looking at her. "What?" Maddie followed his gaze and discovered her parents standing just inside the open door, her mother's hand still on the knob.

"Is it official now?" her mother asked, clasping her hands to her chest. "Have you said yes?"

Maddie knew she should have leaped away from Kit, should have tried to explain the situation. But if months and months of protest hadn't convinced her parents that she wasn't going to marry Kit, a last minute denial wouldn't either. She suddenly felt weary of the whole thing and bowed her head against Kit's chest, closing her eyes.

Her mother, predictably, exclaimed her happiness and ran off to find Mrs. Mathison. Maddie heard her father say something to Kit about settlements in a gruff voice, then he, too, was gone.

"You didn't contradict them," Kit said softly when they were alone again. "Do you want to wed me, Maddie?"

"Would it really be so bad?" Her voice was low, small, as if she didn't want anyone to truly hear what she was saying. "Everyone would finally stop nagging us about it."

He gripped her chin firmly and tilted her head up to meet his blue eyes, so like his brother's. "That is a poor reason to choose a spouse, Maddie Hayward, and you know it."

He was right, of course, but she tried again anyway. "Would it be so awful to have me as your wife? Nothing about our relationship would have to change," she added quickly. "We could carry on as we always have, just living in the same house together."

Kit released her chin, then released her body from his embrace. "We could. If that was what you truly wanted. It would mean you'd never have the chance to work things out with Thomas. And there would be no children."

Maddie's mind wandered back to her conversation with Thomas by the bonfire at the Midwinter Fête and the image of his curly-haired family. She'd unconsciously placed herself in that picture over the past few days, smiling brightly back at Thomas as he taught the children to fish. But that's all it would be if she and Kit were wed—an image in her mind. Kit would most certainly make a good father, but they would have to share a bed to produce children. Yet the thought of even kissing Kit made her mildly nauseated. She loved him, certainly, but as her friend not her lover.

He must have sensed her hesitation, because he set his hands on her shoulders and bent his head to catch her eye. "Would you like some time to think about it?"

"No," she answered immediately. She was sick unto death of thinking about marriage with Kit. Then, "Wait, yes. I would like some time to think about it, and I suspect you would, too. If we're going to do this, we'd better both be sure about it."

"Indeed." He smiled and gave her shoulders a squeeze. "I'll leave you to your thoughts for the night, then. But if you should need anything, I am just a couple of doors away."

"Thank you."

Maddie watched as he let himself out then flopped back onto her bed, staring up at the ceiling with unseeing eyes. She didn't know if Thomas would ever speak to her again, nor was she sure she wanted him to at the moment, even though he'd all but professed his love for her and she for him. Instead, she was actually considering giving in to the pressure society and their families had been putting on her for months—perhaps years—and marrying Kit.

How had things progressed to this point?

Wedding Kit would be the easy way out, of course. She would have a home, a companion she cared for, the independence she longed for, and the ease of never having to worry about money. But if that was all she wanted out of life, she could live out her days with Gran and never think of marriage again.

Did she want more? Did she *deserve* more?

Did Kit?

If she married Kit, she wouldn't just be sacrificing her own chance at love but his, too.

She rolled onto her stomach and buried her face in the red counterpane. Life had been so much easier when the worst thing she could think of was catching a bigger fish than her best friend.

# Chapter 8

Thomas awoke in his old bedchamber, his long legs hanging off the side of the bed. Pushing an aging quilt from his body and pulling himself into a sitting position, he realized he'd fallen asleep laying in the wrong direction.

And fully clothed.

He tried to run a hand through his hair, but met resistance from what was certainly a tangled mess of curls. He'd slept restlessly, plagued with odd, disjointed dreams that disturbed him even though he couldn't remember anything specific about them.

Then the memory of the previous day's falling out with Maddie flooded back into his mind and he sighed, dropping his head into his hands. She'd been upset, of course. But what he could no longer ignore was the shock written on her features when he'd said his state of mind was none of her concern, the pain he knew he had caused when he told her she was better off with Kit because he had money.

"Kit was right," he mumbled. "I am an ass."

The cold of the room crept under the layers of his clothing, and Thomas realized the fire he'd lit the night before had gone out. Wrapping himself in the quilt, he chastised himself for forgetting to bank the fire before he'd gone to bed. Then he chastised himself some more for the way he'd treated Maddie. He'd been so caught up in his perceived inadequacies that he'd rejected Maddie's attempt to help. For that was what she'd been doing when she told him about her grandmother's suggested arrangement. But he'd been too self-centered to see it.

"Have I ruined our future before it could even begin?"

Perhaps not. One of the things he loved about Maddie was her compassionate nature. Oh, she had been the first person to tell him or Kit when they'd done something stupid as adolescents, but she'd also been quick to forgive when presented with genuine remorse and the desire to make the situation right again.

"And I most certainly want to make this situation right again." He clambered off the bed and dropped the quilt onto the floor. "Will she see me if I return to the Haywards' house?"

There was only one way to find out. As he set about tidying his appearance, he tried to plan out what to say to her. "I'm sorry I hurt you," definitely needed to be said, but what else? How to explain the temporary madness that had come over him? Could he assure her it would never happen again?

Another thought halted him in his tracks. What if she wasn't alone?

If Kit was with her—and he probably was—he could be convinced to leave them. But if she was with her parents and his mother, Thomas wasn't sure he'd be able to get her alone.

Dear God, he might have to beg for Maddie's forgiveness while both their families looked on.

A shiver passed through his body. "It should be a private moment," he said to a portrait of his great-grandfather, who probably would have agreed with Thomas's assessment. "But if I have to humble myself in front of the entire county to return to her good graces, then that is what I will do."

When he was satisfied with his appearance, he went hunting for the rose and bottle of scent he'd procured from the shop in the village. He remembered unexpectedly finding both in the pockets of his tailcoat shortly after he'd arrived at the old house, remembered taking them out and putting them somewhere he couldn't see them, where he wouldn't be reminded of who they'd been meant for.

Ah-ha! He discovered both items on top of a tall bookshelf in what had been his father's study. The rose was wilted and rather worse for the wear, but the bottle of scent was intact. That would have to do, unless he found something else on the way to the Haywards' home—unlikely in this weather.

No matter, the scent would do nicely. He'd originally meant it as a gift simply because he'd wanted to give Maddie something, but it would serve just as well as an I'm-sorry offering and a belated Christmas gift.

Thomas located his greatcoat and hat—thrown haphazardly over the banister when he'd entered the house—and headed out into the freezing cold.

"Are you sure you want to do this?" Kit looked down at Maddie, his blond brows raised as he asked the question.

He was giving her the chance to back out. No one else knew about their decision except the two of them, and they didn't have to announce it to their families *now*. But Maddie knew their parents would have to be told at some point. Now was as good a time as any.

"Yes," she said resolutely. It hadn't taken her long to figure out what—or who—she really wanted after Kit had left her to her own devices the night before, and what would be best for all involved. She'd known it since she'd sat down to breakfast with the Mathison brothers the first morning of their visit, and Kit had agreed when she went to him first thing that morning with her answer.

"All right then."

Their parents were gathered in the Haywards' parlor wishing the blustery weather to perdition when Maddie entered the room at Kit's side. All three heads swiveled in their direction and the conversation had died by the time Maddie came to a halt in front of the fireplace, with Kit taking his place to the left and just behind her.

"Mama, Papa, Mrs. Mathison..." Maddie began with confidence, but with three sets of eyes upon her—the eyes of the people who had dismissed her wishes for months and months in favor of their own—her resolve began to melt. She felt Kit's warm hand on her back and took a calming breath, then started again. "Kit and I have an announcement to make—"

"Wait!"

Maddie turned toward the door as Thomas rushed in, still wearing his greatcoat and hat and dusted with snow. "Thomas, what are you—"

"Please don't marry Kit," he interrupted, tossing his hat onto the nearest chair and running a hand through his disheveled auburn curls.

Maddie heard Kit's low chuckle behind her and she managed a smile, despite the thudding of her heart. "I wasn't going to."

"You weren't?" Thomas asked, stopping short.

"You weren't?" Maddie's mother echoed from the sofa. "What announcement were you and Kit going to make?"

"We were going to announce that we'd decided never to marry each other," Kit supplied helpfully. "Maddie and I hoped that you all would honor our wishes if we told everyone together."

Thomas's hands were cold and bare when they enveloped hers, but he was smiling broadly and her body warmed at his touch. "Good. Then I still have a chance to apologize to you."

"As you should," Kit returned with a pointed look at his brother.

"Perhaps we should speak privately," Maddie offered, squeezing Thomas's hands. If there was an apology awaiting her, would there also be an opportunity to have a real conversation about their future?

His smile took on a relieved quality, and his whole body seemed to relax. "Yes. That's a good idea."

With a quick glance at their families, she led him from the parlor around to the dining room, where he'd told her to find a man with money only the day before. Once he'd closed the door behind them, he clasped her free hand once more and rubbed his thumbs over both her hands.

"I'm sorry, Maddie," he said without preamble. "I got so wrapped up in trying to meet some arbitrary definition of worthiness—and failing—that I completely missed the point of courtship."

He stepped closer and the scent of pine and wool emanated from the greatcoat he still wore.

"And what's that?" she asked softly, her blood pounding in her ears.

"To be together," he replied, resting his forehead against hers. "Will you forgive my utter foolishness, darling? Might we resume our courtship?"

She wanted with all her being to say yes, but there were things they needed to discuss first. She pulled back slightly to look into his blue eyes. "I do forgive you, Thomas. But what happens the next time we must deal with a problem? Will you insist on making all the decisions without even talking to me? What about when you and I have a disagreement? Are you going to shut me out until you miss me enough to apologize?"

Thomas drew back as if he'd been stung, then bowed his head. "You're insinuating that I've been a boor as well as a numbskull, and I deserve that. I have been."

"And I deserve answers to my questions," Maddie replied quietly.

He blinked, then lifted his gaze to hers. "You are an intelligent woman, Maddie Hayward, and I was an idiot to dismiss that fact. If I'd have kept my head in the first place, we could have had a real conversation about our future and avoided all this turmoil. I promise you I won't forget that."

"We can still have that conversation," she said, her lips curving into a slow smile. "If you're willing."

"I am, and we should," he replied with an answering smile. "Might we delay it just a few moments longer, though? There's one more thing I would like to do."

He released her and reached into his pockets, producing a small glass bottle in one hand and a familiar clump of leaves in the other.

"What on earth?"

"Belated Christmas gifts," he said, extending the hand with the bottle.

She plucked it from his palm and opened it, closing her eyes in pleasure as the scent of roses filled the air. "My favorite," she sighed.

"Is that why you wore it the night of the assembly?"

Maddie's eyes popped open. "You noticed?"

"You usually wear gardenias." He licked his lips and shifting his weight from one foot to the other. "But the scent of roses will always remind me of you now."

She set the bottle down on the dining room table and slid her arms around Thomas's middle. "That makes it the perfect gift."

He wrapped one arm around her and pressed his cheek to hers. "The second one is for both of us."

"Is that what I think it is?" she murmured, warm and content against him.

He nodded, the stubble on his unshaven face bristling against her skin. "Mistletoe."

She drew back to examine the green mass he held in his other hand, then burst out laughing. "So it is."

"May I kiss you under it?"

"I think that's an excellent idea."

He obliged her, brushing his lips over hers before tossing the mistletoe onto the table and pulling her body against his with both arms. "I love you, Maddie. I can't promise you I'll never let my insecurities get the better of me again, but I'll do everything I can to keep them in check."

"Including coming to me for help?" she asked, tilting her head slightly to one side.

"That," he said, leaning his forehead against hers, "will be my first step. And I hope it would be yours, too, in a similar situation."

"Good." She sighed softly and stroked a hand down his back. "And yes, I would come to you for help if I needed it. I love you, and your support—your emotional support—is important to me."

"Good."

"Like now," she continued with a sly smile. "I think I might need to be kissed again. Can you help me with that?"

He dipped his head, pausing just before capturing her lips once more. "With pleasure."

# Epilogue

Kent, England
Spring, 1814

"They'll be here any moment, Gran," Maddie called from the kitchen in the little house her grandfather had built so long ago. "Will you keep them entertained while I finish up in here?"

"Don't you worry," Gran called back. "Your young men are in good hands."

Maddie exchanged glances with the maid-of-all-work who was chopping vegetables beside her, and they both giggled. Gran would no doubt be talking their ears off before the food had even half finished cooking. And both Mathison men would enjoy themselves immensely.

Kit had offered his brother a home until he could find work or save enough money to open his own office and Thomas had accepted, giving some of the local boys lessons in Latin and Greek to earn his keep. Once Maddie had settled into her grandmother's household, Gran had begun inviting the brothers to dine with them every week and would choose a story from the newspaper to discuss with them.

Maddie wiped her hands on a towel as she walked into the parlor. "What are you going to talk about tonight?"

"Some company is installing gas lighting in Westminster," Gran replied, reaching for the newspaper and seeking out the story she'd marked. "Ah yes, the Gas Light and Coke Company. Gas lighting—can you imagine?"

For a moment, Maddie did imagine it. She'd never been anywhere outside Kent, but she'd seen sketches of the Houses of Parliament and Westminster Bridge, and she pictured herself standing with Thomas under the new gaslights. If they actually were to visit Westminster there would be other people going about their business, of course, but in Maddie's mind the two of them stood alone on the bridge in each other's arms.

"I think it would be beautiful," she smiled, leaning against the door frame.

A knock on the door interrupted her musings, but her smile returned when she answered it and found Thomas and Kit on the doorstep. "You're just in time," Maddie grinned. "Gran's got a good one for you today."

Kit greeted her and gave her shoulder a little squeeze, then moved off toward the parlor to say hello to Gran, giving Maddie and Thomas a few precious moments alone together.

He pulled a small tangled ball of leaves from his pocket and held it over her head. "I believe you're standing underneath some mistletoe, Miss Hayward."

She laughed, pushing his hand away and wrapping her arms around him. "If you keep bringing that stuff every week, there won't be any left for Christmas," she laughed.

"Maybe I'll learn to cultivate it," he returned with a wink.

"You don't need it." She went up on her tiptoes and murmured in his ear, "If you want to kiss me all you have to do is ask."

"May I kiss you, Maddie, my love?" he whispered softly.

"Yes," she breathed.

They had only enough time for a brief brushing of lips before Gran's voice called out, "Did you two get lost on the way to the parlor?"

Thomas chuckled, running a finger down Maddie's cheek and planting a kiss on her temple before holding out his hand. "Her timing is impeccable."

"It always is. I suppose we should go in." Maddie took his hand and starting toward the parlor.

"Wait." Thomas pulled her back to him and wrapped her in his arms once more. "There is something I want to ask you first."

She sighed contentedly, breathing in the faint scent of the leather-bound books and ink he'd been using earlier in the day. "Ask me whatever you want. The answer is likely going to be yes."

"Will you marry me?" he returned softly.

Maddie's heart kicked into a gallop. Whatever she'd been expecting, it wasn't that. Not yet. "Are you sure?"

She knew his answer, of course—if there hadn't been a question of money, they'd probably already be wed. But there *was* a question of money, and she knew tutoring didn't bring in a large sum even when it was combined with her wages from Gran.

"Kit has offered us the old cottage on his property for as long as we want it," Thomas explained. "With that, our savings, and your dowry, we should be comfortable. Not wealthy, but comfortable."

"The old cottage?" She reached back into her memory but couldn't recall anything.

"Downstream from where we used to fish. The structure is sound, and there's room for a small kitchen garden outside. Kit said he'd have the inside cleaned for us, and you can put your new sewing skills to work making curtains and things."

Maddie tried but failed to suppress a giggle. Gran had been trying to teach her how to run a household, and had included lessons in cooking and sewing in her curriculum. The cooking had been going well—their dinner that evening was her biggest test so far—but she'd not taken to sewing quite as well.

"I'm sure I could manage...eventually," she murmured with a half-smile. "But what about Gran? You know I want to marry you, Thomas, but I can't leave her all alone."

"I've thought of that," he grinned, rubbing slow tracks up and down her back. "You could continue to be your grandmother's companion by day, and come home to me and our cottage in the evenings. Or, if you'd prefer to remain living here, perhaps your Gran will allow me to live here as well. I can give lessons from here as easily as I can from Kit's home."

Maddie tried to picture waking up beside Thomas every morning in the chamber she'd been given here in her grandmother's house and ended up giggling again.

"We don't have to decide now," he continued.

"Thank you," she said softly, smoothing back an auburn curl that had escaped his attempts to tame it.

"For what?"

"For giving me—us—options."

He smiled. "It really is more enjoyable when we decide on things together."

She gave a low laugh. The day they'd worked out their current    arrangements    had    included    a    spirited discussion...and was followed by another late night in front of the fireplace. *That* had certainly been enjoyable.

But the decision making had been pleasurable, too, if in a different way. They'd been able to really talk to one another, to share hopes and make plans for a small part of the future. "Yes," she replied softly.

"Wait—'yes' it was enjoyable, or..."

She went up on her toes and whispered in his ear, "Yes, I will marry you."

He sucked in a breath, then lifted her off her feet and swung her around in a full circle. "Sweeter words I'll never hear," he grinned, setting her down. His lips found hers, his mouth opening over hers as he deepened the kiss.

Someone cleared their throat nearby, about a second before Maddie lost all her inhibitions right there in Gran's entryway. With great reluctance, she disentangled herself from Thomas and turned to see who it was.

"I'm sorry to interrupt," Kit said in a half-whisper, gesturing toward the parlor. "It was either me or her."

Thomas laughed. "Thank God for small favors, then."

"Are we to have a new addition to the family, then?" Kit grinned.

"There are still some things to be decided," Maddie said, clasping her hands together in utter happiness. "But yes."

"Wonderful!" Kit practically bellowed. Then, in a quieter voice he continued, "You've been my sister in all but name since we were children. Now it will be official."

Thomas reached for Maddie. "Could you go make our excuses for just another moment, brother? There is one more thing I would like to say to my betrothed." He waited until Kit had disappeared down the hallway before encircling Maddie in his arms.

"What is it that can't wait?" she asked, hearing the trepidation in her own voice.

"I love you."

His voice was low and full of emotion, and her heart fluttered in response. She slipped her arms around his neck and bowed her head against his chest, hoping to hide the tears that sprung unexpectedly to her eyes.

When she could trust herself again, she turned her head and whispered, "I love you, too."

For that moment, it was just the two of them in each other's arms and all was right with the world.

Then Maddie sighed. "We should probably go in."

"How do you think your Gran will take the news?" Thomas asked, releasing his hold on her body in exchange for holding her hand.

"She'll be happy because we're happy," Maddie replied with a smile.

"Will she be disappointed that I'm not Kit?"

Maddie clasped his hand to her heart. "There's no way she could have watched me with you these past months and think that I would want to be with anyone else."

Thomas palmed her cheek and pressed a gentle kiss to her lips. "Then your plan worked," he smiled. "We've finally convinced someone that you don't want to marry Kit."

"Ah, but the most important people knew it all along." She looked deep into his blue eyes, then kissed him one more time. "Now let's go tell everyone else."

# A Kiss to Build a Dream On

**Acquaintances become something more when they each discover the other's true self. Can they find a way to navigate the perils of polite society and their feelings for each other?**

A lady by birth, Margaret Maitland was the toast of the ton until she gave birth to an illegitimate child and raised him without the help of his father. Twenty years later she is received in a few drawing rooms as a favor to her cousin the duke, but misses the friendships and camaraderie she'd enjoyed in her youth.

A gentleman by circumstance, Stephen Eddington is the son of a tradesman who scrimped and saved to give his children every advantage. Twenty years after making influential friends at Cambridge, doors are open to Stephen that his father never imagined, but there are few people in the world that truly understand him...or want to.

When Stephen's nephew invites Margaret's son to visit for the summer holiday, the two families join together to give the boys a care-free month before they return to their studies. And while the younger crowd makes merry, Margaret and Stephen's companionable affection for each other begins to deepen... until their budding relationship becomes the talk of the town. How can they be together without damaging Stephen's tenuous place in society?

# Chapter 1

*The Cotswolds*
*July 1815*

Margaret Maitland sat at her brother's dining table, as she did at least once every week, wondering how she got to this point and where she was going from here.

Not literally how she got there—she walked from the dower house, as usual—but she'd had a letter from her son, Alex, earlier in the day which sent a contemplative wave washing over her. He'd been so small when they'd first moved into that house, and she'd been so vulnerable. But he was a tall, strapping lad now, looking forward to the end of the Easter Term at Cambridge when he could come home and have some fun. Where had the time gone?

"Margaret?"

Margaret's brother Philip, seated next to her, poked her discreetly under the table. "Hmm?" she asked, turning her head toward the sound of her name.

Philip's wife Adeleine frowned across the table and set down her knife with a clank. "I asked if you and Alexander would be attending Natalie's practice ball."

"Yes, of course we will," Margaret answered readily. Adeleine had been hosting a series of informal events over the past several months to give her daughter the opportunity to practice being out in society before her first season in London. Only family and close friends had been invited thus far, but this "practice ball," as Adeleine had been calling it, would be something of a larger affair.

Adeleine's face relaxed and she sat back a bit in her chair. "Good. Natalie has been looking forward to dancing with her cousin."

Margaret chuckled, and Mr. Stephen Eddington, the Maitlands' neighbor sitting across the table from her, lifted a sandy eyebrow in inquiry. "When she was still in leading strings, Natalie decided that Alex was her favorite person in the world, and she's never wavered from that opinion."

"Ah," Mr. Eddington replied with a smile and a nod. "And Alex must return the sentiment, given how much my nephew Patrick includes her in his letters."

Adeleine glanced from Mr. Eddington to her husband, a range of emotions playing out on her face. When outrage made an appearance, Margaret caught Adeleine's eye and shook her head slightly.

"Mr. Eddington's nephew is Alex's closest friend," Margaret reminded her gently. "It's natural that they would speak to each other of the people they care for."

"Yes, that is it exactly," Mr. Eddington added. "Patrick says he feels as if he knows Miss Natalie because Alex speaks of her so often, and so highly."

Adeleine's eyes bored into Margaret's for a long moment. Margaret could practically see her sister-in-law's thoughts—she was afraid her daughter was going to be ruined before she even had a single season. Like her aunt.

Though, to be fair, Margaret had enjoyed three seasons before she had been ruined.

Adeleine nodded faintly, then smiled brightly at Mr. Eddington. "That is good to hear. And oh! Perhaps you would consider attending Natalie's practice ball as well? It will be held right here in our music room in a month's time."

"I would be honored," he replied, his hand going to his chest. "And on the subject of invitations, I came to dinner tonight with my own." His blue eyes slid from Adeleine to Margaret, and a small smile formed on his lips.

"Oh?" Margaret said, taking a sip of sweet red wine, the tide of her contemplation ebbing as a warmer wave washed in.

He grinned, then stifled the expression and cleared his throat. "For all of you. My sister and her children are coming to stay with me for several weeks, and I was hoping to persuade the three of you, along with Miss Natalie and Alex, to join us."

"Like a house party?" Margaret asked, carefully setting her glass on the table.

"A small one," Mr. Eddington acknowledged. "It would just be our two families. I've written to my friend James Fitzsimmons and your cousin Lady Cecilia to invite them as well, but I believe they are otherwise occupied."

Margaret grinned, slicing her roasted chicken and savoring the salty, meaty aroma. Cecilia had recently wed Mr. Fitzsimmons in what was supposed to be a marriage of convenience, but it had turned into a genuine love match. They were spending the summer visiting family and enjoying their new life together.

"My sister has five children, and the oldest girl is about Miss Natalie's age," Mr. Eddington continued over the clinking of silverware against plates. "Since Alex is already friends with my eldest nephew, we thought perhaps the younger ones would enjoy spending some time together while we of a certain age enjoy each other's company."

"That sounds like a capital idea," Philip said, brandishing his fork with enthusiasm. "I don't believe we'll be able to stay, not with all the preparations we must make before we travel to London after the practice ball. But your home is an easy ride, particularly when the weather is fine, and we may be able to join you some days."

Adeleine was smiling as well, but the warmth had begun to seep out of Margaret's body. "I– I'm not sure—"

"My sister has asked for you especially, Miss Maitland," Mr. Eddington replied before she could finish her thought, his voice softer now as he pinned Margaret with his gaze once again. "She wants to meet the mother of her son's best friend."

"Oh, of– of course... And I would be pleased to meet her as well..."

Mr. Eddington smiled broadly. If he heard the hesitation in Margaret's voice, he ignored it. "Wonderful! My sister will be the hostess, of course, and she'll send round the details when she arrives next week."

He turned back to his plate, fairly beaming at his food and, alternately, his companions for the duration of the meal. Margaret found the previously delicious fare chewy and tasteless, and only picked at her entree until they left the table for the drawing room. She tried to focus on the conversations going on around her, but had no luck there either.

When finally Mr. Eddington decided to return home, Margaret jumped up from her chair. "I should also take my leave."

"I'll see you to the gate if I may," he replied, catching her eye.

Margaret nodded her assent. This was their custom if they both happened to be dining with Philip and Adeleine, and it was interesting that he still asked after nearly a year of acquaintance rather than just assuming.

What was he going to say when she refused his invitation?

Neither of them spoke as they made their way through the house and out onto the long drive awash in the reds and oranges of the setting sun. But three steps from the house, she couldn't keep it in any longer.

"Mr. Eddington, are you certain about inviting me to your home, to meet your sister?" she asked, laying a hand on his arm to stop him. A lone songbird serenaded them from a nearby tree as if he had no cares in the world.

"Of course I am," he replied quickly. His brows crowded down low over his eyes. "Why would you ask me that?"

She pressed her lips together, trying to discern just the right words to convey the absolute inappropriateness of her presence in a respectable home. "You know that I raised my son without the help of his father."

Mr. Eddington nodded slowly. "Yes."

"And you also know why."

He nodded again, glancing at her feet for a moment before meeting her eyes once again. Not long after they first met, Margaret had outlined the bare bones of the story —how she had become pregnant without being married and, rather than hide her condition and give the baby to another family to raise, she had elected to keep him, to raise him herself.

It had destroyed her reputation, of course. And though there were a select few people who would now receive her privately in their homes all these years later, Margaret was still not welcome at even the most obscure society functions.

Margaret's voice was rough when she spoke again. "I truly would like to meet your sister, but I am afraid that even after twenty years my reputation would tarnish hers."

"And, in turn, my nieces' reputations as well," he added quietly.

Margaret turned and began to walk down the drive, clasping her hands together behind her back to keep from taking his arm as she often did. She wanted to, but it didn't feel like the right thing to do at this moment. "Exactly so."

"What about your own niece?" he asked, falling into step beside her. He, too, refrained from touching her, which was both a relief and a disappointment somehow. "Does she not suffer from your connection?"

"It's easier for people to overlook a rogue family member when the Duke of Alston is her cousin."

"Mmm. I suppose it's the same for your son as well."

She kicked a small rock to the side. "The stigma is a bit less because he's a man, but yes. Influential relatives outweigh a fallen mother for him some of the time."

They walked along in silence down the length of the drive, accompanied only by the rhythmic crunching of gravel beneath their feet, and Margaret felt some of the tension in her shoulders easing. She feared that she would have to explain to him the details of her situation to make him understand how bad it had been for the family and friends that had supported her, that still supported her.

But he didn't protest any further. When they arrived at the gate, he tipped his hat to her as he always did and held the gate open for her to pass through.

"Good evening, Miss Maitland," he said. His voice was even, and he met her eyes, so perhaps there were no hard feelings.

"Good evening, Mr. Eddington."

A week later later, Stephen rode back to Philip Maitland's home, Eastwood Manor, with two things in his saddle bag: his copy of *Observations on the Theory and Practice of Landscape Gardening* that he'd promised to lend to Philip, and a note for Miss Margaret Maitland from his sister, who was more than a little disappointed to hear that Miss Maitland had turned down the house party invitation.

Hopefully, both things would be well received.

"Eddington—what a nice surprise," Philip said, rising as Stephen was shown into the library by the Maitlands' butler. "Adeleine was wondering earlier about your house party activities, and here you are to ask."

"Ah yes," Stephen replied, taking his usual seat in a sturdy walnut chair. "My sister arrived yesterday with her children, and she is writing up a list. Everything is to be rather informal, but she'll send the details round when she's sorted it all out."

"Excellent," Philip answered, taking his own seat in a chair that had begun its life as the twin of Stephen's but had seen much more wear. "You must thank her for thinking of us, and of Natalie in particular."

"I will do that." Stephen fished around in his inner coat pocket and came up with the note he'd been tasked with delivering. "She also sent along a note for your own sister. Will you pass it along to her the next time she's here?"

Philip waved the note away. "You can give it to her yourself before you depart. She's with Adeleine now walking in the gardens, but they should be returning soon for luncheon."

"Oh." Well, that was unexpected. Though Stephen supposed it shouldn't be—Miss Maitland was frequently here when he was. "Well, that's perfect timing, then. Perhaps I can take an answer home with me today."

Their conversation drifted to other topics, including the book Stephen had brought, and an hour or so later Mrs. Maitland bustled in with a bright smile for her husband.

"I hope you're hungry," she said, touching his shoulder lightly. "Our cook has been experimenting with some new recipes, and there's a mountain of food. You'll stay and taste them all, won't you Mr. Eddington?"

Stephen pulled his gold pocket watch from the custom pocket in his waistcoat. "I'm afraid I cannot, Mrs. Maitland," he answered with real regret. The Maitlands' cook always created the most delicious dishes. "I promised my sister that I would help her with a few things this afternoon. I really only came by to give this note to your sister-in-law."

He produced the note again with Miss Maitland's name written in flowing script on the outside, and Mrs. Maitland nodded.

"Margaret stayed a few more minutes in the garden nearest the house. You can deliver your sister's note to her there if you'd like."

Wonderful—perhaps she could spare a moment to speak with him, too, away from any listening ears. "I believe I will do that. Thank you," Stephen said with a little bow to Mrs. Maitland. "Thank you both."

Eastwood Manor wasn't overly large by aristocratic standards, and he found Miss Maitland with little trouble. She was seemingly lost in thought, admiring a stone statue that appeared to be of a roe deer as the wind tousled the curly brown hair that had managed to escape her bonnet, and Stephen cleared his throat.

"Oh, Mr. Eddington," she said, turning quickly toward him. "What a lovely surprise."

He tried desperately not to react, but he couldn't help the grin that spread across his face. He was a lovely surprise, was he?

"I am here mostly on behalf of my sister," he said, handing her the note Caroline had written. "She would like you to reconsider your attendance at her house party."

Miss Maitland accepted the note and took several moments to read it over. Then her hazel eyes met his. "Do you know what this says?"

Stephen shook his head, shifting his weight from one foot to the other. "Caroline didn't tell me exactly, only that she was disappointed you declined her invitation."

"She talks about how I can't ruin her reputation, how she's the daughter of a master builder married to the fifth son of an inconsequential gentleman, and no one in society even knows she exists," Miss Maitland explained.

"That is all true," Stephen replied, clasping his hands behind his back just to get them out of his way. "One or two society folks may know she exists, as they are aware I have a sister. But she has no dealings with them."

"I see." Miss Maitland's gaze traveled back to the note as a stiff breeze blew through, and she grasped it firmly with both hands. "She also says that she would very much appreciate my company and that of my son."

Stephen nodded, even though she wasn't looking at him. "Caroline has been looking forward to having another woman of a similar age to talk to. And Patrick has been making lists of all the things he wants to show your son while they are here together."

Miss Maitland met his eyes again with a small smile. "Alex may go, of course, and stay until you tire of him."

"And you?" Her mouth turned down and Stephen quickly added, "If you don't feel comfortable staying at my home, you're welcome to come for as many or as few activities as you'd like, or to not come at all. The decision is yours to make."

She pressed her lips together as her eyes searched his face. Even the birds seemed to hold their collective breath, quietly waiting for her answer.

After a long moment, she exhaled slowly. "Might I have a day to think it over?"

"Yes, of course. But don't place more importance on this party than it warrants." He resisted the urge to reach out and touch her, though for some reason it took considerable willpower. "The point of this house party is for our two families to enjoy each others' company for a while, to enjoy having Patrick and Alex with us, and that's all. If that sounds like a pleasant way to spend your time, come. If it doesn't, we will see each other another time."

He was mentally berating himself for adding the last part—perhaps she didn't care if she saw him again—when she smiled faintly. It could have been his imagination, for it was gone as quickly as it appeared, but Stephen didn't think so.

"All right," she said, her voice maddeningly neutral. "I will be here tomorrow helping Adeleine and Natalie prepare for Natalie's next outing. If our paths don't cross, I'll send a note with a footman to your home."

They said their goodbyes and Stephen made his way back to the Maitland stables for his horse. Would she attend? Would she stay in his home?

Stephen couldn't come up with a believable reason to visit Philip Maitland again the next day, so he remained at home, catching up with his sister, playing games with his nieces and nephews, trying not to listen for a knock at the door.

When a footman in Maitland livery did finally arrive, Stephen's stomach did a little flip as he accepted the note with his name printed neatly upon it.

*Dear Mr. Eddington,*

*On behalf of my son and myself, I thank you and your sister for the invitation to your house party. We are both pleased to attend for the duration. If your sister needs any help making arrangements, I am happy to assist her.*

*Margaret Maitland*

"Caroline! She's coming!"

Caroline was at the front door with him a few moments later, clapping her hands together. "Wonderful! I'm so glad she changed her mind."

"I am too," he answered, scanning the note again.

He wasn't quite sure when it had happened, but sometime in the recent past Stephen had resolved to get to know Miss Maitland better. He was her brother's friend, after all, and they met often at Eastwood Manor.

Perhaps this house party was their chance to develop a relationship independent of their mutual connection.

# Chapter 2

On the appointed day, Margaret arrived at Mr. Eddington's home with her son, brother, and niece. Adeleine was feeling unwell, and decided to remain at home to rest. The carriage pulled smoothly up the circular drive and Margaret took the opportunity to stare before she put on her polite company demeanor. It was a modest house for a gentleman—two stories of gleaming red brick, an attic with a gray slate roof, and a few well-placed brick embellishments. Smaller in size than her brother's home, but with an air of understated charm.

The carriage came to a stop in front of the large, white front door just as a man and woman came out of the house and down the stone steps. The man was Mr. Eddington, dressed in a perfectly tailored forest green tailcoat, buff breeches, and shiny black top boots. The woman, who bore a marked resemblance to Mr. Eddington from the sandy brown hair and tall frame right down to the slightly crooked smile, wore a pink day dress with white lace flounces around the bottom.

They both stood back while one footman began gathering Margaret and Alex's baggage from the back of the carriage, and another let down the carriage steps and opened the door. Philip climbed out after Alex and offered his hand to his daughter, then to Margaret as they exited the carriage.

"Welcome," Mr. Eddington said when everyone had their feet firmly on the ground. He shook hands with Philip and Alex, and bowed swiftly to Margaret and Natalie. "Allow me to present my sister, Mrs. Gates. Caroline, this is Mr. Maitland…"

She offered her hand to Philip, who bowed over it politely. "A pleasure, madam."

"…Miss Maitland…"

Mrs. Gates smiled brightly at Margaret. "I'm so pleased you could join us."

Margaret found her enthusiasm charming and couldn't help but smile back. "So am I. It's lovely to meet you."

Alex and Natalie were both presented as well, then Mr. Eddington told them that Mrs. Gates's children were preparing to go fishing and where to find them. With silent assent from their respective parents, Alex and Natalie headed off to go find their companions. The two footmen gathered up the baggage and began carrying things into the house, and Philip and Mr. Eddington, already deep in conversation, followed slowly behind. That left Mrs. Gates and Margaret alone beside the carriage.

"How do you feel about gardens?" Mrs. Gates asked in a cheery voice. "There are four here, and each one has things I've never seen before."

"Wonderful," Margaret grinned. "My brother likes to call me the family's non-farming plant enthusiast, so I would love to see them."

The sun shone warmly overhead, and Mrs. Gates shaded her eyes. "Would you like to rest and refresh yourself first?"

Margaret shook her head. "It was just a short ride. Since the weather is fine, shall we spend some time in one of the gardens?"

Mrs. Gates linked her arm with Margaret's and led her around the side of the house. "This is a bit forward, as we've only just met, but I do hope you'll call me Caroline. With as much as my son and brother talk about you, I feel like I know you already."

Her son *and* her brother? Margaret expected the eldest Gates lad to know a bit about her, of course, as her own son's closest friend. But Mr. Eddington talked about her too?

Interesting.

Margaret ignored the little flutter in her stomach and focused on Caroline. "Then you must call me Margaret," she replied, trying to contain her excitement. Most of Margaret's friends had abandoned her twenty years ago when the rumor of her pregnancy was confirmed to be true. The few that maintained contact had gradually drifted away as their lives became very different from hers.

Perhaps this could be the start of something good, then.

Caroline practically hugged Margaret's arm. "Splendid! There is also something I would appreciate your help with, if you please."

"And what's that?"

Caroline loosened her hold a bit as the pair began to head toward the closest of the gardens. "My brother has held this property for nearly a year now, yet it has no name."

"Oh?"

"The previous owner never bothered to name it, and Stephen is more interested in how things run." Caroline swept her arm wide indicating the land around them. "I'm hoping that as we get to know this place, you and I can come up with a fitting name for it."

That was not something Margaret had ever been asked to do before, and she didn't quite know how to feel about the task. Naming a home was a rather intimate affair and, while she'd known Mr. Eddington for about a year now, they had never shared more than spirited conversation. But Caroline's bright eyes and wide smile suggested she was looking forward to tackling this challenge with her new friend.

"I bet we can," Margaret replied, her eyes sweeping over the verdant landscape. "Let's begin our investigation, shall we?"

Though it wasn't overly large, they spent the next few hours slowly exploring the garden closest to the house with its manicured lawn, its perfectly sculpted shrubbery, its stately old roses, talking and laughing as they shared stories and became better acquainted. They were still there when their flock of children returned with a respectable string of pungent fish carried proudly by the youngest Gates, who was quick to tell his mother all about how he'd been the most prolific of the bunch.

Caroline shot a look at Margaret that said, "back to reality" and took her youngest two by the hands, trying to listen to everyone talk at once. Alex sidled up beside her in Caroline's place, grinning.

"Did you have a nice time today?" she asked her son, tilting her head back slightly to meet his eyes. He looked more and more like his father every day, and Margaret felt a pang in her heart for what could have been.

"I did," he answered, offering his arm like a proper gentleman. "It was nice to be part of a big family for a while."

A thought popped out of Margaret's mouth before she could rein it in. "Did you ever wish you had siblings, Alex?"

She heard the wistfulness in her own voice and was not surprised when he took her hand and squeezed it. "Sometimes I did wonder what it would be like to have brothers and sisters. But then whenever I spend time with large families, like today, I'm very thankful that I was able to find peace and quiet, and time to myself when I needed it."

Margaret managed to partially suppress a smile and took her son's arm as they turned toward the house. "That was a very diplomatic answer."

"I know," he chuckled. Then he became a bit more serious. "But it was also the truth."

"You're a good lad."

He stopped walking and turned to her, studying her face. "Is all well with you, Mama? You haven't seemed like yourself since I arrived home."

"I haven't?" She was genuinely surprised to hear his assessment of her. She'd certainly been a bit deep in her memories lately like a man in his cups, but she hadn't thought anyone had noticed.

"No, you seem... You're quieter than usual, more contemplative."

She brushed a hand across his cheek. "I've missed you, that's all. Then you come home the very image of your father at that age..." She let her voice trail off, not knowing how to explain the painful happiness of a lost love to a young man who had not yet experienced it for himself. "I have been thinking about how different things could have been, but it's time to put that behind me now. We have plenty to look forward to."

"Including fish for supper," he said with a wink and steered them toward the house once more. "Patrick said that we're to have strawberries and cream for dessert, too."

Margaret grinned up at her son. "Now that is something to look forward to!"

Alex and Patrick, who were adults in truth and certainly old enough to eat in the dining room, had elected to spend the rest of the evening with the younger ones eating their catch, so Stephen and Philip met the ladies in the drawing room for a few minutes before going in to dinner rather informally. Stephen ended up sitting beside Miss Maitland, and the looks she shared with his sister across the table warmed his heart. Caroline didn't have many friends outside her own family, but it looked as though she may have a new one before this house party was over.

"You two clearly enjoyed your afternoon together," he remarked, glancing from Caroline to Miss Maitland.

Miss Maitland grinned. "We did." She took a bite of roasted potato and chewed thoughtfully. "It was wonderful to talk with someone who had some of the same experiences I've had. And the formal garden nearest the house is beautiful. What have you and my brother been up to?"

"The usual," Stephen said with an answering smile. "We mostly talked about farming techniques we might or might not try next year. Absolutely stimulating."

She put a hand to her mouth, but he noticed her giggle before she covered it.

"Adeleine has said that Philip speaks much less of farming to her since you took up residence here," Miss Maitland explained, "and for that you should receive a knighthood. The only two things Philip loves as much as his family are farming and politics."

"His love of farming has been extremely helpful to me," Stephen replied sincerely. "I learned how to construct a sturdy wall when I was a lad, but making things grow is not something I understood well. Your brother and my steward have taught me a tremendous amount in the past year."

"Philip is a good man to have around when you need support," she said softly, glancing across the table at her brother before spearing another piece of potato.

Stephen stared at his plate for a moment, continuing to cut and eat his food without tasting it, not knowing what to say. He knew that Philip Maitland had been instrumental in Alex's upbringing, but was unsure how to respond to such a serious statement from a woman he wasn't overly close to.

She saved him from the awkwardness a moment later. "I'm sorry, Mr. Eddington. That was perhaps more sentiment than is called for over dinner with one's neighbor."

"Not at all," he said, releasing a breath. "It's never wrong to heap praise upon someone who deserves it."

Her expression relaxed, as did her fingers which held her fork, and they spoke of more mundane things for a while. But there was one thing he had been wanting to ask her for some time now, and dinner in his own home seemed like the perfect opportunity.

"Will you call me Stephen? At least while you are here?"

She chewed slowly before answering. "Yes," she said with confidence. "If you will call me Margaret."

He bowed slightly from his chair. "It would be my pleasure, Margaret."

She offered him a stately nod. "And mine, Stephen."

The usual small talk permeated the rest of the meal, with the exception of Caroline telling the story about how Stephen's absolute best friend when he was nine years old had been a red squirrel that lived in a tree near their home, and at the conclusion of the last course the ladies elected to have their after dinner conversation in the drawing room.

"I know you will be departing soon," Stephen said to Philip, rising from the table, "but I have an excellent port if you'd like a glass."

"A fine idea," Philip replied, stretching as he stood. "That will give Natalie a bit more time with your nieces and nephews."

They settled in Stephen's library with their glasses of the sweet liquid, Stephen in the old green chair with fraying upholstery and Philip on the sofa near one of the tall windows. The fire that had burned in the grate that morning had been allowed to go out as the temperature rose outside, and a slight smokiness permeated the room.

"I'm going to ask you an impertinent question now that the women are out of hearing," Philip said as he looked around the room. "Why have you never married?"

That caught Stephen off guard. "What? Why?"

"You mentioned this afternoon wanting to be included in the more exclusive circles of society, and not for the first time." Philip added. "One way to do that is to marry into one. I was just thinking that it might be time for you to consider such a course of action."

"Oh, of course." Stephen consciously took a breath in and let it out. "For a moment I thought you had turned into my mother, insisting that it's time I found a wife and gave her grandchildren."

Philip's eyes went round. "Not me. I was lucky enough to meet Adeleine when we were young, and we've had so many happy years together. But I would never tell a grown man what to do with his life. It was merely a suggestion."

"A tried and true one, at that," Stephen replied, his voice and body relaxing into comfort once again. This was a thought he'd had many times himself. "A woman takes her social status from her husband, of course, but a wife's well-placed family members could introduce a man to the right people."

"That's it exactly," Philip said, gesturing with his glass. "You've done an admirable job of improving your circumstances, but if you want to be involved in government and politics, you need to know the right people and know them well. Adeleine's family was an enormous help when I stood for election."

Stephen laughed into his port. "Yes, because you, the cousin of a *duke*, were so very unknown."

Philip chuckled, too. "Third cousin," he clarified. "But yes, my own family name certainly opened some doors. It didn't hurt that I'm on good terms with my titled relations, either. You don't have that arrow in your quiver, though."

No, he didn't. The Eddington name didn't exactly carry a lot of weight in the circles Stephen hoped to one day travel in. If anything, it was a hindrance. "But a wife from the right family could mitigate my own genealogical shortcomings."

"You'll never work for the Prime Minister," Philip said, leaning against the back of the sofa. "You're over forty years of age. In addition to your parentage, you're far too old to be starting out in government—you'll be competing against younger men who have better connections. But you could eventually be appointed to a position that carries a great deal of influence."

Stephen was silent, soaking in those words. Could he reach so high? Even with the help of a wife from a "good" family, it would be difficult. It would be nigh on impossible with anyone else.

"I believe I could live with that," Stephen finally said, taking a large swallow of port. The change he could affect in such a position! Not nearly that of Philip's cousin, naturally, but far more than any Eddington had managed before him.

How much good could he do in the world with a position like that?

They talked abstractly about different positions that might suit Stephen, different families with eligible ladies, before Philip took his leave with promises to return the following day for the next slate of activities. But Stephen couldn't think about the house party, or anything else, for the rest of the evening. Philip Maitland thought he could rise to a high government position, if only he could find the right woman to wed.

His heart thudded as he recalled Margaret debating him over various things during dinner at Eastwood House, taking his arm as they walked toward the gate as they departed. His whole body warmed as he remembered all the times she'd touched him, leaned in closer to share an inside joke with him.

Then Stephen sighed deeply. Margaret, with her reputation, was certainly not the right woman to help him navigate the Beau Monde.

"We're practicing archery this morning, Aunt Margaret," Natalie exclaimed when she and her father arrived the next day.

Margaret was seated at an escritoire in Stephen's morning room writing a letter as sunshine streamed in through the nearby window. She set her pen on the blotter to greet her niece. "Yes, and the butts are to be set up in Mr. Eddington's garden of exotic and unusual plants."

"Well, that will be interesting for you," Natalie replied brightly. "If you get tired of shooting arrows, you can study the plants.

Margaret smothered a chuckle as they headed out to the designated site. She was intrigued by a garden full of unusual plants and could undoubtedly spend many days examining them.

As they walked out, she trailed along behind the crowd, taking in the absolute beauty of the place. The sun was shining in a brilliant blue sky, casting its warm rays over the lush green grass and the multitude of plants that she'd never seen outside of botany texts.

"Did you sleep well last night?" Caroline asked, coming up beside her.

"Like I didn't have a care in the world," Margaret answered with a contented sigh. "I can't remember the last time I was that comfortable, even in my own bed."

"Excellent," Caroline replied, linking her arm with Margaret's as they walked. "Perhaps you'd enjoy a bit of competition, then?"

Margaret turned to look at her companion. "Competition? You mean at archery?"

Caroline nodded and Stephen's voice piped up from behind them, "It's not too late, Philip—your sister hasn't agreed to anything yet."

"What am I about to agree to?" Margaret asked him, noting her brother on Stephen's other side.

Stephen drew even with the two women and slowed to keep pace with them. "Caroline is about to suggest that the two of you could easily shoot better than the two of us, and that we could make things interesting with a little wager."

Caroline grinned. "I wasn't going to suggest a wager, but that is a fine idea."

"I suppose you weren't going to suggest an amount, either?" Stephen asked warily.

Philip shook his head. "Not money. I want to win the ability to do something..."

"Or to make someone else do something," Margaret finished with a grateful glace at her brother. She had some money of her own, but did not possess the fortunes that the other three did.

"I haven't scheduled any activities for Saturday yet," Caroline said, meeting Margaret's eyes and winking.

"Perhaps the winning team could choose how we spend our time that day, then," Margaret finished for her.

Philip rolled his eyes but they were twinkling when he spoke. "You were wrong, Eddington—it *is* too late."

Stephen's gaze shifted from his sister to Margaret and lingered there for a moment before he answered. "I don't see any way around it, then. We're going to have to accept the challenge."

"And be gracious in our victory, of course," Philip said with a chuckle.

"Your victory," Margaret snorted. "We'll just see, won't we?"

When they arrived at the archery butts the servants had set up, the children were already selecting bows and arrows, and arguing over who was going to shoot at which target. The adults took up their equipment and paired off, with Caroline and Margaret choosing the last target in the line and Stephen and Philip setting up next to them.

"Five practice shots, then we start," Caroline announced. Then, quietly, she said to Margaret, "You have done this before, haven't you?"

"Oh yes," Margaret answered with relish. "Philip and I took lessons with the same archery master when we were children. Much to his chagrin, I was as good as he was, though I am three years younger."

"Wait," Stephen called, holding both his hands out in a "stop" gesture. "How are we going to hold each team accountable?"

Philip's mouth turned down in a hard frown. "Is not our honor good enough?"

Caroline made a little waving motion with one hand. "It's me he's worried about, Mr. Maitland, not you or Margaret. Once, when I was very young, I miscounted the number of points I'd scored in some game, and Stephen has brought it up each and every time we are involved in something competitive."

Philip still looked unsettled at the idea of labeling a lady as a cheat, but Margaret had a very sensible way to resolve the problem. "All right then, why don't Mr. Eddington and I use this target? Philip, you and Caroline can use that one. The sexes are separated, as are the sibling pairs."

Stephen's eyes fixed on hers and they shared a... A moment? A thought?

A wish?

Whatever it was, the connection was broken when he looked away to gather up his bow and arrows. "Yes, I think that will do nicely."

Caroline and Stephen switched positions, and Margaret's heart fluttered as he came toward her. But she gave herself a mental shake and tried to relax her body. It was just a game, and she was merely shooting a bow at the same target as her neighbor, her brother's friend. Nothing more.

Unless...

"Thank you for sharing some of your good sense with us, Margaret," Stephen said in a voice only loud enough for her to hear. "Caroline and I are close in age, and did many things together as children."

Margaret offered him a knowing smile. "So you have a long history of watching each other carefully so there are no unfair advantages. Philip and I have a similar relationship."

"I would trust my sister with my very life," Stephen told her, taking a step closer.

"But not with the scoring of a game," Margaret added, the corners of her mouth turning up slightly. "Yes, Philip and I are much the same, and so is my son with his cousins."

Stephen chuckled, leaning on his bow as if it were a walking stick. "A common sentiment among family members, then. I just didn't want you to think..."

His voice trailed off and it was Margaret's turn to step closer. "That you were some kind of scoundrel with no honor? No," she shook her head, as the gentle breeze tousled the loose strands of her hair. "If that were the case, neither Philip nor Adeleine would have ever invited you into their home, let alone ask you to return... How many times?"

"Scores," he replied, the corners of his eyes crinkling up with his smile.

"Well, there you are. My brother and his wife are good, proper people," she said, laying her fingers on his arm for the briefest of touches. "Though they make an exception for me, of course."

Why did she say that? If she could have taken those last words back, she would have immediately. Margaret thought she'd done away with the self-deprecating jokes years ago, as they tended to draw more attention to her situation rather than lighten the mood.

But apparently not.

"That is where you're wrong—you need no exception," Stephen told her quietly. He dropped his eyes to fish around in the pile for an arrow he liked, then met her gaze again, though the intensity and solemnity they had just shared blew away in the light wind. "Shall we?" He asked, gesturing with his arrow toward their target.

"Yes," she answered smoothly, "I think we'd better before we fall behind."

She watched as Stephen took his practice shots, meticulous about his aim and grip on both the bow and arrow, not letting the arrow fly until he was sure everything was satisfactory. Had he been as deliberate when he said she needed no exception to be included in her brother's proper household?

Did he believe her to be a respectable lady despite her past?

Margaret shoved that thought right out of her mind. She was here to seek out the possibility of new friendships, full stop. There was no point in following any other path when it would only lead to humiliation and heartbreak.

After dinner that evening, Stephen and Philip elected not to go off on their own, but joined the ladies in the drawing room.

"No Natalie tonight?" Stephen asked as he took a seat beside Margaret on a hard sofa. He needed to have a word with his housekeeper, or possibly his sister, about replacing the awful thing with something worth sitting on.

"She had a marvelous time this afternoon," Philip answered from his chair opposite the sofa, "but her mother needed her at home this evening."

Margaret sipped her sherry. "I believe they were studying rules of etiquette."

Stephen groaned. "That brings back some memories I'd rather forget."

"For me, too," Margaret said with a chuckle. "Adeleine tries to explain the circumstances rules are meant for, which seems to help Natalie."

"What helps Natalie?" a young man asked.

The joy that overcame Margaret at the sight of her son was palpable. Alex followed Caroline and her eldest son into the room, and Margaret was positively luminous. "Alex! And Patrick! I thought you were spending time with the younger ones."

Alex settled himself on a settee that creaked slightly under his weight. "We decided our time would be better spent with adults this evening."

Caroline sat in the chair beside Philip and practically cackled. "Tired, are you?"

Patrick forwent the creaky settee and brought another chair over from near the fireplace. He sat down in it with a sigh. "Yes. Uncle Stephen, if you ever have children of your own, make sure you have plenty of people to help you take care of them."

"Fortunately, you have your mother, father, a governess, and a nurse to help you take care of your brothers and sisters," Stephen quipped, picking up his glass of port. He didn't take a drink, but he felt as if he needed to do something with his hands.

Alex, thankfully, jumped in and changed the subject. "So who won your archery wager?"

"Oh yes! And what are we doing on Saturday?" Patrick chimed in.

"Believe it or not, it was a draw," Margaret answered, resting her sherry glass carefully on her knee. "So we have to come up with something that all four of us would enjoy."

The conversation turned to different activities they could do in an afternoon from riding to painting to just having an afternoon with nothing planned, and Stephen found his mind wandering. He didn't much care what was planned or not planned, he was simply enjoying spending time with his family and friends.

And perhaps taking advantage of their knowledge.

"Margaret, might I ask a favor of you?" he said, leaning slightly toward her as the others continued to talk around them.

"Certainly," she replied. "How can I be of service?"

Was it his imagination or was that the faintest hint of perfume he detected? He didn't recall her wearing any fragrances for dinners with her brother. "The garden we were in this afternoon is where the previous owner placed exotic specimens and interesting plants that could thrive in our climate."

"Oh yes," Margaret said, her eyes bright. "I noticed some stunning hydrangeas by the statue of Atalanta."

There was only one statue in that garden, and Stephen pictured the white flowers that clumped almost in spheres that evoked the feeling of snowballs even as the sun shone warmly overhead. "Is that what those are?"

She grinned. "Yes. Is that what you need help with? Identifying plants?"

"It is," he said, taking a drink of his port. "Caroline mentioned that you were the Maitland interested in non-farming plants, and I was hoping that while you were here…"

"I would love to," she said when his voice trailed off.

"Marvelous," he said, relief flooding through him. "Neither my head gardener nor his assistant know what most of the plants are in that garden, nor how to take care of them. The previous owner apparently handled that area himself, and would sometimes issue orders but never explained anything to them."

Margaret glanced at the others in the room and must have been satisfied by what she saw, for her shoulders relaxed when she turned back to him. "I have some botany texts at home that may be of help. Perhaps we can walk over one day this week and collect them."

"I appreciate whatever knowledge you have to share," he told her, stifling the urge to punctuate his point by taking her hand. He'd never done such a thing before, nor had it ever occurred to him, but for some reason he very much wanted to now.

"How does that sound to you?" Caroline asked, breaking his thoughts and bringing him back to the larger conversation.

"How does what sound?" he asked cheerfully.

Caroline lifted one eyebrow briefly, but continued on serenely, "Mr. Maitland and I thought an afternoon in the village would be a good way to spend Saturday."

"We can do some shopping, purchase some treats," Philip added. "And I heard that the blacksmith has a litter of puppies who will be weaned soon."

Patrick grinned at the mention of puppies and Stephen winked at his sister. "We'll definitely have to see the puppies."

"I think it's a splendid idea," Margaret said, and Stephen saw her shoot him a look he couldn't quite identify. "Shall we take the little ones or do you think they'd be better off here with their nurse?"

"Do we have enough conveyances for everyone?" Stephen asked. An adult could walk into the village from his home, but it was a long walk and the smaller children wouldn't be able to manage it.

The six of them discussed details, but Stephen was only partially participating in the conversation. With Margaret's enthusiastic agreement to help him identify the unknown plants in his garden—and also because this was an excellent opportunity to do something nice for her in general—he was trying to decide how to repay the favor. His first thought was manual labor, but she lived in the dower house on her brother's estate and Philip had mentioned once or twice that she had her own small staff. Stephen didn't know her exact financial situation, but he gathered that she didn't need help there either.

Perhaps he could find a gift for her when they made their trip into the village in a few days. Did she work outside in her own garden? Was she fond of pastries? Would she appreciate a book or a handkerchief or puppy?

He stopped himself from physically shaking his head since he was surrounded by people, but he was stumped. Margaret Maitland was not one to tell all to anyone except those who were closest to her, and perhaps not even them. He would simply have to pay more attention to the thoughts and feelings she did express.

# Chapter 4

It took three carriages to transport them all to the
village, and they must have looked like a swarming horde
of locusts descending upon the blacksmith's forge: Stephen,
Philip and Adeleine with Natalie, Caroline and her five
children, Alex, and finally Margaret, who allowed her son
to help her down then discreetly stretched her legs and
back. The distance from Stephen's home to the village was
only a few miles, but the older she grew the less
comfortable traveling any distance became.

The younger children were given strict instructions to
remain with at least one person over the age of sixteen at
all times, then the horde dispersed and the carriage drivers
guided their vehicles away. Margaret stood alone and
looked about her in mild disbelief. One would never know
that the people of three separate households had overrun
the place just moments ago.

But all was quiet now and she breathed deeply, filling
her lungs to capacity before slowly exhaling. The smell of
horses and metal permeated the air when she faced the
forge, but she could detect baking bread and grass when
she turned toward the village center. Children were playing
in the distance, artfully dodging adults to retrieve their ball
when it rolled away into the dirt road.

Where should she go? She'd been pondering that
question since they'd agreed to make this trip, yet was still
unsure. Some shops she knew to stay away from—the

dressmaker who wouldn't allow her to even walk through the door, the tea shop where they would happily take her money but snicker and whisper behind her back, the milliner who apologized profusely while explaining that Margaret's presence would drive away too many of her customers.

It all felt petty and mean-spirited after all these years, but Margaret didn't waste energy fighting their decisions now, as she hadn't when her son was born. She was extremely fortunate in the support of her family, both emotional and financial, and simply took her business elsewhere.

Like to the baker who made the most divine shortbread this side of Hadrian's Wall.

"Miss Maitland!" he exclaimed when she entered the shop. "What a pleasant surprise! Oh, and you're just in time —I took a batch of shortbread out of the oven just moments ago."

Margaret couldn't help but rub her hands together with anticipation. She could practically taste the buttery confection just from the smell of the bakery alone. "Mr. Ralston, it's lovely to see you again. How is Mrs. Ralston?"

"She's very well, thank you for asking," he replied, his smile becoming tight. "She asked me to thank you for sending over all those newspapers. They have been her main form of entertainment for the past fortnight, and she's very grateful to have them."

Hmm. If Mrs. Ralston was spending all her time reading rather than her usual knitting, her arthritis must be paining her more than usual. Margaret made a mental note to send her maid over to the Ralstons to help with the household work and whatever else they might need.

She stayed for several minutes to talk with Mr. Ralston a bit more, and to purchase her weight in shortbread, then said her goodbyes and decided to visit the bookshop down the way. Between the financial support of her brother and her cousin Cecilia, Margaret's needs were more than met and she had enough pin money to purchase a few luxuries each month. Books were normally not among them, as she had Philip's entire library to choose from, but her choice of reading material didn't always align with his.

She entered the shop quietly, nodding to a patron in a plain yellow dress who passed her. Margaret saw the woman's eyes widen and watched her immediately rush to another part of the room.

*Blast.*

Would she draw attention to herself if she turned right around and left the shop? Or should she casually circumnavigate the shelves then slip out? Margaret didn't recognize the woman who'd walked past her, but she'd seen that expression too many times before.

"Miss Maitland?"

Margaret turned to find the owner of the shop standing just in front of the woman in yellow. *Too late.*

"Miss Margaret Maitland?"

"Yes, I am Margaret Maitland." There was an edge to her voice that she attempted to soften, but was not entirely successful in doing so.

The owner cleared his throat. "Then I'm afraid I'm going to have to ask you to leave."

Margaret's jaw clenched. "For what reason? I've only just come in. I haven't even had a chance to look at anything yet."

"You know the reason," the owner answered, lowering his voice.

The woman in yellow crossed her arms and cocked one eyebrow as if to challenge Margaret, to goad her into some inappropriate reaction. But Margaret only rolled her eyes. She opened her mouth to speak but was startled to hear a familiar voice only steps behind her.

"Did you just tell this lady to leave?" Stephen asked, coming to a halt beside her. He was tall and broad and glowering at the shop owner.

Margaret's heartbeat thudded in her ears and all she could do was stare dumbly at her neighbor.

"I did," the shop owner said, dropping the volume of his voice another notch. "This is a respectable business, and people like her are not welcome here."

"Is that what *you* think, or what this one told you to think?" Stephen asked gruffly, nodding in the direction of the woman in yellow. "Is there nothing in your past that people might judge you for if they knew about it?"

The shop owner had the grace to blush and look down at his feet for the briefest of moments, but when the woman in yellow poked his shoulder, he shook his head. "My choices are not at issue. Miss Maitland is not welcome here."

Margaret furtively reached over and touched a finger to Stephen's arm, silently willing him to give up the argument and escort her out of the shop. There was nothing either of them could say that would change the owner's mind, and Margaret did not want to spend another moment in a place where she was treated this way.

"That's fine," Stephen replied, his voice as smooth as the Irish whiskey in Philip's study. "No one from my household will shop here again, and I expect Philip Maitland will feel the same way."

He offered his arm to Margaret, who took it with relief and strode out, unable to resist a look back at the dismayed shop owner and the frowning woman in yellow.

When they were far away from the shop, Margaret stopped walking but held Stephen's arm. "You didn't have to do that."

He turned to face her, briefly covering her hand with his. "I have no doubt that you could have handled that situation perfectly well on your own. I'm sure you've done it before, more times than you can count. But fighting the same battle over and over can be tiring, and I thought I might provide some assistance."

She met his eyes, noting that they were several shades lighter than the blue of the sky above them, and gave his arm a slight squeeze. "I always appreciate reinforcements," she said softly.

"I am available any time you might need me," he replied with a small smile.

They resumed walking, their pace relaxed, the distance between them—physical and emotional—shrinking with every step.

⚜

Stephen rode home in his own carriage with Margaret and three of Caroline's children, instructing the driver to detour to the dower house at Eastwood Manor before returning to his own front door. The stop at Margaret's home was a short one—just long enough for her to go in and collect some of her books while he entertained the children. He would have much preferred to walk over with her, as she'd previously suggested, without the company of his nieces and nephews, but this way they avoided the appearance of improper behavior. After the incident in the bookshop he needed to take better care with her reputation, despite her insistence that her reputation was ruined long ago. There was no need to throw any more fuel on a fire that was still smoldering.

Not that the children were fit chaperones, of course, and no one would take their word for anything if someone started an unsavory rumor. But he felt better having someone with them who was old enough to speak about what they saw and heard.

It wasn't until after dinner that he was able to talk to Margaret in a more private setting, though "private" was a relative term. The ladies and gentlemen gathered in the drawing room together again, and Stephen entered after most of the other guests, having a pleasant conversation with Mrs. Maitland as they strolled from the dining room. Margaret had managed to make a two seats in the corner of the drawing room both secluded and public at the same time—two wingback chairs had been pulled close beside one another facing the center of the room. She sat in one with a stack of books at her feet, and gestured him over.

Stephen excused himself to Mrs. Maitland and made his way over to the empty chair beside Margaret, his grin growing as he approached. They hadn't had a chance to discuss the books in much depth in the carriage with three very tired and out of sorts children, so he had been looking forward to this with great anticipation. "What a treasure trove of information you've brought."

"I have some botany books, and some that tend more toward horticulture," she said, setting the one she was reading on the arm of the chair within his view.

"What's the difference?"

"Botany is the study of plants," she explained, a slight wrinkle forming between her eyes as she considered her words. "Horticulture is more specifically the study of gardens."

He shifted in his seat a bit so he could comfortably read the pages of the book on the chair's arm. "Oh, I see. So horticulture is like a specialty within the larger field of botany."

"Yes, exactly." She flipped the pages of the book on the chair arm until she found the one she wanted. "And see here, this looks like one of the plants I saw in your mystery garden the other day."

He leaned forward to study the drawing of plant with long, wide leaves that formed a low mass with a flower spike rising above it, but was distracted by the delicate scent of her perfume. What was it? Had she chosen it specially for this evening?

He closed his eyes for the merest of moments to try to focus on the picture in the book. "It certainly is. There is a group of them in a shady area under a stand of trees."

"They are called hostas, originally grown in Japan and China."

She pointed to a section of text and he read for himself about *hosta ventricosa*, how it could grow up to three feet wide and could not tolerate much sun. "Amazing! Does it say how to take care of them?"

They leafed through her books, marking useful pages with bits of paper so Stephen could go back to them later.

Later, when he was not trying to catalog the fragrance of her perfume with half his brain while the other half tingled at every accidental brush of her fingers as they turned pages.

"Can I ask you an impertinent question?" she asked softly as she opened another book on top of the one they were looking through.

She kept her eyes on the pages before them, her eyelashes concealing the sentiment behind her words, and it took every ounce of willpower he had to answer in a steady voice. "Ask away."

"Why did you get involved at the bookshop this afternoon?" She turned a page slowly. "You could have simply escorted me out to avoid causing a scene or ignored the whole affair entirely. But you didn't."

A sudden rush of anxiety filled his body as memories from his university days came flooding back, and he fought to relax. "I know how it feels to be seen as lesser, to be rejected simply for who you are."

"You do?"

"I am the son of a tradesman, remember?" He tightened every muscle in his body for a moment, then relaxed them. That helped, but didn't slow his pounding heart. "My father worked for a living, which made me an outcast before I even arrived some places. Cambridge especially."

Her hazel eyes slowly lifted to meet his. "Oh, goodness. Yes, Philip and Alex have both told me stories about the treatment of students who attended, but didn't come from the 'right' families."

"The Eddingtons are not one of the 'right' families," he replied, then paused to clear his throat. "It never mattered how much money we had nor how intelligent I was. My father worked for a living, and that meant I was unwelcome."

Her fingers brushed against his once more, but this time she didn't move them away. "And it all came back when the bookshop owner tried to throw me out."

"Yes," he croaked.

She was silent for a long moment, her face completely unreadable, and Stephen began to regret his disclosure. It was the truth, but he could have chalked his actions up to mere gallantry, coming to the defense of his friend's sister. Had this confession been too intimate?

"I was betrothed to Alex's father when I was twenty," she responded. Her voice was steady but her eyes had returned to the book's pages. "Both families were satisfied with the match and we were very much in love—everything was perfect."

"Until it wasn't."

She nodded, swallowing audibly. "One day he just disappeared. His family didn't know where he'd gone, his friends hadn't seen him, no one knew what happened to him. And we'd... anticipated our vows. It wasn't long before I suspected I was with child, and every month that passed confirmed it."

"He got you with child then left you?" Stephen's fingers began to curl into a fist.

"That's what everyone thought," Margaret continued, putting a hand on his sleeve as if to calm him. "It was a full year before he could even get a letter to his family—he'd been impressed."

"Impressed into the Royal Navy?" Stephen asked in disbelief. He knew what impressment was, but he'd never actually known anyone who had been taken.

She nodded weakly. "Forced to serve aboard a ship. By the time he returned to England, Alex was walking and talking." She took a deep breath and blew it out slowly. "Alex's father attempted to pick up where we left off, but the damage to my reputation was already done and he was... He was never the same after his ordeal."

Stephen pressed his lips together, determined that the next words out of his mouth would be supportive, but she beat him to it.

"I was lucky, though," she told him, her voice growing stronger. "I had Philip, my parents, my cousin Cecilia to support me. They were the reason I could even entertain the possibility of keeping my child. I could have ended my pregnancy. I could have hidden it, gone away to some distant relative to have the baby and give him away. I could have pretended the whole thing never happened and returned to my life."

"But you didn't." Most women in her position did end pregnancies or bear their children in secret. To raise an illegitimate child in the open was social death, and for most women of Margaret's class that meant a lifetime of isolation and struggle.

She shook her head and the scent of her perfume swirled through the air. "My family allowed me to make the decision myself and supported me when I did. I knew what I was giving up when I decided to raise my child, but I also knew that he'd never want for anything. Most women in my position aren't so fortunate."

They sat together in a silence that gradually shifted from angry to sympathetic, her hand still on his sleeve, his head bent toward hers.

"I believe we have both been fortunate in our families," he finally said, his voice quiet but steady.

"Yes," she agreed, meeting his eyes once more. "We have."

# Chapter 5

*M*argaret sat at the breakfast table the next morning, picking at the plate of food before her. There were fresh fruits and vegetables from the kitchen garden, crispy toast to which she'd applied a generous coating of butter and strawberry jam, even eggs, which she hadn't had for breakfast in years. A steaming cup of strong tea sat beside her plate, the aroma tickling her mind and bringing back memories of Alex's father, who always drank his tea as strong as it could be brewed.

Her memories contrasted sharply with the scene playing out before her eyes, though. Alex and Patrick sat a little apart from her on one side of the table, with Stephen across from them. The three men were having a spirited discussion regarding Napoleon's recent surrender aboard the HMS *Bellerophon* to Captain Frederick Maitland, a rather distant cousin. Alex's eyes were bright, his hands gesturing as he spoke, as they always did when he was excited about the topic of discussion. Patrick, likewise, was leaning forward, his cheeks pink with the enthusiasm of his words.

But in this instance, it wasn't the younger men that had captured so much of Margaret's attention. It was Stephen. He was just as eager and lively as Alex and Patrick, debating and correcting but also listening carefully to what each one had to say. He was careful to look them in the eye when they were talking, to let them finish their thoughts before countering, nodding vigorously when he agreed. While some of Stephen and Margaret's generation were dismissive of younger adults, continually treating them as the children they no longer were, Stephen responded to Alex and Patrick as if they were his equals.

Margaret lifted her teacup to her lips and realized he interacted with everyone the same way—younger adults, servants, peers, his social superiors.

A lady who had borne an illegitimate child.

"What do you think, Mama?" Alex asked.

She smiled at him, her sweet boy all grown up. "I'm sorry, I was woolgathering. What do I think about what?"

"I ride the entire estate every few days so I can keep abreast of what is happening where. I would like to take Patrick and Alex out with me today, if you don't mind."

"I don't mind at all," Margaret replied, hoping she hid her surprise well enough. Did Stephen realize the symbolism this ride could have? Had she wed Alex's father as planned, *he* would be the one riding out with their son, looking over the property Alex would one day inherit. "I noticed stacks of clouds on the horizon when I was out for my walk this morning—hopefully you don't get caught in the rain."

The men stayed for a few minutes more before pushing their chairs back and bidding Margaret goodbye. She gave them a cheerful wave, meeting Stephen's blue eyes and holding his gaze for a moment. He offered her a small nod, smiled, then turned to follow the others.

She was sure of it now. He knew exactly what he'd asked, and how she would interpret it.

Her heart thudded in her ears and a little tingle ran down her spine. Stephen Eddington was courting her.

"Oh, goodness."

"What's wrong?"

Margaret started, setting her teacup down in its saucer with a clank. "Oh, Philip, I didn't see you there."

He moved from his place in the doorway and settled into the chair beside hers. "I only just arrived. I ran into Eddington on my way in—he's taking Alex and Patrick out to ride the estate?"

Margaret nodded slowly. "He is."

Philip's eyebrows rose. "I see. Well, I came to find you to see if you were all right after last evening, but things have clearly progressed beyond that."

"To see if I was all right?"

"Yes." He folded his hands and rested them on his knee. "You and Eddington seemed to be quite comfortable with your botany books yesterday after dinner. But by the end of the evening the two of you looked as though you'd been through something terrible together."

Margaret sighed deeply. "Both of your observations are true, I think." Philip's forehead wrinkled in confusion, and she continued, "We started off with the books and made good progress identifying some of the plants in his garden. But then..."

She described Stephen's actions in the bookshop, and Philips expression relaxed. "I'm sorry I wasn't there for you myself, but I'm glad he was."

"When we were looking through my books yesterday, I asked him why he'd helped me," she continued softly. "And it turns out that we have had some of the same experiences in our lives."

"Oh, of course. Yes, he's had a difficult time breaking into certain circles because of his parentage," Philip said. "And you have been on the outside looking in as well."

"Yes."

Philip mulled that information over for a moment. "And now he's taking Alex out to ride his estate."

Margaret nodded again. "Yes."

"Are you two...?"

His eyes dropped to the table, to her hand resting near the handle of her fragile teacup painted with delicate little flowers. "We haven't made each other any promises."

Philip leaned forward slightly. "Would you like to?"

"What I would like doesn't matter," Margaret made herself say aloud. Then she glanced up at her big brother. "Philip, I would be such a hindrance to him. He needs a wife he can take to social functions, not one who will be turned away at the door. Someone who will be the perfect hostess for political dinners, not one who is the butt of lewd jokes."

Philip cringed, no doubt remembering several of the instances in which he defended his sister's honor after Alex was born. Then he laid a finger on her chin and turned her head toward his. "But if none of that mattered, would you want to marry him?"

She hesitated. "Perhaps. I... I hadn't thought about it until yesterday." She stood, taking a step away from the table and her brother. "But you told me yourself that Stephen has plans to climb through the ranks of government, so my reputation does matter. It matters a great deal."

Philip rose from his chair and set his arm about her shoulders. "Have you spoken to him about this?"

"No," she said taking a deep breath and exhaling slowly. "I'm not entirely sure there's anything to discuss yet, and I don't want to be presumptuous."

"Given the way he's been looking at you—these past few days especially—I seriously doubt you'd be wrong," Philip replied.

"How does he look at me?"

Philip grinned. "Have you not noticed? He looks at you the same way I look at Adeleine."

Her brother worshiped his wife, and always had. Was that how Stephen felt about her? Margaret sighed again, trying to stem the tide of emotions that threatened to overwhelm her. "Oh."

"Oh indeed."

"Has he said anything to you?" she asked suddenly.

Philip shook his head. "It's not as though he needs my permission, or Father's for that matter. But you will be the first to know if he speaks to me about you."

"Stephen may not need your permission, but I might need your counsel," she said, leaning her head against his shoulder.

"You will have it," Philip promised. "Anytime you need it."

When Stephen returned to the house that afternoon, he managed to sneak away to his study where he could give his neglected correspondence his full attention. He knew he had at least two hours before he needed to dress for dinner, so he pulled the pile of letters into the center of his overlarge desk and started sorting them into piles according to their urgency. Some letters he'd previously read but had put aside to deal with later, and some hadn't even been opened yet. He took the time to at least skim all of them until one massive pile of stationary turned into three: things that must be dealt with now, things that could wait until after his guests returned to their homes, and things that he could hand off to his steward.

He was halfway through answering the letters that required immediate attention when a knock sounded on the stout door. "Enter," he called, continuing to write.

His butler or a footman would have entered and waited to be acknowledged, but the person who opened the door did not. "Are you busy?"

"Caroline." He glanced at his letter and decided it could wait a few more minutes. "I need a break anyway—my hand is starting to cramp."

She made her way across the room, her footsteps echoing on the bare wooden floor, and perched on the edge of the sofa. "I just wanted to check on you. You seemed upset after your talk with Margaret in the drawing room last night, but I didn't want to say anything in front of the children or her family."

He went to sit beside her, and blew out a breath as he lowered himself onto the sofa. "Oh, right. All is well. I interceded on her behalf at a shop when we were in the village the other day, and when we spoke about it last evening it stirred up some memories I'd rather like to forget. That's all."

"You interceded on her behalf?"

Caroline asked the question as if she already knew the details, so Stephen supplied a quick summary of the encounter in the bookshop. "I've been in that position before, been the one who was unwelcome because of who I was. I couldn't just let that happen to Margaret."

"Stephen, I'm going to ask you a delicate question, and I'd like you to answer me honestly."

"Of course I will," he responded, a note of annoyance in his voice.

"Are you in love with Margaret Maitland?"

She spoke the words quietly, as if she were trying to keep them within the confines of the sofa, and Stephen didn't fully comprehend them at once. "Am I... Am I in love with Margaret?"

Caroline nodded. "Yes, that is what I asked."

He slid back, relaxing his body against the back of the sofa. "I don't know."

"That's not a 'no' though," Caroline replied matter-of-factly, turning sideways to face him.

"No, it isn't." His gaze dropped to Caroline's shoulder as he thought about his interactions with Margaret, recently and over the year he'd known her. He certainly felt *something* for her that was different from the friendship he had with his other neighbors. She was kind, caring, generous to others regardless of their station in life. She had taken to Caroline as if they'd been lifelong friends despite the differences in their circumstances. And she understood him in ways not even his own sister did.

Caroline had led a fairly sheltered life. She was educated at home by a governess, socialized with the children of their parents' friends, met her husband through a mutual acquaintance. Thankfully, outside of one or two high sticklers, she had encountered very little opposition in her life.

But Margaret had, like him, been an outsider in her own social circle. They had both committed the sin of being different from the expectations others held for them. He'd had friends, particularly at Cambridge, who were also outsiders for one reason or another, but he could never talk about it with them the way he did with Margaret. Sharing with her the memories, the feelings he'd shoved deep down inside himself had just felt right.

Had Margaret felt it too?

Stephen forced his eyes to focus on his sister's face. "I don't think I'm in love with her yet."

"Yet?" Caroline fairly pounced on the word.

Stephen's answering smile started out small, but when he allowed himself to picture a future with Margaret by his side, it grew into a full fledged grin. "Yet."

"Does she know?"

He shook his head. "I don't think so. We haven't talked about it, at least."

Caroline clasped her hands in her lap, likely to keep herself still. "You'll dance with her at Miss Natalie's practice ball, though, won't you?"

Stephen had completely forgotten about that event, and it was happening in just a few days. "I will ask her for at least one dance yes."

"Wonderful." She rose from the sofa, grinning. "Good luck."

Caroline let herself out of the study, leaving Stephen alone with his thoughts in the rather somber room full of dark woods and heavy fabrics. He could almost feel Margaret's hands in his as they danced a country dance or a staid old quadrille. There was no way Mrs. Maitland would allow a waltz, but perhaps he and Margaret could find a quiet place to admire the stars.

Unless she rejected his advances, of course, for that was a distinct possibility. His heart sank at the mere thought of it, then sank even deeper into the gloom of heartache when he realized the possible consequences of his future actions.

If he did end up wedding Margaret, what would happen to his career in government? Philip had said that Stephen could rise high if he had a respectable wife from the "right" kind of family. The Maitlands were certainly the "right" kind of family, but Margaret herself was looked down upon in society even more than he was. Would her past hinder his future?

Was he willing to risk it?

And what if Margaret was unwilling or uninterested in becoming his wife? His relationship with her brother would surely change, and not for the better. Would his sister's budding friendship with Margaret wither too?

Stephen dropped his head into his hands. Perhaps the best thing he could do for Caroline and himself was to just pretend that Margaret was simply the sister of his good friend and neighbor, to ignore the feelings that had been percolating through his body. Although, based on the ease with which he spilled out the most private parts of his life to her, pretending might not be enough. He may have to avoid Margaret altogether.

"I should have asked Mr. Mowbray's daughter for her hand last year and been done with it," Stephen said aloud, sliding his hands down his face and letting them fall into his lap. Louisa would have been the perfect wife for a person with ambitions of government service and politics, and she seemed genuinely interested in Stephen as a person.

But he never felt comfortable sharing the ups and downs of his life with Louisa Mowbray.

A muffled gong sounded from deeper within the house, signaling the dinner hour. Well, there were three more days until Miss Natalie's practice ball. He had until then to figure out who, or what, was most important to him.

## Chapter 6

Margaret walked over to Eastwood Manor after luncheon with the gown she planned to wear at Natalie's practice ball draped over one arm. The pasture was still damp with dew and she stepped carefully through the grass—this was the favorite grazing site of Eastwood's dairy cows—glad Caroline's lady's maid had thought to wrap her evening gown in an old bedsheet.

She'd promised her niece she would come over early to assist with preparations, but when she arrived Adeleine had everything well in hand.

"Is there anything at all I can help with?" Margaret asked, watching footmen roll up the carpets in the music room and carefully remove most of the furniture.

Adeleine pooched her lips out for a moment, as she often did when she thinking. "This," she said, gesturing around the room, "is all going as planned. But perhaps you could sit with Natalie for a while? I did for a bit this morning, but she's nervous and doesn't want her mother hovering."

"Of course. Where is she?" Margaret asked, relieved. She was ready to pitch in wherever she was needed, but her head was elsewhere and she wasn't sure she could be trusted with details just now.

"She's planted herself in the morning room—away from the commotion, she said."

Margaret chuckled. "So much like her father sometimes. You should have seen Philip before his first ball."

Adeleine laughed. "I remember him hiding in the card room for at least half of it," she said. "He does like to socialize with friends, with people he knows well, but not with strangers."

"I'll remind Natalie that there are no strangers coming tonight," Margaret replied, moving toward the door. "Perhaps that will ease her mind."

Margaret found her niece in the morning room as stated, staring at a blank piece of paper with pen poised. "Are you writing letters? If I'm disturbing you, I can come back."

Natalie set her pen down and sighed. "I thought perhaps writing letters would help to pass the time, but I can't seem to find the words for anything."

"Are the words not coming to you, or are you unable to focus long enough to find the words?" Margaret asked, coming to stand beside her niece's chair.

Natalie thought it over for a moment, then answered, "I can't seem to settle my mind enough."

"You're nervous about tonight."

It was a statement rather than a question, and Natalie frowned. "Yes, but it's strange. I haven't been nervous before any of the other events Mama has organized for me. Why is this one different?"

Margaret found a comfortable chair for herself nearby and sat down, crossing her ankles and folding her hands in her lap. "Balls always felt different to me than any other kind of gathering," she said, studying her shoes. "You must dance and make conversation and look your best *and* eat or drink without spilling anything on yourself."

"Perhaps that's it," Natalie replied, though she didn't sound convinced.

"For me, going to a ball always made me feel as though I was on display," Margaret continued, noting the small hole in her skirt that would require mending. "Even though there were many other ladies of much higher ranking and greater importance than I was, it always felt as though people were watching me."

She raised her gaze and saw understanding dawn on Natalie's face. "I think that's it. Even though all of the guests tonight are people I have known all my life, I feel as though they will all be watching everything I do."

Margaret offered her niece a sympathetic smile. "Some of them will, particularly in this case because this ball has been organized especially for you. But most people will speak with you, wish you well, and enjoy themselves."

Natalie nodded and was quiet for a moment. Then her eyebrows rose. "When was the last time you went to a ball, Aunt Margaret?"

Margaret's eyes dropped to the hole in her skirt once more. The last time she'd attended a ball, she had already been pregnant with Alex and his father had gone missing. The pitying glances behind fans she'd received that night had only been outnumbered by the disgusted sneers.

"It's been over twenty years now," she replied, hearing the edge in her voice. She shifted in her seat and tried again. "Well before you were born."

"Are *you* nervous for tonight?"

Margaret nodded. "A little."

It was Natalie's turn to smile sympathetically. "Then it's a good thing this is just practice."

And practice Natalie did. Margaret beamed as her niece circulated around the rooms designated for the event in her new white ballgown with tiny flowers embroidered all over, making conversation with her guests with poise and genuine enjoyment that evening. Patrick and Alex, in their best tailcoats and breeches, each danced with her at least three times, and Natalie even got her father to partner her in a country dance.

Margaret made a point of staying away from the action as much as possible, unsure if her presence would be distracting and unwilling to risk ruining Natalie's night to find out. She did dance with her brother and son when they asked, but declined all other offers.

And then Stephen discovered her standing alone in one corner of the drawing room where the refreshments had been laid out.

"Ah, there you are," he said with a wide smile.

She couldn't help but smile back as her heart skipped a beat, and she was glad she'd worn the lilac perfume again that she'd impulsively purchased last month. "Mr. Eddington, are you enjoying your evening?"

"Yes," he replied cheerfully. "I have done nothing but dance and talk and laugh since I arrived, and it's been wonderful. You?"

"It's a lovely party, and Natalie seems to be having fun," Margaret said over the din of the orchestra members tuning their instrument between songs.

"But you're not?"

The question seemed innocent enough, but her smile faltered a bit. "I'm tired, I think."

Stephen nodded. "I suspect I'll fall asleep as soon as my head hits my pillow tonight. I was going to take a walk outside—would you like to join me? Take a break from the noise and the people?"

"That's a lovely idea," she answered before she could stop herself. Philip and Adeleine had strategically placed torches and lanterns in several places outdoors, knowing people would want to do exactly as Stephen was proposing, and Margaret was grateful for the opportunity to get away. She also wanted to speak with him alone, and this was likely her best opportunity to do so.

He followed her lead through the house and offered her his arm when they arrived at the open French windows. She took it, her heart beating rapidly in her chest as she tried to summon the right words to start what would either be a very deep or very awkward conversation. But as they strolled peacefully along in the torchlight, her mind rebelled.

Surely it was permissible to savor this walk in the cool air with a man she cared about. They could talk another day.

"May I ask you an impertinent question?" he asked quietly, as if speaking too loudly would shatter the scenery.

She smiled, recognizing the words she'd spoken to him only a few days ago. "You may."

"Why did you change your mind about attending the house party?" He stopped walking and turned to her. "You could have met Caroline here in your brother's home if that was important to you, or chosen not to meet her at all. But you committed fully to the house party after the note she wrote you."

Her arm slid from his as he clasped his hands behind his back and she missed the contact, even with sleeves and gloves between them. "Two reasons," she said, matching the volume of her voice to his. "First, Caroline said in her note that she doesn't travel often, so this might be our only chance to spend quality time together, and that neither she nor her daughters went about in society so there would be no consequences for them."

The torchlight was dim where they were standing, but the moonlight illuminated his satisfied smile. "And second?"

"I thought it would be a good way to get to know you better." An owl hooted from a distant tree, and she took a moment to gather herself. "Since you are our neighbor and a friend of my brother's, it made sense to spend some time with you to see what kind of person you were outside of a dining room."

He took her gloved hand in his. "And what conclusion did you come to about me?"

She tried to slow her rapid breathing, taking deeper, longer breaths. "That I am fortunate to know you. And that I hope our friendship will continue for many years."

He took her other hand and squeezed it gently. "Did you ever consider that there might be something between us in addition to friendship?"

His voice was husky and the little thrill she felt earlier spread through her body. "I... Yes, I have been thinking a lot about that lately. Have you?"

"Yes," he answered softly, stepping closer. "You are a remarkable woman, Margaret Maitland, and I'm disappointed that I didn't notice sooner."

She knew what was coming next, knew she should stop him, but she didn't want to. Here in this moment, all her worries, all her common sense evaporated in the moonlight. When his arms came around her waist, she slid hers around his neck, combing her fingers through his hair.

His lips found hers, tentatively at first, giving her yet another chance to pull away. But she let her heart lead rather than her head, and deepened the kiss, her body awash in tingly delight when he drew her against him.

She wasn't sure who broke away first, but when their lips parted the merest fraction of an inch, her eyes fluttered open to find him grinning.

"Better than botany books?" she asked with a laugh.

"I want to kiss you while we read your botany books," he replied with an answering chuckle.

She palmed his cheek, then reluctantly drew back. "Perhaps we can try that tomorrow."

"I live in hope," he said, breathing in deeply, audibly, before releasing her with a gusty exhale. "You should probably go back in. I'm going to stay out for a while longer."

She nodded, knowing he was right but unenthusiastic about the idea. "I'm staying here tonight so I can help with the cleanup, but we should find some time together tomorrow—without the botany books," she added, unable to keep the smile from her face.

"We should," he agreed. "Can you come to my study around three o'clock? I'll be working on my correspondence, and we shouldn't be disturbed."

Margaret longed to kiss him again, to hold his warm, solid body against hers, but she stepped away. "Yes, I can manage that."

"Then I will see you tomorrow," he said, kissing the back of her hand before releasing her.

"Tomorrow," she echoed, and dreamily made her way back to the party.

⁂

"Stephen, there's a Maitland footman here with a message for you. He says it's urgent."

Caroline's voice broke through Stephen's daydreams. He shook himself back to the reality of lunch with his family as he accepted a piece of paper that was sealed with intertwining M's. That's curious—he and Margaret were going to speak later that day. Why was she sending him a note now? When he broke the seal and read her note, his body ran cold.

*Stephen,*
*Someone saw us, is spreading rumors through the neighborhood. Please come to Eastwood Manor as soon as possible.*
*Margaret*

"Damn," he said quietly, shaking his head.

"Stephen," Caroline scolded. "Watch your language."

He glanced up and noted several of the older children at the table. "Oh, my apologies. Caroline, is the footman waiting for a response?"

"Yes, I believe so."

"Tell him to hurry back to Eastwood Manor and let them know that I'm on my way."

Caroline gave him a quizzical look. "What's happened?"

He glanced at the children again. "I'll tell you later."

She hurried off to convey the message and Stephen practically ran to his study to finish a letter that needed to be sent off that day. He had a feeling that he'd be spending a large portion of his day at Eastwood Manor and doubted he would see his correspondence again before the morning.

When he arrived at the Maitland home, he was shown into the drawing room by a footman. Stephen wasn't sure what he expected, but Margaret sitting alone in the middle of the room, staring at her hands folded neatly in her lap, was not it.

"Margaret?"

Her chin lifted slowly and her eyes slid to his. "Stephen. I'm sorry to have disrupted your day."

He crossed the room and sat down beside her, reaching out to take her hand. "No apology necessary. This is important."

She placed her bare hand in his and her shoulders relaxed slightly. "One of the guests last night saw us together. I'm not sure how much she saw, but she spent the morning calling on everyone she could get to." Her voice caught and her gaze shifted to his feet. "Apparently that Maitland trollop is up to her old tricks again."

Stephen winced. "Oh, Margaret, I'm so sorry... I should have realized... I didn't even think..."

"I should have known better," she said, her voice barely above a whisper. "I thought because it was a very small event, out in the country..."

"We both thought we were being discreet," he said firmly, leaning down to catch her eye. "Some people simply have to insert themselves into everyone's business."

She met his eyes and held them as he straightened in his chair. "Yes, and being out in the country means she can only contact a limited number of people, so we may be able to mitigate this before it gets out of hand."

"And the easiest way to do that is if we are wed," he said, unable to keep the smile from his face. This isn't the way he would have preferred to start their life together, but he couldn't deny that he was excited by the prospect.

"No, Stephen, that's not what I meant."

"It makes sense, though," he replied, his smile faltering. "And I believe we'll do well together. Even if I wasn't honor bound to do so, I would very likely be asking for your hand in the near future anyway."

"Honor bound?" She withdrew her hand from his and frowned. "Stephen, you can't be honor bound to marry someone who was already ruined."

He studied her face for a long moment. "Margaret, you were born a lady. Through unfortunate circumstances, you weren't allowed to have the marriage—the life—you expected. That doesn't make you less of a lady, less of a person."

Her pink lips curved into a smile, but there was only sadness in it. "You are among the few that believe that. My reputation won't change and yours won't suffer if you simply walk away."

"Is that what you want me to do?" he asked in a low voice, afraid the surge of absolute heartbreak would show itself it he spoke any louder. "Is that why you asked me to come here as soon as I could?"

"No," she answered quickly. "No. I thought you should know what was happening. Adeleine has taken Natalie to call on the neighbors that are closest to us, ostensibly to say thank you for attending last night's event, but also to counter these rumors."

"Do you think that will work?"

Margaret shrugged halfheartedly. "Perhaps. If anyone can talk the neighbors round, it's Adeleine. But if she can't, you have options."

"If she can't, my offer stands," he said, covering her hand with his and giving it a gentle squeeze. "I care about you, Margaret, and I meant what I said about asking for your hand anyway."

For a brief moment, her smile radiated warmth and happiness. But it dimmed when she spoke again. "Why don't we both take some time to think things over. I'll stay here today so no one can claim they saw us alone at the dower house, and send you a note with whatever news Adeleine brings when she returns."

He nodded. It was a sensible plan, though every part of him ached to stay. There were consequences for every action, and they both needed to be certain of their decisions. "All right. But if you need me for anything..."

She stood with him and walked him to the drawing room door, touching his arm as they parted. "I will see you tomorrow."

# Chapter 7

$\mathcal{M}$argaret looked up as a footman opened the drawing room door to announce Mrs. Gates's arrival. "Caroline?"

Caroline's smile was tentative as she stepped into the room, fine drops of rain clinging to her dress and skin from a brief downpour after Stephen left. "I wasn't sure if you would want to see me."

Margaret rose but was unsure of what else to do. Should she hug her friend? Should she be cautious because Caroline was Stephen's sister? "You are my friend, and I'm always happy to see you."

The two of them found seats in a pair of wing chairs, then sat in awkward silence for several moments until Caroline cleared her throat.

"I wanted to see how you were, if there was anything you needed," she said in a wavering voice.

"I'm well enough," Margaret replied with a genuine smile, "but bored. I was looking forward to playing games with the children today and whatever other activities you had planned."

Caroline sighed. "I was, too. But perhaps we can resume the house party in a day or two."

"Perhaps." Margaret suddenly found her fingernails utterly fascinating, then realized what she was doing. "I'm sorry, Caroline. I feel like I've let you down along with my niece. I didn't mean to ruin your house party."

"First of all," Caroline began, "Stephen has an equal share of the responsibility, so please don't take it all upon yourself."

Margaret stared at her for a moment, then relaxed a bit when she realized Caroline was serious. "Well that's nice to hear for a change."

"And secondly," Caroline continued, her voice lighter, "you didn't ruin anything. We have simply put our shared activities on hold for a while."

"If I agreed to wed your brother, we could pick up where we left off right now," Margaret said. "Did you know he offered for me?"

Caroline nodded slowly. "He told me. He also said that the two of you were taking some time to think things over before making a decision, and that it's best if you aren't staying with us while you do your thinking."

"Yes," Margaret replied, "and I'm glad we have that option. If this had happened in Town, everyone who was anyone would know about our walk under the stars. At least out here everyone is spread out."

"I'm glad, too," Caroline said, leaning against the arm of her chair. "I would love to have you for a sister, but Stephen is a bit impulsive sometimes. It's a good idea for both of you to be very sure about what you want to do."

Margaret inhaled slowly and sighed. "That's what I told him—that we should both be sure. Having me for a wife will not make his achieving his ambitions any easier."

"You two can settle that between you," Caroline told her smoothly. Then she shifted in her chair. "If you decide not to wed my brother, will you and I still be friends?"

"I hope so," Margaret said quickly. "I view my friendship with you as separate from my relationship with

Stephen, but I would understand if you didn't want to continue it."

Caroline's whole body relaxed. "Oh, I hope we can. I suppose we'll have to wait and see how things turn out between you and Stephen, but I do hope we can still maintain some sort of connection."

Silence fell over them once more and Margaret wondered what on earth they were to talk about after that. Ah, but they didn't need to talk about anything—they could simply have some fun.

"Have you ever played whist with just two people?" she asked, rising and walking to the corner of the room where the bell pull was located.

"How would you even do that?" Caroline said with a giggle. "Whist is for four people."

Margaret grinned. "Normally for four people. Natalie and I got bored one evening when her parents were out and Alex was at university, and we devised a two-handed version. Would you like me to teach you?"

"This I have to see for myself," Caroline laughed.

A footman answered the bell, then went to fetch the deck of cards Margaret requested. While they waited for him, the two women reorganized the furniture in one part of the room so they could play comfortably. When the deck of cards arrived, Margaret seated herself on one side of the table and Caroline on the other.

"For this version of whist, you get twenty cards instead of thirteen..."

Margaret dealt the cards and explained the rules that she and Natalie had invented. They made it through three hands before dissolving into laughter so complete neither of them could continue. When the clock on the mantle struck three, Caroline sighed.

"I'd better be getting back," she said with great reluctance. "I promised I would go with the children to paint this afternoon out in the formal garden if the rain stopped in time, and I can see the sun peeking out through the clouds. Thank you for allowing Alex to join in today—his presence has been a great comfort to Patrick, and to Stephen, too, I think."

"Whatever happens among us adults, we must make sure that Alex and Patrick feel free to maintain their friendship," Margaret said, standing along with her guest. "Alex has had a difficult time making friends, largely due to the circumstances of his birth. But Patrick, your whole family, never cared. That means a great deal to my son, and to me."

Caroline reached out and hugged Margaret tightly. "I agree. And I hope you and Stephen can come to an amicable understanding, whatever it is."

They said their goodbyes, and Margaret wiped tears from her eyes.

"Was that Caroline Gates I just saw leaving?" her brother asked, entering the room.

Margaret could only nod as another tear dripped down her nose.

"Oh no." Philip enveloped her in his arms, and she breathed in the comforting scent of leather and paper clinging to his clothes. "Did it go poorly between you two?"

Margaret shook her head and managed to croak, "No, we had a wonderful time."

"And that complicates things with Eddington."

She nodded again, grateful to have such a supportive brother. "Caroline is a close friend already, and I'm not sure I could bear to lose her. But I'm not going to wed her brother so I can remain her friend…"

"Of course not," Philip replied gently. "And no one expects you to wed Eddington if you don't want to."

Margaret drew back and wiped her face. "Not even Adeleine?"

"No." When Margaret raised one eyebrow, he continued, "She is worried for our daughter, yes. That's why she's out calling on neighbors now. But neither she nor I think you should marry anyone unless you freely wish to do so."

Her arms went around him again. "You and Adeleine are the reason Alex and I had any sort of life. You know that, don't you?"

She felt Philip's mouth curve against her temple. "I think Cecilia would have swooped in and seen to you and Alex if we hadn't. But we were glad to do so. And we're glad to be of help now, if we can. You know Mama and Papa have their own home—that dower house is yours, always, regardless of your circumstances."

The tears that had slowed started to flow again. How different her life would have been without the support of her family!

When she managed to collect herself once more, she released her brother. "I just don't know what to do, Philip. I feel like it's only these past few weeks that I have really started to know Stephen, and that can't be long enough to fall in love. Can it?"

"You've known Caroline only these past few weeks, and you were just crying over the prospect of not having her as a friend after this," he pointed out.

"Friendship isn't the same as romantic love, though," Margaret replied with a frown. "And it doesn't come with the legal requirements that marriage does."

"I did say the dower house would always be yours," Philip reminded her. "Between Cecilia and me, you never have to worry about how you will live, and neither does Alex."

Her brows crowded down over her eyes. "Are you trying to tell me to marry Stephen and leave him if it turns out we're ill suited?"

Philip shook his head. "I'm telling you that you have the freedom to make the choice you believe is best, and that life is unpredictable but you will always have help when you need it."

She laid a hand on his shoulder and smiled. "You are a good man, Philip Maitland. I am very fortunate to have you as my brother."

"You may change your mind after you hear where I'm going," he quipped.

"You're going to call on Stephen, aren't you?" she countered.

He nodded again. "Not on your behalf. I merely want to see how he's holding up. His closest friend, the person I imagine he'd prefer to talk to right now, is unavailable."

"Ah, yes, Mr. Fitzsimmons and Cecilia are enjoying married life on his farm, according to her last letter," Margaret said with a grin.

"And, apart from his sister, Eddington is on his own."

"Go talk to him, or sit in silence and drink port, or whatever it is he needs to do," Margaret said, her smile faltering slightly. "And ask him if we can call on him tomorrow."

"I will."

Margaret stood alone in the drawing room of her brother's home, staring at the door Philip had closed when he departed. The power to decide the direction of her life was in her hands and her hands alone, yet it impacted so many other people.

"What do I do?"

"What do I do?" Stephen asked a stone bust of some ancient Greek figure he'd probably studied at some point during his education.

"Unfortunately, I don't have the answer for you," a familiar voice answered from the door of his study.

"Philip Maitland. You are the last person I expected to see today, unless it was to call me out."

Philip shook his head with a smile. "If my sister were young and impressionable, and you had taken advantage of her, I would. But Margaret passed her fortieth birthday last year—she is certainly capable of knowing her own mind."

Stephen sat down in his favorite chair and noted that Philip took his customary place on the sofa by the window. "Then why have you come?"

"To see how you are," Philip replied, maintaining easy eye contact. "I know I'm not the best person to talk to in this situation, but with your friend Fitzsimmons otherwise occupied, I thought I might make a passable substitute."

"I appreciate the thought," Stephen told him sincerely. "For I am truly at a loss as to what I should do next. I asked your sister to marry me, did she tell you that?"

"She did."

"She also told me I could just walk away and there would be no consequences," Stephen added, his mouth turning down in a hard frown.

"Oh yes, that sounds like her," Philip said with a chuckle.

Stephen's answering sigh was louder than he'd meant it to be. "So she doesn't want to marry me."

"No, if she didn't want to wed you, she would have said so," Philip explained, clasping his hands together and setting them on top of one knee. "She was simply laying out the facts for you. Because of her already ruined reputation, most of society would not judge you for simply going about your life. You are not, nor will you be, forced into marriage with her."

"Is that true?"

Philip must have heard the skepticism in Stephen's voice, for he leaned forward a little to emphasize his words. "Entirely. Right or wrong, our class puts all the blame on the lady when there is an indiscretion, and most of society still has strong feelings about the birth of her son. You could absolutely go about as if nothing had happened, and her life will stay exactly the same. Yours, too, I imagine."

"Not exactly," Stephen responded, leaning against the arm of his chair. "I'm not sure how I am supposed to go about my life as if I don't care at all for her."

"No outward change in your life, then," Philip amended. "Whatever unresolved feelings you have when this is over, you will have to find a way to cope with."

Stephen rested his chin in his hand. "I certainly will. Have you ever been in a situation like this?"

"Not exactly, but Adeleine did ask for time to think it over when I offered for her."

"She did?"

"Mmhmm. It was excruciating." Philip unlinked his fingers and let his hands drop to his sides. "We were very much in love, but she wanted to be certain that marrying was the right thing for both of us, and that it wouldn't have a negative impact on our families."

Stephen pressed his lips together. "Aren't you supposed to figure that out while you're courting?"

"My wife is a very cautious person, Eddington. She needed to prove to herself that the thing she wanted wasn't going to hurt anyone she loved."

Margaret had that in common with her sister-in-law, though whether it came naturally to her or was a learned behavior after the disappearance of her betrothed, Stephen wasn't sure. "There's sense in that. How long did you have to wait for Mrs. Maitland to answer you?"

"Three days," Philip groaned, lolling his head back against the sofa. "I said it was excruciating. But if Adeleine had asked me to wait a year, I would have. She was—she is—worth it."

"So I should just wait for Margaret to make up her mind?" Stephen asked. Were his feelings not even part of the equation?

Philip sat up. "No. You should know what you want, be ready to explain why you want it. If you have lingering questions, ask them. Margaret usually prefers to come to a decision with anyone else affected rather than imposing her will, so she will want to have a discussion with you. She wants to call here tomorrow, likely for such a discussion."

They discussed various options until they reached a mutually convenient time and Philip stood. "Good. I'll leave you to your thoughts then. Oh, one thing before I depart—whatever happens between you and Margaret is between you and Margaret. Unless you wrong her in some way, you and I can remain on good terms if you wish it."

Philip took his leave and Stephen blew out a breath. "Well, that's something of a relief."

"What is?" Caroline asked, shutting the study door behind her.

"Am I never allowed to talk to myself in this house?" Stephen laughed.

"Not if you plan to live here with someone else," Caroline replied with a grin that immediately turned into a frown. "I'm so sorry, I didn't mean..."

He shook his head and walked her over to the sofa Philip had recently vacated, where they both plopped down rather unceremoniously. "I know."

A companionable silence fell between them until Caroline broke it with a question. "Do you love her, Stephen?"

"I think I have for some time now," he answered softly. "I don't know why, but I didn't see it until just a few days ago. I knew I felt some sort of tenderness for her before that, but then at Miss Natalie's practice ball... That day I just knew."

"What about your ambitions for a high government post?" Caroline asked in a low voice. "From what I understand, you need someone of impeccable lineage and upbringing. The people who judge these things will say

Margaret is lacking morals because of her son, and that will make your climb so much more difficult. Perhaps impossible."

"I believe she's worth it." He didn't say anything else—didn't need to. That one sentence summed up his feelings for Margaret Maitland perfectly.

"Tell her that," Caroline said simply. "Whenever you see her next, tell her that. Then she can make a properly informed decision."

Stephen nodded slowly. "Tomorrow at three o'clock she and her brother are coming to call."

Caroline put her arms around him in a fierce embrace. "No matter what happens between you and Margaret, you will always have my love."

"Even if—"

She cut him off, perhaps not wanting to hear words about a broken friendship spoken aloud. "Even then."

He hugged her back just as tightly. "I know we've had our ups and downs, but you have been a true friend to me as well as a sibling."

She placed a big smacking kiss on his cheek, likely to lighten the mood, and released him. "You have as well, and I'm grateful for it. Try to sleep tonight, and try not to worry about tomorrow."

"I will try," he managed gruffly.

She took her leave but Stephen remained rooted to the sofa. He should answer his pile of correspondence, go through his account books, carry on with all his regular duties and responsibilities. But he needed just another few minutes to himself, to think about what his future would look like with or without Margaret by his side.

# Chapter 8

$\mathcal{M}$argaret knocked on Stephen's door promptly at three o'clock, glancing nervously at her brother beside her.

Philip offered her a warm smile. "Just follow your heart," he said quietly.

She smiled in return, but hers was less confident. "I'll try."

The butler opened the door and led them to the drawing room where Stephen and Caroline were waiting, Caroline sitting in a chair jiggling one leg, Stephen standing by the fireplace looking outwardly calm except for one hand fidgeting with the chain of his pocket watch.

"Welcome back," Stephen said, crossing the room to meet them at the door. "I hope you don't mind if we dispense with the pleasantries today."

"Not at all," Margaret answered. "Is there someplace we can talk?"

Stephen nodded and gestured toward the door she'd just entered. "Let's go out into the garden."

Margaret glanced back at Philip, who was settling himself in a chair near Caroline looking perfectly content to stay there for a while. "Good idea."

She left the drawing room with Stephen close behind. When he slid his hand into hers and squeezed her fingers, her heard did a little flip. Now that she truly knew this man, could she spend the rest of her lift without him?

When they exited the house, Stephen drew even with her, lacing his fingers with hers as he led her to one of the gardens she hadn't yet spent much time in. It was informally styled, with flowers of every color happily intermingling and an old stone bench set beneath an arbor alive with honeysuckle.

"Would you like to sit?" Stephen asked, nodding in the direction of the bench.

"Probably a good idea," Margaret answered, inhaling deeply as they approached the arbor. "The fragrance of honeysuckle is always stronger at night, but this one smells divine even at this hour."

He grinned. "I hoped you would appreciate it."

She touched his arm with her free hand as they settled onto the bench. What a thoughtful gesture it was to find a place that was both private and appealing to her for what could be a difficult conversation. "I do."

"How did Adeleine fare with the neighbors?" he asked.

"Things went well, from her account," Margaret answered, suppressing the urge to smooth a lock of hair back from his forehead. He'd forgotten to wear a hat and his hair looked rumpled, as though he'd been running his hands through it. "The people she and Natalie visited talked about how much they'd enjoyed the evening, and mentioned that the person attempting to spread rumors was a busybody."

"Oh good," he said brightly.

Margaret continued, "There are likely other guests who are absolutely appalled by our behavior, but they are not Philip and Adeleine's close friends."

"So Adeleine and Philip should escape this incident unscathed."

Margaret nodded. "Natalie, too, though we won't know for sure until she arrives in Town."

They sat together for several long moments in silence that could have easily been uncomfortable, but strangely wasn't, holding hands and enjoying the warmth of the sun. But when the silence stretched on even longer, Margaret began searching for the right words.

Stephen spoke before she could find them. "I am going to ask you a question, and I'd like you to answer as honestly as you can."

"All right."

He clasped both her hands in his and slowly slid his thumbs across them. "If there were no complications, no consequences, would you wish to marry me?"

Straight to the point, then. Well, she could get straight to the point, too. "Yes."

Stephen had been studying their entwined hands, but his eyes darted to hers. "Yes?"

"Yes," Margaret repeated with a light laugh. "I don't wonder at your surprise—I wasn't sure myself until just last night. My affection for you has certainly grown over the past few weeks, and I hope that was obvious at least. But I wasn't convinced that a strong, romantic love could develop between two people in such a short time."

"Until last night," Stephen repeated, squeezing her hands.

"My brother pointed out that I was mightily upset about the prospect of losing Caroline as a friend, and I had known her for only a few weeks. I've known you for the better part of a year and just didn't see it until Philip practically pointed it out to me."

Stephen grinned. "Remind me to send him a bottle of his favorite port."

She laughed again and slid closer to him. "He will be very pleased."

"Does that mean that you love me?" Stephen asked with a slight waver in his voice.

"Yes," she replied, sliding closer to him. "I do love you."

His arms went around her and he pressed his lips to her ear. "I love you, too," he whispered, trailing delicate kisses across her cheek until his mouth met hers.

She twined her arms around his neck and drew him closer, combing her fingers through his hair. But all too soon the sensible voice in the back of her mind reminded her that there were more things to discuss.

Margaret broke the kiss and leaned her forehead against his. "Stephen," she breathed, her eyes fluttering open, "we live in a world where complications and consequences are very real. We can't just run off to Gretna Green because we're in love."

"I know you're right," he murmured, his eyes still closed, "and I'm very glad one of us can be practical when necessary..."

"But?"

His lips captured her once more. "But I don't want to let you go."

"You don't have to," she replied softly. "We can stay just like this and talk about how to forge our future together."

Stephen grinned. "Excellent. I had an idea last night, also."

Margaret tried to command her heart to slow to a normal pace so she could think, but it refused to obey. She took a deep breath and exhaled slowly, palming his cheek. "What is your idea?"

"You and I will live here and socialize with friends and family," he told her, his grin widening. "We never have to go to London if you don't want to."

"What?" She sat back and let her hands fall to his shoulders. "Stephen, what about your career in government? You must be where they are if you're to have a post."

"I don't need a government post," he said, loosening his arms around her. "It occurred to me last night that it wasn't rank and privilege I wanted, especially if it meant putting you in a distressing position."

Margaret stared at him in disbelief. "What is it that you want, then?"

"Other than you?" he asked with half-smile.

She acknowledged the quip with her own half-smile. "Other than me."

His expression softened. "I want to do some good in this world. In a high enough government position I would have influence and the ear of men with even more influence—I could enact changes in this world for the better." He stroked her back. "But I don't need to be part of the government to change things."

She blinked. "Are you sure? What will you do instead?"

Stephen pulled her closer again. "I'm going to be a country gentleman and a good husband, first and foremost."

"Well that's a relief," she said, not quite able to keep a straight face. "But seriously Stephen, you can't just give up your entire plan for me."

"That's what I realized last night," he said, his grin returning. "I only ever had half a plan—I was going to get myself into a position of influence and 'do good' but it was never more specific than that. Perhaps," he continued, pressing a kiss to her temple, "you can help me figure out the details."

"No plan?" She wanted to simultaneously kiss him and throttle him. She'd been plagued by the notion that her mere presence as his wife would weigh him down like an anchor on a sinking ship. What a relief that they could work together, as partners in life and in occupation! "And you didn't realize this until last night?"

He shook his head. "Something my sister said. When I told her I loved you, she, as you just did, asked how I could reconcile marrying you and climbing the ranks of government."

"What did you tell her?" Margaret asked, tilting her head slightly to one side.

"That you were worth giving up a high ranking position for," he answered in a low voice. "If I had to make the decision one hundred times, I would choose you every single time without hesitation. And that's when I realized that there are other ways to make a difference in the world."

She smoothed his hair back from his forehead. "Remind me to send Caroline a selection of her favorite desserts."

He chuckled. "Our siblings have been rather helpful, haven't they?"

"They're good people," Margaret agreed. "Shall we go tell them the good news?"

Stephen scooped her up and slid her onto his lap. "They can wait a few minutes more..."

Stephen opened the door to the drawing room for Margaret, unable to keep the foolish grin off his face. As soon as they entered, Caroline rose from the chair she'd been sitting in and Philip turned from the painting he'd been studying.

They were both smiling.

"I told you we wouldn't be able to surprise them," Margaret chuckled.

"We don't know the details yet," Caroline said cheerfully, fairly bouncing over to the happy couple.

Philip followed at a more normal pace, but was grinning almost as widely as Stephen. "So we're to have a wedding, then?"

"Yes," Margaret answered, squeezing Stephen's hand. "As soon as the banns can be called."

"I'm going to speak to the vicar tomorrow," Stephen added, glancing at Margaret. His heart swelled so much he thought it might burst, but he contented himself with squeezing her hand back.

"That's wonderful!" Caroline exclaimed, hugging Stephen first, then Margaret.

Philip hugged his sister, then put his arm around Stephen's shoulders. "I'm glad everything worked out for you both."

"She's worth it," Stephen replied quietly.

Philip nodded once, his smile softening, then cleared his throat. "We should celebrate. Eddington, do you have anything special in your wine cellar?"

Stephen summoned the butler and consulted with him for a few moments. "We'll have wine and cake shortly, a footman is on his way to Eastwood Manor to fetch Mrs. Maitland and Miss Natalie, and another is going to find the children. We can have a proper celebration with both families."

"Splendid," Caroline said with a little clap of her hands. "I'm so glad everyone is nearby."

Philip took Margaret aside and Stephen tried valiantly not to listen in. Fortunately, Caroline hugged him again and provided a welcome distraction.

"I'm so glad for you, for both of you," she said with a particularly tight embrace.

Stephen grunted under the pressure of her hug, then grinned. "You'll stay for the wedding, won't you? I know you hadn't planned to be away from your husband for so long."

"Yes, of course I will," she said, releasing him. "Ambrose won't mind spending an extra fortnight or so with his brothers—this is the only time of year when they're able to all be together."

Stephen opened his mouth to reply, but stopped when Patrick entered the drawing room with Alex. Margaret met her son halfway across the room and took his hands. A moment later Alex was grinning.

"Good," Stephen said to his sister.

She waved a hand in front of his eyes. "You only have eyes for your betrothed, don't you?"

"My future stepson has just heard the news," Stephen said softly.

"You should go talk to him," Caroline urged.

Stephen nodded, his gaze lingering on Margaret and Alex. "I will, after he's spoken with his mother."

The siblings talked a bit more, mostly about when Stephen and Margaret might be able to travel to Essex for a visit to Caroline's home, until Alex approached alone. Caroline patted Stephen's shoulder and went to speak with her own son, taking Stephen's ability to think along with her. There was so much he wanted to say to Alex, but the words just wouldn't come.

"So you and my mother are to be married," Alex said. His voice was even, his posture straight but relaxed...and he was smiling.

Stephen took his cue from the younger man and allowed the grin to return to his face. "We are. I'm sorry I didn't mention the possibility to you sooner."

"Mama and I talked yesterday," Alex replied, shifting his weight from one foot to the other. "I just wanted to say that I'm glad. She's so happy when she's with you, when she talks about you..." He paused again, put his hands in his pockets, then took them out again. "She seems more like herself lately, and I think that's because of you."

"I'll do my best to keep her happy," Stephen managed gruffly. "And you will always be welcome here. In fact, I'm hoping you're still interested in learning how to manage a place like this. You made some good observations when we rode out together, and knowing how to run an estate of any size gives you options when you're ready to forge your own path in the world."

Alex grinned. "So you're going to take on Mama *and* me, are you?"

Stephen chuckled, but then became serious. "The offer is yours to accept or not. Your mother has made her decision about me, but you are your own person and you're certainly old enough to make your own decisions. If estate management doesn't interest you but there's another way I can be of help, all you have to do is ask."

Alex nodded, and just as the conversation was about to turn awkward once again, a footman arrived with the promised wine and cake. The two men joined the rest of their families and helped to pass around plates and glasses.

"Thank you for making time for Alex today," Margaret said, accepting a piece of cake. "I realize that he's old enough now to be wed himself, so it's not as if his life will change much with our marriage. But he's still my son."

"It was my pleasure," Stephen replied—an honest assessment, as he truly did enjoy Alex's company, though hopefully they would become more comfortable with each other again once the newness of the situation wore off. "I told him I would help him in any way I can, though I don't know what the assistance of a builder's son is worth."

She pressed a kiss to his cheek. "It's worth a lot."

Caroline sidled up beside her brother and grinned at Margaret. "Did you tell him yet?"

Margaret's eyes went round. "Oh, not yet—should we wait?"

"No," Stephen cut in with a chuckle, "whatever it is you should tell me now or else it's all I will think about until you do."

"We've come up with a tentative name for this place," Caroline said, between bites of cake. "What do you think of Woodbine Lodge?"

"What is woodbine?" he asked, his eyes shifting from his sister to his betrothed.

Margaret's smile blossomed slowly, dreamily. "Woodbine is an old name for honeysuckle."

Stephen locked eyes with Margaret and his grin matched hers. "Excellent choice."

Caroline bounced away to ask the rest of the guests for their thoughts on Woodbine Lodge, and Stephen had his betrothed all to himself for the first time since they re-entered the house.

"You're sure about this?" he asked quietly. "It's not too late to go back to the way things were."

"Oh but it is," she replied with a small smile. "Now that I know what it's like to love you, I can never go back to merely being your acquaintance."

He glanced around and, noting that everyone seemed occupied with other things for the moment, dropped a light kiss on Margaret's lips. "Neither could I."

# Epilogue

*London*
*June 1816*

"You're sure about this?" Margaret asked, the trepidation in her voice evident even to her own ears. The last time she was a guest at a ball, things hadn't exactly gone well. "It's not too late to go back home."

They sat in their carriage, on loan from Margaret's cousin Cecilia, outside a moderately sized townhouse in Brook Street. A friend of a friend had suggested Mr. and Mrs. Eddington as guests to the hosts—Margaret couldn't recall their names now—and after a great deal of thought, they had elected to attend.

"I'm slightly terrified," Stephen answered, taking her hand in his and giving it a squeeze.

They were only in London to see Philip and Adeleine, who were there for Natalie's second season, and a friend of Stephen's from his Cambridge days, who was an MP and in Town for the parliamentary session.

They had no obligation whatsoever to attend this ball.

Margaret looked at her husband in the dim light of the torches held by footmen as they directed carriages and people to their proper locations. He was the most steadfast man she had ever known, defending her when she was maligned by neighbors or merchants, helping her settle into her new life as a wife and mistress of her own life, loving her deeply and fiercely. They'd received this invitation because word of the work he'd been doing at Woodbine was beginning to circulate among the gentry and lower aristocracy.

The least she could do was attend a ball for him.

"Let's go in and see what refreshments they're serving," she said lightly. "If the food is lacking, we'll go home."

He chuckled. "That's the spirit."

When their carriage reached the front of the line, a footman opened the door and let down the steps, assisting Margaret down to the pavement. Stephen hopped out behind her and offered her his arm.

They waited their turn to go through the receiving line and made their way into the area set aside for playing cards. The house was too small for a proper ballroom, but there was enough space for dancing with refreshments set up in an adjoining room, and a string quintet playing a country dance with gusto in one corner.

"Well, there are the refreshments," Stephen quipped, nodding toward a lady carrying a small plate of pastries and a glass of what appeared to be lemonade.

A few guests looked scandalized to see them in public, some turned up their noses, and one lady even yanked the train of her dress to one side when Margaret's gown brushed against it, as if Margaret had some highly contagious disease.

Her chest tightened and her heart began to pound. "Let's see what they have, then, shall we?"

Stephen pressed his lips together and led her through the crowd to the tables laden with pastries and cakes, drinks of all kinds, and even a pineapple placed in the center of the main table on some kind of pedestal.

"Eddington?" a deep voice called.

Margaret and Stephen both turned toward the sound. "Yes?" Stephen answered, scanning the assemblage.

"Eddington!" the voice repeated genially. "I'm glad to have found you in this crush."

"McAlister," Stephen replied warmly to a tall, thin man heading toward them. "I didn't know you'd be here tonight."

"I wasn't going to come," Mr. McAlister confessed, shaking Stephen's outstretched hand, "but when I heard you had accepted I talked myself into it."

Stephen glanced at Margaret, who shrugged. She didn't know this man at all, let alone why he would want to attend an event with her husband.

"I want to introduce you to someone..." Mr. McAlister said, craning his neck to see around the people nearest to them. "Bradford? Bradford! I found Eddington..."

Margaret had let go of Stephen's arm as they made their way through the house, but she reached out and clasped his hand for a moment, giving it a squeeze.

"Mr. Bradford, this is Mr. Eddington, the one who is building the schools in the Cotswolds."

Margaret beamed with pride as the men exchanged pleasantries, then peppered Stephen with questions about his schools. He'd built two so far, with a third one under construction. They were ostensibly for the children of Woodbine's employees and those of the near neighbors, but there were also lessons on Sundays for adults who wanted to learn to read and write. Margaret taught some of the reading classes herself, but the number of pupils had swelled after the first month and other teachers were hired to make sure everyone who wanted to learn could do so.

Margaret squeezed Stephen's hand one more time, giving him a slight nod when he met her gaze, then heading off to circulate on her own. She wasn't particularly excited to do so, but it was one of the unwritten rules of society functions—couples can not spend too much time together, or be too affectionate with each other.

She filled a plate with delicate cakes, nodding to acquaintances who acknowledged her, answering each snide remark with a cheerful smile. She stopped to talk with a friend of Adeleine's who had always treated her like a person worth knowing, and helped two young ladies with the flounces on their gowns. She wandered into the dancing area and leaned against a wall, listening to the string quintet move smoothly from country dance to Scotch reel to waltz.

"May I have this dance, madam?"

She turned, laughing, to find her husband offering her his hand. "I don't feel much like dancing, sir, but would you care for some cake?"

He took a bite of the square she held up for him and closed his eyes. "We need to get the recipe for that one."

"I thought you'd like it," she said, turning to watch the musicians and leaning back against her husband. "How did things go with Mr. McAlister and Mr. Bradford?"

His gloved hand slid down her arm, and his lips brushed against her ear. "Bradford is interested in building a similar school on his estate in Sussex, and he had questions about how we went about building and staffing ours."

"Oh, that's wonderful," she replied, closing her eyes to savor his touch. "I'm sure you had a lot to tell him."

"I did," Stephen said, "but I promised to meet him at his club tomorrow afternoon for a more in depth discussion. I would rather spend this evening with you."

He practically whispered that last sentence and Margaret shivered deliciously. "We have tried the refreshments. Or I have, anyway. Did you want to render an opinion as well?"

"No," he murmured, slipping his arms around her waist. "I trust yours."

"Then let's be off," she replied softly, giving her plate to a passing footman and taking Stephen's hand. They made their way out of the house and into the cool night air, where Margaret pulled him to a stop. "What shall we do while we wait for the carriage to come round?" she asked, wrapping her arms around his shoulders.

"We could completely scandalize any guests that happen to see us," he suggested, pulling her against him.

"Scandals are what I'm known for," Margaret replied. She managed to keep a straight face just long enough to get the words out, then giggled. "May I kiss you, my love?"

He bent his head to hers and grinned. "Yes, and please be thorough."

His lips were warm on hers, his arms secure around her. In the flickering torchlight, she combed her fingers through his short hair and sighed happily. "Better than botany books."

His laugh was low and gravelly. "Definitely better than botany books."

# WHEN I FALL IN LOVE

**Childhood friends reunite in their mutual struggle against their financial burdens. What magic might they find together under the Harvest Moon?**

Ever since Kit Mathison took control of the modest estate he inherited, he's had nothing but setbacks. When the roof of his house caves in and makes the place unlivable, he's frustrated but not surprised. How much will this disaster cost? Where will he stay while repairs are made?

Sylvie Devereaux has remained in her childhood home to help her aging grandparents with their farm, only to realize they need as much care as the crops and livestock. But while love and laughter are prominent in their home, money is not. And the never-ending rain is drowning their wheat along with any hope they have for financial recovery.

When Kit returns Sylvie's wayward goose, they re-ignite the friendship they'd kindled as adolescents and put a plan into action to relieve each others' burdens: Kit will board with the Devereaux family while his home is repaired, providing money and labor in exchange for their hospitality. But when Kit proposes a marriage of convenience to make the arrangement permanent, Sylvie balks. She has always wanted to marry for love, and they don't love each other...do they?

# Chapter 1



Sylvie Devereaux sat in her usual place on the brown sofa, lightly rubbing the worn spot on the arm. Her grandparents occupied the wooden chairs on either side of the fireplace, where a small fire burned to try to combat the unusual chill. The low, red light of the evening sun filtering through the windows wasn't quite bright enough to see by anymore, so Sylvie lit the oil lamp on the table beside her, hoping to get some mending done before she went to bed.

Her fingers lingered on the lamp a moment, the smooth metal cool to the touch for a few moments before it began to warm. This particular lamp had been a rather costly wedding gift to her grandparents from both their families, the result of a numerous relatives pooling what they could spare to purchase something truly beautiful...and useful. Sylvie's grandparents had brought it with them when they emigrated from France, a symbol of the family they left behind and the hope they cherished for their future.

Was this the future they had envisioned?

"How does the field look, Grandpère?"

It was a topic they had discussed at least once each day during the growing season, usually in this fashion around the fireplace or while they ate supper, for as long as Sylvie could remember. Grandpère would inevitably talk about the height of the wheat, the color and strength of the stalks, or a myriad of other tiny but important details that signaled the health of their crop.

But this season had been different. This *weather* had been different.

His silence stretched out so long that Sylvie put down her needle and looked up at her grandfather. His eyes had met his wife's, his mouth turned down into a hard frown that didn't ease when he finally answered.

"Not good, ma chérie. We may not have much of a crop this year."

Not a surprise and yet wholly surprising all at the same time. Sylvie had been half-expecting this bit of news for the past several weeks now, but to hear her grandfather say it aloud was like a physical blow to her chest.

"Still too wet," her grandmother added, returning to her own sewing. "The kitchen garden has been struggling all summer, too."

Sylvie had noted the lack of production in the kitchen garden herself, trying to find enough produce to eat with each meal. There was never enough, and what was growing was undersized and slow to ripen.

Grandpère nodded. "And too cold. Wheat doesn't like a great deal of heat, but it needs some warmth."

"And sun." Sylvie pressed her lips together, recalling the abnormally high number of dark, rainy days they'd had this year. Even this day they'd only seen a bit of sun as it set, and that was more than most. "Do you think we'll be able to pay rent this quarter?"

The fire gave a loud pop and sent out a plume of thick smoke as he sighed heavily. "For the first time since you were a little girl, I don't know. If we get enough sun in the next few weeks, there may be something to harvest. But if the rain keeps falling…"

He didn't have to finish his sentence. If the rain kept falling, any wheat that had managed to grow in their field despite the conditions would rot at the root and there would be no harvest. Sylvie also didn't need to ask if he'd thought of borrowing money—her parents might have a little to spare, but likely not enough to cover rent for the farm. And they were in France with no way to send money or to return to England themselves. A bank loan might be a possibility, but without a crop to use as assurance…

"Try not to worry," Grandmère said, turning in her chair to meet Sylvie's gaze, her face partially cloaked in shadows. "There is still time to figure something out."

There was a measure of comfort in her words, but Sylvie was too practical to be swayed very much by them. If Grandpère said things were looking dismal, then there was reason to worry.

"There are always my animals."

In addition to the three people and the wheat fields, the farm housed a flock of geese, a few goats, some laying hens, and a dairy cow, all of whom would need to be fed through the winter. They weren't truly hers, but Sylvie had taken over caring for the farm's livestock as an adolescent and had hand raised many of the goats and geese herself. As a result, Grandpère had taken to calling them hers.

He raised a hand to object, but she held up her own to stop him. "Not Moses, of course." She suppressed a shudder at the thought of sending her special pet, a goose that she'd raised from an abandoned egg, off to someone's dinner table. "But the others should fetch a good price. That is why we keep them, and if it means keeping our home…"

Grandmère sent her a sympathetic look, then sighed herself. "Hopefully it won't come to that."

"But if we need to," Sylvie continued, turning their alternatives over in her mind, "it wouldn't be that different from other years. We've sold animals before."

"Yes, when we run out of room for them," Grandpère answered gruffly. "I will go to London and talk to his lordship myself before we sell off your entire collection."

Sylvie was certain Grandpère wouldn't even know what their landlord, the Marquess of Whitby, looked like, let alone find the wherewithal to go and speak to the man, but she kept that to herself. She also noted the red creeping into Grandpère's cheeks that couldn't all be attributed to the fire and turned the conversation to a new topic. "Perhaps I can take in some mending, then, or do some cooking for the neighbors. Mr. Mathison next door is a bachelor, and so is Mr. Ross across the way—I could speak to them both tomorrow."

Grandpère nodded, his face returning to its normal color. "I suppose it wouldn't hurt to inquire. And if we do end up with enough wheat to pay the rent, you'll have a little money put by for your future."

Her future. Sylvie suppressed a shiver and tried to focus on her needle going in and out of the soft, worn fabric of her second best dress. When Grandpère died, her father would likely be allowed to take over the copyhold on the farm if he chose to, but there was no telling when he and her mother would return, or if they'd even want to take up farming again. What if they decided to stay in France? They had a comfortable home there now with her mother's parents. What was there to come back to here except unending hard work and rain?

Sylvie gave up on her mending and said goodnight to her grandparents, trudging slowly up the stairs to the bedchamber she'd occupied all her life. How much longer would it be hers?

What would she do when it wasn't?

Cold water dripped onto Kit Mathison's face, which was occasionally accompanied by a chilly breeze. He blinked his eyes open but quickly squeezed them shut again, pulling the blanket up over his face to block out the small deluge. But instead of soft, dry blanket, he was met with sopping fabric that threatened to drown him before he could rise from his bed.

"Thomas, you've left the tent flap open again," he said with a yawn, his eyes still tightly shut to keep the water out of them. "It must have rained last night."

He felt about for a patch of dry cloth to wipe his face with and found part of his nightshirt that was unaffected. Rolling over onto his side, he pushed the blanket off and struggled to a sitting position as the dripping continued to wet his hair and clothes. "Thomas?"

Kit opened his eyes to find that he was not, in fact, in a tent behind the house with his younger brother, as his sleep-addled mind had believed, but alone in the big bed in the master's chamber.

"What the devil is going on?"

Another cold stream landed in his lap and he leaped out of bed. What the devil *was* going on? He held his hands out, palms up, eyes wide as he looked around the room.

Yes, it was definitely raining inside the house.

*His* house.

And there was a very large hole in *his* roof.

He stood in the corner of the room for a moment, unmoving except to blink, staring dumbly at the raindrops falling through the ceiling. How did this happen?

How much would it cost to repair?

Kit shook himself and set about dressing in dry clothes, thankful that the rain hadn't damaged his wardrobe...yet. He made his way down the stairs and stopped in the kitchen to butter a piece of bread, shifting the bread from one hand to the other as he put on his old, patched tailcoat and hat.

"All right, let's see how bad it is."

The rain had abated and the bread was reduced to crumbs by the time Kit stepped out the front door. He managed to wrestle the tall ladder and a large tarpaulin out of the barn with the help of one of the stable lads and hauled them one at a time to the house. When the two of them had propped the ladder against the house as close as they could to Kit's bedchamber, Kit climbed resolutely to the top with a rope tied to the tarpaulin while the stable lad held the bottom of the ladder steady. The ladder was just tall enough to reach the second story of the house, forcing Kit to scramble up onto the roof to survey the damage.

"How does it look?" the stable lad called?

Kit stayed low, crawling from the edge of the roof toward the hole, his eyes growing wider as he drew nearer.

"Oh no."

A large portion of the roof had collapsed into the attic space some time ago, judging by the weathering of the timbers poking out. And each time rain fell from the sky during this very wet summer, it had collected in the newly bared attic—he could see the water stains on the attic floor —weakening the structure.

The rain that morning was merely falling through a ceiling that had been rotting away for weeks.

Kit sighed wearily. "How could I have missed this?"

He spent a few more minutes surveying the damage, then pulled the tarpaulin up to the roof and secured it over the gaping hole, trying to commit the details of the damage to memory so he could make a sketch later. A careful check of the other parts of the roof he could reach yielded even more information—three other places where shingles were loose or damaged, and water was likely already getting in.

When Kit reached the ground again, his stable lad wasn't the only one waiting for him.

"Moses! Have you come to swim in my bedchamber?"

The big white bird looked up at Kit and turned sideways, asking to be scratched the way Kit's childhood dog had done once upon a time. Both Kit and the stable lad obliged before hefting the ladder once again and hauling it back to the barn, with Moses waddling alongside them.

Once the ladder was stowed, the stable lad went back to his usual work and Kit headed back to the house, walking slowly around the perimeter looking for other issues.

"The roof was damaged, you see," Kit explained to the goose as they circled the house, "and I didn't realize it until just today. It's made a terrible mess inside the house, and I fear it's going to take a long time to restore."

A gust of wind blew through, ruffling Moses's feathers. He resettled his wings with a little shake.

"Indeed."

With another sigh, Kit made note of a couple of places under the eaves that were showing early signs of water damage. "Do you want to come in while I write these all down? Or shall I walk you home first?"

The first few times Kit had met Moses, he'd felt rather silly talking to an animal that most people would make into Christmas dinner. But the bird's owner, Kit's neighbor, had insisted that Moses had a personality and enjoyed conversation, and Moses had begun wandering over to Kit's farm on his own from time to time.

Apparently he liked the company here. And the stream that ran across one corner of the property. And the scratches. But he never seemed to be able to find his way back without a human escort.

Moses looked around, then met Kit's eyes and huffed a sigh.

"Home it is then, lad."

Kit started off toward Broadstone Farm, the home of Mr. and Mrs. Devereaux and their granddaughter, with Moses waddling along beside him.

When Kit was halfway up the drive of Broadstone Farm, a woman dressed in a faded green gown and matching bonnet came around the side of the house and stopped, raising a hand to shade her eyes in their direction.

He waved at her. "That's your mama, I think," he said to the goose.

Moses continued to waddle stoically along beside Kit for another minute or two until the woman called to them.

"Moses? Is that you?"

The bird perked up at the sound and honked in return, his little webbed feet moving faster and faster until he was half running, half flying toward the woman.

"Indeed, that's your mama," Kit said with a chuckle, following along behind.

By the time he caught up to Moses, the woman was crouched down beside the goose scratching the back of his long neck. She gave him one last pat before rising.

"Ah, Mr. Mathison brought you home again," Miss Devereaux said to her pet, wiping her hand on her skirt. The bird must have been wet from the light rain that still fell. "Did you say thank you?"

"He never does," Kit replied with feigned exasperation. "I don't know what kind of bird you raised."

She laughed a little, even though they'd had this same exchange numerous times over the past two years. "I think he's jealous of your navigation skills. You can find your way back and forth between our two homes without any help at all. For all his intelligence, Moses still hasn't quite mastered that skill yet."

Kit smiled in return, wondering briefly if this would be the sum of their relationship from now on—small talk about a bird. "Well, his timing was good today. I needed to get away for a while."

"Oh?"

"My roof caved in."

Miss Devereaux gasped, her eyes widening. "No!"

"On top of me. While I was sleeping."

"Oh, Kit," she breathed.

He started momentarily at the use of his nickname. In the time since he'd moved back into his childhood home she'd only ever called him "Mr. Mathison," despite having called him "Kit" for all the years they spent in each other's company growing up.

"How awful. Come inside and sit down for a moment or two, won't you? Have you eaten yet this morning? Grandmère is just about to put breakfast on the table."

Mrs. Devereaux could make shoe leather taste good, and Kit put a hand to his empty stomach. "I believe I will. It's too hard to think when one is hungry."

He followed Miss Devereaux and Moses up to the house where the bird veered off toward the barn, and the two humans entered the kitchen where the smell of eggs frying in butter washed over them.

Kit's stomach growled.

"Grandmère, we have one more for breakfast," Miss Devereaux said to the gray-haired woman at the stove, removing her bonnet and hanging it on a peg behind the door. She pushed a lock of glossy brown hair behind her ear. "Mr. Mathison has had a trying start to his day, and I've asked him to join us."

Mrs. Devereaux slid the pan she was tending to a cooler part of the stove. "Christopher," she said with a bright smile, enunciating each syllable of his name in her French accent. "How good it is to see you!"

He swept his hat off his head and bowed like a proper English gentleman, but couldn't keep the grin from his face. "Madame Devereaux, the pleasure is all mine. What can I do to help?"

Mrs. Devereaux directed him to a towel and the stack of plates behind her. He gathered them up after drying his hands and followed Miss Devereaux out to the dining room.

"How bad is the roof?" she asked, laying forks and knives next to the plates he set out.

Kit's shoulder slumped. "There's a hole a couple of feet across that goes through the roof, into the attic, and through the ceiling. And it looks like there are a few weak spots elsewhere."

"That sounds like fairly extensive damage." Two forks clinked together in her hand as she separated them. "Will you need a completely new roof?"

"I won't know for certain until I can get a builder out to have a look," he set the last plate down and looked over at her, "but it seems likely. Until then, I'll have to cover the holes as best I can and hope the rain lets up."

Miss Devereaux met his gaze. "Less rain would be ideal, yes. In the meantime, you can't stay in a house with a hole in the roof, especially when it's so wet."

"What was that?" Mr. Devereaux asked, entering the dining room as his granddaughter headed back to the kitchen. "Christopher has a hole in his roof?"

Kit recounted the events of the morning for Miss Devereaux's grandfather, trying to keep his voice matter of fact when his mind was spinning.

"Sylvie is right, you cannot stay in that house again until it's properly repaired." The smell of bacon permeated the room and he waited a moment for Mrs. Devereaux to enter the room with a platter of sizzling hot food. Then he continued, "You should stay here for a few nights."

Mrs. Devereaux's eyes met her husband's and she nodded. "Yes, I was thinking the same thing."

Miss Devereaux followed her grandmother in with four cups. "What?"

"What?" Kit said at the same time.

Mr. Devereaux took the platter of food and set it on the table, then held out a chair for his wife. "You'll have a warm, dry place to sleep until your bedchamber is serviceable again," he said to Kit, as if the decision had been made.

"That does make sense," Miss Devereaux added, taking her seat at the table. "And we have plenty of room."

Kit looked at the three of them, offering up their home to him as if it was something they did every day. It was true they'd known him since he was in leading strings, but the years he'd spent in Scotland after his father died had added a measure of reserve to their relationship that they had yet to fully put aside.

"Thank you," he said simply, pulling out his own chair and settling himself at the table. "I will spend the day assessing and cleaning and patching, and I'll join you for supper tonight."

Mrs. Devereaux smiled brightly. "Excellent."

Mr. Devereaux nodded once and turned his attention to his food.

Kit's eyes met Miss Devereaux's and he smiled to cover the flash of longing that washed over him. Would these couple of days be awkward between him and Sylvie? Or could they perhaps use this physical proximity to start rebuilding their friendship?

Sylvie sat across the table from Mr. Mathison once again that evening, wanting to inquire about the state of his house—and himself. But his speech was slow and his eyelids drooped, and he excused himself to bed not long after they'd sat down. She led him up the stairs and down the hallway to the extra bedchamber she'd helped her grandmother prepare earlier in the day. He mumbled his thanks and disappeared inside, closing the door behind him.

The second evening of his stay, Mr. Mathison managed some small talk at supper but was otherwise quiet, almost dull—wholly unlike the boy she remembered from her childhood.

Of course, the boy never had to worry about the time and expense involved in repairing his crumbling home.

He once again excused himself to bed early, and Sylvie watched him trudge up the stairs alone, wondering what she could do to make him feel better. She turned the thought over in her mind as she cleared the table and washed the dishes, unsure of what kind of gesture would be welcome. They had been friends as children due to the proximity of their homes, but not overly close ones. Kit was the eldest son of an English landowner, while Sylvie's grandparents were immigrants who paid for the privilege of running Broadstone. The two families hadn't exactly moved in the same social circles.

But Kit had always been kind to her, and they had spent some time together as affable companions when they were children and into their adolescence. She grinned momentarily remembering the time Kit had wanted to learn to bake a cake and her grandmother had obliged him, showing him how to measure out ingredients, what to mix together when, and how hot the oven needed to be. With Grandmère's guidance, Kit's cake had been a tasty treat. When he'd repeated the action at home the following week, it had resulted in a blackened brick.

"Do we have any of that pound cake left?" she asked herself aloud, wiping her hands on her apron and searching through the larder. "Ah-ha!" She found half of the pound cake her grandmother had made the day before and a few undersized strawberries from the kitchen garden. "That will do just fine."

Sylvie waited for her grandparents to go up to bed, then waited another quarter of an hour. She crept quietly into the kitchen and cut two slices of pound cake, then carried them slowly up the stairs.

Was he even awake?

There was a faint light shining under his door, and she took a chance, knocking softly. "Mr. Mathison?"

There was a rustle of fabric and the creak of the floor, then the door swung open. "Miss Devereaux? Is everything all right?"

"Yes, everything is fine." She offered him one of the plates. "I only thought that if you were still up, you might like some cake."

He glanced from her to the plate, then back to her, and a wide smile spread across his face. "That was very thoughtful, thank you." When he accepted the plate and took a bite of the cake, his features melted into an expression that was part bliss and part relief. "This is so good."

"Grandmère's special recipe," Sylvie replied with a smile of her own. It was good to see him happy, even if it was only for a moment.

Mr. Mathison chuckled, leaning against the door frame. "Do you remember the time she tried to teach me to bake?"

"Yes," Sylvie grinned, taking a bite of her own piece of cake. "The first one turned out rather well, if I recall."

"But not the second." He breathed in and let out a long sigh. "I fear the same thing is happening with the house, and that I'm not as good at taking care of my home as I should be."

Sylvie almost made a joke in an attempt to return the joy to his face, but elected not to. Perhaps he needed a sympathetic ear more than a quick smile. "Is it that bad?"

"I think it might be." He took another bite of cake and chewed it slowly. "I will know for certain in three days when the builder comes out, but I already know that it will not be good."

She wanted to reach out and touch him, to try to impart whatever comfort to him that she could. But she didn't know how to do that for him anymore. In that moment, she wasn't sure she ever did know. Instead, she said, "You can stay here as long as you need to. I know it's not the same as sleeping in your own bed in your own home..."

"But I very much appreciate your kindness," he finished for her. "These past few days have been exhausting. Coming home to good food, a dry bed, and people who care about me has been exactly the thing I need to keep going."

Sylvie's gaze dropped to the floor for the briefest of moments before meeting his blue eyes again in the dim light emanating from his bedchamber. "I'm glad we could provide that for you."

They stood in a slightly awkward silence for another moment before she spoke again. "I should seek my bed. I may not have a leaky house to repair, but I do have a list of tasks as long as my arm to start in the morning."

He gave her a half-bow, holding tight to his cake plate. "Good night, Miss Devereaux."

"Good night, Mr. Mathison."

Kit said goodbye to the builder and headed slowly for Broadstone Farm. When he was about halfway up the drive, Moses came waddling toward him, honking a greeting.

"I'm glad one of us is in good spirits," he told the bird, stooping to scratch the base of Moses's neck.

The pair walked up to the house together in companionable silence and met Miss Devereaux, who was sitting in the grass with her back against the rough bark of a large oak tree. She raised her eyebrows in an unasked question, and Kit sat down beside her as the leaves rustled quietly in the slight breeze.

"The whole roof has to be replaced."

"Oh no."

"And the amount of time it will take will depend largely on the weather."

It was dry currently, but there were thick gray clouds gathering on the horizon, and Miss Devereaux's brown eyes shifted to them. "Oh no," she repeated with a note of dread.

It was the same feeling he'd had when the builder had broken the news. Putting a new roof on a house in the summer should have been a fairly straightforward procedure, but this summer had been everything except straightforward.

"Well," she continued, returning her gaze to him, "I meant what I said the other night. You can stay with us as long as you have the need."

He turned his body toward hers and offered her a small smile. "Thank you."

# Chapter 3

"Let me get that one," Kit said, stooping to heft a large rock before Mr. Devereaux could make the attempt. They were repairing a stone wall that separated Broadstone Farm from the property behind it, but Mr. Devereaux was the embodiment of a willing spirit with weak flesh.

Instead of loudly lamenting the loss of his strength over the years, as some men might, Mr. Devereaux took a step back and leaned against a sound part of the wall. "You're welcome to it, Christopher."

Kit scooped the rock up and nestled it carefully into place, then picked up two smaller rocks to fill in holes on either side.

Mr. Devereaux watched him appraisingly. "I was young and strong like you once," he said with a note of wistfulness.

"I think you were stronger," Kit replied with a grin, bending his knees to heave another large rock into place. "Those didn't put themselves there."

Mr. Devereaux's eyes followed Kit's to a series of small boulders that served as the foundation of the wall. "Ah yes, I remember setting those. You and Sylvie must have been, what? Eight? Nine? And you wanted to climb on them after I put them in place."

The laugh escaped Kit before he could suppress it. "I remember that! Sylvie asked me to help her climb up, then challenged me to a race, with her on the boulders and me on the ground."

"Yes," the older man grinned, his eyes crinkling up at the corners. "She fell off the second one, but wouldn't give up!"

"She gets that from you, I think," Kit chuckled. "Never one to give up if there's a still a chance."

Mr. Devereaux sobered, leaning more heavily against the wall. "And a blessing it's been these past few years. We haven't had all the help we've needed since her parents went back to France, but my Sylvie does everything that she can to keep the farm and the house running."

"Well, perhaps I can relieve some of the burden while I'm here," Kit replied, continuing to fit rocks together and build up the wall.

Mr. Devereaux nodded thoughtfully. "We would very much appreciate that, including Sylvie. She should be getting her animals ready for the Harvest Festival. She takes at least one prize every year, but she's been too busy this year." His eyes met Kit's and held them. "When she's not working in the house or on the farm, she has begun to take in mending and sewing for some of the bachelors in the area. She has a friend in the village that she visits when she drops things off to her customers there, but it makes me sad that even her social engagements involve her working somehow."

Kit paused, resting his hand on the wall. "How long have things been this bad?"

"We have had to tighten the purse string the past few years, but this year..." Mr. Devereaux's whole face sagged.

He didn't have to finish the sentence. The ever-present rain was the first thing anyone spoke about after "How do you do?"

Kit nodded and resumed piling rocks in strategic places on the wall. He was a member of this household now, even if only temporarily, and his mind searched for ways he could provide some comfort to the people who offered him sanctuary. They wouldn't take money, even though he was effectively a boarder and should be paying for the privilege, but perhaps he could purchase some things they needed in addition to offering his labor.

And maybe he could find a way to remind Miss Devereaux what it was like to be carefree. For some reason, that felt very important to him.

Kit packed that feeling away for examination another time and said instead, "As long as I'm here, I'll do whatever I can to be helpful."

"You always were a good boy, Christopher," Mr. Devereaux said, his features lightening considerably. "And it appears you've grown up to be a good man."

"My mother will be pleased you think so."

"How is your mother?"

They talked of family and old times for a while longer while Kit continued to repair the stone wall, fitting rocks into crevices just the right size. When a light drizzle began to fall and the rocks became slippery, Mr. Devereaux declared that work was done for the day and that they should head back to the house.

Miss Devereaux's voice greeted them when they entered the kitchen. "I picked up the post while I was in the village, Grandpère. There's a letter from Papa." She shifted the wooden spoon she was stirring something with to her other hand and met Kit's gaze. "There's a letter for you, too, Mr. Mathison."

"Oh?"

Kit followed Mr. Devereaux to the stack of letters on the dining room table and grinned the moment he laid eyes on his. The handwriting was that of his best friend turned sister-in-law, Maddie, who had written to him regularly after his family had left Kent for Scotland and continued to do so now that they lived considerably closer together. He took it up to his bedchamber, washing his face and hands and putting on a clean shirt before returning to the dining room to help set the table for supper.

After the food was eaten and the table cleared, Mr. and Mrs. Devereaux settled themselves before the fire, and Miss Devereaux sat down on the sofa to sew some buttons onto a shirt. Kit retrieved his letter and brought it down, seating himself at the other end of the sofa near the oil lamp and cracking open the plain seal.

He must have had a serious expression, because Mrs. Devereaux turned to him after a few moments and asked, "Is everything well, Christopher?"

"Hmm? Oh, yes." He grinned. "My brother's wife has written to tell me about the repairs he's made to their home. He managed to re-hang a door, and there was much celebrating."

"Thomas married Maddie Hayward, didn't he?" Miss Devereaux asked, glancing up from her sewing.

Kit nodded. "He did. They live with her grandmother about two hours' ride from here."

"Who is she?" Mrs. Devereaux inquired. "That name sounds familiar."

"Her parents are Kit's neighbors on the other side. You should remember Maddie, Grandmère," Miss Devereaux prompted. "She was Kit's closest friend when we were children. The one who—" She stopped abruptly and pressed her lips together.

Kit put his letter down and turned his gaze on her, filing away the feeling that washed over him when she called him "Kit," and chuckling when she looked away with an awkward smile. "The one who everyone thought *I* was going to marry," he said slyly. "Is that what you were going to say?"

Miss Devereaux nodded sheepishly and Mrs. Devereaux's eyes lit with recognition. "I remember her now. She was the one who caught a fish bigger than Christopher's, yes?"

Miss Devereaux laughed aloud, then hastily covered her mouth with one hand to stifle it. "I'd forgotten about the fish," she said after a moment, dropping her hand into her lap. "You sulked here for days when that happened."

"But you took me in and comforted me," Kit replied, the memory of Sylvie's arm around him, the biscuits Mrs. Devereaux had given them, forming in his mind. "Then promptly told me to go congratulate Maddie on her catch."

Miss Devereaux grinned. "To your credit, you did exactly that."

Mrs. Devereaux turned back to her husband to ask him a question, and Miss Devereaux leaned toward Kit. "Grandpère told me about how you helped him with the stone wall today, or rather, how you did all the labor. Is there something I can do to return the favor?"

Kit's first instinct was to say no, that he was the one who owed them and hadn't done it in order to get something in return. But perhaps he could give her the chance to slow down and relax while still feeling useful. "I could use some help with some new arrivals in my barn, and you've always been good with animals. Can you go over with me tomorrow?"

She thought for a moment, then nodded slowly. "As long as I'm back in time to help prepare supper."

"Excellent."

They talked about unimportant things for a while longer while she sewed, then Kit excused himself to his chamber. Climbing the stairs two at a time, he held in his mind that picture of a young Sylvie, who had been there for him when he'd needed a friend, and told him when he needed to discard his childishness. It had been exactly what he needed.

Could he be what she needed now?

Sylvie entered Mr. Mathison's barn beside him, with Moses close on their heels. "What can I do?" she asked, casting her eyes over the large interior.

"Will you take a look at these kittens?" he asked, gesturing to a nest of hay in one of the horse boxes. "This is the mother's first litter, and I don't think she quite knows how to care for them."

"Of course. Let's see what we have here..." She entered the horse box and knelt down just close enough to see the kittens, but not close enough to upset their mother, her heart swelling at the sight of their tiny faces. "Do you know how old they are?"

"A fortnight, I think," came the reply as he approached and knelt down beside her. The heat radiating from his body felt good in the cool damp air.

Sylvie nodded, watching the mother cat approach her and sniff at the hem of her skirt. Moses, she noted, had gone off to another part of the barn. "Their eyes are all open but they're still very small, so that fits."

The mother, a stocky tortoiseshell cat, approached Mr. Mathison, sniffed him briefly, then rubbed her body against his legs. "Good morning, Leto," he responded, scratching her back gently. "This is Sylvie. She's a friend. Would you mind if she looked over your babies?"

Sylvie instinctively suppressed the smile that threatened to form on her lips, then realized what she was doing and relaxed her expression. "How do you do, Leto?"

The cat rubbed on Mr. Mathison one more time, then eyed Sylvie as if to judge whether or not her kittens were safe with this stranger.

"You have so many babies!" Sylvie continued, slowly stretching out a hand toward Leto. "Do you need help looking after them?"

Leto sniffed Sylvie's fingers, then took a few steps toward her and pushed herself against Sylvie's palm. Sylvie reciprocated by scratching Leto's neck and was rewarded when the cat arched up into her hand.

"I think she likes you," Mr. Mathison said cheerfully.

"You trust me, so she's decided to trust me...for the moment," Sylvie replied, scratching Leto's face. "I'm going to take a look at your babies now, Leto, but I promise I won't hurt them."

Sylvie slowly made her way toward the nest in the hay, keeping one eye on Leto lest she decide to strike out in defense of her young. Leto, too, kept her eyes on Sylvie, moving with her as she peered over the edge of the nest. There were seven in total: one tortoiseshell like her mother, two orange toms, three gray-and-whites, and a diminutive all-black that appeared to be the runt of the litter.

Her knees began to protest and Sylvie carefully shifted to a new position sitting in the hay, locking eyes with Mr. Mathison for a moment before reaching into the nest and picking up the black kitten.

Leto watched Sylvie intently with wide green eyes.

"Don't worry," Mr. Mathison said gently, stroking the cat.

One by one, Sylvie lifted and studied each kitten, checking their overall condition, to see if they were getting enough to eat and being cleaned properly. Each time Leto got too tense, Mr. Mathison would touch her, or scratch her in her favorite spot, and she'd relax again.

"Here you are, Leto," Sylvie said, placing the last kitten back in the nest, "I'm quite finished now."

She rose with Mr. Mathison's help and brushed the hay from her skirt as Leto went immediately to her kittens and began to bathe them.

"How do they look?" Mr. Mathison asked, leading her out of the horse box.

"Fairly good," she responded, noting that he didn't release her hand until they were halfway to the entrance of the barn. Last time he'd held her hand they'd been perhaps ten years old. "The black one is a bit on the small side, even for as young as they are, and Leto isn't cleaning them overly well. But on the whole they look normal for their age."

A sigh of relief whooshed out of Mr. Mathison and he put a hand to his chest. "Oh good. They looked awfully small to me, and I was afraid she wasn't feeding them properly."

Most people wouldn't think twice about a litter of barn cats, and Sylvie found his concern touching. "I can show you how to clean them up, and how to feed the black one to make sure she's getting enough to eat, if you'd like."

"Excellent," he grinned. "Will you help me look after them? When you have a spare moment, of course."

Sylvie's mind traveled over the list of tasks she needed to complete each day and sighed inwardly. She didn't really have time to take on another responsibility. But it wouldn't really be her responsibility—Mr. Mathison would be doing the lion's share of the work. "Help Kit with his kittens?" she asked spontaneously, then giggled. "I could do that."

"I'll make it worth your while," he answered with a grin, offering her his arm and leading her toward the house. "Wait until you see…"

She clasped his arm firmly and allowed him to whisk her into his kitchen, where he had laid out a cold luncheon on the table.

"What is this?"

"A meal that you didn't have to prepare."

She took in the slices of bread and block of cheese, the plate of what looked like ham flanked by four oranges.

Wait. Oranges?

"Where did these come from?" she asked, letting go of his arm to pick up an orange and inspect it as closely as she had the kittens.

"From a friend of mine who keeps an orange tree in his conservatory," Mr. Mathison answered, closing the gap between them again. "I thought you might enjoy them."

She tilted her head back to meet his blue eyes. They hadn't had much interaction in the two years he'd been back, outside of him walking Moses back home. Was he still the boy she'd capered with when they were children? The one who had made a point of continuing their friendship into adolescence despite the difference in their stations?

"If not, I'll be happy to eat them all myself.," he continued, his baritone voice breaking her train of thought.

She laughed lightly—that sounded like the old Kit. "That was very thoughtful of you. Thank you."

He handed her a plate and picked one up for himself, pausing when a series of loud bangs filled the room. "How do you feel about eating outdoors? Then we won't have to listen to the noise of the builder's men working on the house."

She agreed and, after serving herself, followed him outside and across the farm. "Where are we going?"

"You'll see."

She briefly considered taking his arm again—she craved the feeling of safety and comfort that came with his touch —but couldn't ascertain how to do so while holding an orange and a plate. Instead, she inched closer to him as they walked, taking care not to get so close they would bump into each other, but close enough to detect the scent of hay that clung to his clothing.

"Here we are," he proclaimed, stopping at the edge of a stream. "And look! Someone has left a bottle of lemonade here in the cold water."

Kit set his food down and pulled a stone bottle out of the cool water, shaking the drops from his hand and holding it out to her.

"You planned this."

"I did," he grinned. His expression sobered a bit, and he continued, "I know you have a long list of things that need to be done, but you never seem to have any time to just rest."

She didn't reply for several moment, trying to discern what exactly she was feeling. Her grandparents, her friends, they were all wonderful, generous people. But when was the last time anyone had thought to provide her with the luxury of *rest*?

Sylvie set her plate and orange on the ground and took the cold bottle, uncorking the top and breathing in the sweet, lemony smell with a soft smile.

"Thank you," she said again, her voice full of emotions she still couldn't name. "This is a tremendous gift."

His eyes caught hers and held them. "It's my pleasure to give it."

They sat on the grassy bank of the stream under a cloudy sky, eating in companionable silence as the water bubbled along beside them and the birds called back and forth to each other. Sylvie forced the list of tasks from her mind, the tension in her shoulders slowly releasing with every sip of lemonade.

It was exactly what she had needed.

# Chapter 4

For the next several weeks, Sylvie continued her regular routine with the addition of visits to Kit's barn to check on the kittens. It was difficult to justify spending the time away when there was so much to be done, but Sylvie found herself looking forward to the visits, particularly since Kit went to the trouble of providing a quiet luncheon by the stream when the weather allowed, and in his own kitchen when the rain returned.

The kittens grew strong and healthy, including the little black runt, and they were great fun to play with, of course. But sitting with Kit, sometimes talking about their shared past, sometimes speculating about the future, was a somewhat unexpected delight.

Especially when he answered her impertinent questions.

"Why did you never marry Maddie Hayward?" she asked one day. "I always thought you would."

Kit was lying on his back, his plate empty beside him, gazing up at a rare blue sky. "She was my closest friend—she still is—but what we share isn't romantic. I did offer once, though."

"You did? When?"

When Kit didn't elaborate, Sylvie poked him in the shoulder. "You can't just say you once offered for Maddie and leave it at that. What happened? Or," she continued somewhat hastily, "is it too painful to speak of?"

Kit shook his head. "No pain at all, in fact. It was over two years ago now, and she despaired of ever finding a husband because everyone thought she was waiting for me to speak. I told her that if she wanted to marry me, I would be willing. That's all."

"But she wed your brother instead."

"Yes," he confirmed with a grin. "They hatched some plan together to free her from everyone's expectations, and ended up falling in love."

Sylvie sighed, her mouth curving into a dreamy smile. "How lovely. And you're truly not bothered?"

Kit rolled onto his side and met her gaze with another smile, this one softer. "Not at all. They are two of my favorite people in the world, and I'm glad they've found happiness together."

Sylvie opened her mouth to reply but caught Moses waddling toward them out of the corner of her eye. "I suppose we should get back to the house," she said instead, reaching for their plates and the stone bottle with the last of the lemonade.

Kit flopped onto his back once more and sighed heavily. "Yes, I suppose we should."

He helped her gather up their things and carry them to his kitchen, then walked beside her back to Broadstone Farm with Moses between them. Sylvie found herself wanting to reach out to Kit, to hold his hand or take his arm, but judged both actions too intimate for now.

Maybe in the future...

The Devereaux home was strangely silent when they entered with no sign of Grandmère, who was usually working in the kitchen at this time of the day. Sylvie exchanged a look with Kit and instinctively took a step closer to him.

"What's wrong?" he asked quietly.

"I'm not sure. But something isn't right."

She crept through the house, Kit close behind her, and finally stumbled upon Grandmère standing in the sitting room with her face in her hands, Grandpère with his arms about her. Sylvie immediately turned to leave, but Grandpère motioned them to come into the room.

"This effects you both, too."

"What's happened?" Sylvie asked, grateful for the support Kit's presence lent.

Grandpère took in a breath and let it out slowly, releasing his wife. "There will be no crop this year."

The room began to spin, and Sylvie couldn't make it stop. "Nothing?"

Grandpère shook his head. "Not a single stalk of wheat. It's all rotted."

Sylvie rocked backward slightly, but was steadied by the warm pressure of a hand on her back. Her mind was spinning as fast as the room, and she closed her eyes to concentrate better. "I have some money from—"

Grandpère raised a hand to stop her. "We will make plans later. Right now, let us simply come to terms with it."

But for Sylvie, making plans and trying to solve the problem were what helped her come to terms with bad news. And, though not unexpected, this was still the worst news she'd ever been given.

"I'm going to take a walk," she said as Grandpère went back to consoling Grandmère.

"Would you like some company? Or would you rather be alone?"

Kit's voice was gruff but strong, and pierced her heart. "Company would be nice," she managed thickly. The last thing she wanted right now was to be alone.

They walked out through the kitchen and Sylvie automatically started toward the wheat field, but halted. She couldn't bear to look at the rotted plants wasting away in the soggy ground.

Kit came to the rescue. "Why don't we walk over to the stream?"

She nodded, numbness replacing the spinning feeling she'd experienced inside the house.

They walked without speaking, arms brushing from time to time with the rhythm of their steps, the singing songbirds and sun shining brightly overhead irritating Sylvie like a grain of sand in her eye. Why did the sun have to show itself today of all days? Didn't it realize her world was about to end?

The first fat tear rolled down her face, and was followed by another and another in short succession. She brushed them away but they were replaced by a sudden horde of others, flowing down her cheeks and splashing onto the bodice of her dress.

Kit took her hand and pulled her to a gentle stop, then pulled her to him and enveloped her in his arms. Sylvie sunk into his embrace, circling her own arms around him and holding him tightly against her as she sobbed.

"What are we going to do?"

Late that night, after Mr. and Mrs. Devereaux had gone to bed, Kit sat beside Sylvie on the worn brown couch in the sitting room with only their clasped hands between them. The fire burned low, throwing off little light, but neither had bothered to light a candle or lamp to lessen the darkness.

Kit breathed slowly in, then let out the breath with as little sound as possible. He was grateful for the dark, truth be told—it gave him a measure of courage for what he was about to do.

"Sylvie," he said softly, hoping she couldn't hear the slight shaking in his voice. "I know you're worried about what will become of your home..."

She turned to face him, the outline of her nose and mouth visible in the dim light but her eyes were lost in shadow. "But you have an idea," she finished for him.

Was she smiling? Was she tense? He couldn't tell, but he plunged ahead. "Yes. I was thinking that if you and I were wed, all our problems would be solved."

She didn't reply immediately, but her fingers tensed around his. "How would our problems be solved?"

"Well, for one thing, I can pay the rent for Broadstone," he said, trying to infuse more confidence into his voice. "You and I could live here if your grandparents were amenable, and I could have some other repairs done on my house while the work continues on the roof."

She was nodding slowly, but didn't speak.

"Once the repairs on my house were completed, you and I could live there. You'd still be close to your grandparents and able to help out if they needed you, or us. But they would have their privacy and we would have ours."

She stilled, and replied quietly. "If you marry me, you are tied to me until one of us dies."

"Yes, I know that." He grinned, though she likely couldn't see it. "I am tied to you by friendship already. One more bond will not change things all that much."

Sylvie's hand slipped from his. "You don't think *marriage* would change our relationship?"

Kit started to speak but stopped, turning his hand palm up on the sofa. "Practically speaking, things would not be so different, no. Emotionally, though..." He paused. What exactly did he think would happen if Sylvie became his wife? "I would hope that marriage would add another dimension to our relationship."

She nodded again once, and Kit desperately wished he could see the expression on her face. Was she happy? Shocked? Insulted?

"You have property that you'll want to pass down," she finally said, her voice carefully even. "Do you anticipate having children?"

This question Kit was prepared for. "My property is not entailed, so I can leave it to whomever I wish."

"But do you *want* to have children?" Sylvie repeated slowly.

Well, perhaps he wasn't as prepared as he thought. "I always expected to, but no one has ever asked me what I wanted. Do you want to have children?"

"Yes," she answered without hesitation. "If my health and our family finances could support such a notion, I think I'd like to have a large family."

"Oh." The word fell from his mouth before he could think of a better response, but he really didn't know what else to say. Sylvie would make a wonderful mother, certainly, and being a father would be an adventure to look forward to. But he'd have to bed Sylvie to get her with child.

They hadn't even kissed yet.

What would it be like with Sylvie? Would it be a chore, like it was for some of his friends and their wives? Would it be awkward because they had known each other as children? Or could it be pleasurable, even fun?

"You haven't really thought this through, have you?" she asked, disrupting his thoughts. "Is this what happened when you asked Maddie, too? Do you just go around asking women to marry you to help them out of a difficult situation?"

Kit bristled a bit at that. "Perhaps I didn't give it the consideration it was due, but I did not make this offer lightly. I think you and I could make a good life together, and our marriage *would* solve several problems for both of us."

"But those things you listed—you paying rent on the farm, living here while your house is repaired, moving back into your house when it's ready but still being available to help out here—those can all happen even if we never see the inside of a church together."

"Oh." Apparently that was going to be his standard response to everything she told him now.

She turned toward him, lacing her fingers together as she slung one elbow over the back of the sofa. "Did that truly never occur to you? Or did you simply want me to be your wife and the circumstances made it convenient to ask?"

She sounded curious now, and Kit was rather curious himself. "Honestly?"

"Please."

"I believe it was some of both." He longed to take her hand again, to stroke her hair, to have her in his arms, but instead he settled his hands on his knees. "I miss the friendship that we used to have, and if we were wed we'd have the opportunity to spend more time together. I also want very much to help you and your family keep your home."

Sylvie placed her hand on his for a brief moment, then rose from the sofa. "I appreciate your candor, and your generosity toward my family, Kit, but I can't marry you. Not this way."

She lingered a moment longer then headed toward the staircase, leaving Kit alone in the dark with his thoughts.

Sylvie closed the door to her bedchamber with a sigh that was half fatigue and half bewilderment. The fire that she'd laid earlier in the evening burned cheerily in the fireplace, casting long, flickering shadows over everything in the room.

Kit had asked her to marry him.

Kit had asked her to marry him!

He said he meant it, and that it wasn't only a convenient way to solve their financial problems. But Kit's circle of acquaintances included several rungs of society that Sylvie, the granddaughter of glorified tenant farmers, could never aspire to. Perhaps he expected to have a more formal alliance with his wife, where they would come together for procreation and light conversation, and live their separate lives the rest of the time.

But Sylvie wanted her husband to be her partner, her lover, not just a man she was legally bound to.

She leaned back against the door and sighed again, this time with the tiniest bit of disappointment. It was unlikely Kit could be that man to her, though a part of her wanted to explore the idea. What would it be like to have their half-opened flower of a friendship blossom into a strong, devoted partnership? To know that he loved her and held her best interests in his heart, and that she reciprocated those feelings?

To know what it was like to be kissed by Kit, touched and caressed, to lie with him in the bed they shared...

She shook herself mentally and pushed away from the door. She was not going to marry Kit, to gamble her future on a fantasy coming true, so none of those things mattered.

What mattered was figuring out how to pay the rent this quarter for the farm.

# Chapter 5

*H*eavy rains raged across Kent the next day, flooding the already sodden landscape and forcing Kit, Sylvie, and her grandparents to remain indoors. Sylvie spent most of her time on the sofa in the sitting room mending clothes, and Kit tried desperately to occupy himself in ways that didn't include watching her. He finally resorted to going through his accounts, spreading out the big leather-bound books and various other papers on the table in the dining room with a deep sigh that was equal parts regret and resignation.

Kit's inheritance from his father was, strictly speaking, an estate. The parcel of land he owned was large enough to require account books and a man of business, but not large enough for him to rank among the more important landed gentry. He had the house and farm, and just a few small investments—plenty to live on when times were good, but lately he'd begun to economize in order to afford the repairs required on the house.

As he worked his way through the columns and papers, though, he knew he'd need to do more than economize this time.

He must have groaned aloud, for the door opened and Sylvie came in, her eyebrows raised and her mouth drawn into a frown. "Is everything alright?"

He blew out a breath, pushing away the awkwardness of seeing the woman who'd rejected his proposal of marriage just the day before. She was still his friend, and he needed a friend right now. "No."

"Would you like to talk about it?"

A small smile tugged at his mouth. This must have been difficult for her, too, perhaps even embarrassing. But when she thought he needed help, she was there to offer it.

Kit pulled out a chair near his and gestured for her to sit down. "My crops have failed, too," he began. "There might be enough to harvest for personal use, but there certainly isn't enough there to sell, so I'll have no income from the fields this year."

" 'From the fields' meaning you'll have income from other sources?"

"Yes, exactly." He picked up a letter he'd received the previous day from his man of business. He'd tossed it on the wash stand in his chamber and blithely went about asking for Sylvie's hand, forgetting all about it until he sat down with his account books. "The estate could survive a bad yield or a year with no yield at all—I made sure of that. But this…"

She took the letter when he offered it to her and read silently. After a moment, her eyes widened. "Oh, Kit. The whole ship?"

His father had regularly invested in the import of goods from outside the realm, a practice Kit was content to continue when he took the reins.

"I knew the risks," he said, a note of defeat creeping into his voice despite his efforts to keep it out. "Storms, pirates, blockades—there are many ways a ship's cargo can be lost. I thought it was a risk worth taking, but now…"

"Now you've lost your whole crop and this investment," she finished, setting the letter on the table.

For a moment he thought she would touch him, possibly to comfort him, but her hand slid into her own lap instead.

"And I'll have to lower the tenants' rents so they can afford to remain in their homes. Perhaps it's good that you refused me, Sylvie," he said quietly. "I can't do any of the things I promised you now."

She shook her head, tutting at him like an old hen. "If you think my only interest in you was ever for your money, then it *is* a good thing I refused you. You ought to know me better than that."

He did know her better than that, and it was a stupid thing for him to say. But his fortune, while not large, had always been a point in his favor. Losing even part of it felt like a strike against him in everyone's eyes—including hers —regardless of their actual feelings towards him.

"I do. And I apologize," he managed, clearing his throat. "I'm not good company just now, I think. I'll..." Where could he go? He longed to go sit by the stream running across his meadow, but the weather was fit for neither man nor beast, so he was confined to the house. "I'll go lie down for a while."

She remained motionless in her chair as he gathered up his papers and account books, laying a hand on his back briefly as he exited the room. Once he made it to his bedchamber, he set his pile of work on the wash stand and flopped onto his bed, trying to still his swirling thoughts.

He could no longer provide financial security to Sylvie and her grandparents, nor any of the people who worked on the farm. He wasn't even sure he would be able to pay the builder for the work done on his roof. Could he keep the farm running without going into debt? Would anyone lend him money if he couldn't?

Kit rolled over and buried his face in the peacock blue quilt covering his bed so no one would hear him moan. Perhaps he would take a page from Mr. Devereaux's book and just come to terms with this loss before trying to find a solution.

If only he'd invested more carefully!

He laid there for a while, eventually turning onto his back again, staring up at the ceiling with unseeing eyes, ignoring the pelting of the rain against the windows. The only thing that seemed to quiet his mind was recalling the feel of Sylvie's hand on his back in the dining room, fleeting as the contact had been. It meant that she still cared about him, that she would be there if he needed her.

And he needed her now.

He clambered off the bed and flung open the door to his bedchamber, only to find Sylvie standing at the threshold.

"Sylvie?"

"Kit?"

He froze, his brain overwhelmed with the sheer number of actions he could take.

"Are you well?" she asked, slightly confused, and that seemed to break the spell.

He reached for her, sliding an arm around her waist and pulling her into the room. "Will you hold me for a while, Sylvie Devereaux? I need to borrow some of your strength."

Her arms came around his neck in a warm embrace, her cheek resting against his. "You may have all the strength I can give you."

⁂

The light pressure of Kit's hands on Sylvie's body, the soft sound of his breathing—his embrace was warm and comforting, even though she was supposed to be comforting him. The faint fragrance of Grandmère's homemade soap combined with the scent of his skin and slowly enveloped her, setting her heart off at a gallop. When he sighed deeply, his body relaxing around her as his chest rose and fell, she finally understood what other women meant when they talked about butterflies in their stomach.

She tightened her arms around his neck and combed her fingers through his short blond hair. "Stronger now?" she asked, her voice a near whisper as she tried to conceal the emotions coursing through her.

"I don't know how I'd face this on my own," he replied quietly.

"You don't have to. You never have to."

His heart was beating as fast as hers now—she could feel it reverberating through his body pressed against hers. Was he experiencing the same things she was? She pressed her lips to his temple, his cheek, and his breathing hitched.

"Sylvie..."

Her name was almost a moan, and it ignited a flame somewhere inside her. "Yes?"

His lips brushed her earlobe. "I want to kiss you," he whispered, his voice husky. "May I?"

"Yes," she breathed, closing her eyes as he repeated the sequence she started, kissing her temple, her cheek, then capturing her lips.

"Mmmmm." Her hands slid down his back and cupped his derriere.

He broke the kiss, his eyes wide. "I did not expect that."

"Do you not like that?"

"I do, actually," he said with a grin. "I just didn't think you'd do it. Is there something you like that I can do for you?"

Her mind whirled, but she stopped it with the thought of her grandparents sleeping just down the hall. "Yes, but you'd better not. Kiss me again and I'll say goodnight, then we can talk things over in the morning."

He did as she bid him, kissing her thoroughly before loosening his arms around her. "Goodnight, then, my Sylvie. I look forward to tomorrow."

He kissed her hand and opened the door for her, checking the hallway quickly before she crept quietly back to her own chamber.

"What was that?" she demanded of her small desk as loudly as she dared. "I went to see if he was well, and ended up kissing him!"

Her body was still hot from the embrace and she picked up a letter to fan herself. "This is merely a physical attraction, though. I don't love Kit, and he certainly doesn't love me." She paused and touched a finger to her lips, then dropped her hand. "No, it doesn't matter what it was or what it meant. We have to figure out how to save our homes."

She washed and undressed, donning her nightdress and climbing into bed. But sleep was elusive. Too much had happened in too short a time, and Sylvie was completely overwhelmed. She turned onto her stomach and buried her face in her pillow, pushing aside everything to focus on paying rent for the quarter. She had a bit of money saved from the extra mending she'd taken in, so that was a start. She knew that Grandpère and Grandmère had a little, too.

They could talk tomorrow about how much the combined sum was and how much they would still need to raise.

Sylvie turned onto her side and suppressed tears. Her animals would have to be sold, there was no question now. But would they bring in enough?

She fretted through most of the night, only sleeping for a couple of hours before it was time to rise and begin another day. Fortunately, the first person she saw when she descended the staircase was her grandfather. Good. They could talk over their situation and Sylvie could stop thinking about Kit.

"Good morning, Grandpère," she said with as much cheer as she could muster.

"Good morning, ma chérie," he returned with equal enthusiasm. "Your grandmother and I would like to talk to you this morning."

A bolt of panic shot through Sylvie. Did they know about her tête-à-tête with Kit?

"Since Christopher has already gone out for the day," he continued, "we thought breakfast would be a good time to discuss our financial situation."

"Oh, yes of course." She tried not to visibly deflate, but her relief was surely noticeable. But there was nothing to be done about it now. "I have some ideas."

Grandpère smiled, a genuine expression of happiness despite their current trials. "I knew you would."

Sylvie followed him to the dining room where her grandmother was already waiting, and settled herself at the table. As they ate their eggs with the last small, watery vegetables from the kitchen garden, Sylvie and her grandparents talked about how much money they needed, how much they currently possessed, how much the animals were likely to fetch, and what would be the best way to sell them.

Sylvie noted the various amounts on a scrap of paper, adding in estimated earnings for Mr. Ross's mending and the pies Grandmère planned to bake for the tea shop in the village with what remained of last year's apples.

It still wasn't enough, but they were getting closer to their goal. Sylvie set her pencil on the table and blew out a breath. Perhaps they would be able to manage after all. She stood, gathering plates and silverware to take to the kitchen for washing, and felt some of the tension leave her shoulders.

"Wait," Grandpère said after the door closed behind Sylvie, "we must put something aside for the Harvest Festival."

Sylvie almost turned around to go back into the dining room, but Grandmère's voice had a hard edge to it when she replied that stopped Sylvie in her tracks, with the door to the dining room open a tiny crack.

"We don't—"

"I know," Grandpère interrupted. "But a few pennies for Sylvie to have fun, when she's given up all of her own money for us..."

They were silent for a long moment and Sylvie couldn't see them from her vantage point. They were likely giving each other the same meaningful looks they often traded during their evening conversations in front of the fireplace, trying to converse without giving away their thoughts to anyone else in the room.

Grandmère broke the silence. "You are right, of course. This winter will bring many hardships, and Sylvie should have what enjoyment she can find before then."

Sylvie quietly closed the door the rest of the way and leaned against it. Even now, when she was well into adulthood and they were facing terrible difficulties, her dear grandparents were plotting to ensure she had some fun.

She must make sure they found some enjoyment at the Harvest Festival, too.

# Chapter 6

A week later, they came for the animals. Grandpère and Kit had made joint arrangements to have their livestock transported to the temporary market set up for the Harvest Festival near the village. There was a rumor among the local farmers that the Duke of Alston was looking to add to his herds and flocks, and some of his wealthy friends might be, too. If it was true, Grandpère and Kit both had a chance of making the money they required.

As Sylvie had been the one to care for the Devereaux animals, she was tasked with supervising their removal and making sure a select few—a few chickens for eggs, a goat for milk, and Moses for himself—remained on the farm. She segregated the keepers into one corner of the barn and made sure all persons involved in the transaction knew which animals were to go and which were to remain on the farm.

The whole process took longer than she expected, but it seemed to go smoothly enough. The animals were loaded onto wagons with the appropriate tags, then the transporters headed down the road to repeat the whole procedure a second time. Sylvie resettled the chickens, goat, and Moses in their regular homes, then headed back to the house to help Grandmère with the extra baking.

"How are you holding up?" Grandmère asked when Sylvie entered the kitchen.

"It was sad to see them go," Sylvie replied, trying to keep her voice steady as she tied on her apron. "I always knew they'd be sold or butchered at some point, but…"

"But you took care of them every day of their lives," Grandmère said, putting a hand on Sylvie's shoulder. "It's not surprising you'd grow fond of them."

Sylvie covered her grandmother's hand with her own and gave it a squeeze. "I suppose not."

She kept herself busy for the rest of the day in an attempt to keep her mind from simultaneously missing her livestock and worrying about how much money they would bring in. After the pies were baked, she set about cleaning every inch of the house, then sat down to work on the dress she planned to wear to the Harvest Festival. It was in need of new cuffs, and she wanted to add some embroidery to the hem to hide the worn spots and give the garment a bit more adornment overall.

It wasn't until Grandmère interrupted her later that she realized she'd been working on her dress for hours.

"Has Christopher returned?" her grandmother asked.

Sylvie shook her head. "Not that I'm aware of, no."

"He's always come back to us in time for supper or sent word that he would be late," Grandmère replied, squeezing her hands together. "I wonder what has happened."

Sylvie put her needle down and flexed her fingers, wondering too. It wasn't like him to simply disappear. "Perhaps loading the livestock took longer than anticipated —ours certainly did. I'll walk over and see."

"Thank you, my dear."

Sylvie put away her sewing things and went first to the barn. The noise and heightened activity of the repairs at Kit's home had caused Moses a fair amount of distress, and the bird had elected to remain closer to home for the past week or so. But perhaps if he had an escort he'd feel more comfortable amid the hustle and bustle.

"Moses, would you like to go for a walk?" she called, entering the barn.

He normally would come running at the word "walk," but there was no sign of him. The chickens and goat were where she had left them earlier in the day, but Moses was not.

"Not so unusual," Sylvie said to the goat. "He's never been shy about going off on his own."

She searched the rest of the barn and the surrounding area, discovering several frogs socializing around a newly formed pond filled with rainwater and a hedgehog family passing by, but no Moses.

"Maybe he went to Kit's after all."

The doubt was evident in her voice, even to her own ears, but she couldn't think of a better explanation. Well, then she would go to Kit's to look for her friend *and* her pet.

She covered the distance between the two homes in record time, stopping partway up the drive to catch her breath.

"Sylvie?"

Kit's large frame came down the drive and stopped before her. "Is everything alright?"

"I've solved one mystery," she said with a half-smile. "It's nearly time for supper, and Grandmère was worried that you hadn't returned."

Kit grinned, offering his arm to her. "Your grandmother was worried? But not you?"

She hesitated for half of a second, then took his arm and walked with him up the drive. It was the first time since their late night kiss that they had touched each other, were alone together. They'd continued to live in the same house, of course, but between the added work of selling the livestock and the presence of her grandparents, there had been no time for a private discussion.

She glanced up the drive at the horde of people either loading up the last of Kit's animals or working on the house. They weren't alone now either.

"I was curious," Sylvie answered, trying to push the feeling of Kit's lips on her skin out of her mind, "and now I've found you."

"Excellent. What's the other mystery? You said I was one."

She held his arm just a bit tighter. "Moses is missing. He hasn't come here, has he?"

"I don't think so. At least, I haven't seen him. But let's have a look." The last wagon of livestock trundled down the drive, and Kit steered Sylvie to one side, using the movement to disguise his light kiss on her temple. "We'll find him."

They searched the grounds, questioning each member of the builder's crew and Kit's laborers they came across.

"He should be pretty memorable," Sylvie pointed out after a half dozen men didn't remember seeing the bird, "you don't keep geese, so it's not as if there were a flock he could have disappeared into."

"You don't keep geese, Mr. Mathison?" one of the nearby farm hands asked. "Not even one?"

"Have you seen one?" Kit countered quickly. "Miss Devereaux is correct—the Mathisons have never kept geese, but we are currently looking for one who was all on his own."

The farm hand's eyes widened. "One all by himself? I put him on one of the early wagons."

Sylvie gasped, but Kit remained calm. "Do you remember which wagon? What else was on it?"

The farm hand gave Kit as much information as he could recall before Kit sent him to saddle a horse. He turned to Sylvie, taking both her hands in his. "Don't you worry. Go back to your grandmother and tell her I'll be home late tonight. I'll go fetch Moses."

She hesitated for the briefest of moments, glancing at the assembled workers, then put her arms around him. "Be careful," she murmured. "I need both my lads back with me."

He grinned again and kissed her cheek. "We'll both come home safely. I promise."

Sylvie remained long enough to see Kit off, then practically ran home to let her grandparents know what had happened.

Supper was a quiet affair, though Sylvie noted the significant looks Grandmère was giving Grandpère. The looks continued into the evening as Sylvie took up her accustomed place on the sofa with her sewing, but couldn't seem to focus on the task.

"If Moses is on one of those wagons, he's not in danger," Grandpère said in a soothing tone. "Those animals will be treated like lords so they're in the best condition possible for sale."

"I know," Sylvie replied, putting her needle down. "But what if he's in with some of the larger animals? He could be trampled. Or sold before anyone can find him, and end up on someone's dinner table." She shuddered at the thought, then had another that was equally horrifying. "What if he isn't in any of the wagons at all?"

"Christopher will find your pet," Grandmère said with a sure smile. "He always comes through for you."

Kit did always come through for her. Every time she needed him, he was there to help, to comfort, to do everything he could to make the situation right.

"I hope I'm half as good a friend to him as he has been to me," Sylvie said, more to herself than anyone else.

Another hour passed and the sun began to set, raising Sylvie's anxiety level even further. Dark country roads were no place for a single rider with no lantern. It would be easy for his horse to misstep and injure itself or Kit.

"Ah, there he is, coming up the drive," Grandpère finally said after entirely too much time had passed.

Sylvie should have waited for Kit to take care of his horse, but she couldn't. Rushing out into the damp air, she picked up her skirts and ran into the barn. He was dismounting as she arrived, muddy and defeated.

She knew before he said the words that there would be no happy ending tonight.

"He wasn't in any of the wagons I checked," Kit said, wrapping his arms around her, "but there were two I couldn't get to before the light faded. They'll be at the market by now, and I can ride out tomorrow to see if he's there."

She kissed him then, heedless of who might see or know. He'd gone to great lengths to find a mere bird, for no other reason than said bird was important to her. "Thank you, Kit," she said softly, resting her cheek against his. "Thank you for trying."

Kit couldn't sleep that night thinking of how Sylvie's heart would break if Moses were lost to her. Every indication was that the goose was safely ensconced in a market stall with Kit's livestock, warm and comfortable for the night.

But what if something happened to him before Kit could get there?

As soon as the sky began to lighten, Kit washed and dressed, then headed to the barn to saddle his horse.

The ride to the Harvest Festival market was uneventful, even peaceful so early in the morning. But Kit urged his horse on, anxious to return the smile to Sylvie's beautiful face and, if he was totally honest, to see Moses himself unharmed. The bird had been something of a companion during the past two years, and had brought Kit and Sylvie together on many occasions.

One could even say Moses helped them fall in love.

Because Kit was certain now that he loved Sylvie. How could he not? She was kind and generous, not only with material items but with her time and her heart. She was practical and hard-working and lovely, and he didn't want to imagine his life without her.

Kit dismounted when he arrived at the market, walking his horse among the stalls as he looked for his livestock.

"Ah, there you are," he said aloud to them when he found the first group. "I've never been so happy to see a bunch of goats before."

He tied the horse to the corner post and began systematically searching the stalls containing his animals. But his heart sank a little more as each stall turned up chickens, goats, cows, and pigs but no goose.

"'Scuse me, mister, can I help you with something?" a man asked as Kit was leaning over the half-door of one stall examining the chickens within.

The man was dressed in work clothes, but wore a pencil behind his ear and carried what looked like a ledger. "Are these all the Mathison animals that were brought in last night?" The man looked askance at him, but Kit clarified, "I'm Christopher Mathison."

"Oh, yes, of course." The man flipped open the ledger, searching for the page he wanted, then tried to reconcile the information on the page with the animals in the stalls. Twice.

"No, it appears we're short." He went back to the ledger a third time, then nodded. "Oh, of course. The Duke of Alston's man was here yesterday afternoon when the first wagon came in. Apparently His Grace wants to add to his collection, and his man bought up that whole bunch."

"What?"

"Wanted to take possession of them immediately, and paid a pretty penny for them, too. Your man who came in with the animals authorized it, but wouldn't take the money with him when he left—we have it in the strongbox."

Well, that might come in handy. Because now he was going to have to ride thirty miles to retrieve a wayward goose.


Fortunately, the weather was clear for once and the roads were reasonably dry. Kit reached Orchard Lake, the Duke of Alston's home in Kent, by mid-afternoon. If all went well, there was time to find Moses, rest the horse, and still get back home to Sylvie before nightfall.

If all went well.

Kit was met by a groom who gave him directions and led his horse away to be cared for, then found himself standing before the great front door, suddenly conscious of his worn work clothes that smelled of the stables. But there was nothing he could do about it now.

A footman opened the door and left him to wait in the entryway when Kit asked for the steward.

"I must look like a beggar," he muttered, removing his hat and sliding a hand through his bristly hair.

"Not quite," a male voice answered crisply, "but the footman thought you were one of our tenant farmers."

Kit looked down at his frumpy tailcoat and the frayed cuffs of his trousers. "I can see why. Mathison is my name. You are the steward of this estate?"

"Jacobs," he said, shaking Kit's hand. "My office is this way."

Kit followed the steward through a series of hallways and into a darkly paneled room with little in the way of furniture, but floor to ceiling windows that let in much of the afternoon sun. He took the chair Jacobs offered him, and waited for the man to settle in his own seat behind the stout wooden desk.

"Now, what can I do for you, Mr. Mathison?"

"I'm here about a goose."

Jacobs gave him a quizzical look, and Kit told him about the transportation of his livestock to the market along with Moses's probable though mistaken inclusion.

"You came all the way from the Harvest Festival market for one goose?"

"Yes."

"Truly?"

Kit's chair was becoming uncomfortable, and he shifted slightly. "Yes. Do you have him or not?"

"Let me check the inventory." Jacobs stood, straightening his immaculate waistcoat and tailcoat, and walked slowly over to a table that held stacks of papers and what looked to be ledgers or account books. He selected one of the oversized ledgers, turned to the relevant page, then laid it on the table and began shuffling through a stack of papers.

And continued to shuffle.

Then went back to the ledger, ran his finger down the page, and returned to the stack of papers.

Was he being deliberately slow? Trying to impress the grandeur of the operation on Kit? It was difficult to believe he possessed any level of incompetence and still kept his position as the steward of a ducal estate.

After several more minutes of going back and forth, Jacobs located the item he was searching for and brought it back to his desk. "My apologies—we purchased several loads of livestock at the market yesterday. But yes, there was one white goose in the group of animals we purchased from C. Mathison."

Relief flooded his body, but his posture remained straight, his face—he hoped—expressionless. It could be the wrong goose, and even if it was the right one, Kit hadn't secured him yet. "Excellent. I will take him off your hands, with adequate compensation of course, and be on my way."

Jacobs smiled tightly. "Perhaps."

They negotiated for several minutes, but in the end Kit decided that Sylvie's happiness and Moses's safe return were worth more to him than time spent arguing over how much said goose was worth. "Ten percent over market value. That's far more than what you paid for him."

Jacobs hesitated, and Kit knew the man was toying with him.

"That's my final offer," Kit said, rising. "If you aren't interested, then our business is concluded."

He turned to leave, his heart in his throat, hoping that the steward didn't call his bluff and let him walk out the door with no bird.

"Ten percent over will do," Jacobs replied, a note of satisfaction creeping into his voice.

"Good. I'll see the bird first, then you'll get your money."

When they reached the barnyard, the steward spoke to one of the stable lads and stood to one side while work bustled on about him. "Bryant will fetch your goose."

Bryant was apparently much more efficient at his tasks than Jacobs, and returned with a ball of gleaming white feathers tucked under one arm.

"Moses?" Kit called.

The bird's head went up and his feet began flailing. Bryant shifted the goose against his chest and held on with both arms.

"Moses! There's the lad I'm looking for."

The flailing became whole-body thrashing accompanied by a series of excited honks.

"Satisfied?" Jacobs asked.

Kit grinned and reveled in the relief. "Yes. Very."

# Chapter 7

*I*t had begun to drizzle, but Sylvie sat outside under the big oak tree along the drive waiting for Kit to return. She dearly hoped that he would return with Moses, but knew that if he returned alone he'd have a plan to try again. As long as she'd known him, if Kit Mathison could solve a problem for someone he would do it.

It was a trait she'd come to cherish over the past several weeks. Not just because she benefited from it, but because he didn't do it for recognition or attention. He simply wanted to make her life easier because he cared about her.

Was there something she could do for him?

Shortly before sunset, a lone rider trotted up the drive and Sylvie jumped to her feet. "Kit?"

"We're home, lad," he said to the dark bundle tucked against him. A white head popped out and glanced around, then began honking.

"Moses!"

Kit handed down the bird, wrapped in a rough blanket, before he dismounted, and Sylvie hugged the bundle to her. After just a moment, Moses expressed his displeasure at being unceremoniously crushed and she unwrapped him, setting him loose to become reacquainted with his home.

Then she threw her arms around Kit.

"I don't know how you did it," she said softly, pressing a kiss to his wet cheek, his temple, "but I'm so glad you did."

He held her tightly, reciprocating each kiss she gave him. "I'll tell you the story later tonight, if you want to hear it. I'm sure your grandparents are anxious to have you back indoors, out of this rain."

The mention of her grandparents, who had a clear view of them from the sitting room, cooled her enthusiasm slightly, but she nodded. Whatever this was—or wasn't—between her and Kit, they did not need to play it out for an audience.

She did take his arm as they walked up the drive, and helped him stable his horse, unwilling to go inside until he was ready to do so. Moses came running into the barn behind them, honking happily with his wings spread, asking for neck scratches before darting back outside.

"Look how happy he is," Sylvie exclaimed, clasping her hands together. "Kit, I don't know how to thank you."

He stole one more kiss, murmuring, "We can talk about that later as well."

The butterflies returned to their fluttering in her stomach and she shivered deliciously. "Looking forward to it."

They somehow managed to go inside and eat supper with Sylvie's grandparents, then to sit side by side on the sofa in the sitting room afterward, as if they were two friends who were merely excited to have a special pet returned safely home.

Or at least, she thought they had. When Grandpère decided to go up to bed, Grandmère decided to follow but paused at the sofa. "Enjoy the evening," she said quietly, giving them a little wink.

Apparently they hadn't concealed their eagerness as well as she'd thought.

Well, no matter. The hour had finally arrived when Sylvie could thank Kit properly for bringing Moses back, and perhaps to figure out how she felt about this man who had, until very recently, been little more than an acquaintance to her these past two years.

She scooted closer to him on the sofa and took his hand in hers. "You must tell me how you managed to find Moses."

He gave her hand a squeeze, then explained his stop at the market, his negotiations with the steward at Orchard Lake, and having to wrap Moses in the blanket in order to carry him on horseback.

"All that just to bring a bird back to me," she said when he finished.

Kit cleared his throat. "For you, yes."

His words squeezed her heart. "And I know that steward didn't just give you Moses. You will let me repay you for that cost at least."

"Absolutely not," he replied firmly.

She pressed her lips together for a moment. "I saw the roof yesterday, I know that it's nearly completed. You'll need to pay the builder very soon for everything you still owe him."

"You and your grandparents need every penny you can save," he reminded her. "I will have enough from the sale of my livestock to pay for the repairs to the house."

"Kit—"

"No," he said, turning to her, "I'll not budge on this point. If you feel that strongly about it you can owe me a favor, but I won't take your money."

She slid an arm around him and drew him down to her, capturing his lips with all the emotion she'd been suppressing. "You stubborn man," she mumbled, pulling back just a fraction of an inch before kissing him again.

His arms came around her, one big hand splayed across her back, holding her securely. "Yes, but you love me for it."

He was grinning, and likely joking, but her heart jumped into her throat and she rested her forehead against his. "I do love you, for your stubbornness and many other reasons."

"What?"

"I love you," she said softly, combing her fingers through his hair. "I can no longer pretend I don't."

Kit didn't pull away, but he didn't celebrate the news either. In fact, he didn't react at all. If it weren't for the increased thumping of his heart in his chest, Sylvie might have thought he hadn't heard her at all.

She loosened her arms about him. "I don't expect you to return my feelings—I've only just realized myself that I had them. But please don't say we can no longer be friends."

His eyes met hers in the light of her grandparents' treasured oil lamp and he traced a finger down her cheek. "I would never say that. You've caught me by surprise, that's all."

"You're sure?"

"Yes," he said with a nod. "I've also thought of a favor you can do for me, if you're willing."

"What's that?"

"Let me escort you to the Harvest Festival next week," he said. His voice was a bit rough and his breathing rapid, but his eyes were locked on hers.

Her hands found his shoulders. "That hardly seems like a fair trade after you rode half the county to bring Moses back to me."

"It's more than enough," he assured her. "Will you?"

His arms were still around her, his body warm against hers, and she wanted badly to kiss him again. But he'd spooked like a frightened horse when she told him she loved him, and she didn't want to spook him further.

Instead, she simply said, "It will be my pleasure."

The day before the Harvest Festival, Kit moved back into his own home. The repairs had been finished for several days, he'd hired a local woman to thoroughly clean the interior, and there was no longer any reason to continue staying with Sylvie and her grandparents.

He gathered his clothing and personal items together along with the loaves of bread Mrs. Devereaux had baked for him, and carried them to his house through a fine mist that emanated from low, dark clouds. Sylvie had offered to help him, but he'd declined. He wanted to get his head and his heart sorted out before spending time alone with her again, to decide what he wanted and what his next step should be. He had nearly burst with joy when she said she loved him, but no words would come when he'd attempted to summon them.

And now he was afraid he might well be too late.

Arriving at the house, Kit left the bread in the kitchen and headed up the stairs to the master's chamber. The last time he'd been there, water had poured from the ceiling and soaked everything within its reach. But when he opened the door, the room was freshly plastered and painted, the hole in the ceiling no longer even visible.

He put his things away, then sat down on the upholstered chair he kept by the large window and sighed.

"It cost me every penny I have, but I have my house back."

There were other problem areas the builder had identified which would need repairs sometime in the future, and the farm wasn't producing the way it had when Kit was a boy. He ought to sell it to someone with the means to restore it to its former glory, but despite the money and effort he knew he would be putting in—had already put in—he couldn't bring himself to do it.

Would Sylvie love this old heap as much as he did? Would she wish to preside over a home that was constantly in need of expensive repairs?

Did he want her to?

He had no doubt in the world that he loved Sylvie. He was less convinced that her declaration was true. Not that she would purposefully mislead him, of course, but he had returned her beloved pet to her thereby saving the goose from a fate as someone's Michaelmas dinner. Had she only thought she loved him because she was so relieved?

Or was she truly sincere?

Kit leaned his forehead against the cool glass and closed his eyes.

The memory of Sylvie in his arms overwhelmed him just then and his breath caught in his throat. Ye gods she was an amazing woman! What would it be like to wake up beside her every morning? To discuss the workings of the estate together, reinvigorate this house together, handle account ledgers together?

Handle account ledgers? If he thought that was romantic pastime, he *must* be in love.

What if she really did love him in return?

He stood and gave himself a mental shake. "I can't just sit here brooding all day. Even with the livestock sold and the crops ruined, there is still work to be done."

When Kit returned to the house later that evening, he was tired and sweaty, looking forward to washing, eating a quick supper, and going to bed early. But just as he was about to head upstairs, a knock sounded on the kitchen door. He trudged over and opened it, then rubbed his eyes. Had he conjured her with his thoughts?

"Good evening, Kit."

"Good evening, Sylvie." He opened the door wider and gestured for her to come inside, but couldn't help making a joke as she entered. "Miss me already?"

"Yes," she said with a grin. "But that's not why I'm here."

She touched his shoulder as she passed by him and his stomach did a somersault, then he cringed. He hadn't had a chance to wash or change yet, and he must smell like an ox.

But Sylvie didn't seem to notice or care. "I have a favor to ask of you."

"I'll do it."

She laughed lightly. "You don't even know what it is."

He took one of her hands and gave it a gentle squeeze. He didn't care what the favor was. He would do anything for this woman. Didn't she know that? "Very well then, what is your favor?"

"My grandparents' wedding anniversary is tomorrow, and I'd like to surprise them at the Harvest Festival. But I need a partner."

"Come sit down, and tell me what I'll need to do."

He led her into the sitting room, careful to choose an old, tatty chair for himself, pulling it closer to hers. She explained her plan, her eyes shining with excitement and love for her grandparents, and he couldn't help but love her more.

"I would be happy to," he said when she was finished. "And you're welcome to use the kitchen whenever is convenient. I'll be out most of the morning, but I'll leave the door open for you."

"Oh, Kit, thank you," she replied, clasping her hands together on one knee. "It's not much, but I think they'll enjoy it."

"I think so too." He paused, desperately wanting to tell her how much he loved her but unable to find the right words. Ah, but there was one thing he could do. "I'm glad you came over tonight, because I have something for you."

He excused himself and went to the room his mother used to jokingly call the conservatory because it was the sunniest room in the house. He returned with a slip of a plant in a small pot.

"It's not much to look at yet," he said, the slightest hint of trepidation creeping into his voice, "but I'm told that roses take some time to root properly from cuttings."

She stood and accepted the pot from him, curiosity written all over her face. "It's a rose cutting?"

He nodded, gaining confidence from her interest. "From the rose bush on the south side of the house. The variety is called 'Duchess of Portland.' My mama and papa planted it underneath the window of the master's chamber when they were first married. Apparently this variety was rather rare at the time, and neither of them would tell me how they happened to obtain one."

Her lovely eyes went wide. "What a wonderful way to celebrate their marriage. And you're giving me a cutting?"

"I took that cutting the day after our first kiss," he told her softly.

Her reaction was slightly delayed, as if it took her a moment to fully understand what he had said. Her gaze dropped to the nearly bare stem in the pot then back to Kit, her mouth forming a small o.

She set the pot on the floor, then stepped close to him and slid her arms around his neck, heedless of the sweat and smell. "Thank you," she whispered.

He closed his eyes and held her close against him, thankful that his gift could say what he couldn't.

# Chapter 8

Sylvie took Kit's hand and climbed up into the old gig that he'd hauled out especially to drive her to the Harvest Festival. The day was overcast but dry for a change, so she'd planned to walk. But when Kit realized she'd be carrying the cake she'd baked in his kitchen earlier that day, he'd insisted on driving her. Grandmère and Grandpère had gone on ahead, smiling at her then at each other when she said she'd arrive with Kit a little later.

Kit clambered up onto the seat beside her, dressed in one of his finer tailcoats for the occasion, and took up the reins. "Ready?"

She nodded and the conveyance jerked into motion. Unfortunately, their conversation remained at a stand still. What did one say to the man who couldn't tell you he loved you in so many words, but did everything in his power to *show* you?

Nothing, apparently. But perhaps she could do a little showing of her own.

His hands were occupied driving and hers held the cake, but she slid closer to him on the seat so their arms and thighs were pressed lightly together. He glanced at her and grinned, and his body visibly relaxed.

When they arrived at the festival, Kit helped her down and kissed the back of her hand. "Go prepare and start letting people know. I'll see to the horse and find your grandparents."

She almost kissed him then, but now that they were in public they had to abide by the rules of propriety. Instead Sylvie squeezed his hand. "Excellent. I'll meet you near the musicians."

She skirted the festival grounds with her cake, covered with a kitchen towel to disguise its true contents, until she reached the area where a group of local musicians had arranged themselves. They had left room for dancing, though at the moment there were only a few small children bouncing around in approximate time to the music.

As promised, a small table had been placed there for her with a borrowed linen tablecloth folded atop it. She set the cake down carefully beside the table and spread the cloth across it, aligning each of the four embroidered clusters of wildflowers with the four corners of the table. The cake she placed at the center, but left it wrapped in its towel.

"What's all this, Miss Devereaux?"

Sylvie turned to see Mr. Norris, who lived just a few miles away from Broadstone, gesturing to the table. "This is a surprise for my grandparents—we're going to celebrate their golden wedding anniversary today."

"Oh, lovely! Can I do anything to help?"

"Yes," she said with a wide smile. "Can you help me spread the word? I'd like everyone to meet here. After the Duke of Alston makes his speech, we'll congratulate them and have some music. But my grandparents mustn't find out."

Mr. Norris gave her a little salute and headed off. Sylvie surveyed the table, gave the musicians a nod, then headed off herself to the flower sellers. The offerings were meager this year and her purse was light, but she managed to put together a modest bouquet of late-blooming pink peonies interspersed with stalks of dried lavender for her grandmother and a smaller peony for her grandfather's buttonhole.

"Aren't the flowers lovely, Mr. and Mrs. Devereaux?" came Kit's voice from some distance.

Sylvie turned hurriedly toward the sound and spotted him trying to steer Grandmère and Grandpère toward the animals. She flashed him a smile and darted in the opposite direction, talking the long way round to return to her cake, hoping she'd escaped unseen.

Finally, as the sun began to set, the Duke of Alston arrived in his grand carriage with his wife and son. He was the predominant landowner in this part of Kent, and he or one of his family had welcomed people to the Harvest Festival for as long as there had been one. Sylvie wondered momentarily at the man's health, as he needed to be helped from his carriage and was slowly escorted to the musicians' box by Her Grace and a sturdy footman.

The crowd began to gather around, and Sylvie searched the multitude of faces for Kit and her grandparents.

"There you are," came Grandpère's voice from behind her. "I was starting to suspect that Christopher was deliberately leading us away from you."

"Nonsense," Sylvie replied, trying to keep a straight face. "Why would he do that?"

"I don't know, but it certainly feels like he did."

Grandpère led Grandmère to one side of Sylvie, and Kit took up a position on her other side, brushing his fingers against hers.

His Grace made his welcome speech with a surprisingly strong voice, thanking everyone in attendance for all the hard work they put in this year even though the unusual weather had overwhelmed so many fields. He urged them to leave off their worries for one night and to enjoy the festival.

The assemblage applauded and Sylvie assumed the duke would take his leave, but he waited for the applause to die down and added one more thing. "I believe there is also a golden wedding anniversary to celebrate this night. Miss Devereaux? Are you ready?"

Sylvie's heart pounded and her eyes must have been as round as coins, but Kit's hand found hers and gave it a reassuring squeeze. "How's that for an introduction?" he whispered.

She squeezed back and made her way through the crowd, curtsying before the duke and allowing him to bow over her hand. "Thank you, Your Grace."

"Tell your grandparents I hope they have many more happy years together."

"I will."

The duke gestured for the duchess and footman, and allowed himself to be escorted away. Sylvie stood watching him for a long moment, wondering how on earth he'd found out about the anniversary.

Taking a deep breath, she turned to the festival goers and smiled brightly. "His Grace is correct—my grandparents, Monsieur and Madame Devereaux, are celebrating their fiftieth wedding anniversary today. I hope you'll join me in congratulating them on so many wonderful years together."

Kit parted the crowd for her grandparents, gesturing for them to stand beside her near the musicians' box. Sylvie presented them with the flowers and unveiled the cake, brimming over with happiness for the two people that had raised her.

"One more thing," she said, looking to the musicians and giving them a nod. "Will you lead off the dancing?"

They looked at each other as the musicians tuned their instruments.

"Will you do me the honor?" Grandpère asked, offering her his hand.

Grandmère grinned. "It will be my pleasure."

Other couples joined in when the music began, but Sylvie hung back to just watch them enjoying the moment.

Kit found her, slipping an arm around her. "They look like they're having fun."

She leaned against him and sighed. "Good. That was the plan."

"Would you like to dance?" he asked softly.

She took his hand in both of hers and drew his arm more securely around her waist. "I'd rather stay here," she replied. "With you."

Such an intimate pose was highly improper in public, but Sylvie didn't care. For once she was going to do what the Duke of Alston had suggested—forget her worries and enjoy the evening.

The last note of music died away in the moonlight, and the dancers began to go their separate ways. Kit sat off to one side watching them. Some left as soon as the music stopped, some took a moment to say their goodbyes, and some lingered together as if they were reluctant to part.

Sylvie had been dancing with her grandfather, laughing through the steps of a country dance that neither of them executed very well. When the music ended, they bowed and curtsied to each other, and Kit expected Mr. Devereaux to escort his granddaughter away. But instead, Sylvie came to Kit.

Alone.

"That turned out rather well, don't you think?" she asked when she reached him.

"The festival or your grandparents' anniversary?"

"Both." She sat down close beside him but didn't touch him. "Did you enjoy yourself?"

He nodded, aching to have her in his arms again but electing to remain still for the time being. "I did. I wasn't sure I wanted to come this year, but I'm glad I did."

Her gaze met his as the last of the clouds drifted away revealing a sky full of dainty, twinkling stars, and for the briefest of moments he thought she might kiss him. When she didn't, the disappointment nearly overwhelmed him.

"Are you returning home with your grandparents?" he asked.

"I think they could use some time to themselves," she responded, her smile softening. "Would you mind driving me?"

"Not at all. Shall we sit here for a while and let them get a head start?"

Sylvie twined her arm around his. "That's just what I was thinking.

Kit's heart began to pound as hard as the hammers that the builder's men had swung during his roof repair. "Good. There's actually something I'd like to speak to you about, and I think it will be easier to do if neither of us is focused on directing a pair of half-ton animals."

"Oh?"

He glanced around, noting the only people still nearby were the musicians packing up their instruments. A handful of other festival goers remained, but they were attending their own affairs. "A few days ago, you told me that you loved me."

The big full moon was bright overhead, and Sylvie's deep blush was evident. "Kit—"

"To my everlasting shame, I didn't say it back to you then," he continued, covering her hand with his. "I wanted to, and I'm still not sure why the words would not come. Because, Sylvie, I do love you."

"You do?"

Her eyebrows were raised, her head tilted slightly and he chuckled. "I would be skeptical, too, if I were you."

"No, it isn't that I don't believe you." She slid her hand down his arm and laced her fingers with his. "In fact, I know you love me. I just didn't expect you to say it."

"What do you mean you know?"

She grinned, and laid her head on his shoulder. "I knew for certain when you went to find Moses. You're a kind man, but that was more than even you would do for most people."

Kit thought back to those two days, searching wagon-loads of smelly animals crowded together, bargaining with that smug steward. "I absolutely would have done the same thing for Thomas or my mother. Maddie, too." He kissed the top of her head. "I didn't think twice about doing it for you, either."

She nodded. "I thought that when I told you I loved you that night, you'd return the sentiment. When you didn't, I suspected you either needed more time or you just weren't a man that expressed his emotions in words."

"Well, you were right," he murmured against her hair. "I needed time. I wasn't sure you were actually in love with me or just grateful I brought Moses back."

She straightened and met his eyes. "Oh, I hadn't even considered that."

"But when I gave you that rose cutting..."

Her expression turned dreamy and her body softened. "Any doubts I might have had about your feelings for me were put to rest right then."

The grounds were nearly deserted now. He released her hand and slid his arm around her, drawing her even closer to him. "Good," he said, his voice gruff with emotion. "That's what I had intended."

They sat together in the moonlight for several minutes, relaxing against each other. But all too soon, Sylvie sat up and turned to face him.

"There is something else I wanted to ask you about."

"What's that?"

"A few weeks ago, you proposed marriage to me." She clasped his free hand in hers and dropped her gaze to her lap as if to gather her courage, before meeting his eyes once again. "Is that offer still available?"

Kit shook his head, but couldn't keep the grin from his face. "That proposition was for a marriage of convenience. We were going to pool our resources to pay the rent on Broadstone and repair my house, remember?"

She searched his eyes, and her grin matched his. "Then let me make you a better one. I propose a marriage based on love and partnership and trust."

"We may have to work on our communication skills a bit more," he laughed, the joy of the moment breaking over him in the most delightful waves.

"I agree," she replied, her grin widening, "So I'll be plain. I love you, Kit Mathison, and I would very much like to have you as my husband."

"I love you, Sylvie Devereaux, and I would be honored to be your husband. Will you be my wife?"

The words had rushed out of him as if they were trying to escape, not in the measured manner he had tried for. But it didn't matter. Sylvie's arms came around him and her lips brushed his ear as she whispered her answer.

"Yes."

# Chapter 9

$S$ylvie's heart was soaring as her betrothed handed her into the gig for the trip home. But there was one nagging voice in the back of her mind that kept asking questions she couldn't answer.

Would her grandparents be able to take care of the farm without her?

Could they pay the quarterly rent without the money she was earning?

Would her parents finally return to England to care for her grandparents when Sylvie went to live with Kit?

Kit was driving with both hands, but one arm was entwined with Sylvie's and she held it tightly.

"What's wrong?" he asked.

"How do you know something's wrong?" she countered, trying to make her voice light.

He bent his head toward hers. "Your fingernails are going to leave marks in my arm through my coat."

Sylvie immediately loosened her grip. "I'm sorry. I'm just worried about the effect this marriage will have on us and our families."

"It's time for practicalities, then," he said, pressing a kiss to her temple, then straightening to watch the road. "Very well. What is your biggest worry?"

"My grandparents," she said without hesitation. She listed off her questions regarding their welfare and was surprised when he smiled.

"We can't predict what your parents might do, but once we're wed you'll only be next door. And so will I. We can work out how to ensure your grandparents won't be overwhelmed by work."

He said it in such a matter-of-fact way that her heart rate slowed almost to normal. "It's that easy?"

"That part is." He pressed his lips together, squinting at the small patch of road that was illuminated by the lamps hanging from either side of the gig. "My estate is not in the same financial health that it was when I offered for you the first time, but we can sit down with your grandparents and sort things out together. Pool our resources, even if it's not exactly how I'd originally planned."

A measure of relief flowed through her. She expected no less from this man than to care about the people important to her, else she wouldn't be marrying him. But it still felt good to hear the words aloud. "That's an excellent idea."

The questions in her mind didn't vanish, but they quieted enough that Sylvie could enjoy the rest of the drive. They decided to go to Kit's home first to unhitch the horses and put them to bed, then took the lanterns from the gig and walked the familiar path to Broadstone Farm.

As they approached the house, Sylvie became jittery, fairly bouncing up to the door.

"Nervous?" Kit asked, taking her hand and giving it a reassuring squeeze.

She squeezed back and grinned broadly. "Excited. They love you almost as much as I do, and I'm looking forward to telling them that you'll be their grandson by marriage."

They entered the house and found Grandmère and Grandpère in their usual places in front of the fire.

"We've returned," Sylvie said brightly as they came into the sitting room, "and we have news."

Grandpère was holding a small damask bag in his lap. "So do we." He eyed their clasped hands and grinned. "Let us tell our news first. Then we can spend the rest of the evening celebrating yours."

Sylvie's face warmed but Kit was standing tall, his chest puffed out proudly. "Certainly. What is your news?" she asked.

"We received an anniversary gift from the Duke of Alston," Grandpère told her, handing her the damask bag.

Sylvie released Kit's hand and took the bag, pulling open the draw strings. "These are gold guineas."

"Five of them," Grandmère chimed in. "One for each decade we have been married, the card said."

"Five guineas?" Sylvie repeated incredulously.

"Not enough to get us through a winter with no crops," Grandpère clarified, trying—and failing—to maintain a serious expression, "but between those, the sale of your animals, and our savings, we'll be able to pay the rent and have money left over."

"That's wonderful!" Sylvie exclaimed. "Kit, do you know what this means?"

Kit grinned broadly. "We can be married as soon as the banns are called?"

Grandmère sat up straighter in her chair. "Married?"

Sylvie looked to Kit then nodded, unable to keep the smile from returning to her face.

Grandmère jumped up from her chair and enveloped Sylvie in a warm embrace. "Oh, my sweet Sylvie, I'm so happy for you!"

Grandpère rose, too, and put an arm around Kit's shoulders. "I hope you have as many happy years together as we have."

Grandmère embraced Kit as well, jubilant tears in her eyes. "Oh yes! If you are as happy together as we have been, what a marvelous life you will have together."

After another round of hugs, they sat before the fire and made plans for a wedding later that autumn when the leaves would be deep oranges and reds. Kit wrote a letter to his mother and one to his brother, promising to keep them informed of the exact date when it was chosen.

But soon enough, Grandmère and Grandpère gave each other a knowing look and declared they were tired.

"You may stay for another hour, Christopher," Grandpère told him. "Anything left unsaid after that will have to wait until tomorrow."

"We will expect you for breakfast, though," Grandmère said cheerily. "And for supper, too."

Kit accepted both invitations, and Sylvie's grandparents went up to bed. Then at last, Sylvie was alone with her betrothed. The long day was wearing on her, but there was one thing she wanted to do before attempting to sleep.

"Kit," she said, wrapping her arms around his waist, "may I kiss you?"

"I wish you would," he murmured, sliding his arms around her shoulders.

She had to reach a bit, but she captured his lips once, twice, then slid her hands down to cup his backside as she kissed him a third time.

He drew back a fraction of an inch and grinned. "You remembered."

"I did," she said, matching his grin. "I want to learn all the contours of your body...and your heart."

"You know the contours of my heart already," he replied softly, caressing her cheek. "Tonight, when you said yes, I realized you've held my heart for far longer than I knew."

Her throat closed with emotion, and this time it was Sylvie who couldn't answer in words. Instead, she slid her arms around him and pulled him tightly against her, sighing with a contentment she didn't know was possible when he reciprocated.

"I love you," she managed to whisper.

"I love you, too," he whispered back.

**Other Books by Cora Lee**

Sweet & Traditional:

Save the Last Dance for Me (Maitland Maidens #1)
Back In My Arms Again (Maitland Maidens #2)
Kissing by the Mistletoe (Maitland Maidens #3)
A Kiss to Build a Dream On (Maitland Maidens #4)
When I Fall In Love (Maitland Maidens #5)

Spicy and Suspenseful:

No Rest for the Wicked
The Good, The Bad, And The Scandalous
The Duke of Darkness

# About The Author

Cora Lee is National Bestselling author of Regency romance. She went on a twelve year expedition through the blackboard jungle as a high school math teacher before publishing *Save the Last Dance for Me*, the first book in the Maitland Maidens series. She then followed it up with six more novels and novellas, ranging from sweet and traditional to spicy and suspenseful.

When she's not walking Rotten Row at the fashionable hour or attending the entertainments of the Season, you might find her participating in Regency Fiction Writers events, wading through her towering TBR pile, or eagerly awaiting the next Marvel movie release. If you'd like to find out more about Cora or her books you can visit her website, sign up for her newsletter, or connect with her on Bookbub, Facebook, or Goodreads.